You Won't Forget Me

Mazey Eddings

HEADLINE
ETERNAL

Published by arrangement with St. Martin's Griffin,
an imprint of St. Martin's Publishing Group.

First published in the UK in 2026 by Headline Eternal
An imprint of Headline Publishing Group Limited

1

Cataloguing in Publication Data is available from the British Library

Paperback ISBN 978 1 0354 0404 9

Offset in 10.32/14.4pt Adobe Garamond Pro by Six Red Marbles UK,
Thetford, Norfolk

Printed and bound in Great Britain by Clays Ltd, Elcograf S.p.A.

Headline's policy is to use papers that are natural, renewable and recyclable
products and made from wood grown in well-managed forests and other
controlled sources. The logging and manufacturing processes are expected
to conform to the environmental regulations of the country of origin.

Headline Publishing Group Limited
An Hachette UK Company
Carmelite House
50 Victoria Embankment
London EC4Y 0DZ

The authorised representative in the EEA is Hachette Ireland,
8 Castlecourt Centre, Dublin 15, D15 XTP3, Ireland (email: info@hbgi.ie)

www.headlineeternal.com
www.headline.co.uk
www.hachette.co.uk

Mazey Eddings is a *USA Today* bestselling author, dentist, and (most importantly) stage mom to her cats, Yaya and Zadie. She can most often be found reading romance novels under her weighted blanket and asking her husband to bring her snacks. She's made it her personal mission in life to destigmatize mental health issues and write love stories for every brain. With roots in Cleveland and Philadelphia, she now calls North Carolina home.

To learn more, visit: www.mazeyeddings.com
or follow Mazey on Instagram: **@mazeyeddings**

By Mazey Eddings

A Brush With Love
Lizzie Blake's Best Mistake
The Plus One
Tilly in Technicolor
Late Bloomer
Well, Actually
You Won't Forget Me

To Stevie Nicks, for singing "Silver Springs (Live)" at Lindsey Buckingham like that in 1997. I'll never get over it and I hope he doesn't either.

Content Notes

To my beloved reader,

The following romance has a hard-won happy ending with plenty of longing and laughs along the way, but please be aware that the following are portrayed/discussed throughout:

- Depression
- Compulsions, particularly around social media
- Compulsory heteronormativity

As always, I've done my best to handle the above with respect and care, and I encourage you to take care of yourself while reading. If you'd like a bit more context on how the above became themes in a rom-com, please see the Author's Note at the end of the book. (I can't even begin to tell you how long I've worried over whether to put that note up here or back there, but I refuse to be accused of spoilers, so read at your own risk, etc.)

All my love,
Mazey

You Won't Forget Me

Prologue

Five years ago

"I think Connor's going to kiss me tonight," I say, staring into my bedroom mirror, my face an alarming shade of gray-green. My eyes flick to the corner of the glass, locking with the reflection of my best friend, Darcy. She blinks at me from where she's sprawled on the bed.

"Enjoy," she drawls, scrunching up her nose before turning back to her phone.

I whip around. "Like, he's going to *kiss me* kiss me."

"Congratulations," she says through a yawn. "Would you like a gold star?"

"Darcy, I'm serious." I stand, pacing the room to the beat of my nervous energy.

My lovely, giving, *exceptionally* compassionate friend manages to turn off her phone with a sigh and sit up, watching my movements with a bored expression. "I'm serious too. I'm so sorry I don't have a cake prepared. I'll run to the shops while you're on your date. CONGRATS ON SMOOSHING YOUR FACE AGAINST SOMEONE ELSE'S FOR THE FIRST TIME! or something like that written in icing. Invite your brother and mums to join the celebration."

"I hate you." I throw a pillow at her head, then collapse on the mattress next to her.

"Sure you do, Cubby love."

I scowl as she slides down to level her face with mine, a playful smile tugging at her wide mouth.

"Let me make sure I'm following," she says, voice velvety but wrinkled with teasing. "The boy you've been friends with for five years, in a band with for three, had a crush on for one, and been obsessively texting for six months is going to kiss you tonight and you've worked yourself up so much you have the complexion of a zombie because . . . ?"

"Because I'm eighteen and I've never done it before and you know that and I probably should have loads of kissing experience by now and what if I screw it up or what if I'm awful at it or what if—"

"Your breath smells terrible or you move in too fast and break his nose?"

"You are truly the worst. Why do I talk to you?"

"Because you love *meeee*," she says in a singsong, tapping my nose.

I slap her hand away then snatch it back up, holding it against my chest, my steady anchor as insecurities jangle through me.

Darcy stares at me, features dropping from light and teasing to something careful. "So this whole thing's real, then, yeah?"

I frown. "You've known I've fancied him for a while." Connor moved from Ireland to our small corner of Surrey during primary school. It wasn't until a few years later, when Darcy and I were in choir with him and our other friend Harry, that we bonded. It didn't take long for our love of music to cinch a lasso around us, our world shrinking to the four of us but expanding with our boundless dream to make music.

"Yeah, no. I mean, I knew, like, conceptually you liked him. But it seems like you *really* like him."

I shrug. "I guess so?"

Darcy shakes her head, something sharp flashing behind her eyes, gone before I can read it.

"What?"

She schools her features, fixing me with a bland look. "I'm fairly certain there's a textbook's worth of examples of what a terrible idea it is to date a bandmate, but follow your heart or your knickers or whatever."

I shove her, and she laughs. "Well, if I'm as horrible a kisser as I'm assuming I'll be, there won't be any dating, just awkward tension in a fissured friend group."

"Which everyone knows is great for a band's sound."

"I'm glad our music outranks my personal romantic happiness on your list of priorities."

"You could practice," Darcy says suddenly, sitting up and crossing her legs, that serious look back.

My mouth twists. "On what? A pillow? Is all of this not embarrassing enough?"

"No, you weirdo. On a person. On . . . me."

My heart stutters for a beat, then kicks into overdrive, a flood of warmth suffusing through me to the tips of my toes and fingers at the image that flashes in my mind. I shake my head, clearly misunderstanding her. "What do you mean *on you*?"

Darcy tucks her blond hair behind her ears, the ends recently dyed blue in her latest act of rebellion. "Hear me out. I've kissed loads of guys, right? I know what makes a good kiss and a bad one. I can give you . . . pointers."

I stare at her, my mouth falling open as all words leave me. Her eyes flick to my lips and I lick them without thinking, then bite down hard on the lower. "Wouldn't that be, um . . . weird? For us to, er, do?"

Darcy clears her throat, giving a nonchalant wave of her hand. "'Course not. It's you and me. Nothing's weird with us."

She's right. Darcy's been my best friend since we were both in nappies, having grown up next door to each other. I have a twin brother who I'm very close with, but I've always felt equally close to Darcy, sometimes even more intensely. She's like family, but it's more than that. She's someone I *choose* to spend time with, share everything with, tell my deep dark secrets to, listen to hers in return. It makes sense we'd share this too.

"Okay," I say slowly, looking at her glinting blue eyes, my stomach clenching and heartbeat vibrating in my palms. "If you're sure you don't mind."

Darcy's smile is dazzling as she shifts onto her knees, leaning toward me. "'Course I don't mind. What are friends for?"

I swallow, anticipation rising from my belly to rest as a shimmering ball in my chest, the glow radiating down my arms. I nod, scrambling up so I'm mirroring her position.

We stay like that for a moment, looking at each other, something delicate but electrifying weaving in the space between our bodies. My heart is beating so hard I wonder if she can see it through my shirt, can feel the reverberations against her own chest like ripples in a pond.

"To kiss, you generally need to be closer," Darcy whispers, a tiny laugh in her voice. I can tell it isn't at me but in response to the strange volts of giddiness between us.

"Right. Yeah. 'Course." I shuffle nearer, a few centimeters separating us now. "This better?"

Darcy's grin is crooked, a dimple popping out on one side. She puckers her lips like a fish and makes a popping sound, then frowns. "Was that a good kiss for you?"

I roll my eyes, and she snorts.

"Like this," she says, one hand reaching out to land on my hip. With a light tug, she brings our bodies together—thigh to thigh, chest to chest. Now I *know* she can feel my heart pounding.

I look between us, her hand still on my hip, both of mine somehow on hers, holding tight. I don't remember putting them there.

Fundamentally, this is no different than a hug. No different than how we cuddle close when she sleeps over on the weekends. I can't figure out why it feels so charged, every nerve ending a trip wire ready to detonate. But then again, things with Darcy always feel gleaming and hyperfocused, like she absorbs all the light in a room, then reflects it back tenfold.

"Okay?" she asks gently. I look up, and all teasing is gone from her face. I nod, my throat dry and tangled in a knot so tight I can't get any words out. My stomach swoops like I'm cresting the highest hill of a roller coaster, limbs tingling with adrenaline and excitement and a tinge of fear that maybe I've made a mistake that there's no turning back from.

With all the care in the world, Darcy lifts her free hand so her palm cups the side of my neck, thumb brushing the angle of my jaw. I watch her watch where she touches me, brows knitting for a moment like something about it confuses her.

"Are *you* okay?" I echo.

She blinks, coming back to herself, a bit of that teasing resurfacing in slow degrees. "'Course," she says, tapping her forehead against mine. "I'm just taking my role as a teacher very seriously. I can't be responsible for the neighborhood youths being lousy snogs."

Some of the tension eases in my chest as we land back on familiar, sarcastic ground. "Darcy Burton: bassist and kissing instructor. Your CV is glowing."

"Mum and Dad will be so proud," she says with a tinkling laugh. I feel that laugh—the way the warm air of her exhale dances across my skin, vibrates into my chest, every sensitive cell in my body absorbing the sound waves like they can hold on to her forever.

Something about that laugh unlocks me.

Before I can process the movement, I press my lips to Darcy's, searching and hungry, wanting to taste her joy before it evaporates.

She tenses, and I do too, pulling back just as suddenly. "I'm sorry," I bumble out, eyes wide. "So sorry. I think you were supposed to do that part. I—" She cuts me off, molding her mouth back to mine with urgency.

My mind clears like the extinguishing of a candle flame while the rest of my body catches fire. Darcy is so soft, so warm, her hands sliding up to tangle in my hair in a gentle, desperate grip, urging my head to tilt slightly to the side. I follow her guidance and she deepens the kiss. An involuntary noise vibrates at the base of my throat, and she hums back, the sound both needy and satisfied.

We break apart on a sharp intake of breath. *Oh my god*, one of us whispers. I'm so lost and dizzy and delirious I don't know who. Then, like magnets colliding, we're kissing again, messy and rough and a little bit frantic, like a ticking clock hangs over our heads and we only have moments to indulge in these bursts of sensations zipping between us. Darcy's tongue gently glides across my lips, shocking my system, and I open on another gasp.

I feel like I'm flying, like a thousand tiny butterflies have unfurled from my skin, their beating wings lifting me *up*, *up*, *up* as I sink *closer*, *closer*, *closer* to Darcy. I hold on to her like I'll float away if I let go, and she holds me back, tight and flush against her.

"*Cubby*," Darcy murmurs against my lips.

"Cubby!" a voice parrots through the door, followed by three quick knocks.

Darcy and I break away, noses still touching as we stare cross-eyed at each other, breaths coming short and sharp.

"Cubby?" the voice repeats, doorknob starting to turn.

Oh crap.

My mum.

We rip apart, plummeting backward off opposite sides of my bed and landing with a loud crash. My head starts to spin, lips tingling and skin scorched with heat.

"Cubby, my love? Are you okay?" my mum says, entering the room in a hurry. She hovers over me, eyes wide as I try to bring her into focus.

"Christ, what happened?" Oliver, my twin, materializes in the doorway. "Sounded like the whole house was coming down."

"Are you two all right?" Mãe, my other mum, pushes past Oliver to look at Darcy.

I'm frozen, wind knocked from my lungs and head still swimming as I blink past a few stars.

From the fall.

Obviously.

Not from the kiss.

It would be weird for my head to still be swimming from the kiss . . .

"We were practicing a song and got too into it," I blurt, lurching up like a vampire rising from a casket. "We were, uh, standing on the bed and got too excited and fell."

"I didn't hear any music," Oliver, the delightfully aware menace, says.

"Maybe you weren't listening." I give him a warning glare that he completely misses.

"You two are very loud." He looks between me and Darcy. "It's more difficult not to hear you even when I don't want to." Oliver is autistic and while his honesty and candor are some of my favorite things about him, they're absolutely drowning me in embarrassment right now.

"Did you need something, Mum?" I turn to her, praying there was a reason for the interruption.

Because it needed to be interrupted.

Obviously.

Not because some weird part of me is furious that we were interrupted.

Mum blinks a few times. "Oh. Right. I was coming to tell you Connor's here to collect you. He's waiting downstairs."

Connor? Oh my god, *Connor*. How did I forget about my date with Connor?

"I've got to go." I jump to my feet, grabbing my black denim jacket from where it hangs on the chair as I dash to the door. "Love you all."

"Are you not going too, Darcy?" Mãe asks.

Christ, how did I forget about *Darcy*? What is wrong with me? Why does it feel like my brain is splitting in two?

"Nah. I got caught sneaking out last time," she says with a flippant wave, already back in her relaxed sprawl on my bed. "Only just got ungrounded. Not willing to risk it to watch a group of boys make farting noises."

Darcy's a year younger than me, and her parents keep her on the shortest of leashes, not allowing her to go out at all, tracking her phone and making surprise calls to the parents of whoever's house she's supposed to be at and asking to speak to her. They're über-conservative, and certainly wouldn't have picked me, with my piercings and "vulgar" music collection, as their daughter's best friend. It's only because I live directly next door and Darcy and I would burn the entire block down if we were separated that they let her stay here as often as they do.

Darcy regularly jokes that her parents spend their days wringing their hands that my mums will initiate her into the demonic cult of lesbianism, but I see the way their strictness eats at her, leaves her dimmed and dulled some days when they've really dug their claws into her.

"Besides, Cubby has herself a bit of a date tonight," Darcy continues, her voice calm and its usual level of bubbly. I cut her a warning glance, and she smiles that radiant smile of hers. She doesn't look flustered and frantic and blown to bits like the inside of my head does right now. The only thing ever so slightly off is her lips, a shade redder than they usually are. She's . . .

Darcy is unfazed.

Which makes sense. Total sense. Honestly, it's weird that *I'm* so frazzled. What's there to be frazzled about? It was just two friends practicing kissing. It must be my nerves from my date with Connor.

"I'm gonna crash here tonight if that's okay with you, Mrs. Clark," Darcy adds, shooting a puppy-dog look to my mums. They melt.

"Of course it's okay, darling," Mum says with a smile. "I'll order you some takeaway. Just tell me what you want."

"You're the best mums ever," Darcy croons. I know she means it. Darcy's mum, Doreen, makes Cruella de Vil seem like a top-rate caregiver.

A text buzzes on my phone.

u coming or what

"I've got to go," I say, jarred by the fact that I forgot about Connor *again*.

"Bye, darling. Have a good time."

"Be good."

"See you later, Cubby love." Darcy's soft goodbye is the one that snags my attention, and I spare one more second to look back at her between the slats in the staircase I've started descending. Our gazes lock, and my stomach lurches in that same way it did before. "Knock 'em dead," she says with an exaggerated wink, and I realize any charge was just in my head.

I roll my eyes and bound down the rest of the stairs to the guy I like waiting below.

This "date" is a lot like all the other times I've hung out with Connor outside of school or band practice: awkward, loud, and sparse on much interaction between us.

I'm extremely aware of my limbs and how I have no clue how to arrange them in a way that seems cool and alluring while I watch Connor chug beer bought by his older brother, then chuck the bottles at a low wall in an abandoned lot, his mates cheering from the side when they shatter.

At least Harry's here. He's also in our band, having moved to our town from Dublin several years ago. He's one of the best pianists I've ever heard, and it helps that he doesn't suck like most people in this village.

"You look nice tonight, Cub," he says, sidling over to me. "Is that a new shade of black you're trying out?" He gestures at me from head to toe.

I scowl as I give him a light shove. He knows I'd rather die than introduce a color besides black into my life. "Piss off, O'Connell." He laughs. Harry always laughs with me and it always creates a glow in my cheeks. We watch the guys throw rocks and bottle shards in quiet comfort.

"We still on for practice tomorrow?" he says after a bit.

"Unless the world ends, I suppose so." Our band—we're in between names at the moment—is the central part of our lives. Harry, Darcy, Connor, and I are all very different people, and I've often wondered if we would even talk to each other if it weren't for music binding us together, the sounds we create weaving between us like shared DNA.

We practice every second we can because we *want it*—that elusive *it*. That creation of a sound, a story, that takes the jumbled mess inside your head and turns it into something beautiful. Something others connect to. We want to be heard, and we'll do whatever it takes to make that happen.

"I've been fiddling with that transition to the bridge on our new song," he says. We've been pulling our hair out for a week trying to perfect this melody. I give him an excited look.

"Well, go on, then," I say, expecting him to hum it for me.

He smiles, grabbing my hand and propping it up so my forearm is parallel to the ground. He places his fingers on me like I'm a keyboard, pretending to play as he intones what he's come up with. He ends with a flourish, swiping across my arm like he's hitting every key, making me laugh.

I squeal, throwing my arms around his neck. "I love it! You're so right. We needed that major there to give it the—"

"What's this, then?"

Connor's voice is a physical thing, knocking Harry and I apart.

I blink for a second, not sure why I'm so startled. "*Connor*," I say, coming back to myself. "Connor, you have to hear this. I think Harry figured out the part we've been stuck on. Harry, go ahead—"

"Come on, Cubby. We're leaving." Connor's voice is devoid of any inflection, face stony and jaw working as he stares at Harry. Harry looks down at his shoes. I don't know why, but the tension is thick and dark as it looms over us.

Connor reaches out and grabs my wrist, tugging until I stumble next to him. He starts walking, hand moving to lace with mine in a too-tight grip as he tows me away. I trip as I look over my shoulder at Harry, who's still staring at the ground.

I've known Connor long enough to understand that when he gets in one of his moods, it's best to let him shake it off in his own time. He's one of the most charming guys I've ever met, but he has an artist's soul, one that's deeply sensitive, prone to moodiness. He's so brilliant, it's best not to push him, instead letting him linger in his emotions as he needs to. It's where the best art is made. We all know at this point to let him ride out a dark cloud. But this is wrong. Different. I can't parse out why.

He continues to hold my hand as he marches me home, but when we're a few blocks away, I dig in my heels. "Connor, what's *wrong*?" I pull on his arm so he'll stop. So he'll look at me. He turns, jaw set, and I flinch at the thunder in his expression, taking a step back. I return his stare, apprehension ticking at the back of my neck.

After a moment, he curses, dragging a hand over his mouth. "I just don't like the way he looks at you."

"The way who looks at me?"

"Harry."

I blink at him. "*Harry*? Our friend *Harry*?"

"*Yes, our friend Harry*," he snaps, mimicking my voice in a high-pitched tone. He shakes his head, glaring off to the side.

"How does he look at me?"

Connor's gaze flicks to me, lip curled, eyes dark, and I watch his face change—melting from stern and angry to something wolfish. My pulse picks up. He continues to look at me, his eyes tracing up and down my body, slow like honey, like an animal sizing up its prey. Heat flashes through me, making my skin prickle and my muscles tense.

"Like that," he murmurs, taking a step toward me, backing me up till my heels touch the lamppost behind me.

"Harry definitely doesn't look at me like *that*."

Connor chuckles, one hand coming to rest on my hip, warm and gripping tight. I'm probably supposed to touch him back, but I lock up, arms glued to my sides. "I had a lot of fun tonight," he says, eyes roaming my face.

"Yeah?" I stutter out as he leans closer. I can smell the beer on his breath, see the slight glaze in his eyes. My heart squeezes from the whiplash of his moods. But that's good, right? That he had fun?

"Yeah. You're . . . you're really cool, Cubby. I like spending time with you."

"I like spending time with you too," I whisper. His lips are near my throat, and I swallow. "I love making music with you." Connor, for all his moodiness, is a genius, the kind of guitarist I could only dream of being. We both know he's better, but it pushes me. Makes me strive and work at this thing I love, this raw form of creation. He brings out this need in me to impress him. I feel his smile at the spot right below my ear.

"I'm glad," he murmurs, pulling away to look down at me. "Because we're going somewhere. The band, I mean. Somewhere huge. We're going to be the next big thing, I can feel it."

"You shouldn't jinx us."

His look is pure mischief. "With people as good as me and you around, luck has nothing to do with it."

My smile is outrageous, but there's no dimming it. I bask in his praise like a plant seeing the sun for the first time after a brutal winter.

"One day, I'm going to write the biggest song in the world about you," Connor says, dragging a hand down my cheek, letting it rest on my throat.

I'm about to respond, mouth open, when he crushes his lips to mine. Our front teeth bang together, my head rocking back and hitting the lamppost with a crack. Connor doesn't seem to notice as he presses against me harder. It takes me a moment to realize that this is a kiss. Connor is kissing me. And I don't know why, but my immediate thought is that it's nothing like it was with Darcy.

It isn't soft. No warm lips and hesitant touches. It's gruff and wet and he's hurting my jaw with how hard he's holding it to keep my mouth propped open. He sticks his tongue down my throat, and I feel like I'm drowning.

After a moment, I roll my head to the side, desperately gulping at the cool night air. Connor's still there, lips at my neck. Along my collarbone.

These are better, gentler, and I force my muscles to relax a bit, lifting my shaky fingers into his hair. He lets out a small grunt of approval.

Something in me stirs, and I lean into the feeling, wanting it to erupt through me—craving the butterflies and the free-fall rush and the tingly cheeks from blushing and smiling. Because this is what every girl wants, right? A hot, brilliant guy telling her he likes her. Writing songs about her. Holding her hand and kissing her under streetlights.

He travels back up to my lips, and this time I'm prepared and brace for impact. I kiss him back, trying to keep pace. I must do an okay job because when he pulls away, he's smiling, cheeks flushed. He's so cute like this, grin boyish and broad, so different from the usual smirk he wears. I want to keep him like this forever.

"Let's get you home," he says, taking my hand and leading me the last few blocks to my door. He kisses me twice more before I go inside, my lips raw from the intensity.

I tiptoe to my room. Darcy is curled up in bed, fast asleep. I stare at her outline for a minute, my jaw clenched and eyebrows furrowed, an ache pulsing at my temples. I can't trace the knot of feelings in me, this tangled mass of misfiring nerves since kissing Connor. Is this what it feels like when you kiss the person you fancy? Confusing and hectic and leaving your brain doing somersaults?

It must be.

Relationships are never easy, that's what everyone says. Shows and movies and books always talk about how much hard work it is . . . This must be part of that.

With a sigh, I throw on my pajamas and snuggle up next to Darcy, creating a protective shell around her curved back, how we normally arrange ourselves when she sleeps over. Darcy stirs, looking over her shoulder at me. She blinks a few times, eyelids heavy, then she smiles, nuzzling closer.

"How was it?" she asks, voice thick with sleep. She reaches behind herself, finding my arm and pulling it over her, holding my hand to her chest.

"Really great," I say. And I'm pretty sure I mean it. I clear my throat. "He kissed me."

Darcy squeezes my hand. "Atta babe," she cheers through a yawn. "I knew you could do it."

"Practice makes perfect."

She chuckles, then yawns again, burrowing deeper into the sheets. Into me. There's that swooping feeling again, like my heart's a balloon, lifting me into the clouds and leaving my stomach behind. I feel a bit sick from it.

It's okay that I didn't feel that with Connor. Totally fine. Just because I didn't, doesn't mean I won't. It'll take time. More closeness. Maybe a few rounds of snogging when he isn't buzzed.

"Darcy," I whisper after a few minutes. "Did . . . did our practice feel different to you?" I have no baseline, no metric, to know how I'm supposed to be feeling. How a kiss is supposed to *make* me feel. And kissing my best friend, well, *obviously* that will create a funny feeling. It's a funny thing.

Darcy doesn't answer, her breathing deep and steady with sleep.

Which is fine. I don't need her answer. I'm too in my head, too lost in my thoughts, per usual. It's a knot of brambles up there, and I'm better off not fertilizing the weeds.

She's my best friend, that's all.

Things with her will always feel different.

Chapter 1

Now

Funny enough, the lyric *I hope you herniate a disc shaving your ass hair and stumble into traffic, Connor McCabe* doesn't lend itself to a decent melody. This fact hasn't stopped me from dedicating the past four grueling hours of band practice to making it even vaguely musical.

"Cubby, I'm not sure if you're aware of this, but screaming directly into the mic doesn't create a very good sound," Harry says, pulling off his headphones and stepping away from his keyboard. "So if we could move on . . ."

"Never took you for a traitor, Harry," Darcy says, eyeing him closely as she wraps a protective arm around my shoulders. "Do we need to add your name to the lyrics too?"

He throws his hands up in surrender. "I'm here, aren't I? If I were a real traitor, I'd be pissing around America on tour with Connor, selling out venues and making snow angels in all that studio money."

Darcy hisses, and I roll my eyes, pretending the truth of it doesn't slice me in half.

"Jesus Christ," Kale, one of our newest members, grumbles. "This is so boring." He slopes off to the corner, sliding down the wall to sit on the floor while he scrolls through his phone. His name is actually Harry Kale, but that is absurd, and we couldn't possibly keep track of two Harrys, so bitter vegetable it is. I frown in his general direction, and he ignores me per our usual routine. So cute! So fun!

I sigh, rubbing my knuckles against my eyes as a headache looms. It's moments like this that hurt the most—looking around and seeing this mess we're trying to call a band when, a year ago, Connor, Harry, Darcy, and I were a cohesive unit. While becoming successful musicians is the delusional pipe dream of countless people, we actually made it happen.

. . . Sort of. We were *close*, at least. We were called . . . well, we've cycled through quite a few names over the years. Rabbit Hole, Tongue-Tied, Ivan on My Mind—our inability to land on one doesn't matter. What matters is we were on the brink of really making something of ourselves after years agonizing over every note, practicing till our fingers bled, playing at any crap-hole pub that would let us through the door. We even finagled shoestring-budget tours, playing dive bars around Europe and gaining some recognition on social media.

Well, *Connor* gained recognition on social media. Pretty privilege is a very real thing, and he had no problem taking advantage of that. *For the good of the band*, he'd say. Now, his chronic flirting with girls in DMs seems less a selfless act to build a fanbase and more another brilliant red flag I ignored. Hindsight blah blah blah.

Regardless, we were honing in on the dream—bigger gigs, opening for bands we love, generating enough buzz and attention to sign with a label. Granted, that label is based in Iceland and only has a handful of other bands on their roster and we had to relocate to a new country to record, but we had stars in our eyes at the promise of a professionally produced album with real backing, nonetheless.

And then Connor, human wet wipe that he is, mucked it all up, cutting the rope as he reached the peak of the ladder, our deadweight plummeting back into a pit of insignificance.

Now we're once again nameless, with two new random band-mates our furious producer threw in to replace Connor as we watch his solo star rise.

"Okay, we need a reset," Darcy says, setting down her bass and rolling out her neck. "Let's talk it out. Jökull, would you like to start? Any input you want to give the group?"

Jökull, our new drummer, stares from behind his kit, slowly blinking his heavily lined eyes. "No."

He is the embodiment of the most stereotypical goth person I could ever conjure, and I catch myself frequently wondering if he's for real or just exceptionally committed to some sort of bit. He's the cousin of the owner of our label, Ring Road Records, a tiny "boutique"-style studio in what many call the music capital of the world: Reykjavík. (No one calls it that.) (Even my record deal is sad.)

Jökull never offers much in the way of input, ideas, or general conversation, but he is an excellent drummer, I'll give him that.

"Okay," Darcy says, smile never wavering. "Kale? Do you—"

"Actually," Jökull interrupts, voice deep and Icelandic accent strong, "I do have something to say." He unfolds his lanky limbs from his stool, rail-thin frame reaching an outrageous six foot six. He drags chipped black fingernails through similarly black bangs, shoulders hunched. "I've thought about this for a while now," he says, eyes fixed on the ground, voice a rumbly whisper. "And I'd like you all to call me Skull."

He's definitely committing to a bit.

"Skull?" Harry echoes. "As in—" He points to his head, and Jökull—sorry, *Skull*—nods.

After an extended moment of silence, he sits back on his stool.

"Right," Darcy says, drawing out the word. "Wonderful. Welcome . . . *Skull*! Thank you for sharing that with us. Does, er, anyone else have anything they'd like to add?"

"Yeah, I do," Kale says from the corner.

"Shocker," I mumble.

He shoots daggers at me, then stands, arms crossed and mouth twisted in a sour frown as he looks at the room at large. "Cubby is one more meltdown away from me walking. I'm an artist. My job is to make *art*. I can't work in an environment with more melodrama than a twelve-year-old's diary."

My anger spikes, and I step toward Kale. "First of all, there is nothing more melodramatic than saying your job is to *make art*, you pretentious roughage. Secondly, I'm not melting down. I'm—"

"I agreed to join this band because you had a unique sound. A clear vision of what you were trying to create. Not this disjointed bullshit," Kale spits back.

"You joined because you had a few viral videos playing violin and jumped at the first offer someone sent your way to join a band to get over your ex-boyfriend dumping you," I snap. "You'd still be in a basement in Ohio if it weren't for us."

Kale scoffs. "You really need to reevaluate who needs who in this situation. I've gained us more social media hits in a month than you've had in the three years since you released a single on Spotify."

"Don't flatter yourself," Darcy says, her own temper flaring. "Connor screwing us over accomplished that. It's only from morbid fascination that anyone gives us a listen now."

The room goes silent as a crypt, the truth of Darcy's statement oozing through the cracks in the cinder block walls. Connor went behind our backs, pursuing an invite from a stateside producer to record an EP about our messy relationship while he was still the lead of our band.

We ended our relationship eight months ago after being on-again, off-again for four and a half years. And it was amicable. Totally fine. Took him all of two weeks to start bringing random girls around, but I played the cool-girl role to a T. I'd spent the years we were together learning over and over again that showing any strong feelings was a surefire way to look pathetic and foolish so that by the time we were officially done, I didn't feel much at all.

And while I'd come to terms with the fact that I was too difficult to put up with in a relationship, too needy to love, I never for a second doubted that Connor would be faithful to the band in a way he could never be faithful to me.

This band has been our everything for so long, the idea of abandoning it is gross and sacrilegious. But apparently that was one more thing I subscribed uneven feelings toward. Now he's using the brutal tumult of our time together to fuck with the band I've put so much of myself into creating, and it makes me want to burn cities to the ground. But I can't. I have to still be the cool girl because any huge display of emotions will only magnify the microscope Connor's stunt has put me under.

You wouldn't think the lyrics "*You roared like a bear, caught my attention / Was that just reality suspension? / Cuz now you're meek as a mouse in our bed / Touching you fills me with dread*" would land with anyone with two brain cells to rub together, but the label execs liked the song so much, they offered him a fat deal, which he jumped at immediately.

The single hit number five in its first week.

I'm teetering between lashing out further at Kale or collapsing into my black hole of self-pity when Sigrún, the owner and CEO of Ring Road Records, walks in. She's also our producer. And publicist. And artist relations manager.

When we were first courted by Sigrún to sign with Ring Road, it was continually mentioned how the label has an intimate approach to creating an album . . . A more accurate term would be *one-woman-operation*.

"You need a name," she says without ceremony, pushing aside our long-forgotten tea to plop her large binder and computer on the shabby table near the door. "A band is nothing without a name. You are a gaggle of starry-eyed nobodies playing pretend at being rock stars without one."

"Good to see you too, Sigrún," I mumble. I like Sigrún, I really do. She's young and sharp and has built a label that—while not huge—is genuinely creating cutting-edge music and slowly attracting more attention. She doesn't take any bullshit, which is one of the reasons I was so excited to work with her. But she's also the most painfully honest person I've ever met—giving my autistic twin a run for his money—and sometimes I want to beg her on hands and knees to stop challenging the strength of my stiff upper lip.

"How about the Moody Loser's Club?" Harry chimes in, fingers tapping a lazy melody on his keyboard.

"How very helpful," Darcy says, lips pursed.

"Tell me it isn't accurate." He gestures at our defeated faces, then strikes a minor key.

"I'm looking for real suggestions here, Harold," Sigrún says. Through a bit of cyberstalking, I know she's twenty-nine, only six years older than most of us, but she acts like our mum, sharp glares and all.

"How about Cubby Clark and the Bad Apples?" Harry tries again.

I flinch, mouth dropping into a sour frown. "Why my name?"

He shoots me a confused smile. "Because you're our fearless leader, Cub."

No. He's wrong. So wrong. I *used* to be our leader. There wasn't a song or riff or key change I didn't have an opinion on. I organized gigs and accommodations and delegated anything else I was simply too exhausted to manage, but I led it all. Now it's hard to even get myself out of bed, let alone lead anybody anywhere.

"That's the cheesiest name I've ever heard," Kale sneers. We ignore him.

"Why not Darcy's name?"

"Darcy Burton doesn't have as lovely an alliteration," she says, knowing what a sucker I am for the way words balance and bounce.

"I don't think Cubby's name should be front and center. We're all equally contributing members here," Kale presses.

"Right. Because you bitching and moaning from the corner about how miserable you are really adds a lot to our collective morale." I don't generally like being an asshole, but fighting with Kale is the only time I feel anything but blue lately, so I'll take it.

"And you cursing out your ex into a microphone for hours on end is much better?"

"Oh, bugger off, you cabbage. No one asked you."

"Would you both shut up?" Sigrún barks, rubbing her temples. "I'm sick of this incessant bickering."

"Sorry, Sigrún," we mumble, looking down at our shoes.

"Don't be sorry, just knock it off. This isn't some open mic night at a shithole bar. You all pursued a music career because you apparently wanted one, so start acting like it." Sigrún's piercing gaze sweeps across us once more. "Right. Now that's settled, I'm going to pick a name and you're all going to shut your mouths about it." She looks around for a moment, eyebrows furrowed. Her attention locks on the mugs of stale tea. She snaps her fingers and points at it. "Tea Time Tantrum. That's your new name."

"Oof," Harry whispers from the corner. "That's . . ."

"A bit shit, innit?" Darcy mumbles back from her spot next to him.

"It's a fitting description of you," Sigrún replies dryly. "It's all you seem to know how to do. Lord knows you haven't been making any music."

While we have some home-recorded demos from the last few years up for streaming, we don't have anything professionally produced, and nothing without Connor credited. We're in a mad dash to get a song out while we're still benefiting from his betrayal. This isn't at all a horrifically bitter pill for me to swallow and doesn't eat me alive every night as I try to go to sleep.

"Good," Sigrún says, absorbing our silence. "Glad that's sorted. Now let's focus on the other elephant in the room. How is the new song coming?"

"Really great, thanks," I lie. Kale snorts.

"Can I hear it?" Sigrún asks, arching an eyebrow.

"Sorry, what now?"

"The song that's going really great. Can I hear it?"

It doesn't exist. "Still not finished," I reply, chewing on my lip.

"I don't care." She waves her hands. "Play me what you have so far. I can help brainstorm where to take it." Kale lets out another snort, and I'm seconds away from personally stripping the strings from his precious violin and strangling him with them.

I'm frozen, Harry's eyes fixed on me, Kale's smug grin burning into my cheek, Skull's . . . well, Skull is in his own world at the moment, where he tends to primarily exist, balancing a drumstick on the tip of his long finger.

Darcy's phone beeps, and she fishes it out of her pocket, murmuring a "Sorry" as we all turn to look at her. She glances at the screen, and her sharp intake of breath ripples across the room.

"What's wrong?"

Darcy shakes her head, shuffling backward as she looks at me. "I—No. Nothing. Nothing at all . . . I . . ." She collides with the soundproof wall, a small grunt tumbling from her full lips.

"What are you on about, Darce?" Harry asks, closing in on her with me.

She clamps her mouth shut, shaking her head like a wild thing, shooting out waves of panic that we all feel. "Nothing. I swear," she squeaks, phone clenched to her chest.

I narrow my eyes, then grab for her phone, but Darcy knows my tricks, her palm pressing squarely against my chin as she pivots away, my hand accidentally slapping her tit. She lets out a squawk of surprise, and I duck under her arm, only to be met with her elbow near my eye.

"Cubby, stop it," she hisses, trying to roll away along the wall. I stick out my foot, our calves twisting together until we tip into a jumbled mess against the ground. We squirm for a few more seconds, arm wrestling for the phone until I take a cheap shot and tickle the soft skin between her shoulder and jaw, a spot I know is incredibly sensitive. Her hands dart to her throat in protection, and I snatch up the phone, tapping in her passcode and squinting at the screen.

Connor's face glows back at me, black hair the perfect mix of styled and disheveled, green eyes glinting with mischief yet somehow also looking desperately bored. One corner of his mouth is tipped up, the hint of a dimple making his smirk just approachable enough that it's dangerous.

Dickhead.

I scroll to the headline, heart sinking like a stone in water as I read.

SPECIAL GUEST: CONNOR McCABE!

Connor McCabe, overnight musical sensation, is making a surprise appearance on *Evenings with Evening* where he's slated to debut a new song and offer up a few hints at the album he's rumored to be releasing any day now. Connor went viral after his first single "can't bear it" dropped, the internet buzzing over his angsty sound and unarguably gorgeous appearance in a simply shot black-and-white music video. But what really fueled the frenzy was the plethora of hidden messages in the lyrics. In the age of social media, almost any couple has the potential to become global gossip if the drama is juicy enough, and Connor's coded references to former girlfriend and bandmate, Cubby Clark (lead singer of a band that apparently doesn't have a name), has everyone intrigued, his use of intricate Easter eggs creating a storm of excitement and guesswork online.

Okay, I literally just threw up in my mouth. It is a musical hate crime to offer any praise to lyrics like "*Tease me up, wear me down / Promised paradise didn't feel that nice / You're an empty vase with a pretty face.*" It doesn't take a genius to pick up that he's speaking of my apparently disappointing vagina, pop culture sleuths requiring all of four seconds to decode that hidden meaning. High fives to all the brainiacs who took the time to tag me in their revelations.

"Cubby love, leave it. He doesn't matter," Darcy says, reaching around me to try to grab her phone, her chest plastered against my back. We've been here so many times before, Connor slicing me open and Darcy trying to hold the edges of the wound closed.

"What's going on?" Sigrún says in a clipped tone, snatching the phone from me. Her eyes flick across the screen, Harry and Kale coming up behind her to read. I don't bother checking on Skull. I'm sure he's still fully engrossed in his stick.

Sigrún lets out a deep sigh, closing her eyes and tapping the corner of the phone against her forehead.

"I'm sorry, Cubby," she says, rolling her neck, then fixing her weary gaze on me, "but we're going to have to watch."

Chapter 2

Bleary-eyed and cranky, we crowd around a laptop in one of the studio's conference rooms. It's four AM here in Reykjavík as we tune in to Connor's New York appearance, and I add being awake at this ungodly hour to my endless list of grievances against my ex—above him telling me acknowledging a six-month anniversary was cringe but below him suggesting I "do something about my mustache."

The opening theme for the late-night talk show *Evenings with Evening* trills from the tinny speakers, and we all flinch. Applause erupts as Danny Evening, the charming host, steps out from behind the curtains and grins. The introduction plays out as Danny waves at the crowd, the announcer mentioning Connor's name as the special guest, generating some screams. My body is a live wire of anticipated rage, poised and ready to detonate the second Connor opens his smug mouth and says something deeply cutting to me on a personal level—artfully disguised in a tone that's kind and magnetic and will make everyone believe he's a good guy.

It's so simple, almost boring, how he'll accomplish it: Connor will come out, waving in a way that's tentative, somewhat aloof, but endearing all the same. There will be a tender awkwardness to him, something sort of precious in the way he carries his long limbs, like he's just recently grown into a man's body he isn't quite sure how to carry, shoulders ever so slightly curled, smile somehow sinful yet earnest.

He'll sit in the overstuffed armchair, looking around, wide-eyed, until he catches himself, fixing his attention back to the host. He'll push his hands through his hair, maybe miss a beat or talk over Danny Evening, color rushing to his cheeks as he risks a quick glance at the audience who will whoop at his effortless allure. He'll make a self-deprecating joke, prop one ankle on the opposite knee, an obvious show of ease that the audience will pick up on, knowing that *deep down* he's nervous. A beautiful, talented, *nice guy* wanting to make a good impression.

It'll all be absolute shit.

Connor is the most absurdly confident person I've ever met. He disguises his cockiness as dazzling charisma, but that boy could sit in a meeting with the prime minister and feel like his input on foreign policy is a godsend. The nice guy is the greatest myth of the twenty-first century.

Danny Evening drags out his opening monologue, the climax marked with a clap of his hands and a sly grin to the camera. Darcy toys with my hair from her spot behind me, twisting a strand around her finger, dragging the pad of her thumb over the fanned ends. Her gentle touch is the only thing that keeps me from storming out right now.

"Unless you've been living under a rock for the past month, you've definitely heard of tonight's first guest. Now, at this part of the show, I generally go into a little bio on the star, talking about their claims to fame, their accolades. But why talk when I can"—someone throws him an acoustic guitar from off-camera—"introduce him in song."

Danny strums the guitar, clearing his throat a few times as the audience applauds. He starts playing the rough melody of Connor's chart-topping hit, and the crowd erupts in more screams and cheers as he parodies the lyrics:

> *Who knew that you could top the charts*
> *Of pop art*
> *By singing of lackluster sex*
> *With your ex.*
> *It helps to have a handsome face,*
> *If I drop names, I'm a disgrace.*
> *Give great applause to our guest,*
> *It's safe to say, he is the best.*
> *At sex? We cannot say, but hey!*
> *With a face like that, I'm sure he'll get to try again someday.*
> *Please welcome—*

Danny whips the guitar to his hip, throwing out his hands. "Connor McCabe!"

The curtain rises, and my villain origin story appears, walking out in well-tailored black trousers, a white T-shirt, and the leather jacket I bought for him for his eighteenth birthday.

"Damn," Kale mumbles. "Sometimes I forget how hot he is." I punch his shoulder.

Connor makes his way across the set, shaking Danny's hand before sitting. It takes a ridiculous amount of time for the crowd to stop cheering, anger churning through me with every passing second.

"I feel incredibly uncool sitting next to you," Danny says, toying with his tie covered in daisies. "Should I be sporting more leather? No one gave me the memo."

"You seem like a chaps guy," Connor quips, Irish accent dripping with good humor. He leans back in the chair, crossing one ankle over the opposite knee. Called it.

Danny shoots the audience an impish look. "My wife has specifically requested I don't comment on any assless paraphernalia I may or may not dabble in. Some things are supposed to stay between a couple."

The crowd erupts, Connor grinning as he chuckles along. "Smart woman."

"But seriously, look at you," Danny says, roping the audience back in to Connor's orbit. "So damn cool. You have that quintessential rocker vibe. That indescribable thing."

"Careful, mate, my head won't fit through the doors leaving here." There's more laughter, a few high-pitched cheers. Connor winks at the audience. I want to put my fist through the computer screen.

"Does this come naturally?" Danny asks, gesturing with a flourish at Connor. "Have you always been like this? Or is it something you're stepping into with your new fame?"

Connor's expression shifts to something thoughtful. Serious. He leans forward, uncrossing his legs and planting his elbows on his thighs, fixing his gaze on Danny in a way that gives the sensation that we're listening in on something intimate and important shared between friends. We all hold our breath. "I'm not trying to be anything but myself."

"Liar!" I slam my hands on the table, wanting to break the laptop in two.

Harry, ever so delicately, restrains me. "Easy, Cub. It'll be okay," he murmurs into my ear as he squeezes my shoulders. I shrug out of his grip.

"Don't lie to her," Darcy says to my left. "There's no telling what shit he'll spew next. This could *easily* get worse."

"Will you all shut up?" Kale snaps. "The whole point is to hear what damage he's going to do."

Skull snores from the couch in the back.

"So your single—this single—" Danny holds up a posterboard of Connor's derivative black-and-white EP cover. "It has everyone in a chokehold. You've become an overnight sensation, bringing in record-breaking streams of your music video, hitting number *five* on the *Billboard* charts . . . What's that like, man? How does it feel?"

"I hope it feels like a boiling enema, you talentless clown," I spit at the screen. Everyone shushes me.

Connor shakes his head, tilting his face up toward the ceiling for a moment before fixing an earnest look at Danny. "It feels"—*bleep*—"ing incredible, mate. I never expected this. All I've ever wanted to do was make music, put pieces of my soul into a melody. And to have that embraced by fans? It's unreal."

"Okay, I'm sorry, but, like, is this legal? Is it legal to lie this much on a late-night program?" I say, deranged gaze bouncing around the room. "Does America not have some alliance to prevent this kind of bullshit? Because that dickhead has wanted fame and fortune since I've known him."

"Cubby, please, I'm begging you to shut up," Sigrún says, placing a hand on the nape of my neck. I think it's supposed to feel comforting, but it's like a vise. "We need to hear what he's saying."

"You were in a band before going solo, right?" Danny asks.

Connor nods, features slipping into a pensive expression. "I was, yeah."

"What happened there? What made you set out on your own?"

Connor sighs like the weight of the world sits on his shoulders. I hope he gets crushed by a piano. "Music is a fickle beast, yeah? Creating it, you can almost lose yourself, if you aren't careful. You need to be in the right place, the right frame of mind, with the right people. It'll be work, don't get me wrong, but something about that work *works*, if that makes any sense. Like you feel things settling into place when you've found your sound. Your flow.

"And, listen, I have nothing but the greatest of love for my old band. We're still close, we still talk, there's no bad blood between us, so I really don't think they'll mind me saying this, but it wasn't a good fit. They were searching for a sound that wasn't right for me. And I sincerely hope they find what they're looking for. There's so much peace in finally discovering the thing that clicks."

"And you certainly found that, didn't you? Your first single, and you shoot up the charts. How does something like that happen? What inspired that song?" Danny slants a knowing look at the audience, garnering a few more whoops.

I'm twenty-three. Is this forty-year-old man truly asking on live TV for the inspiration of a song obviously written about me losing my virginity to be spelled out for him?

Connor laughs, a light blush staining his stupid perfect cheekbones. "Well, I can't say they're the most subtle of lyrics, mate. You can go ahead and fill in those pieces yourself, yeah?"

Danny throws his head back and laughs like Connor is a stand-up comedian. "A very diplomatic answer. They have you trained well already."

"I'm not looking to ignite discourse." Connor holds up his hands.

"It's rumored the muse of the song was a member of your old band. You sure there's no bad blood?"

Connor laughs again, blush deepening. He plays to the crowd, looking around while he plucks at the collar of his T-shirt. "Christ, did it get hot in here?"

"Touchy subject?"

Connor shrugs, some of that composure coming back. "Listen, the muse of the song, she's a great girl. I'll always love her. And what she taught me about myself? Can never thank her enough for that. I won't say who she is, specifically, but there's no bad blood. I think when you're foolish, young teenagers you kind of hold this idea that you're immune to heartbreak, in a way. Like if you give love everything you have, there's no way it can turn around and hurt you. I've come to realize that I'm just as susceptible to heartbreak as everyone else. It happens, and we learn and we grow from it, healing around and preserving that love that was once there."

My head jerks back, smacking into Darcy's chest from where she stands behind me. I tilt my chin up to look at her with wild anger on my face.

Darcy's mouth hangs open as she stares at the screen. "Did he—"

"Imply *I* broke *his* heart?" I finish for her. "Yeah. Seems like it."

"Wow. You really can't spell *manipulation* without *man*," Darcy growls. A startled laugh bursts out of me, and I turn fully around to face her. Her eyes are already on me, something soft and charged about them that makes my heart squeeze. For half a second, as she looks at me and I look at her, all of this feels . . . okay. Funny, even. I have Darcy and I'm not sure what else a person needs in life. Then Kale shushes us and Connor starts talking again and the rage regains its footing.

"We both know we're better off as friends," Connor continues. "And we'll always have a mutual respect for each other as artists. I truly believe she's not bitter."

Not bitter? You bet your ass I'm bitter. I'm so bitter, I could be a lemon at this point. And Connor knows this. He knows my every scar and bruise. He knows how I hold grudges. He knows the dark cloud that lurks around my bones and the constant ache in my jaded heart. And he made no secret of how unpalatable all of it was. I used to believe Connor would be the person to know me better than anyone, but now all I know is how much he resented my dark, ugly pieces.

"And there's a real beauty in that, yeah?" Connor carries on, my blood boiling. "In that pain of caring so deeply about something—someone—but letting go because it's what's best for everyone. That idea—that nostalgia for a love you want with a partner so badly but realize they aren't the person you made up in your head—the beauty in letting them go, has really inspired my next single."

"Are you going to play that single for us tonight?" Danny coaxes. The crowd goes wild.

Connor blushes again, dragging a palm across the back of his neck. "Only if they want me to." He flicks a wrist at the audience. The applause could rupture an eardrum.

"I think that's a yes," Danny says with a smile that belongs in toothpaste commercials.

Things move quickly from there, the cameras switching to the house band as they play a jaunty beat before fading out. The shot focuses on a dark stage, the lighting midnight blue, Connor's tall silhouette looking otherworldly in the center.

With a striking flourish, the lights illuminate his face. One hand cradles the microphone as he adjusts it, the other gripping the neck of his guitar.

After a dramatic pause, both hands move to the guitar, and he starts strumming, the acoustics deep and rumbly, an accompanying piano joining in after a measure. There's something familiar about the melody, like a rhythm from a dream, warped somehow but tugging at a memory all the same. My eyebrows furrow, shoulders hunching forward as I lean toward the speakers. Where do I know it from?

A gentle percussion joins in, and the notes swirl in my head, even more familiar, but swollen in a way I don't recognize. What damn song is this?

Connor grips one large hand around the mic again, leaning in, voice raspy as he presses his lips close and begins to sing:

> *The cracks in my ceiling*
> *Are a map to our memories.*
> *The innocent first days*
> *All the things we could be.*

The tempo is slower, but realization slams through me.

> *It strikes deep in my chest,*
> *A bolt from the blue.*

I should lay it to rest,
But damn, how I wanted to love you.

I see red as the instruments pick up emotion, Connor stepping forward so he's straddling the mic stand as he (over)sings the next verse:

You weren't my dream, just an illusion,
A house but not my home.
On shaky ground with perpetual frown
I watched you tear down my delusion.

The truth twists through me like a knife, white hot and violent as betrayal rips down my spine. There's no way he could be this evil.

There's a guitar solo here, one I could play in my sleep, despite that bastardized beat and addition of a major key. And then he sings the next lines:

That you were the one,
Oh baby, why'd you have to run?

I feel Darcy's and Harry's eyes on me, my skin burning with an anger that can't be safe for a single body to hold. I jerk to standing, hands tensed into claws at my side as I continue to stare at the screen.

"Oh, Cubby," Darcy says. Harry puts his hand back on my shoulder, but I flinch away, his pity not helpful.

Nothing will ever be helpful.

Because Connor McCabe just stole my lyrics on live TV and is singing them to millions of viewers.

Chapter 3

"We need to take action. A cease-and-desist. Sue him into oblivion," I say, pacing the length of the room, hands tearing through my greasy brown hair.

"*You* need to calm down," Sigrún warns from her chair in the corner.

"Calm down? Calm down? My ex-boyfriend deserted our band, became an overnight star on a song about how bad I am in bed, then stole my lyrics and sang them on an internationally beloved talk show viewed by millions every night. Where in that absolute disaster is calm supposed to fit in?"

I'm not sure if it's my hysterics or the truth of what I say, but Sigrún backs down. Even Kale has sense enough to not be an absolute tit at the moment. He never played with Connor, so this isn't as appallingly personal, but he *has* worked on old songs we've been trying to repurpose for our EP. Who knows how many others Connor has planned to snatch from us? He's probably ready to drop a surprise album of my life's work on Tuesday.

What twists the knife even deeper is that of all the songs Connor could have stolen from me, *that* was the one he picked. I wrote it when I was eighteen and heartsick, reeling from my first of many breakups with him. We'd played our first London show a week before, and I caught him snogging a girl in the bathroom after our set.

I stayed in bed for days, devastated and inconsolable. The only moments I felt remotely human were when I was writing about the pain eating away at me. When I completed the song, I foolishly played it for Connor before band practice, expecting some sort of vindication and empowerment like when Stevie Nicks sang "Silver Springs" at Lindsey Buckingham on live TV. But instead of staring at me with remorse and heartbreak and need, he stared at me like I was a proper idiot and he was embarrassed for me and of me.

"It's a bit much, don't you think?" he'd said, a few seconds after my voice broke on the final lyric. "All the theatrics . . . Comes across rather desperate. I don't think it would play well for a crowd."

Connor had needled at my songwriting since we started working together, but I'd always seen it as him pushing me to new levels of creativity. But that was the first time he was breezily brutal, showing me how excessive my feelings are, how stupid they make me look when I share them. It was then that I learned to tailor away the gross enormity of my emotions.

We got back together a week later.

With shaky hands, I click into a social media app, needing to stare directly into the pit of hell. I only have to type C-O-N before Connor McCabe pops up as the first suggestion, an obscene number of hits about him from the last hour noted in the search bar.

I wish him the worst, I really do.

Can Cubby Clark fight? Cuz i'll go at anyone that hurt my
bb Connor McCabe

no but did you guys *listen* to those lyrics? The man is
fucking brilliant

Connor McCabe is the only man that could ask me to
smile and I wouldn't punch him in the face

I know we've all moved on from his first single and are making his new song our entire personalities but the offer will forever stand for Connor McCabe to fill my empty vase any day.

Okay but fr are we not going to talk about how Cubby Clark was wearing blue in that first pic Connor posted of them on IG and then deleted? "A bolt from the blue"??? Like PLEEEEEASE

I'm sorry but Connor McCabe could spit in my face and I'd be like thank you daddy i'll have another. it is truly insane to me that Cubby Clark would ever fuck that up like girl what?????

My phone drops from my numb fingers and I press my forehead against the wall, praying for a black hole to open up and swallow me.

"How could he do this to us?" I whisper. The question loops around my mind, rage chiseling through the hurt. "Seriously, how could he do this to us?" I whip around, eyes frantically searching for Harry and Darcy, the ones who have been there from the start. "We wrote that together. Those are *my* words. *Our* music. How could he violate something as sacred as that?"

Harry's face is stricken as he looks back at me, slowly shaking his head. His lips part but no words come out, and he drops to his piano bench, elbows propped on his thighs as he buries his head in his hands.

Darcy is similarly collapsing in on herself from her spot on the floor, legs tucked to her chest and forehead pressed against her knees. I have the impulse to go to her, to wrap my arms around her shoulders, to sit next to her and let her lay her head in my lap, holding her tight until the world stops spinning out of control.

But my anger churns up a restlessness, something sharp and desperate with snapping jaws in my chest, moving my feet. I pace the room, vision blurred. I feel Sigrún's eyes tracking me, Kale's and Skull's too, but I can't look at them. I refuse to acknowledge the pity on their faces, the reality that we're even more behind now with this album than we originally thought.

Sigrún grabs my hand on my next pass. "Take a beat. Sit down and we'll talk this through."

I shake my head, slipping out of her grip. I can't stop. Stillness is the scariest thing to face. If I give in to the stillness, it'll leave the door wide open for sadness, which will take me to my knees, lay me on the ground, and never let me back up. It's the law of inertia. It's better to move—vainly try and satiate that manic restlessness—than be trapped under the weight of numbness.

"Let's look at this rationally," Kale pipes up. "Cubby, I get it. I get why you're upset and it's a really shitty thing he's done, but it doesn't actually change that much for us."

This stops me in my tracks. If looks could kill, Kale would be dust in the wind right now.

He holds up his hands, gaze steady but not challenging. "I swear I'm not trying to fight you. I'm *not*. But we have to take emotions out of this for just a second as we figure out the next move."

Take out emotions? Take out *emotions*? Music is nothing *but* emotions. It's the language of feelings we don't have names for. It has the power to lift you up or drag you down. It's memories set to melodies. Without emotions, there is no music.

I'm about to say all this to Kale, but he clasps his hands in front of his chest in a mock beg. "I'll let you yell at me in a second but please let me get this out."

I scowl but wave him on.

"Here's what we know: Connor stole your song. There's no getting that back. And it also means he's not above stealing other songs."

I nod, teeth grinding together.

"Sorry, but couldn't we make a statement? Go to the press with the truth?" Skull surprises me by asking from the corner.

We all look to Sigrún. She shakes her head, pinching the bridge of her nose. "It wouldn't do much. You never recorded or released the song, so there's no real legal action. Making a claim that the moment's hottest pop star stole a song from a no-name band—quite literally up until yesterday—he was previously a member of would only be setting Cubby up to be called the crazy, vindictive ex. The optics aren't good."

"Fuck the optics, it's about telling the truth," Darcy says from her spot on the floor, indignation flaring crimson across her cheeks. "Those are Cubby's words. She deserves the credit for them."

My gaze locks with hers, something fierce and frightening in its intensity burning in her eyes. She doesn't smile, or soften, or give me an encouraging nod, but that look lets me know she'll always have my back. She'll do whatever it takes to make things okay.

Sigrún shoots her a pleading frown. "I agree, Darcy. Believe me, I do. But I'm telling you the reality of the outcome. It wouldn't hurt Connor or get the music back to Cubby. It would only increase public support and infatuation for him. People love to be on the side of the 'nice guy' being publicly slandered by the 'crazy ex-girlfriend.' It's awful but it's the truth."

Bile burns up my throat, head swimming. Even before this new song, I would regularly get hate for being associated with Connor. DMs and tags calling me a whore, a prude, a bitch. YouTube comments on our old performance videos saying how glad they are that we're broken up. That I never deserved him. That he was way out of my league. That I'll end up miserable and alone. Strangers on the internet somehow hacked into the meanest, darkest things I whisper to myself in the bad times and confirmed they're all true.

"We won't make a statement," I say, knees giving out as I fall into a chair. "But it's too risky to include anything we wrote when he was around on our album."

"Unless we drop the songs first, yeah?" Harry says. "We could put them out right now? Lay down four or five tracks we like well enough and put it out there?"

I shake my head. "Still too risky. We could put weeks into producing it for him to beat us to it. And I refuse to put out anything in an unpolished rush because Connor's gone and strapped a ticking time bomb to our chests."

Harry opens his mouth to argue, but Kale cuts him off. "Cubby's right. We've been disconnected as a band as is, even before this was hanging over our heads. There's no way we could even get an EP produced in a way we all agree on."

"So, what, then? Where does that leave us?" Harry asks, an edge of desperation in his voice.

I take a deep breath, then another. It takes work to swallow down the anxiety knotting in my throat, pressing at my ribs, but I square my shoulders, meeting the eyes of each person in the room with a rueful look. "It leaves us at the beginning. So we better get started."

Chapter 4

I've been staring at the studio ceiling for so long my vision has gone fuzzy, like I'm in the center of a blizzard, trapped on all sides by suffocating white.

Someone threw out the idea that we head back to our apartment to rest a few hours ago after I calmed down, but none of us made any actual moves. Something about a forty-five-minute bus ride out of Reykjavík's city center to our shoebox-sized apartment we all cram into didn't seem that great.

Instead, we're taking turns lying on the studio's worn-out couch, kidding ourselves that any second we'll initiate the grueling work that needs to be done.

Skull is spread across the cushions, his long body relaxed, eyes closed. I'd think he was asleep if it weren't for the drumstick twirling gracefully between his long fingers. I have my back pressed against the base of the sofa, Darcy's head resting in my lap as I play with her hair, looping the pink strands around my fingers, feeling the smooth glide of it across my palm. She holds my other hand near her stomach, twisting my rings and fiddling with my bracelets. Kale tunes his violin from the corner, Harry tapping a piano key sporadically for him to work off. The inability to keep our hands still might be the only thing we have in common, music radiating from our bodies, inevitable even when we'd rather avoid it.

Kale runs out of strings and places his instrument to the side, a low, haunting echo vibrating through the room before silence closes around us like a curtain.

I know I should be working, leading us to make something, but I can't. I can't open that vein—feel and feel and feel in the hopes I create something someone else feels too. I'm supposed to say something in my music, but I don't have any story worth sharing that isn't mortifyingly vulnerable. Even the idea of getting up and grabbing my guitar, strumming a few notes, exhausts me.

That's the part that's most grotesque about depression—how it binds your limbs so you can't move to do the things that might make you feel, might take you out of the numbness. Instead, it keeps you chained down as you rot in the stupor. I know so many artists use their depression for something achingly beautiful—create masterpieces from the hurt—but mine is too dark and wet and grimy. Too consuming. More and more often, I wonder if I'm too sad to make good art. I know I'm too sad to be loved. Connor proved that time and again.

We sit in silence for a few more minutes, a dark cloud hovering over the room, then Harry turns fully to his piano, staring at the expanse of keys before cracking his knuckles and wiggling his fingers.

With the bravado of a concert pianist, he bows his head and lays his hands to the ivory, the notes reverberating around us. A swelling melody fills the room as he plays, and it takes me two bars to recognize the beat, Cardi B's "WAP" resonating through the room with a deeply emotional undertone, slowed way down to add drama.

I let out a bark of surprised laughter, and Harry looks at me out of the corner of his eye, lips twitching before he tilts his head, putting his entire body into the performance, hands moving with an ostentatious flourish as the chorus plays out. The words *wet ass pussy* loop through my mind with the chords.

I'm fully giggling now, Darcy's head bouncing in my lap as she laughs too. After a few more bars, Kale picks up his violin, adding an enchanting somberness to the notes. Darcy sits up, clearing her throat and belting lyrics about doing Kegels with an emotional punch that would make Adele proud. That's when I properly lose it, tipping to my side and grabbing my stomach while I cackle. Skull quietly snorts from his spot on the couch above me, tapping his drumsticks against the wall in time to the beat.

They amp up the theatrics, Darcy singing with her entire soul, Harry standing as he pounds into the keys. He cocks his head to look at me, a lock of his chestnut hair falling across his forehead as he grins. I shake my head as I smile back, and that earns me a wink before his focus returns to the piano.

Darcy's face pops up above me, lined with emotion. She straddles my hips while I continue to lie in a giggling heap on the floor, her hands moving to cup my cheeks in a dramatic grip as she sings to me about how profoundly she's a freak bitch. Warmth balloons in my chest, knowing she'll do anything to make me laugh like I'll do anything to make her smile.

When the song finally comes to a close, Darcy slumps against me in a boneless heap, panting as she presses her cheek against my sternum. Our bodies vibrate together as we continue to laugh, every nerve ending in me lighting up, the stale sadness temporarily lifting from the room. After a few seconds of silence, Harry starts at the piano again, playing around with the keys so the quiet doesn't linger. I watch him toy with his instrument, the way his hands spread and stretch, how he keeps his lower lip held between his teeth as he tries something new.

Harry is beautiful in a way of contradictions. Wavy, reddish-brown hair that's always a few inches too long, sticking up in angles from how often he runs his hands through it. His nose is on the larger side, sharply defined and drawing focus, a crook in the bridge from a childhood fight. It balances his wide mouth that's always kicked up in a boyish smile. And those eyes. Flame-blue and framed by dark lashes, his eyes could stop anyone in their tracks. Everyone talks about how gorgeous Connor is, and that's true, but I've always thought Harry was the beautiful one between the two.

Harry taps out a stilted melody—moody and slow—repeating it a few times. He trips over a key, but something about it clicks a mental gear into place.

"Add an A minor to that?" I say, sitting up suddenly and causing Darcy to topple off me. She shoots me an undignified pout. I distractedly pat the vicinity of her shoulder, my eyes locked on Harry.

Without pause, Harry seamlessly does as I ask, and the notes wrap around me, my focus turning inward, a golden thread looping through my mind. I trace the progression. Track where it should go next.

"Take the E minor, B minor to the five?" I scramble on hands and knees across the carpet toward him. The chords play out, something intimate and sad with an almost hopeful note at the end. "Minor two, to the five, to the one?" I say, eyes fixed in a trance while fuzzy lyrics dangle in my periphery. I know better than to grab at them. They'll slot into place when they're ready. He keeps playing, hands spread across the keys as he explores further up the scales. There's something vulnerable in the way Harry plays, pouring raw emotions into the tips of his fingers.

"Darcy, can you—"

A deep rhythm vibrates from her bass, creating a ripple through my brain and down my spine, causing me to shiver. She reads my mind, amplifying the whisper in my head, playing it so perfectly a lump forms in my throat. Sometimes I wonder if she knows my thoughts better than I do.

Pieces start to crystallize, the colors of the song inking into my vision—dark blue, streaks of gold, a violent splash of pink, the same shade as Darcy's hair. I whip around, eyes spinning as I try to pinpoint Kale, but he already has his violin to his shoulder, chin lovingly cradled at the base. He drags the bow across the strings, something quivering and sharp mixing with the swelling music around us. Skull moves to his kit and joins in, his offbeat drumming grounding the sound, making it fuller, richer.

Harry continues leading us, the piano melody becoming stronger, surer. He's added an optimistic lilt, something that starkly contrasts against the drama of the chord progression.

I stand, snatching up my guitar and slinging the strap over my shoulder, following their lead. Darcy winks at me, and my heart could burst from the excitement, the smile spreading across her face. I fish out my phone from my back pocket, tossing it on the table after hitting record on a voice memo.

I start to mumble-sing, humming along to the melody as I search for words. For the first time in a long time, I don't hold myself back, I don't bite my tongue to pieces in fear of the inevitable imperfection.

> *A fool of me and a fool of you,*
> *I regret you now, but what's a girl to do?*

Phrases continue to tumble out, some good, some nonsensical, others undeniably awful, but I don't care. This moment isn't for perfection, it's for creation.

> *Dreams of us stuck in my mind,*
> *but you always mocked the things that shined.*

Darcy's voice joins the sound, rough and lovely, a bit higher than mine:

> *Wore your empty promises like a tattoo on my skin,*
> *Your losing battles, I just can't win.*

My focus flashes to her, our eyes hooking and holding as the music continues to dance around us. Her smile is equal parts joy and disbelief. It's been so long since we had a moment like this—one that feels almost otherworldly, like we're making something more than music with how in sync we are, how starkly and terrifyingly rooted in the present we are. Darcy and I have always toyed and played with music like this, but the purity of creating in this way has dimmed over the past few years, so much of my focus centered on trying to impress Connor, make something that would win me a rare smile or crumb of praise.

I smile back at her, nose stinging and pressure building behind my eyes. Which is stupid and dramatic, but I've felt so disconnected from music, from the thing that makes me whole and human, that it's like gasping in a breath after nearly drowning.

Harry trips over a key change, and we all share a shaky laugh, Kale's quick hands covering the hole. Skull carries the rhythm, his brows knitted in concentration as he plays. We continue to toy with the sound, taking it down different twists and turns, aimless lyrics thrown in and out.

The song builds toward the inevitable bridge, and I watch Darcy's clever fingers pluck notes straight from my heartstrings as I fumble out words that rise to the surface of my throat before I can question if they work.

> *Stab myself in the back, just to prove to you,*
> *Go ahead, ask me to do it again, and I would.*
> *Who else are you going to find to stand where I stood?*
> *They may love you, but no one will ever treat you half as good.*

The early melody repeats, and Darcy and I bumble out a choppy chorus, trying to remember what we sang earlier, smiling with a laugh at the curled edges of our voices. Finally, when it feels like this thing we're making has embedded under our skin, we come down, the last few notes of Harry's piano echoing in the room.

It's silent for a few moments, all of us staring in bewilderment at each other, panting and flushed like we ran a marathon.

Then we burst into screams of excitement.

"We made something. We actually fecking made something," Harry cheers, sliding off his piano bench and charging at me. The second my guitar hits its stand, he wraps me in a hug, lifting my feet from the ground and spinning us around.

"I'm so excited I could cry," Darcy says, lying flat on her back, one hand ostentatiously draped across her forehead. When Harry lets me go, I trip over to her, planting my hands on either side of her shoulders, touching my nose to hers before collapsing on top of her in a tangle.

"I didn't think we actually had it in us," Kale says with his usual level of snark. But when I look at him, his smile is genuine.

"Skull, I loved how you brought it all together," I say, trying to roll off Darcy. She doesn't let me, cinching her arms around my middle and hugging me closer. Skull's solemn mouth is kicked up on one side, and he bows his head slightly, which is basically the equivalent of him jumping up and down, shrieking with joy.

"All right, that's enough chatter, innit?" Darcy says, wiggling out from under me. She hops up, clapping her hands like a bubbly little drill sergeant. "Places, everyone, let's keep at it." She grins down at me, grabbing my hand and hoisting me to my feet.

She drapes her arms over my shoulders, eyes twinkling. I sometimes get lost in those eyes of hers. They aren't startling blue like Harry's. No, they're much darker. Easy to overlook if you don't study her closely. Her irises are an indigo so deep, they're nearly black, like the inky darkness of the sky right before dawn. But they change with her mood—little cracks of silver threading through like bolts of lightning when she's intensely focused; pure violet when she lifts her face to the sun; dark and stormy like the ocean when she's mad.

My twin brother, Oliver, is a walking encyclopedia of color theory, and he once tried to tell me which Pantone shade her eyes are when I was describing them to my mums over dinner. I'd told him to piss off, explaining that her eyes held so much depth and nuance, they could never be defined by one silly color swatch. He'd stared at me like I spat in his supper. But I've spent so much time looking into Darcy's eyes over our years of friendship, it would be impossible *not* to notice stuff like that.

Harry starts up the melody again, tugging me back down to earth, and we assume our spots, trying to re-create what we did. We take it slower this time. And the next. Pausing between verses, tweaking bars, rewinding the phone recording and arguing over what chord progression we hear, what chord progression we think would be better.

We strip that magic down to its bare bones, building it back up, note by note. We play with it until our fingers are stiff and our heads ache and we have something close to done.

We know better, though.

No song, no piece of art, is ever truly finished. There's always one note, one chord, one beat of silence that you chase, desperate for perfection. But that's the beauty of art: It's a snapshot of imperfection poised at the threshold of everything it could but never will be. And it's lovely for that all the same.

"All right, lads, that's class," Harry says, rolling out his neck and cracking his knuckles. "But I can't hear that song one more time or I'll lose it." Skull nods in agreement, setting his drumsticks down and resting the back of his head against the wall.

"We actually did something," Kale says, the slightest hint of pride in his apathetic voice.

"That we did," Harry agrees, smiling at him. "So let's get to the pub to celebrate."

Chapter 5

Harsh wind at our backs doubles our pace to the nearby bar, and Darcy shrieks, burrowing into my side as we hustle along. But not even Iceland's late-spring cold front can chill our giddiness. Well, the band's giddiness. My smile has worn thin and aches at the corners, cheerfulness draining with each step away from the studio like a wet footprint on the sidewalk.

I *wish* I could join in their reckless hope that we can make something that shines outside of the shadow Connor has cast. No matter how hard I try, the happiness refuses to embed, bubbling off me like oil in water. I can shake myself as hard as possible, let it sink into me for a moment, but it's fleeting at best.

Inside, we huddle at the bar, and Harry orders us shots. We cheers, the alcohol a welcoming burn that I feel in the tips of my fingers and toes. Harry talks us into another round, and within half an hour I'm feeling relaxed and lazy, sitting on a barstool near the window, alternating between sips of water and beer.

I use my sleeve to scrub the fog off the window, staring into the graying evening. Music thumps through the cramped space like a heartbeat, the crowd packed in tight to take advantage of the bar's infamously low prices, my friends scattered around the room, enjoying the night in a way I envy.

We've lived in Reykjavík for about three months, but every time I stop to take it in, it's as breathtaking as the first day. Iceland is unearthly, beautiful in a brutal type of way. Even in the city center, it's like navigating a stunning new planet. Technicolor buildings and vibrant murals decorate the streets, the gray ocean and imposing snow-capped mountains a dramatic backdrop.

But as beautiful as it is, the experience has been equally jarring—living in a *new* place, creating something as intimate as music with *new* people, all while adjusting to my *new* status as single and publicly scrutinized. I don't know if it's the change of country or plans or relationship, but I can't seem to settle, even for a moment.

And I hate that I'm thinking about Connor. He's occupied so much of my brain space over the past five years, I've probably grown a malignant lobe just for him, and I want nothing more than to cut it out.

What makes me the most furious is that I don't even miss him. I miss that there was a version of me, before him, that didn't exist solely for his approval. That at some point I was blissfully unaware of how imposing my feelings are and I could let their pressure out through music without a second thought. I'm not sure I can create anything that matters to anyone now that I know how unrelatable and unsuitable this mess in my head is for public consumption. Anger pierces like a wasp bite, and before I can think better of it, I gulp down the remainder of my drink and fish my phone from my pocket, thumbs pounding on the screen as my vision blurs. I step out of my body as I do it, a rational, wispy version of me shaking her head as she takes in my hunched back and sour face in the furthest corner of a bar while I should be celebrating. That rational version of me calls this exactly what it is: a horrific moment of weakness.

And that version of me can fuck right off. Righteous indignation feels way better than sensibility ever will.

How dare you? I type.

Too soft. Delete.

just wanted you to know how much I hate you, you useless prig

Delete. Need something with a bit more razzle-dazzle.

You wouldn't even have a hit song about our lackluster sex if you'd taken all of ten minutes to figure out how to make me come, you hamfisted miscreant

I think for a moment.

. . . and your breath always smells like butter. Find a dentist for fucks sake.

Getting closer to a winner, but a bit too specific. Delete.

you're a real piece of shit, you know that?

Ah. That's the one. Short, sweet, and straight to the point. I stare at the screen, adrenaline zipping through my finger as it hovers over the send button.

"Who ya texting?" Darcy's breath is warm on my cheek, and I yelp, jolting out of my seat and sending my phone flying. She fixes me with a bemused smile before stooping down to grab it. I contemplate pushing her out of the way so she doesn't see the screen. "Why are you sulking alone in the corner? That's usually Skull's job," she says, popping back up and glancing across the bar at Skull, who is surrounded by three devastatingly pretty women. The inexplicable cool-rock-star aura is an amazing thing.

I grab for my phone, but it's too late, Darcy's clocked Connor's name. "Cubby, *no*," she says, looking at me with pure agony. "Not unhinged rage texts."

"I wasn't going to send it." I swipe for it again, but she dodges me.

"Yeah, I don't believe you."

"I swear. I just needed to live out a bully fantasy for a moment. It's one of the healthy stages of grief or closure or whatever." And I mean it. As good as it would feel to send that text, that would only last for a second. I can picture Connor's expression reading it—the bored eye roll, the heavy sigh, the smug twitch of his lips that I'm once again proving him right that I'm too dramatic to handle.

Darcy makes quick work of deleting the text and locking my phone, sliding it in her back pocket. I reach around her with both arms in an attempt to retrieve it.

"Jesus, Cubby, buy me a drink first."

It's then that I realize my face is cradled between her breasts, my hands fully cupping her ass. A memory morphed into fantasy shakes the locked box I keep it in, but I shove it away, ignoring the way my skin prickles from a sudden flush of heat.

I drop my hands, trying to move away, but she holds me close, tucking my head under her chin, fingers tracing through my hair. I lean my full weight into her, allowing myself to be soothed by her gentle touch, the pace of her heartbeat.

"He's a line in your songs, Cubby. Nothing more," she says softly.

"I know," I whisper. "But it eats at me that he's won. That he doesn't have to feel this embarrassment and betrayal and hurt that I do."

"Ah, come on now, Cubby love. He hasn't won. It's all just beginning."

My face twists. "That was somehow both deeply ominous and very live, laugh, love of you, and I mean that in the most derogatory way possible."

"Your kindness is unrelenting."

I let out a hollow laugh, releasing her go and turning back to my empty glass.

"I'm proud of you," Darcy murmurs.

"For what? Almost calling him a piece of shit?"

"Well, yes. But also for not completely melting down."

"You can't be serious. What do you call literally any part of today? What do you call what *just* happened?"

"A *partial* meltdown," she says with a devastatingly bright smile. "That's tremendous growth."

"The bar is on the ground, Darce." I try to fight it, but my mouth mirrors hers in a grin.

"But you didn't show up with a shovel, and that's worth celebrating."

"Why does your face look like that?" Kale says, sidling up to us with a sneer.

"Like what? A smile?"

He blinks. "Damn. So much teeth. It's very off-putting."

"Don't worry, a few more seconds subjected to your losing personality will kill it, I'm sure," I reply sweetly. "You have the same effect as a particularly rancid fart."

"You truly are the most charming woman I've ever met. Stunned that you're single." Kale lifts his beer in a mock cheers before tipping the bottle to his lips.

Narrowing my eyes, I decide messing with him is better than wallowing. I tumble off my stool, throwing my arms around his neck (in an affectionate way, not a strangling way, despite the latter crossing my mind many times). "My precious little superfood," I croon, rocking us back and forth. "I know all that snark is just a desperate cry for attention. I'll dote on you more, don't worry."

Kale chokes on his beer and I pretend to burp him like a fussy baby. He squirms out of my grip, and I snicker at how flustered he is, his reluctant smile winning out as he looks at mine. "You're the worst," he says.

"I know."

"She knows."

Darcy and I speak in unison, gazes whipping to each other. Our foreheads touch as we break into giggles. Kale pretends to be annoyed.

"Do I not get any of this love?" Harry says, placing more drinks on the table and sliding one to me before plopping down on the seat at the end.

"Consider yourself lucky," Kale says, massaging his neck. "They're brutal in their affection."

"We'll make a softy of you yet, darling," Darcy chirps, playfully pinching his cheek. She's on her third drink, pink kissing the tips of her ears and the bridge of her nose, her telltale signs of tipsiness. But as our group titters like fools, I realize that's probably true for all of us.

"I'm feeling thoroughly neglected," Harry says, accent softer at the edges, a pout fixed on his mouth.

With a teasing smile, I skip over to him, collapsing in his lap and throwing my arms around his shoulders. His palms land on my rib cage as he holds me. "There she is," he murmurs. "I feel like I haven't seen you in ages."

"Whatdya mean?" A hiccup pitches my voice, and I pull back to look at him. "We spend at least nineteen hours a day together."

Harry rolls his eyes, smile loose and lopsided. "I know *that*. But most of the time, it isn't the real you. I miss her."

His statement is a kick to the chest; a phantom me materializes at the edges of my vision—happy and peaceful and fists lowered, willingly unprepared for a fight. I know it's the me Harry sees right now. I wish it were the me I always was.

But I don't want to slip into the deep dark of that thought. My heavy emotions aren't for Harry. Aren't for anyone but me to sink under when I can't sleep, wrestle with in my brain that won't shut up. The only other person who's caught a glimpse is Darcy.

"Hush your pretty mouth," I say to Harry, pinching his lips playfully between my thumb and forefinger, tapping into empty reserves of energy to push away the numbness that always hovers on the surface of my skin. His smile breaks out of my finger trap.

"Such a bossy wee thing," he says, digging his fingers into my sides and pulling a squeal from me.

"I hate you."

"Oh, wise up, Cub. You adore me."

I scrunch my nose, trying to shake my head, but I end up nodding at that outrageous smile of his. I lean in to whisper that maybe he's not so bad, my head swimming a bit, but I end up letting out a breathy laugh directly in his ear, making him jump and turn his head.

"Cubby!" Darcy calls my name right as his skin presses against mine, my lips somewhere below his cheek, and in my fuzzy state, I turn, eyes on her, mouth dragging loosely against Harry's, our parted lips notching together. Warmth dissolves through my skin, arrowing for my chest, my heart squeezing at the sudden intimate touch. It's been so long since I've been gently kissed, my nervous system doesn't know how to react.

Darcy gasps, phone held at the ready as she snaps a picture, the flash blinding me. I jolt back from Harry, my eyes shooting wide and jaw crashing open. We stare at each other for a moment that's equal parts shock and horror, then Harry slowly reaches out, placing his fingers under my chin and closing my gaping mouth.

"Well . . . that was different," he says, pressing his lips together. They waver, and, for a split second, I think he's going to cry.

And then I realize he's laughing.

"Oh my god, don't try and cop a feel and then *laugh* at me." I punch his arm. "My ego's bruised enough without your help."

"*I* copped a feel?" he says with an indignant crack in his voice. "You threw yourself at me, Cub!" Harry laughs harder, and it pulls me a bit further out of the shock. I manage to laugh too, combing out my tangled nerves.

I've kissed Harry before. Granted, on the cheek, but the mechanics of it are all the same; this isn't something to make weird or even a thing. We're a touchy group in general, Harry, Darcy, and I.

The problem is, the warmth of his lips still lingers on mine, tugging at the frayed edges of a memory I keep tucked away. My brain transports me to five years ago, a moment that's sharp and luminous and wasn't an accident but somehow a hundred times more shocking, one that, for some reason, my thoughts like to grab at when it's late at night and I'm trying to sleep. A memory I keep sealed in a small box because something confusing knots in my chest and throat if I look at it too closely—look at it at all.

My eyes flick to Darcy.

Her arms are still lifted with her phone, smile frozen. It falls in slow degrees, eyebrows tracing down with the corners of her mouth, lips parting. Something about that look plucks me toward her, but Harry's arm is still circled around my waist, and I wheeze at the sudden pressure.

My movement makes her blink, and she shakes her head, beautiful grin back in place as she glances from us to her screen. "Ooh la la. That's a keeper. Very sultry seventies vibe."

She flips the phone to show us, and it takes more work than it should to pull my attention from her smile to focus on the photo. Harry takes the phone from her, zooming in with an incredulous sound. I understand why.

Darcy took the picture in black and white, and it's startling in its intensity. My shoulder-length brown hair is wavy and messy, dark-rimmed eyes heavy-lidded as I glance at the camera like it's the most tedious of interruptions, lips parted against Harry's like I'm ready to devour him. Harry, for his part, looks smugly delighted, the corner of his mouth cocked in a devilish grin.

"Oh, that's class," Harry says, laughing as he stares. "That's like . . . iconic album cover shit."

Darcy claps her hands in glee but I scoff.

"We have to use this," Harry says, cheeks flushed and eyes glinting. "This really would make a craic cover. Or at least promo graphic. So dark and moody and like you're about to eat me alive."

"Never doubt I will," I reply, my startled heart settling back into a normal rhythm.

"I'm serious, we should use this," Harry presses, turning the phone around for Kale to look at. Darcy nods so fast her head is a blur. Kale shrugs.

"Oh my god, piss *off*, Harry. We aren't Cigarettes After Sex. We can't pull off a look like that."

"No, we're Tea Time Tantrum and we just *did* pull off a look like that," he argues. "I say we let the public decide."

I watch him AirDrop the photo to himself, then hand back Darcy's phone as he fishes his own from his pocket, lifting his hips and bumping me from his lap. Resettling, he pulls up Instagram, thumbs flying across the keyboard before he angles his phone to show me the caption, eyebrows raised and smile broad.

Settle a debate for us: new album cover? Yes or fuck yes?

"You're ridiculous," I say, turning back to him and pressing *post*. His smile somehow widens.

I pull out my own phone, clicking into the app, Harry's post the first thing on my feed. Biting my lip, I comment: **some photos are supposed to stay in the camera roll, dickhead ♡ ♡**

"Connor will love that," Darcy says, reading over my shoulder. The ends of her hair tickle the sensitive skin of my neck, and an odd heat spears through me, making me shiver. "Spent five years making us all miserable with his accusations at you two."

I roll my eyes, but a vindictive smile wins out. "He can chew on glass."

Connor lived with a chronic undercurrent of doubt that Harry and I really could be *just friends*, always telling me it was impossible for a girl and a guy to be as close as we are without there being some sort of attraction. He'd get nearly belligerent about it when he smoked or drank too much, screaming at us that we were deceitful little liars. In the most terrible of ironies, he was the one chronically cheating on me, DMs and hookups with women who would come to our shows. Anytime I'd confront him about it, he'd deny it, telling me I was overreacting and crazy. If I'd push the issue, he'd turn it all around, saying the only reason I'm so suspicious is because I'm secretly pining for Harry.

Harry has never been someone Connor needed to worry about.

"Sigrún messaged me," Skull says, materializing at Kale's shoulder, making us all jump.

"And?" Kale asks.

"She loved the demo. Says with a few more tweaks we may even be able to release it as a single."

We cheer, smooshing together in a group hug. While we may have loved what we created today, we're still beholden to the approval of others, and it feels nice to get the validation that we're on to something.

"She said if we can get some more tracks like this, she could see the album making a decent splash."

"Maybe we aren't completely useless after all," Kale says, which is the closest thing to exuberant praise we could ever hope to get from him.

"Oh, how I adore this beautiful brain of yours," Darcy says, gripping my face between her palms and placing a sloppy kiss on my forehead. That radiating warmth is back, a current spreading down to my toes as her touch weaves into my muscles.

I pull away from her grasp with a smile. "Stop it. You know that would have never happened without Harry's melody. And you wrote most of the lyrics."

"Cubby?" Darcy says, eyes a little glassy as she stares at me.

"Yes?"

"Shut up and take the compliment."

"Make me."

She doesn't have to be told twice, grabbing my face again and peppering more kisses along my hair. Temples. Nose. I giggle like a little kid.

We don't drink often—mainly because we can't afford the cost of alcohol in this expensive city—but when we do enjoy a pint or a glass of wine, Darcy gets playful and touchier than usual. I generally indulge her as any best friend would.

"I love this song!" Darcy squeals as a deep beat pulses through the speakers. "Let's dance." I groan, shaking my head, but Darcy ignores me, dragging me to the dance floor, my fingers laced with hers.

I hate dancing—I feel awkward and uncomfortable and lose any sense of how to move my body—but Darcy loves it, bringing music to beautiful life any time she moves.

She ducks under my outstretched arm, spinning around and around before rolling into me. I squeeze her tight, then dramatically dip her. She snaps back up, her laugh of delight a warm puff against my neck. We rock back and forth like a pair of fools for a few moments, then the beat picks up, and she slips out of my arms, jumping up and down with the crowd. I watch her move, eyes closed and hair flying around her shoulders as she loses herself to the rhythm.

Her eyes flash open and land on me, a sudden charge cinching us together so we're chest to chest, hip to hip. Her smile shifts from wide and broad to something smaller, private. She leans heavily into me for a second before pulling herself back, surprise notching her face as she continues to stare. I'm hooked by her expression—a little bit confused, a little bit enthralled. The tips of her ears turn pink as the seconds tick on.

With a tiny shake of her frame, the tension disperses, and she catches her lower lip between her teeth, turning so her back is flush to my front, her hips swaying against mine in time to the music.

My body goes taut at the odd circus of feelings that fire through me—my pulse kicking against my chest, stomach yo-yoing through my torso. It must be from the mix of exhaustion and beer.

Darcy glances at me over her shoulder, arching an eyebrow, something a little bit daring, a tiny bit reckless, glinting in her dark irises. She tips her head back so it presses against my shoulder, then reaches up and cups her hand around my neck, tugging me down so her mouth brushes the shell of my ear. "I need to tell you something," she says over the music.

I swallow. "Yeah?"

She takes a deep breath, her exhale tracing along my cheek. "You're a terrible dancer." My jaw crashes open, and she snorts.

"I'm an excellent dancer!" I lie. "I . . . I'm very cutting-edge with my moves." She laughs even harder. "I'm a passable dancer," I try. No one would ever accuse me of being a triple threat.

"You need to loosen up. You're as stiff as uncooked spaghetti," she says, turning around to face me, the fluid sway of her hips continuing to keep time to the beat. "Let me teach you."

She plants her hands on my waist, trying to move me with her. My head starts to swim, and I suddenly feel like I'm free-falling. I hold on to her, hands twisting into her shirt, feeling the warmth of her body in my palms.

"That's a bit better," Darcy coos, one palm slipping up to cup my rib cage, the other lower at the flare of my hip. "Perfect."

The song fades into the next, the bass deepening, the tempo picking up, and Darcy guides us through the change, smile brilliant and eyes holding mine. She shifts her hands, dragging them up from my waist to rest around my neck. I fight a shiver at the ticklish sensation that lingers for too long. The pulse of the music makes it feel like we're sharing a heartbeat as we move together. She leads us through two more songs, giddy and carefree and unraveling me like thread from a spool until I'm jumping and swaying with her, self-consciousness deserting me.

Darcy leans close again, lips brushing my cheek as she says, "I think we've uncovered a new hidden talent of yours."

Maybe dancing isn't so bad after all.

Chapter 6

Darcy and I trip off the midnight bus, waving to the driver before crossing the street to our apartment. We clutch each other as we stumble up the stairs to our third-story unit. The others kept their good times rolling, heading for a nightclub to see some hot new DJ. Darcy had been outraged at the idea of missing the last bus and having to pay taxi fare home, and I wasn't about to leave her side.

Kicking off our shoes and shucking our coats, we make our way to our shared bedroom. The place is pitch black, and I collapse onto one of the two mattresses, Darcy next to me, head on my shoulder, arm around my waist.

It's Darcy's bed, I realize, as we squeeze together on the narrow frame. I briefly wonder if I should move to my own, but she hugs me tighter, and I melt into the sheets. She hums one of our old songs, the sound sweet and rough near my ear as the words dance in my head.

You know ignorance so I'll never know bliss.
All I've ever waited for, wanted for
Is the feel of your kiss.

Something dizzy and bright presses through me until I feel it in the tips of my fingers. A hiccup fractures her pretty voice, and we both honk with laughter like it's the funniest thing in the world.

"Tonight was so fun," Darcy says, rolling to her back, hand dragging over me to rest on my stomach as she smiles up at the ceiling.

"I don't want to go to bed," I say through a yawn. "I don't want it to be over." I hate the idea that if I close my eyes, I'll slip away from this lovely night where everything's a mess but somehow that's okay.

"It doesn't have to be," she says, giving me a mischievous smile that, for some reason, makes my mouth go dry. "Wanna watch *Love Island* and judge everyone as though we aren't the same level of trash?"

"Always." I scramble over her, my stomach draped across her lap as I fish for my laptop on the floor between our beds.

"Arch that back, baby." Darcy whistles as she slaps my ass, and my entire body lurches, stomach clenching tight. An odd heat surges through me, and I drop my computer back to the floorboards with a clang. Darcy hoots with laugher, and I finally grab it, jolting up to a sitting position, posture ramrod straight as I let out an indignant sniff.

"I will be taking that up with HR," I say primly.

"Right. I can see it now. *Why did you spank Cubby?*" she says, imitating Sigrún's voice. "*It's not my fault, Sigrún! She shoved it in my face! What else am I supposed to do but give it an appreciative pat?*"

"The entirety of second-wave feminists just turned in their graves. Even the living ones."

She clucks her tongue, waving me away. "Oh please. They'd all agree that your ass is exceptionally spankable."

I smile in spite of myself, feeling both pleased and bashful. Gaze turned from Darcy, I open my laptop and cue up the show. We *oontz oontz* to the theme music and settle against the pillows, pressed close from the lack of space. It takes us approximately thirty-eight seconds to get hooked by the drama.

"His beard looks like it's buffering," Darcy says halfway through the episode, pointing at one of the contestants running around in swim trunks arguing with everyone.

"Don't ask me to explain it, but I feel like he'd only eat the cauliflower on a veggie tray," I say back.

"Big-headed, pale, and causes indigestion flare-ups? Like calls to like. Makes perfect sense to me." We really start to lose it when the group has a talent show and one of the contestants whips out a recorder and gives everything she's got to a musical performance.

The episode takes a turn for the boring, and my eyelids droop. Darcy snickers during a bland confessional, and I glance at her, ready to be ruthless over whatever she picked up on that I missed. I'm caught off guard that she's looking at me.

"What?" I say, eyes narrowing at the dangerous tilt to her smile.

"Nothing," she says. "Just thinking . . ."

"Don't hurt yourself."

She smooshes a pillow in my face. "Piss off. I was thinking, I can't believe you kissed *Harry*."

I make a choking sound. "I didn't *kiss* Harry!"

"It certainly looked like a kiss."

"It wasn't! My lips fell against his lips."

"Which is the definition of a kiss."

"What are you, twelve?" I throw the pillow back at her, but she dodges it.

"Harry and Cubby sitting in a tree, k-i-s-s-i-n-g," she croons.

"Stoppppp," I groan, grappling for another pillow.

Darcy catches my wrists, pinning them to the bed and hovering over me. I squirm against her, and her smile grows, sparkling and teasing in a way that makes my heart squeeze. She leans so close the tip of her nose brushes mine. "First comes love," she chants. "Then comes marriage. Then comes—"

I press up, silencing her with my mouth against hers.

The world screeches to a halt, the second splitting open, time elongating, zooming in on the softness of her lips, the warmth of her shocked exhale as it fills my lungs. My thoughts evaporate as heat rolls through me. Darcy's soft, full lips slotted against mine. Thigh notched between my legs. Hips and chest pressed against my own.

A tiny gasp tumbles out of me, and time clicks back into rhythm, my brain spinning to organize what's happening.

My eyes flash open, and Darcy's mirror mine in shock.

Oh my god. Oh my god. *What the fuck am I doing?*

We rip apart, Darcy poised over me, hands still pinning my wrists, our breaths so short and sharp our chests thump against each other with every inhale. I try to pull my arms free, but it's a mistake, dropping her closer to me. She clambers away, kneeling between my legs, eyes wild and cheeks seared with red.

"I'm sorry," I blurt out, each word tinged with panic. I prop myself up, my inner thighs brushing against her, and sharp heat scorches through me. My fingers press against my lips like I'm trying to make sure they're still there. Trying to keep the warmth of Darcy's mouth imprinted on mine.

"I . . . You . . ." she splutters, face creased with confusion. Horror.

"I'm so sorry," I say again, voice pinching as I search for an excuse. "I was . . . being silly. So silly. I didn't mean . . . I shouldn't have . . . That was . . ."

Something in Darcy's eyes shift from confused to—

Her hands fist my shirt, jerking me toward her, closing the few breaths of distance between us. Her mouth is hungry and wild and the slightest bit hesitant as she presses it back to mine in a kiss that rushes through me like a tidal wave, drowning out all thoughts, all reason, leaving only an aching sense of want that has my toes curling, fingers scrambling for purchase along her back as I pull her just as hard against me.

Desperate, I realize in a haze as a low, greedy sound comes from one of us, both of us. Darcy's eyes were *desperate*.

I lose control of my body, one hand knotting in her hair, the other at the side of her throat, holding her to me. Her tongue slips out, tracing across my lips, and I open to her on a gasp. Darcy shocks me by biting down on my lower lip like she wants to mark me. Keep me. Own me. Consume me.

The world stops spinning, this moment the center of gravity as her body wraps around me, one hand sliding to the curve of my spine as she pushes me back against the mattress, pulling my pelvis against hers, my legs falling open, her thighs pressing tightly between where they're splayed. My touch is soft and hesitant, hands moving frantically like a butterfly in flight as I try to figure out where to touch her, if I'm even allowed to.

I don't know what's happening, I really don't. I could blame it on the drinks I finished over an hour ago or the slumber-party giddiness or just being stupid. But all I know is there's a clawing ache of need spearing through my chest, up my throat, down my stomach.

All I know is I don't ever want this to stop.

Any pretense of hesitancy is obliterated, my body turning inside out with hunger as I tremble and squirm and clutch her to me and do anything, *anything* to get closer to her, like the world is ending and this is my last chance to touch her like this.

Maybe it is.

She tastes sweet and electric, and she kisses me harder, rolling us so we're on our sides, facing each other, legs tangled together, one of hers over my hip, heel pressing into the back of my calf. My thigh slips to the crux of hers, and she lets out a gasp at the pressure.

Her hand traces from my back to my rib cage, thumb settling below the swell of my breast, index finger resting along the side, framing me. Waiting. Hovering. Making my teeth ache with need.

"Is this okay?" Her breath in my ear.

"*Yes*." A thrilled and shocked syllable in the back of my throat.

Of course it's okay.

It's Darcy.

Darcy.

My fingers skim from her throat to the center of her chest. I feel her heart pound against my palm, and I move my wrist, cupping her breast, plumping its softness as stars swim in my vision and she presses into my hand with a groan.

"And you?" I gasp out. "Are you okay?"

"Yes. God, yes," she says, her hand mirroring my own, her thumb circling my nipple, teasing it into a taut peak.

Her touch. Her lips. *God*, the softness of her skin, my hand snaking under her shirt, hers doing the same to me. Exhale on my cheek. My chest.

My closest friend.

Hair dragging across my throat as she rolls me to my back again. Fingers skating up my leg as she licks along my collarbone.

I'm clumsy. Shaky. An absolute mess as I fumble for the buttons of her jeans, her deft fingers already pulling my zipper down. Time is slipping away. I've stumbled into some alternative universe and reality will rip me back by the ankles any second now, and all I know is I need more of Darcy and her skin and her heat and her lips searching and wanting and searing against mine while I'm here.

"Lift your hips, Cubby love," she whispers, voice rough as she impatiently tugs at the waistband of my jeans. I do as she says, cool air kissing my bare thighs as she drags the denim to my knees. I crunch up enough that she moves back an inch, and I work her jeans down too, hands desperate as I grope handfuls of her skin, falling back against the pillows and drawing her closer to me. Chest to chest. Our hearts clanging against each other in a jagged rhythm. It's my new favorite sound.

"Want you," Darcy says on a harsh groan as my hands curl around her ass, squeezing and kneading as she wriggles her arm between us, and I realize she's dragging her underwear off her hips. I was wrong before. Her saying *that* is my new favorite sound.

Her fingers—rough and callused and so familiar I whimper—curl into the elastic of my underwear, gripping tight, but not moving the last shred of fabric that separates her touch from the place I want it most.

Suddenly, everything comes into sharp focus. My heart beating so hard, so fast, it feels like it might rip me apart, like I'll be torn to shreds if she doesn't touch me where I'm slick and desperate, already mindlessly shifting in search of friction.

All of this feels inevitable, like I've been running with a resistance band slung around my waist and it's finally jerking me back into place, exactly where I'm meant to be.

"Need you," I plead into her mouth before pressing my tongue against hers, silently begging for her to consume me. She does as I ask, kiss decadent and wild.

At the same moment, we touch each other, our knuckles brushing between our bodies as we move our hands. My fingers glide through her wet folds, finding her clit, giving a light, questioning press to the swollen bud. Darcy cries out into my mouth, her fingertips slipping to my entrance, circling and swirling as the heel of her hand rubs against my most sensitive spot.

Our mouths break apart, and we stare in wide-eyed wonder as we continue to touch each other, explore this forbidden, sweet territory. Darcy's eyebrows fix in fascinated, hazy focus as she finds a spot, a rhythm, that has my entire body trembling, my head spinning as pleasure spikes through me. My hands move like they belong on her, like they were designed solely to bring Darcy pleasure, wring out those sharp whimpers and desperate cries that are punctuated by her hips pressing harder into my touch, her teeth biting my lip. I'm instantly obsessed with the way her face creases in need when I put two fingers in her, my thumb circling in a steady, firm pressure against her clit.

"Tell me again," she commands, her hips bucking against my hand.

I try to focus but she hits a spot so good, starbursts of color obscure my vision and my head falls back, an agonized moan ripping from my throat. "Tell you what?"

Darcy's free hand snakes into my hair, fisting it and tilting my head so I'm forced to look at her, look into those big blue eyes that are somehow both sharp and eclipsed with pleasure.

"Tell me that this is okay. That all of this is okay," she pants.

Despite the frantic heat clawing through me, I pause, my pulse pounding in every corner of my body. I look at her. Stare. Her lips red and bee-stung, hair a mess, cheeks flooded with color, and expression wrecked. I fall so deeply into my body, every feeling magnified—her breath across my cheek, our feet tangled, the heel of her hand against my clit, fingers deep in me.

I'll never recover from this.

In a rush of movement, I flip us, Darcy falling to her back, her hair spilling across the pillow, chest moving rapidly as she stares at me. I adjust us, using my knees to open her legs wider, sitting back on my heels to see where I touch her. Her hand moves from between my thighs to my knee, but I can't even be bothered by the lack of stimulation, not when this new position allows me to watch the smooth glide of my soaking fingers as I move in and out of her.

Her head rolls back, throat exposed. I curl over her body to kiss the spot where I see her pulse fluttering.

"Darcy," I say, placing a soft bite to the spot. "It's perfect."

She cries out, her hands moving to my hair, holding me tight against her. "Is this normal?" she whispers against my temple.

A gasp tumbles from my lips as I press my legs together against the mounting pressure. "Is what normal?"

She levels her face with mine, eyes dark and wild and a little bit terrified. "Is it normal to feel this much? This much want?"

I nod, my nose dragging against hers. "I think so."

"How do you know?" Her voice is a soft but firm demand, hands gripping my shoulders.

I clear my throat, ignoring the warning bell in the back of my mind trying to stop the dangerous words pressing out of my overly earnest mouth. The truth can't be swallowed down. "Because I feel it all too."

Our touches become frantic, like this is the last chance we'll ever have to know the comfort of another person's skin. Clashing teeth and bitten lips and pounding hearts and her fingers back on me, in me. We rush together over the cliff, a shared, sharp cry into each other's mouths as we tumble over.

We break apart, only for a moment, collapsing on our backs, chests moving from disjointed breaths. Then we turn back to each other with the inevitability of magnets, like no single kiss will be good enough to end the night on.

We press our lips back together as if it's the most natural thing in the world, something we've done every night and we'll continue to do till we're old and gray. We rest there, not kissing exactly, but our lips still touching, still brushing against each other, the delicate warmth of Darcy's every exhale on my skin.

My head is swimming, heart tripping over itself about what this means and how we shouldn't have touched each other like that and how it seems impossible we've never touched each other like that before and . . . and . . .

Sleep pulls me under as I nestle deeper into the circle of Darcy's arms.

Chapter 7

"My arrrrm. Get offfffff." Darcy's voice is coarse as sandpaper and way too close to my ear.

Uuuugggghnnnnn, I gargle in response, trying to push her away, eyes still closed. My palm makes contact with something that feels like her jaw.

"My arm is asleep! Get off it!" She pushes me right back, and I fall like a sack of bricks to the floor.

Uuuugggghnnnnn, I repeat when I can breathe again, head pounding.

"Sorry," Darcy says, eyes peeking over the edge of the mattress. "All right?"

I wave her away, dragging my useless body to my own bed and clawing my way up. I pull the quilt over my head and turn on my side, squinting through the crack at Darcy's similar form. We're both the worse for wear, her eye makeup smeared in dark rings, pink hair sticking up in frizzy angles.

"Hi," I whisper, voice scratchy.

"Hi," she echoes back, gaze fixed on me.

We stare at each other for a moment, a bright triangle of sun slicing through the window between us. The night floods back, memories glaring in the morning light, the replay of every touch creating a spike through my chest that's terrifying in its intensity.

I can't . . . I can't believe we did that, that any of last night was real. It's like a fever dream, like sense and reason gathered their things and fled my brain, my body overtaken by a mindless want. I feel it still, that want, morphed and changed but pulsing under my skin nonetheless.

What *is* this? What do I *do* with it?

Darcy's lips part, eyebrows dropping. She sucks in a breath, but the trill of her phone cuts off whatever she's about to say. Her gaze flicks to her nightstand, confused look hardening to one of panic as she takes in the name lighting up the screen. Reaching out like she's about to stick a fork in an outlet, she palms the phone, staring at it for another few rings before answering the call.

"Mum?" Her voice drips with apprehension, face twisting like the word is sour on her tongue. She blinks twice as she listens to her mum, Doreen, on the other end. "Sorry. Yeah. I'm fine. Just waking up."

Silence.

"I mean, it's only nine here. Not like I've wasted a—" She sits up, tucking her messy hair behind her ear as tense lines form across her forehead and between her eyebrows. "I'm not taking a—" Her mouth slams shut for a moment as she grimaces. "I'm not taking a tone," she says through clenched teeth. "I'm just saying I—"

Silence again, her energy draining away and eyes glazing over. "I'm sorry. I didn't—Okay. Sorry. I know. I'm sorry."

More of that heavy silence.

"It was a joke. I wouldn't have worn it if I'd known they'd be taking pictures. I . . ."

Darcy flinches as her mum's fussing grows so loud I can hear it across the room.

"I really am sorry. I didn't—" More indecipherable yelling. "I wasn't thinking. I'm so—" Darcy swallows, biting her lower lip as she hangs her head. "Okay. Yeah. Talk to you soon. Sorry again. Lov—"

Darcy pulls the phone from her ear and stares at the screen, lips blanching as she presses them into a fine line. After a moment, she clicks the screen off, tossing it on her pillow.

Tension lingers in the room and, because I'm a dumb bitch, I have to break it with sarcasm. "That sounded like a lovely chat."

Darcy shoots me a pained look, then blinks away, shaking her head as she lies back down.

"What was she on about this time?" Darcy's mum calls her regularly, but it's always to let Darcy know about a new way she's let her parents down.

"The paper back home printed the profile on us," Darcy says numbly. Sigrún arranged an interview with our hometown newspaper a few weeks ago, trying to drum up some local pride as if Connor wasn't their new golden boy they'd be feasting on for years.

"What's so bad about that?"

Darcy sets her jaw, letting out a long breath through her nose. "They took pictures from the video call, and I'm wearing my SLUTS' RIGHTS shirt."

I snicker. "I love that shirt."

"I know you do. You gave it to me." She fixes me with a look so angry I choke on my remaining laughter. "Mum called to let me know I'm the town slag and have embarrassed her and Dad to no end."

"Christ, it's just a shirt," I mumble, anger rising in me. I hate Doreen, I really do. Darcy shines so brightly, but a few choice words from her mum snuff her out like a candle. It's a crime against nature to smother someone so vibrant. "It's not like they published a video of you giving a foot job to Father Joe or something. Even then . . . sexual autonomy, et cetera, et cetera."

"I don't want to talk about it," Darcy says. "Would rather not ruminate on what a fucking disappointment I am."

My heart sinks. She's usually pretty good at bouncing back after a call and compartmentalizing her parents' cruelty, but I feel her slipping away like water through the cracks between my fingers.

"You okay?" I ask gently, moving off my bed and padding to hers. I expect her to scoot over, make room for me like she usually does, but instead she tenses.

She looks at me, pain lining her face, eyes lingering for a beat too long on my mouth, sending a rush of heat through me. Her frown deepens, and she squeezes her lids closed. "Don't feel well."

I stare at her, echoes from last night ghosting through my head—the grip of her hands on my hips, the rasp of her breath against my chest, the softness of her kisses on my skin—and those heady delights tangle with the utter insanity of it all.

What the hell were we thinking? Why the fuck did I, a straight woman, hook up with my similarly straight best friend? Why am I a tangled mess of emotions I can't parse out when the *only* thing I should be feeling is regret at indulging in such a bizarre, careless whim? What is wrong with me?

I let out a deep breath through my nose, trying to steady my racketing pulse. I need to calm down. Granted, I've never been calm in my entire life, but now would be an excellent time to try it out. Maybe this isn't as big a deal as I'm making it out to be. I have a tendency to catastrophize things . . . just ask my ex; he's probably releasing a whole studio album on that next week.

I mean, truly, what's a little . . . kissing and heavy petting and . . . and shared orgasms between friends . . . right?

Shit.

Uninvited, I crawl onto her bed, sitting cross-legged at the end near her feet. I anticipate her usual response of poking my thighs and knees with her toes until I pick up one of her feet, massaging her arch until her head rolls back and she lets out a tiny sigh of relief. Instead, she snatches her legs up, tucking her knees to her chest as she lies on her side, wrapped in her bedsheets. I wonder if she can smell me on them. Fucking hell, I've gone mad.

I clear my throat, searching for words that will somehow make this less horrifically awkward, but none come.

Plucking at invisible fuzz on my pajama shorts that I changed into sometime in the middle of the night, my eyes snag on a small maroon spot blooming on my inner thigh. My blood turns to smoke when I realize it's Darcy's thumbprint, her mark on my skin. A few inches away the stain of her other fingers show where she gripped my legs. Every kiss crashes through me as if Darcy were touching me right now, and I flinch, closing my legs and hugging my knees to my chest in the hopes that if I make myself small enough, I can stop whatever scary emotion is trying to crack through me.

I let out a deep breath, screwing up my courage and closing my eyes as I attempt to face the mess of it all head-on. "So, uh, last night . . ."

"What about last night?" Darcy asks in an even tone.

I blink at her, trying to figure out the subtlest phrasing to remind her that her fingers were in me and on me in ways not particularly usual for us. "Umm . . . just that last night was—"

"Such a laugh," Darcy says, offering a bastardized example of the noise. She brings her blanket more tightly around her. "I really loved that bar."

More blinking.

"What's wrong with you?" she says, twisting her mouth into a tight smile. After a beat, she does extend a leg, nudging my shin. "Are you super hungover?"

"What? No. I-I'm talking about . . ." I make a jerky gesture between us and the bed.

Darcy's eyebrows furrow with her frown, like she's digging deep into her memory, then her eyes widen. "*That's* what you're on about? Oh my god, don't be silly."

Confusion and an odd sense of panic has my heartbeat pounding in the crooks of my elbows and down to the tips of my toes. "Silly?"

"I mean, yeah, sure, that was definitely a *weird* way to end the night. But . . ." She shrugs. "We were probably both just lonely, or whatever. Not a big deal." Her tone is light and airy, but her face is a hardened mask.

I blink again, my lips parting. I'm suddenly . . . empty. Blank. All of my feelings deserting me except for a tiny knot of dread in the pit of my stomach. I've been here before, and the mortification makes me want to keel over.

The first time Connor and I had sex, I cried. I'd built it up in my head, and the moment felt huge and emotional for me. I caught him rolling his eyes as soon as he pulled out and dealt with the condom. He left while I was asleep and when I tried to talk to him about it (in what was an admittedly alarming state of weepiness on my part), he stared at me with horror. When I finally calmed down enough to swallow my gasps and wipe the snot from my nose, he said, "Christ, Cubby. Try not to be so fucking earnest all the time. It's just sex."

Just sex. That's all we ever had, truthfully.

And that's all this was too.

The idea of reliving that kind of embarrassment makes every muscle in my body tense and tears claw at my eyes. Last night I was lonely and stupid and made a really dumb decision because of it, and Darcy and I should never *ever* talk about it. What would be the point?

"Yeah, I don't remember much after we got home," I lie. Anxiety, guilt, shame—they all twist like a knife between my ribs, stomach roiling and bile burning my throat, my hand clenching at the base of it.

In a swift movement, Darcy sits up, something wild and terrifying in her eyes. "Really? Yeah?"

I stare at her, lips parted, trying to decipher her rapidly shifting expressions. That's when it clicks.

Darcy knows me. Better than anyone. Which means she knows what a messy fucking shitshow I could turn this into if given even an inch. It's what Connor always talked about, my ability to ruin a good thing by overthinking it, attaching so many ridiculous feelings to it. Darcy sees that now too and she doesn't want to be stuck in the crosshairs of it just because she was bored and horny and wanted to get off last night without any guys around.

Darcy loves sex, a new guy on her roster every few days, but she doesn't deal in any emotions with those hookups. This was no different. I was a warm body that showed her a good, if not "weird" time, and that's all.

What else are friends for?

My spine rounds, muscles collapsing as some of the tension releases. This is good. This is the best outcome for this absolutely terrible situation. But some strange, foreign part of me wants to rebel against that—fight and snap and confess every soft, scary thought that's pulsed in the back of my mind since that kiss all those years ago.

But I can't mortify myself further. I take all that sharp, gnawing want for answers and crumple it into a ball in my chest, lighting it on fire and burning it to ash before it can ink itself too deeply on my skin.

Nails digging into my chest, I whisper, "Yeah. I don't remember much at all."

Darcy's pinched profile eases, and she lets out a nearly silent sigh of relief. I look away, trying to blink past the pinpricks of tears trying to surface, eyes fixed on the harsh white wall and the ratty scraps of paper we've taped there while sharing this room. A lot of it is scribbled notes between Darcy and me—discarded song lyrics with doodles in the margins, gossipy notes filled with inside jokes we passed in school that we couldn't bear to toss after all these years, Polaroids of us smiling, cheeks smooshed together from our dive-bar tour last summer. I fight the impulse to rip them all down.

Darcy clears her throat, snagging my attention. Her eyes flick down to the duvet, then back up to my face, and I realize I'm still on her bed, a spot I'm no longer welcome. I scramble off and burrow under my covers, turning to the wall and clenching my jaw against the choked cry knocking at my teeth.

I'm terrified to move, to even breathe, to cause any more ripples that will fuck up my world further. My ears are pricked to every noise Darcy makes, the cadence of her breathing. Like a broken, piercing record, the question *How did this even happen?* loops around my mind.

She's right, it must be the loneliness—Connor's betrayal still torturing me as if he's holding a scalpel to my spine. The loss of my art, my ability to create, that has me choking on air.

"Cubby?" Harry's voice is high, barreling through my muddled thoughts and making me jump. I turn toward the door, Darcy similarly disturbed as she lifts to her elbows. He bangs on the door, the poor old wood rattling in its frame like he's about to knock it off the hinges.

"Cub, I think something's happened," Harry calls. "Something kind of . . . I'm not sure *bad* is the right word, but something big. With the potential to be bad." He pounds his fist on the door again.

"Bang on that door one more time and I'll make sure something bad happens to you, Harry O'Connell," Darcy yells.

The door swings open, Harry framed in the center in a ratty T-shirt and shorts, eyes wide and phone clutched to his chest. My stomach plummets.

"No," I growl, pointing at him. "Whatever is on that phone, I don't want it. Take it elsewhere."

"You need to see this, Cub. It involves you."

"Yes, I figured as much by your incredibly loud wake-up call and frantic expression. Now, piss off, this is a safe space." Or, at least it was, up until twenty minutes ago.

Instead of doing as he's told, Harry scurries across the room, sitting on the edge of my mattress and hovering over me with pure panic. I sink deeper into my pillows and sheets. The silence is oppressive, his big blue eyes locked on mine. With absurd slowness and caution, he holds his phone out to me. I stare at it like it's a severed limb.

When it's clear he's not going anywhere, I take the phone, holding the screen up to his face to unlock it, then flip it around to find the Instagram post of us from last night pulled up.

Harry makes a choking noise. "So, uh, yeah. That picture. It's . . . well . . ."

"Spit. It. Out. Man," Darcy snaps, clapping with each syllable.

"That picture kind of blew up last night. In a way I've never had a picture blow up, or anything for that matter, and there are so many comments and shares and I'm starting to get DMs from people claiming to be pop culture journalists for a statement and I—"

I jolt up to sitting, eyes bulging out of my head as I scroll down on the post. The picture has upward of three hundred thousand likes, and over five thousand comments. My hands shake as adrenaline leaches through my system.

There's no way this can be good.

We have a modest social media following as a band, most coming from our unsavory (dis)attachment to Connor. Harry probably claims the biggest following besides Kale's hefty TikTok reputation. But it's not this level. Nowhere near this level.

Swallowing past the knot of panic in my throat, I view the comments.

The first few aren't terrible. Actually kind of nice . . .

omfg slay bestie

icon

Hi hello @womenpostingtheirwins

But it derails quickly from there.

Damn all the boys of that band are running the train on her huh 🤭

she's a four that thinks she's a nine
It's sad that young girls think they have to act like whores
    to get attention nowadays
        Reply: I don't think she's acting lmaoooooo I'm
        sorry but this is just so desperate??? like be serious
        Reply: no fr it's sad at this point
        Reply: came here to say the same thing
        Reply: she knows what she's doing. Timing is so sus
Am i the only one totally losing it over this tho? Like I
    KNOW there's massive connor x cubby issues and based
    on that interview she royally broke his heart but I've been
    following the band for a long time and always thought
    cuby and harry would be soo cute together
        Reply: nahhh I've ALWAYS shipped darcy and harry
        Reply: ya'll trying so hard at being fake fans as if
        you gave a shit about the band before any of the
        drama literally yesterday
        Reply: how can anyone be a fake fan of a band
        that's had like six different names over the past
        year? It doesn't seem possible for anyone to be a
        real fan if the band itself isn't real
        Reply: you literally don't know what your talking
        about. Just because a band's name changes
        doesn't mean it's not a real band.
        Reply: you're*
        Reply: go fuck your*self

Harry's phone slips from my cold, clammy hands. I feel Darcy move to sit next to me, Harry shifting to make room for her on my tiny bed, but I can't bring myself to look at her. I can't look at anyone or anything, the comments blurring through my brain. Darcy grabs the phone, and her sharp intake of breath confirms it's as bad as I thought.

"There's more," Harry says, voice hoarse.

I shake my head. "No. I refuse for there to be more."

He takes his phone back from Darcy, typing for a moment before showing us the screen. A massive headline from a gossip rag glows back at us.

> Cubby Clark uses new boy toy to take swing at ex, Connor McCabe

My gaze shoots to Harry, whose face is lined with worry.

"They think we did this for publicity?" I ask, voice grating over the words.

"I think so, yeah."

I grab for my own phone, barreling straight to the viper pit. Similar headlines pop up with a search for my name, one in particular snagging my attention.

NICE TRY, CUBBY CLARK, BUT HEARTTHROB
CONNOR McCABE COMES OUT ON TOP

The headline has the picture of Harry and me next to what appears to be a new one from Connor, posted this morning, black and white as well, his guitar cradled in his hands, eyes fixed to the side with a sly grin. The curve of a hip and the hem of a lacy nightgown disappear at the edge of the frame in his line of sight.

My stomach clenches, bile rising in my throat, as I skim a few sentences, reading out loud.

> . . . In a world that stunts men from ever sharing their feelings and emotions, Connor McCabe has set out to break the mold, dropping track after swoony track of vulnerably raw lyrics chronicling the hardship of a love that didn't last. But while social media has lauded the chart-topping, angsty, good guy's novel

approach, some are dead set on striking back. Ex-bandmate and ex-girlfriend, Cubby Clark, is the most aggressive in the campaign, trying to bait Connor by posting scandalous pics of her getting cozy with her band's piano player, and Connor's reported childhood bestie, Harry O'Connell, no doubt to stir up trouble in the hopes of a jealous rage. No luck here, as Connor seems more than happy to explore his feelings with a mysterious woman in a subtle and tasteful response post. No doubt, she'll serve as a more agreeable muse.

"Well, that's utter shit," I say, indignant rage bubbling through me as I look up at Harry. "You're the one that posted the damn picture."

"A bit beside the point, Cub."

"I think that's exactly the point. I'm supposedly leading an aggressive campaign to stir up jealousy from a picture *you* posted."

"People probably think you made Harry post it," Darcy says, brow furrowed as she continues to read over my shoulder.

My phone starts buzzing with a call, and I'm so on edge it makes me jump, and I lob it away, accidentally hitting Harry in the throat. I watch Sigrún's name flash a few more times before going to voicemail.

"Thanks for that," he says, rubbing the spot. A few seconds later his phone starts ringing. Wearily meeting my eyes, he accepts the call and puts it up to his ear.

"How ya, Sigrún?" A long pause. "I'm good, yeah. Slept a bit funny on my neck, but fine all and all. Does look like we'll be getting some nasty weather, though, yeah?" More silence. "She's here." Silence. "Right. Yeah. Okay. Bye. Right. Bye. Okay. Yeah. Right. Bye."

He ends the call, head hanging as he lets out a deep breath. Darcy and I stare at him, bodies held tense like slingshots. He lifts those baby-blue eyes to us. "That was Sigrún."

Darcy reaches out and punches him on the shoulder. "No shit. What did she say?"

Harry rubs his arm, face scrunched as he glares at her. "Christ, woman, you've got an arm on ya. She wants to meet us in the studio in an hour."

"Is it about—"

"Our stunningly problematic rise to viral fame? Seems so, yeah." He stands, dragging a palm across the back of his neck as he heads to the door. "I guess I should go inform the rest?"

"Send Kale my disdain," Darcy says weakly, burying her head in her hands.

Harry slumps away, mumbling something that doesn't sound exactly kind as he goes.

We're quiet and still, too afraid to move, like any ripples we make will set off another tidal wave of controversy.

"You okay?" Darcy asks.

Hmmm, let's see, I'm being called a slut on the internet, blamed for breaking the heart of the guy who broke mine, and filled with the highest degree of humiliation by hooking up with my best friend last night and making everything exceptionally weird by having jumbled-up feelings that won't get out of my head. No, I wouldn't say *okay* is a good word to describe where I'm at.

"Fine," I say through numb lips. I feel Darcy's stare but I don't look at her. "I mean, no, not really. I'm actually pretty fucking stressed and panicked, but that won't change much, will it?"

She's silent, and I risk a glance at her. Her expression is unreadable, something held tight in the corners of her mouth and eyes. In a movement that's jerky and hesitant and so counter to every embrace we've ever shared, Darcy does the one thing I wish she wouldn't: She gives me a hug.

Actually, *hug* is a generous term. This is stiff and awkward, her arm looped around my upper body while managing to touch me as little as possible. A contactless vise that makes my muscles lock up, shoulders rising toward my ears like I'm anticipating a blow.

"I'm sorry, Cubby," she says after a beat, her voice cracking on my name. For a second, I let myself imagine that her *sorry* isn't pity for this shit storm I've found myself in. A miraculous fantasy unravels in my mind that she's sorry for this morning, sorry for not telling me she's having confusing feelings too. That she's sorry for this brand-new spiky wedge between us and she wants to dislodge it. But I know I'm the only one confused.

I want to cry, a knot swelling in my throat, every cell tugging me to lean into her familiar embrace. The impulse is too much to ignore. I suck in a sharp breath, my body relaxing a fraction, giving in to temptation. But the second my skin brushes hers as I move to hug her back in something tentatively tender, she drops her arms and slips off my bed, eyes fixed straight ahead as she moves to her dresser and rifles through it.

I want to say something. Anything. Everything.

If she looks up at me right now, I think I'll crack open. I'll tell her I remember everything and I know she does too. I'll tell her I remember that first kiss from five years ago as well. I'll ask her why we never talked about it. I'll ask if, when she lets her guard down, her mind always wanders to it like mine does. I'll tell her I'm scared, petrified, but I can't figure out if it's from the storm brewing on the internet or the idea we'll never again reach the level of closeness we had up until this morning. The intimacy of last night.

But she doesn't look at me.

So I keep my mouth shut and watch her walk out the door.

Chapter 8

Sigrún doesn't acknowledge us as we file into her office, her focus darting between two computer monitors, an iPad, and a phone. Her bloodshot eyes have unease skittering up the back of my neck. We stand there in silence, watching her violently type.

I spent the entire ride here combing through social media, reading every ugly sentiment written about me until I felt the words carved into my skin, salt rubbed into the raw edges. *Bitch. Slut. Desperate. Pathetic.*

Harry steps closer to me, and his warmth at my back tempts me to lean into him, turn and bury my face into his shirt and beg him to hug me tight and make this building dread go away.

Instead, I move away from him and toward Sigrún's desk. "I'm sorry," I blurt out. I'm not sure what I'm apologizing for—I never really am—but I feel like there's always some reason for me to say it. Absorb whatever blame lingers in the air.

Sigrún finally clocks our presence, head snapping up, blond strands of hair falling out of her messy bun. "You're sorry?"

I swallow, then nod, forcing myself to keep looking at her. She's probably going to drop us from the label for stirring up too much drama and keeping the attention on Connor's bullshit instead of our music. I wouldn't blame her.

She looks less frazzled now, but I can tell her brain is still hopping between a million different places. For some reason, she smiles. "Cubby, there's nothing to be sorry for. This is great."

I recoil. "What?"

"*Great*," she repeats, enunciating every letter. "Do you have any idea how many media requests are flooding my inbox? Journalists, producers, music vloggers . . . They're all rabid to get a bite of this. A bite of you. And Harry, of course."

My stomach drops. I'm feeling a bit ripped at the seams as it is, not sure there's much left of me to sink their teeth into.

Sigrún glances at her ringing phone, smile spreading even broader across her pale lips. "See, there's another one. This is *huge* for you. For the band."

"How?" Kale's voice is sharp and cutting. "Seems like a mess, if you ask me."

"You aren't getting it." Sigrún drags her hands over her face, scrubbing hard. "This kind of publicity, viral-level press, is a young band's dream. Overnight, you put yourselves on the map. Are you aware of how many streams your old stuff is getting right now? How many hits your name brings up? Your little photo plopped you front and center of attention."

"I don't want the attention," I say, voice somehow steady for all the panic dripping through me. "Not this personal kind, at least. It should be on the music."

She shrugs. "You've got it whether you want it or not. You might as well capitalize on it."

"Capitalize how?" Darcy asks, voice slow. Intrigued. I shoot a horrified glance at her, but she stares straight ahead.

"That's the spirit," Sigrún replies, pointing at her. "Fans are invested in this little love triangle you created with Connor," she continues, swinging her finger between me and Harry. "And like I said, your streams are skyrocketing. But we need more to give them. In the age of social media, every hour counts when it comes to content creation."

"Love triangle?" I turn to Harry, whose mouth is pressed in a firm line as he listens to Sigrún. "There is no love triangle. We aren't a couple."

Sigrún shakes her head, rolling her eyes with a grin like we're the silliest little things she ever did see. "Doesn't matter. For the foreseeable future, you need to pretend to be. And document it."

I gape at her. "Are you mad?"

She shakes her head again. "No. *Listen.* You need to keep this up, keep playing this game on social media—"

"Why would we do that?"

"Because it focuses attention on you. On the band. And you'll want that attention—need it—for this tour to be a success."

"*Tour?*" My head is spinning so fast I worry I might faint. Or projectile vomit.

"It's not only media requests I'm getting. Bookers and promoters are begging to get you on their venue lineups. And fast."

Skull surprises me by laughing. "What venues? Húsavík's biggest club for all ten people that live there?"

Sigrún glares at her cousin. "Try Boston. Cleveland. Philadelphia. Atlantic City. New York. Any of those cities sound familiar?"

"You're joking," Darcy says.

"Does any of this seem funny to you?"

It's probably because my life seems to be rapidly spiraling out of control, but I do laugh (a bit hysterically, I'll admit). "You're mad." It's no longer a question.

Sigrún pins me with a level stare. "I'm about to make you very famous if you listen to me and let me do my job."

My stomach twists, breath getting cut off at the top of my throat.

"Pretend to be a couple, go on tour, watch your career take off in ways you can't even imagine. Anyone have objections to that?" she says, looking around the room.

Harry is silent, and I'm ready for him to jump in and say what a horrible idea this is any time now. "What would the rules be?" he says instead, ripping the rug from under me, my head bashing to the floor.

"Are you joking?" I turn on him. "Rules? How about objections? I have plenty of those."

"Oh really? We weren't aware. You keep your feelings so under wraps," Kale quips.

"What kind of rules are you looking for?" Sigrún asks. I want to duct-tape everyone's mouths shut.

"We'd need a specific timeline we're going to carry this on for . . . A plan for how it would wrap up," Harry replies.

"An easy timeline would be not doing it at all and wrapping the idea up here and now," I yell.

Harry's look is pleading, a little conspiratorial. I can't tell if he's trying to be in cahoots with me or Sigrún. "Come on, Cub. What she's saying makes sense. Who are we to say no? To turn down this chance?"

"Fully autonomous individuals?"

"We're artists. Artists always have to suffer."

"And fake dating me would be suffering, would it?" I say, planting my hands on my hips.

Harry hangs his head and laughs. "For how much I think you'll torture me with it? Yeah, probably. But in the grand scheme of things, it isn't really that bad, is it? At least from my perspective, there are way worse things they could be asking of me than pretending to date you."

"I'm sorry, but do we not get a say in this?" Kale asks, lip curled.

"Yes! Of course! Say what a horrible idea this is!" I beg.

He rolls his eyes. "Don't delude yourself. Sigrún's right—when will we ever get an opportunity like this again?"

My jaw hangs open like a rusted screen door on broken hinges.

"An opportunity to *what*? Create a massive lie that we hope people on social media are dumb enough to believe?"

"If it gets us famous, yeah."

"Fame isn't why we do this."

"Come on, Cubby, you know the reasons we do this . . . It's not just about the music."

"It's *only* about the music!" I shout, hot tears pricking at my eyes. I refuse to let them fall. "Creating something special, something real, is why we do this. And you want to generate a massive lie to tie on to that? We don't even have an album completed, and we're supposed to go on a tour? While also pretending to be in some big romantic scandal? Do you not see how far off that is from the music, it might as well be a different dimension?"

"This band isn't about you and your feelings," Kale snaps back. "There are four other members here all working for success like you."

"Only one of you four is also being asked to parade yourself like an asshole on the internet for attention."

"Grow up, Cubby. Sometimes we have to do things we don't like for the sake of the greater good."

"Who are you, John Stuart Mill?"

Kale blinks at me. "What?"

I am not even remotely calm, but I do take a moment to look at him like the dense prat he is. "You're the greater good, then?"

"We all are." He gestures wildly at the group.

Scoffing, I scan their faces, hoping, expecting to see expressions that match my disbelief at this ridiculous idea.

I don't.

Sigrún nods at Kale, Skull doing the same. Harry's eyes are fixed on the ground, but there isn't a morsel of defiance in his frame. And Darcy—the person always on my side, the one I can always count on to have my back—she's looking at me with a pained expression.

"Really?" I whisper, a mortifying crack in my voice. "You think this is a good idea?"

"I think it's the hand we've been dealt," she whispers back, reaching out for me. I let her extended hand wither in the space. "It isn't ideal or fair, but it makes sense. It's the right move if we want to really do this thing."

"Give me the summer," Sigrún says, clasping her hands in front of her chest as she looks at me. "Give me the summer to take advantage of this for your career. Book you more shows. Get you headlining big bands. You don't even have to say you're dating. Play coy on social media. Post more cute photos. Banter back and forth in the comments. Then, when the summer's done, we can reevaluate. Stage an obvious but amicable parting of ways. Let it fizzle out altogether in a way we can tease a reconciliation for decades to come. My point is, let me capitalize on this for us. For *you*. This could be game-changing for your trajectory as a band."

"What about the album?" I bring up again, searching for any reasoning that will talk them out of this horrible idea.

"You wouldn't leave for a few days yet, maybe even a week," Sigrún says. "Still a lot of logistics to sort. You can come up with some songs by then, I know you can. Put out an EP, at least. Keep writing while you're on the road. People love surprise releases."

"Maybe even use that to hype up the tour? New song at every venue?" Harry asks, blue eyes flicking up from the ground to absorb Sigrún's excited nod. A tiny whimper tears from my throat.

"Cubby, it's okay. Why are you so upset? This is an amazing opportunity," Sigrún says.

I'm blinking rapidly now, heat radiating off my cheeks from the force of holding in a cry. The gentle, cooing sound Sigrún makes as she approaches me with outstretched arms has indignation swelling low in my belly. I sidestep her embrace, wrapping my arms around my middle. I watch her face fall as I shake my head, trying to find any words in my flooded mind.

This is too much, too soon, too fast, and for all the wrong reasons. Did I want *fame* when I started pursuing a music career? I mean . . . I guess that's the simplest word for it. But making music has never been about the glitz of stardom.

It's something so much more elusive than that, this amorphous idea of self-preservation, that if I play hard enough, good enough, devastatingly enough, I don't have to feel my feelings, I can make others feel them instead. A bridge from my broken, too-sad heart to those more able to endure the emotions.

Sigrún's expression hardens, and she straightens her shoulders, hands planted on her hips. "You're forcing my hand here, Cubby. I'm sorry, but as the owner of this label, I'm telling you, you have to do this. It's what the majority wants, and makes a hell of a lot of sense for your career."

My vision blurs, walls shuttering down around me. They've already seen too much; I can't let them watch me break apart further. I storm to the exit and push through the small building's maze of hallways until I find my escape.

Out on the street, the cold bites my cheeks and bare arms, sucking the last bit of air from my lungs. I stop, my wobbly legs folding beneath me as I drop to the dirty sidewalk, back pressed to the wall of the studio. I pull my knees up to my chest, forehead resting on them as I cry.

And it's so damn pathetic. Why am I *crying*? I don't feel *sad*— sadness is useless, it's soft. I feel *angry*—rage swelling up in me with so much pressure I could burst at the seams, raze this city to the ground with the force of it.

But instead, I'm huddled against a wall, curled up as small as I can make myself, quietly weeping into my knees and praying no one notices. My world has been slowly falling apart for months, but now the foundation has snapped and I'm plummeting so fast, I feel sick from the jolt of it. I lost the guy I spent years giving every ounce of my energy into pleasing. I've lost my spark, lost my creativity that let me untangle these feelings, numbness cementing me down.

Connor stole my words. My identity. My own stupidity last night stole the only good thing I had going for me—my seamless friendship with Darcy. And now I have to pretend that all of it hasn't cut me to the bone, bleeding me dry in a slow death—paste on some heart eyes so our band can get attention on the internet when all I fucking want is for someone to care about what I have to say and be patient enough for me to find the words for it.

The outrage continues to spill out of me in silent, wet sobs that no one but me and the ground have to deal with. I cry until I'm a sniveling mess, as useless as the tacky gum stuck to the sidewalk next to me.

I don't hear Darcy walk up to me as much as sense her, like I always do. You know when you're lying in the grass on a bright day and someone hovers over you, blocking out the sun, and everything goes dark and the tiniest bit cooler? Darcy is the opposite of that. Her presence eclipses my gray skies, simply standing nearby lifting my clouds.

She doesn't say anything, sitting down next to me and dropping my coat over my shoulders before hugging me—a proper hug, one with her arms cinched tight and head on my shoulder, the hesitancy from this morning gone. Thank god for small mercies.

It feels so comforting, so right, a tiny whimper tears from my throat, but I stay rigid, trying to avoid my natural response of melting against her. Darcy's always been the one I lean on when I sink low, but after the confusion of last night and the absurdity of what happened in the studio, she feels like a stranger to me.

"It'll be okay" she whispers, rubbing her hands up and down my arms. "I promise."

"How do you know?" I blubber back, softening a bit. I try to stiffen my shoulders, but it's no use, she's too warm. Too familiar.

"Because we'll make it okay. You and I, together. Like we always do. We'll go to America—go on tour—and make music and kill performances and play pretend at this ridiculous scheme and laugh at everyone we fool along the way."

I let out a doubtful snort.

"Think about it this way," she says, a small spark in her voice. "What better way to get back at Connor than needle at his jealous streak? It will eat him alive to think something's going on with you and Harry."

That hooks me, a vindictive little monster in the center of my brain purring at the idea. I lift my head and look at her, swiping at my tear-stained cheeks.

She smiles, mischievous and delighted that she got to me. "It's just for the summer. One summer. We survived twenty-two together so far, what's one more with a bit of mayhem thrown in?"

I soften further. That's the thing about Darcy. She can make even the worst situations seem a little bit wonderful.

Like any good hunter, she senses my rapidly deteriorating resolve and pushes. "We'll take this shite hand and make something beautiful from it. Like it or not, this may be our one chance. I don't want to regret not taking it."

A bitter laugh scratches out of me. "That's the problem: I hate that *this* is our chance. This isn't *right*, Darcy. This isn't how things are supposed to happen. It was never supposed to hurt this much and feel so raw and exposing and humiliating."

Darcy stares at me, midnight-blue eyes sharp and invading, like she can see into me. And god, does it feel good. Normal. Like all the mess of last night has been packed up into a box and forgotten. It proves that pretending it didn't happen really is the best thing we can do to preserve this friendship.

"You're right," she says, gripping my shoulders. "It's not fair and it's not right. But it's happening regardless, and it'll only hurt that much if you let it."

Those silly tears start falling again. Darcy's thumbs are on the apples of my cheeks, softly swiping them away. "They'll rip me apart," I whisper.

"They won't ever get their hands on the real you."

I scoff. "What kind of new-age bullshit is that?"

Darcy giggles, the sound so sweet and warm, my heart skips a beat. "It means that this Connor-Harry thing is a game. A role. Any pretending you have to do will be like putting on a suit of armor. People might claw at that version on the internet, but it's not the real you, right?"

"Who's the real me?" It's pitiful how desperate I am for her answer. For someone, anyone, to tell me who I am or who I'm supposed to be because life is so hard and scary and I feel entirely lost in it.

Darcy stares at me again—studies me so intensely my cheeks warm. Her eyebrows notch, lips parting. Those eyes of hers trip down to my mouth, lingering there for half a second too long, before skimming back up.

For a moment, I imagine her leaning in to kiss me.

For a moment, I want her to.

God, what is *wrong* with me? What is this absolutely ridiculous, inappropriate fascination I have with Darcy and kissing? It's because I'm a mess, that's all. I'm vulnerable. I'm emotional. I'm a total mess. I turn away from her, dropping my chin to my knees.

"You're my best friend," she whispers after a moment, hand resting between my shoulder blades. "There's no challenge we can't beat."

My heart sinks, and I swallow past the lump lodged heavily in my throat, fighting for a smile. I can do this for Darcy. If it's what she wants, there's no way I'll say no. "Okay." I sigh, blinking away the remaining poke of tears still trying to fall. "We'll do it."

Darcy chirps, throwing her arms around me in a bear hug, rocking us side to side. "It'll be amazing, I promise."

"I think we need to get a manager," I say after a beat. "Things felt overwhelming enough before this and all we really had to focus on was making an album. With the tour and social media stuff, we need someone to look out for our interests and handle the big picture."

Darcy nods, biting her lip as she thinks. "We could ask your mum to do it?"

"Which one?" Louise (Mum) is an art curator, and Beatriz (Mãe) is an artist; neither knows the first thing about music.

"Louise. She's managed all those galleries and hosts all kinds of posh events. I'm sure she could handle us on tour."

"To point out the obvious, there's something rather inherently uncool about bringing your mother on tour with you."

"Planning on letting loose with some good ole American sex, drugs, and rock 'n' roll, are ya, Cubby?" she says with a laugh.

My face burns, stomach clenching. "Well, I'd certainly like to keep my options open." I'm surprised to see color rush to Darcy's cheeks, and I press on, eager to skip over the weird flip it causes in my chest. "Should we bring your mum along, then?"

Darcy's smile drops, eyes shooting wide. "You know that's not a fair comparison. Your mums are effortlessly chic and brilliant and mine keeps her eyes glued to the telly all day howling praises for conservatives and their traditional family values."

I concede her point with a knowing frown. Darcy's parents are . . . tight-laced, to phrase it nicely. Bigots with their heads stuck up their arses to phrase it plainly, and it's only gotten worse over the years. "It'd be better to have an outsider anyway. Anyone with even an ounce of connection to me would cause Kale to scream favoritism first chance he gets."

"Human equivalent of a pimple, that one," Darcy mumbles. "If he weren't so damn good, he'd be on the curb. But you're right. We'll find someone. Probably have our pick of the litter if we've gained as much notoriety as Sigrún claims."

My stomach sours at the reminder of our rapidly growing infamy.

"Right, let's get inside, we have songs to write," she says, hopping to stand and helping me up. With one last sigh, I turn and lead us toward the door. "Sigrún mentioned she has an instrumental arrangement she's been toying with that maybe we could package into a love song or something."

I stop in my tracks, Darcy smacking into my back. "No love songs," I say, spinning on her.

"What?"

"No love songs," I repeat, leveling her with a serious look. "Only spite songs."

"Spite songs?"

"If I'm going to do this, I refuse to be happy and lovely about it."

Darcy rolls her eyes and shoos me toward the door. "Of course. I shouldn't have expected anything different."

Chapter 9

The next week moves at a brutal pace—meetings and emails and endless hours in the studio, working on songs until our eyes are bloodshot and fingers stiff. We come up with five solid tracks to release on an EP. Some, like that golden day in the studio that feels like a different lifetime, are fully from scratch. Others are built from half-finished arrangements Darcy and I fiddled with years ago that I never bothered to share with Connor. He didn't pull any punches when it came to giving me feedback on my lyrics and compositions, most deemed painfully derivative and weak. I learned quickly what was better kept to myself to be spared his brutal honesty.

But even with a framework to go off, reworking an old song is like ripping each word out by the roots from frozen ground and planting new seeds in the barren space, leaving my brain feeling dried out and withered.

Today's meeting about final details for the tour has forced us into a break. We file into Ring Road's conference room, Sigrún at the head of an imposing oval table, so large in the tiny space that I feel claustrophobic as I squeeze into a seat. Sigrún doesn't acknowledge us at first, her eyes zipping between her computer screen and phone as she pounds on the keyboard.

Sticky anticipation oozes through me, and I swipe open my phone, doing a quick circuit of various apps, thumb flicking in a blur as I scan comments and tags. I exit out of the last site, shoving my phone between my thighs and watching the seconds tick by on the clock above the door, my legs bouncing.

I only get to a count of eight before I grab my phone again, repeating the loop, the chronic tension in my chest growing tighter as I see nothing's changed, and I lock it once more.

Sitting still is the worst thing for me right now. It gives me too much time to think, to play on loop the parade of degrading opinions shared in comments, to manifest even worse sentiments about myself into existence.

Harry and I have been equally feeding the relationship rumors like good little soldiers—pictures of the band where we're caught looking at each other, video clips of him playing the piano while I sit pressed close to him on the bench, singing in rough harmony; actual candid moments someone snapped during sessions where he says something that makes me scrunch up my face and laugh—but I'm the one getting hate. Mean comments telling me I'm a manipulative man-eater toying with the emotions of two wonderful guys.

But Harry? I haven't seen a single bad word against him.

I sneak a glance at Darcy, but she's staring straight ahead, a bored look on her face as she traces Sigrún's frenetic movements. She's right there but feels miles away.

On the surface, everything between us is friendly and normal, if not a little strained from the whirlwind of stress we're under. That normalcy makes me want to shake her, ask her if I'm crazy, if it's all in my head, or does every interaction between us feel tame and cautious, each word analyzed before spoken to make sure it's stripped of any possible misinterpretation to her too?

Which, obviously, can never happen because she's made it pretty obvious she doesn't think about that night.

I grab my phone once more, clicking into an app, then catch myself, catch the itch of the compulsion to complete the circuit, and slam it back between my thighs.

My jiggling legs pick up speed, the sturdy wooden table vibrating. At the same moment, Darcy and Harry, sitting on opposite sides of me, reach out a hand, each giving my leg a gentle squeeze under the table.

My body locks up in surprise.

It's amazing that an identical gesture can split me down the middle with different feelings. Harry's hand is large and soft, the lightest pressure right above my knee before slipping to my wrist and tracing down to where my hand is sandwiched under my thigh. He pulls it out, threading his fingers through mine under the table.

Darcy, on my other side, lingers on the center of my thigh, fingers spread wide like she can pull all the nervous energy out of me and hold it in the palm of her hand. My gaze flashes to her, lips parting, a surge of emotions clawing up my throat. She looks back at me, startled by the intensity in my expression. I hold her stare, everything blurring at the edges as my body singles in on her touch, the heat of her scrambling my nervous system so every circuit reroutes to the spot.

On impulse, my eyes flick to her hand on my leg—like I need visual confirmation she's actually, willfully touching me—then back to her face. With a start, she looks to my lap, then jerks her hand away like she's touched a hot stovetop. She pivots away from me, knees pointed in the opposite direction, palms resting on the tabletop. She starts to drum a rhythm with her fingertips, and a tiny, rough noise escapes my lips.

Everyone turns to me, and I try to disguise the small, pained gasp in a fake coughing fit, pushing my chair back and pulling my hand from Harry's.

"Are you okay, Cubby?" Sigrún asks, joining us in the real world.

I open my mouth like a fish reluctantly trying to survive on land, but nothing comes out. I nod instead.

"Kevin should be joining us any moment," Sigrún says, tapping a few times on her laptop until a Zoom call pops up on the large monitor mounted on the wall.

After an excruciating number of video interviews for a manager—ranging from lackluster to downright horrifying in both personality and vibe—we finally settled on Kevin Cho, the son of a successful talent manager looking to make his own name in the industry. While he's rather green—we're only the second band he's represented—there's something genuinely earnest about his excitement for our music (i.e., he's actually listened to it). Plus his commission rate is reasonable enough we can actually afford him.

"Heyyyy, everyone!" Kevin says, cheeks flushed and expression exuberant as he pops up on the screen. "How're my favorite rock stars?"

"We're more of folk-pop band," Kale says with a grimace.

Skull stares straight ahead, unblinking and in a world all his own.

"Catch yerself on," Harry says, clicking his tongue as he frowns at Kale. "We're not *pop*. We're indie folk rock."

"Why are you saying it like that, Harry?" Darcy chimes in, leaning across me with a frown.

"Like what?"

"Like you're putting *derogatory* in parentheses after *pop*."

"Oh, come off it, Darce. I'm not having this fight with you again."

Kevin has the expression of a clubbed baby seal at the sore spot he accidentally pressed.

Darcy rolls her eyes. "For it to be a fight, you'd actually need some ammunition in that arsenal. Need I remind you—"

"Can we focus?" Sigrún says, clapping her hands. When she's satisfied with Harry and Darcy's chagrined silence, she carries on, "We've ironed out the details of the tour, so let's dive in."

A tiny thrill shoots through me as she splits the screen and brings up the meeting agenda and info sheet. Over the next eight weeks, we'll be touring the East Coast of America, headlining some small but historically iconic venues in big cities.

I've always been in love with music—my mums have home videos of me pressing my slobbering baby face up close to their speaker as Fiona Apple played, my wobbly legs bouncing to the beat while my twin, Oliver, stared like a loris at the noise. But since I can remember, I've also been fascinated by musicians, ingesting every documentary and interview I could get my grubby hands on, diving into their memories like they're my own, seeing the twists and turns and the crucial nights at special venues that changed their careers forever.

Maybe one of these venues will be that for us.

"Kevin will meet you at Boston Logan International Airport," Sigrún says, eyes skimming over her screen. "You'll check into the hotel, rest up, then get to the Paradise Rock Club around five for sound check, then the show that night. The next day you'll open for a band called Dubstep Anarchy at the Lizard Lounge in Cambridge."

"Dubstep?"

"Lizards?"

Harry and I speak at the same time, glancing at each other in horror. Sigrún arches an eyebrow. "Someone pull out their phone. These are the cute moments we need to be capturing for social media."

My stomach clenches, a buzzing growing in my ears as Sigrún chuckles, then continues talking through our tour. I hate these moments, the unwelcome reminder of the tangled mess I'm in, that I have to lie about who I am—attach myself to the likability of another person—to get anyone to listen to the thing that means the most to me.

"You'll finish the tour with the Jersey Shore Pride Festival in Asbury Park."

"Asbury Park? Like the Springsteen album?" I ask.

Sigrún nods. "And the song. In fact, Kevin and I were discussing, and we think it would be great for you to do a cover of 'Sandy' during your set to pay homage. Maybe then have it lead into a mash-up with the release of your own brand-new love ballad. Go out with a bang to keep the spark alive."

I grimace. "Is that song some sort of touchstone in America's queer culture?"

Kevin and Sigrún blink in unison at me. "Not that I'm aware of?" Kevin says, like this is a test and he's terrified of answering wrong. "Why?"

"Because you said this is a Pride festival?"

More blinking. "I'm not sure I follow your point?" Sigrún hedges.

I slant a glance at Kale, who looks equally perplexed at their confusion. "Isn't the point of Pride sort of, er, queer pride? Honoring that? It'd be one thing if you told us to perform something on the nose like a Lady Gaga mash-up, but an old, white, hetero, cis man seems . . ."

"Wrong unless it's Tony Soprano?" Kale finishes for me. "It's giving Walmart in June."

Sigrún purses her lips. "Oh. I think you're missing the point. The song is a reference to where you'll be location-wise for the festival."

I inwardly groan but drop it. "Regardless, we don't have a brand-new love ballad."

"You will by the time the festival rolls around."

I open my mouth to argue, but Darcy's touch is back, a gentle pressure, the whisper of her fingertips at my forearm.

"We'll come up with something," she whispers out of the corner of her mouth as Sigrún continues. "It will be surface-level fluff with plenty of hidden barbs in there, don't worry."

I nod, keeping my eyes fixed straight ahead. I'm terrified that if I look at her, she'll see how much I don't believe her. How I don't want to. I don't want to do fluff. I don't want to do any of this fake shit.

"I have some exciting news," Kevin chimes in as Sigrún wraps up. "With your latest audio release gaining some traction, we've had a few branding opportunities pop up."

Sigrún wasted no time getting a polished soundbite of our song from last week that we've titled "fool," up on social media. While it hasn't broken any records, it's steadily growing, people lip-syncing the crescendo lines "*Wore your empty promises like a tattoo on my skin / Your losing battles, I just can't win*" while pounding on their chests and pretending to cry.

"This newer fashion company, Zuuli, they're starting to take off too, very in, very trendy, doing the whole upcycled vintage, anti–fast fashion thing. They've signed on for tour exclusivity of your wardrobe!"

"What does *tour exclusivity* mean?" I ask, defenses perking up.

"Which word confused you, Cubby?" Kale deadpans.

"Lick rust, you repugnant vegetable."

"How clever," Kale says, rolling his eyes. "The kids from my high school would be so impressed by your originality."

"Anyway!" Kevin, our king of perpetual cheeriness, says. "Zuuli has offered to sponsor the band and the tour by providing you all with wardrobes for the shows and associated events. You'll just have to tag them in posts and do some outfit-of-the-day stories in recognition. Hype them up a bit. The deal is all set!"

"We don't even know what these clothes look like and we're already committed to wearing them all summer?" I say, mouth twisting.

"Oh, but they're actually really cute," Darcy says, eyes scanning her phone. She tilts the screen to me, scrolling through.

I hate to admit it, but the clothes do look rather nice. An eclectic mix of simple nineties pieces and more boho seventies gear. It fits our vibe rather well. But still, not only am I being told what I have to write and post on social media, but now they're telling me what I have to wear too.

"This is class," Harry says, leaning across me to look too. "Great job, Kev."

"Can I get one of these denim shirts for my portion?" Kale asks, waving his phone around.

"Send me the link, I'll see what I can do," Kevin says with a grin.

"I like this whole look. Especially the boots," Skull says, showing us an all-black look complete with platform combat boots.

"I'll try to work some magic," Kevin says. "So pumped you all are excited."

Excitement isn't even in the top ten of emotions I'm experiencing, but I already feel like such a wet rag with this group, I keep my mouth shut. I don't need to leak the dull emptiness of my depression onto my friends. And Kale.

"My girlfriend will be meeting us at the airport. She will come on the tour with us," Skull announces using the most words I've ever heard him string together.

We all blink at him.

"Skull . . . *what*?" Kale finally asks, face drooping with confusion.

"You have a girlfriend?" Darcy says, leaning over the table toward him. "In America?"

"Where is she going to sleep?" I love Harry, he always asks the important questions.

"My American girlfriend, Deja. She is a tiny woman, she will sleep in my bed," he says with finality, something about his sharp accent daring us to try to argue.

"Where did you find this tiny girlfriend who's going on tour with us?" Darcy asks, heart in her eyes. She's a hopeless romantic and loves seeing people in love. I'm sure every cell in her body is sighing wistfully right now.

"Internet," Skull says. Truly the new frontier. Someone should probably push back on this a bit, or at least ask some logistical questions about our next eight weeks on a bus with Tiny Deja, but Skull asks for so little, moving like water with the flow of everyone around him, we silently agree to let him have this one thing.

"Well . . . all right, then," Sigrún says. "That wraps up everything on my end. Kevin, you have anything you want to add?"

Kevin grins. "Only that I can't wait to see you all tomorrow—the first day of your new life as a band. I have no doubt it will be epic."

Darcy offers a bubbly round of applause as Kale and Skull stand.

Harry leans close to me, nose brushing the side of my cheek as he whispers, "Let the adventure begin."

Chapter 10

At an ungodly hour the next morning, our plane barrels down the runway, lifting us up as I leave a piece of my heart behind. I lean over Darcy, who's in the window seat, staring down at Reykjavík, the streets and roads and jagged coastline sprawled beneath like the closing words of a love letter.

We're subletting our sublet, and I imagine I can see the apartment building as clouds haze the view. The water took ages to heat to lukewarm and traffic from the street sounded like it was happening in the living room and we were constantly on top of each other in the cramped place, leading to countless arguments. And I'm sad to say goodbye to the shithole.

Darcy nudges me out of her personal space, and I wriggle in my uncomfortable middle seat, Harry on the aisle. Darcy hoists her backpack onto her lap, rifling through the absurd amount of books she *had* to pack in her carry-on for in-flight entertainment. She hands me a small stack as she digs to the bottom, and I thumb through some of the pages. When she finally finds what she's looking for, she shoves all the books back in and kicks her bag under the seat.

"What'd ya decide on?"

"I'm in my cowboy-romance era," she says, putting on a Southern American drawl and flashing me the cover. "Save a horse, ride someone's dad, or however the saying goes."

"I think you nailed it."

With a smug smile, she settles in and starts to read. I watch her from the corner of my eye, see her melting into the pages, leaving me behind for a fictional world with a hero and romance and a lot less complication.

Early-onset nostalgia has our shared room popping into my head again, Darcy's narrow mattress pushed against the wall, duvet rumpled and a precarious stack of books perched on her nightstand. She liked to curl up against her pillows and read while I strummed my guitar at the foot of her bed, creating a soundtrack as she lost herself to other worlds. How many hours did we spend on that bed? Laughing or crying or making music?

It's rather jarring that such an unassuming-looking corner could be the spot my mind won't stop circling.

I mean . . . it's not that I think about that terrible night *that* much. Hardly at all, really. It just creeps in at the edges, flits across my mind when my defenses are down.

My phone is on airplane mode, but the impulse to check it anyway has a physical grip, tightening the muscles in my neck and palms. If I can stay on top of what's being said on there, maybe I can learn how to control it.

My leg starts bouncing, and Darcy's reluctantly pulled out of her book, looking around at the plane like it's about to break apart, then down to my thigh. She places a hand on my knee.

"You okay?"

I fight the urge to shake my head, shrugging instead. "I'm fine. Just tired."

"Try to get some sleep."

I shrug again, giving her a resigned look, gesturing around the stuffy, loud plane, Harry lightly snoring next to me.

"I'm too wired to sleep too. This feels like the start of everything, doesn't it?" she whispers, notes of excitement and hope dancing across the syllables.

I stay silent, not wanting to burst her bubble. I'd like to tell her she's wrong. Everything is wrong. This isn't the start. We're smack dab in the middle of the end. The end of making music for the sake of creation, for the joy of sharing it. The end of simplicity, of having a neat little box that contained the definition of our friendship to something confusing and messy that, no matter how hard I try, I can't stop my finicky brain from turning back to. But instead, I swoop up those feelings, compress them into a tight knot, and kick it far out of my brain, leaning back toward the numbness that is safe and keeps me whole.

I feel her eyes on me, searching out the lie, to call me on my shit like she always does. I can't let that happen, can't have her seeing what a mess I'm making of us in my head; it would only take her further away. "Guess I'm worried about the social media stuff."

The tension evaporates with a small sigh from Darcy. "It'll be fine, Cub. It's already going well. The pictures of the band have tons of likes and comments, and we even sold out that venue in Cleveland."

"Yeah, you're right."

"I know it's not ideal," she says, voice soft like a lullaby, "but I hope you know how much we all appreciate you and Harry doing this, playing the game like you are. It's creating something big for us. It . . . it means a lot."

I grind my teeth. Not like I had much choice in the matter. "Don't mention it."

The silence stretches, and Darcy goes back to her book, turning the pages in a steady rhythm that eventually lulls me into a light, choppy sleep for the rest of the flight.

We land in Boston a few hours later. With a stiff neck and bleary eyes, I navigate customs and eventually get my phone to connect.

Harry, bougie ass, woke up in the second half of the flight and bought Wi-Fi access, and I shoot him a glare as a flood of notifications drill through my phone. Apparently, I've been tagged in a post.

"Just doing as I'm told, Cub," he says with a pitiful frown. I wish I could be mad at him, but I know his intentions are good. I scroll way back to see what he posted.

The photo is black and white again, my head resting on Harry's shoulder as I doze on the plane. Harry's lips are quirked in a small smile that's both playful and serene, cheek pressed against my hair. He's captioned it with a cute bear emoji and a line of Zs. I study the picture closely, and it makes something in my chest ache. If I didn't know better I'd actually believe the lies and think Harry feels something for me.

What the camera doesn't show is my right side, Darcy's head on my arm and hand gripped tight in mine as she sleeps too. That aching feeling expands for a moment, cracking like glass down to the tips of my fingers, then snaps back with a sharp throb right below my sternum.

With the usual impulse that congeals with dread, I start scrolling the comments.

So fucking cute

Okay but seriously does she know how lucky she is?

This made me have my first feeling in six months

Poor Harry :(she's going to use him like she used Connor.

> **Reply:** no fr but if she's smart she'll realize what thin fucking ice she's on

Reply: she's way too self-centered to realize that
we're all on to her. It's sad

"You okay?" Darcy asks, resting her chin on my shoulder. I quickly swipe out of the app.

"Yeah. Fine." I slide away from her touch, pretending to stretch after the long flight. My limbs are tight and swollen with a sickly anxiety that makes me want to crawl out of my skin.

I have the excruciating urge to find something, anything, that I can throw at the wall of the internet to make me more likable. Acceptable. Anything to fight against this vulgar misconception of who I am. I scroll deep into my camera roll, hoping I can find a cute throwback picture, something innocent and endearing I can post that will remind people I'm a human and see the awful things they're saying.

I land on a screen full of Darcy and I, hundreds of rapid-fire photos from my eighteenth birthday. We're dressed in skimpy outfits and an alarming amount of glitter, the backdrop of the club blacked out from the flash. Darcy and I looking at each other, faces screwed up as we laugh, her arms thrown around me and nose pressed against my cheek as I blush. That ache is back so sharply, so acutely, a tiny gasp is pulled out of me, my hand rubbing against my chest.

An exuberant shriek across baggage claim snaps me out of my misery, making us all turn, and I blink as a pocket-sized woman around our age barrels at us full-speed. Faster than I've ever seen Skull move, he drops his backpack and runs to meet her halfway, picking her up and spinning her in his arms with a movie-worthy kiss. It's so beautiful I feel inclined to clap.

When the kiss starts to border on obscene, her thighs wrapped tightly around Skull's trim waist, his hand inching up her skirt, I glance away. Kale, Harry, and Darcy are similarly staring in shock with their jaws on the ground. With breathtaking tenderness, Skull gently lowers the woman in his arms, who I have brilliantly deduced must be Tiny Deja.

Hand in hand and grinning at each other, they walk toward us. I blink rapidly as I fully take her in. Skull's tiny, internet, American girlfriend is, quite possibly, the most stunning woman I have ever seen. She has dark brown skin and full lips curved in a perfect smile. Her hair is pulled into twist braids that fall to her waist, and her coffee-colored eyes are framed by full thick lashes that belong in a Maybelline advert.

"Everyone," Skull mumbles, "I'd like to introduce you to—"

"Let me guess!" Harry interrupts. "Your sister?"

Deja lets out a bubbly laugh, beaming at us. "I'm Deja," she says, touching a hand to her chest. "It's so good to meet you. Skull has told me so much about all of you. Honestly, he never shuts up about you."

"Really?" Darcy blurts out, the skepticism palpable. The idea of Skull talking at length about anyone or anything requires quite the suspension of reality. She clears her throat. "I mean, hiya! We're so pleased to meet you too. I'm Darcy."

Deja, friendliness personified, wraps Darcy in a huge hug like she's greeting her best friend after years apart. She does the same to me, then turns to Kale as he eagerly introduces himself— even Beelzebub incarnate wants to absorb some of Deja's warm attention.

I'm probably being rude at this point, but I can't stop staring at her. Harry and I share a quick look. He leans close to me, inconspicuously whispering, "Is Skull's girlfriend . . ."

"Outrageously hot?" I whisper back.

"Holy God, I thought she was a mirage. Glad you see her too."

I feel like doing a slow clap for Skull.

Harry's expression as Deja hugs him slips from shock, to stupefied, to downright envy as he glances over her shoulder to Skull, whose mouth curves in a knowing smile. I bite my lip hard to hold back my laughter.

"Hey, superstars!" Kevin's voice calls from the bank of exit doors. He struts toward us with exceptional swagger, arms outstretched. "How was the flight?"

"We didn't end up on the news, so fairly boring," Darcy says, shaking his proffered hand.

Kevin throws his head back as he laughs. He's decked out tip to toe, a trendy blazer over a loose-fitting pink button-down, well-tailored trousers that lead to exceptionally posh suede loafers. The outfit would look douchey on most people, but there's something so endearingly earnest in the way Kevin smiles at us, I feel like it's more armor than anything else, dressing for the job he wants (established manager of actual superstars) and not the job he has (inexperienced manager of D-list disasters). He goes around the group, initiating an awkward handshake-half-hug thing with each of us.

"Great thinking on that post during the flight, by the way, Harry," Kevin says, clapping us both on the back as we watch the luggage being spat out onto the carousel. "Keeping that rumor mill churning. Very smart."

"Yeah, what a mastermind. Learned how to tie his shoes last week too," I say, turning to Kevin. "We'll make sure you have a chance to sign the congratulations card."

"Thanks, Kev," Harry says with a smile, inconspicuously digging his elbow into my side. "Just trying to do as Sigrún advised."

"Such a good little soldier," I coo, swerving away from his arm, then turning to smartly pat him on the cheek.

"One of us has to be."

I roll my eyes. While I'm going through the motions of throwing stuff up on my stories and posting pictures, I haven't taken initiative with any of it, only doing what I'm told when I'm explicitly ordered to, spending more of my time lurking in the comments section, committing to memory all the harsh sentiments being shared. I don't see what the big deal is—the response is exponentially more positive when Harry posts anyway.

We collect our bags and Kevin orders us a car that takes us to our accommodations where we'll stay for the next two nights before switching to the tour bus that will take us to Vermont. I stare out the window, excited to see a new city—cobbled alleys nestled between skyscrapers—but we head away from downtown.

"Much more reasonably priced outside the city," Kevin says in a chipper voice as the skyline disappears behind us.

We're dropped at an inn on a plain-looking street. It's an old, Victorian-style house with hideous plastic siding in desperate need of a power wash. The inside isn't much better, the lobby/sitting room smelling like someone chain-smoked for multiple decades, then dumped lavender essential oil into the old pink carpeting to cover up the stale stench. A bored-looking woman around my age reluctantly looks up from her laptop and checks Kevin in, handing him keys and flicking her wrist toward the rickety stairs, eyes already back on her screen.

Skull stops Deja on the second floor, scooping her into his arms as she lets out a breathy shriek of delight.

"What are you doing?" she asks.

"Own room," he replies with a grunt, carrying her into the first door on the right. "We do not share with others."

The door shuts with a *thump* behind him, and it takes all of point-two seconds till we hear bed springs creaking, punctuated by a raspy moan (from Deja) and what can only be described as a lusty giggle (from Skull).

Kevin blinks at their door for a moment before his eyes skip to the room next to it. "You all are upstairs," he says with a defeated sigh, head hanging low as he lets himself into his room.

Kale, Harry, Darcy, and I bumble up the next flight, hauling all our crap with superhuman strength to escape the growing amorous volume. Sigrún booked us two rooms—Kevin and Skull splurged on their own spaces—and we were promised the arrangement would mean none of us have to share a bed with anyone, so we didn't put up too much of a fuss. Kale and Harry carry on down the hall to their room, while Darcy and I unlock the door to ours. We share a grimace as we take in the space . . . Maybe a fuss would have been warranted.

"What a shithole," Darcy whispers as if she's worried she'll disturb the film of dust coating the questionable decor.

While Sigrún was more than ecstatic to capitalize on the momentum and send us on tour, she did warn us that some accommodations would be less than ideal on Ring Road's tight budget, and our room paints a clear picture of just how economical she's being.

The air is somehow even mustier up here, Boston's humidity leaching through the windows. The decor is coastal grandma but without any of the chicness and all of the mounted fish eternally gaping for their dying breath. An alarming amount of thick rope decks the walls, while the bust of a wrecked-looking mermaid that may have belonged on the mast of a worse-for-wear ship or a poorly designed strip club lurches over the bed.

The bed is its own anomaly, not matching the . . . *style* of the rest of the room. The frame is a jarringly white four-poster monstrosity, a heavy, sagging mattress wrapped in a bubblegum-pink duvet sitting on top of short, skinny legs. Somehow, I instinctively know that if I lie on that bed, a cloud of dust will poof through the room like an atomic bomb.

But the alternative . . .

A threadbare rollaway cot sits next to it, the mattress as thin as the other is thick, and so compressed lengthwise that my legs would dangle off the edge.

We stare at the beds in silence, neither of us breathing. And, like the climax of a horror movie, our eyes slowly trace to each other, locking in fear. The fear shifts to realization. Then determination.

"Dibs," we screech in unison, then make a mad dash across the room.

"Get off me," I grunt as Darcy grabs my elbow, trying to jerk me back and use the momentum to fly ahead. I shake her off, giving her a decent shove into a floor lamp shaped like an anchor with so KNOTTY written on the shade in letters made to look like rope.

"I called it first," she lies, tripping me so my knees land on the carpet, something crunchy in the fibers sounding with my impact. I wrap my fingers in her belt loops as she tries to leave me in the dust, and she joins me on the ground.

"I'm taller," I pant as we tussle. "The cot is the perfect size for you."

"I will saw your feet off if you try to stick me on that piece of plywood," she snarls back.

We manage to stand, still tangled as we move. We leap at the same moment for the bigger bed, colliding in midair so we land on the edge of the mattress, hanging like Mufasa in his final moments.

I claw into the duvet, using some of the ostentatious buttons as hand holds, Darcy scrabbling next to me. We've both nearly dragged ourselves to the top when a loud groan cuts through our struggling, a wail of warning before a *crack* echoes through the room.

We only have half a second to look at each other, eyes widening in fear. Then, with the jerk of a roller coaster, the bed collapses down, the skinny legs splintering to twigs as the crash thunders through the bones of the house, the entire structure shaking.

Everything is silent for a moment, Darcy and I still locked in a horrified look, and I'm fully convinced this bed is about to fall three stories through this dilapidated house and we will die in the wreckage of this hideous bedding.

I think my life is supposed to flash before me when faced with imminent demise like this, but the only (ridiculous) thought I can muster is that I'm so glad Darcy's big blue eyes are the last thing I'll see before I perish. That I'll go out doing something ridiculous with my favorite person on the planet.

The bedroom door flies open and bangs against the wall, snapping me out of my fanciful final moments, the house settling back into place.

No death today. Not even bodily harm. Maybe the tour won't be so bad after all.

"What the hell are you on about?" Harry shrieks, barreling through the room, the rest of our gaggle of misfits—minus Skull and Tiny Deja, who apparently can't be bothered enough by cataclysmic sounds to stop shagging—close on his tail. "Are you okay?"

Darcy and I share another look. "The bed broke," we whine in unison.

"Clearly this was faulty construction," Darcy says, gesturing at it. "We can't be blamed for that."

I nod emphatically, locking eyes with the front desk girl as she mounts the final step and enters the room. She could not look more unimpressed.

"Okay, everyone keep calm," Kevin says, not very calm at all. "We can figure this out. Discuss the damages."

I'm guessing massive ancient bed destruction wasn't budgeted for.

"I literally do not care," the front desk girl says with a yawn. "That bed is a thousand years old, and the legs have been replaced so many times. Just, like . . . keep it down? I'm trying to study for my bioethics in the age of consumerism exam tomorrow."

"Right. Sorry. Wow. Bioethics in . . . That sounds . . . Yup, she's walking away," I say, watching her disappear down the steps.

"You two need to get your shit together and not die before our first show," Harry says, sounding like a mother hen. "You nearly gave me a heart attack."

"Cubby's untimely death would keep us trending for at least another week, so it wouldn't be the worst thing in the world," Kale says, eyeing the damage.

I bark out a nasally fake laugh, flipping him off with both hands.

Kevin looks the worst for wear, frazzled and sweaty as he continues his wide-eyed appraisal of the room. With a deep sigh, he hangs his head and says what we're all thinking. "This is going to be a long summer, isn't it?"

Chapter 11

The Paradise Rock Club is standing room only, featuring a stocked bar to the left that I can already imagine packed with bodies, judgmental eyes fixed on my every move. The wraparound balcony overhead makes me feel like I'm under a microscope during sound check. My voice is wobbly as we rehearse a few songs, sweat budding on my forehead and pooling under my arms until my skin prickles.

"Great job, everyone," Kevin says, clapping his hands and smiling at us as we finish up. "Let's get you all cleaned up and presentable." I want to strangle him by his stylish silk scarf for the extra long glance he bestows upon me.

In an edgy haze, I follow the group backstage. They sprawl out around the green room—Harry and Kale slouched on the couch, Deja perched on Skull's lap as he lounges in an armchair, Darcy planting herself in front of one of the mirrors and applying a dramatic swoop of pink eyeshadow across her lids. I stay hunched in the corner, something sticky and dark with fear rooting my feet to the ground.

They laugh and chat, an excited current zipping between them while my nerves envelop me in a throbbing bubble, the noise reaching me like it's traveling through water. Rather fitting, I suppose—I do feel a bit like I'm drowning.

We've played plenty of shows before, and it used to be my favorite part of the job—taking this wonderful, terrible, magical thing we've labored over and sharing it with anyone willing to listen; losing myself in the addictive thrill of handing something so deeply personal over to strangers.

But this show is different. Tainted and messy and already a rotten memory. It's my first without Connor. The first with a substantial crowd. The first where I know people are here to size me up as a spectacle, not as a musician.

I'm still fading into the cinder block walls when Kevin rolls in a few racks of new clothes from Zuuli, the others swarming like moths to a flame to collect their spoils. When the frenzy disperses and everyone heads to their mock modesty corners to change, I flick through the clothes designated for me.

There are few things I hate more than admitting when I'm wrong or that I maybe, ever so slightly, overreacted to something, but Zuuli did come through with some amazing pieces for our shows. Still don't love the exclusivity part, but I'm learning not to look a gift horse in the free crop top.

Darcy's wardrobe hangs on one half of the rack next to mine, and the difference is comical. Her side is short hems and bright colors. Sequins and outrageous patterns and plenty of feathers thrown in.

So entirely her.

My side looks more like a display for an incredibly trendy funeral. Black, black, black, exactly how I want my clothes, matching my emotions and cold, shriveled heart. I pick a piece at random and throw it on.

"Whatdya think of this one?" Darcy asks, doing a quick spin and making her pink miniskirt flare around her hips. She's paired it with a lavender halter crop top and a stack of necklaces. She laughs as the skirt continues to sway when she stops in front of me. I swallow past the knot in my throat, mouth going dry.

"Stunning," I answer, honestly. Hopefully she can't tell how honestly.

"Will it look like I'm just in my knickers when I'm holding my bass?" she asks, swiping her hands back and forth across the pleats before grabbing the instrument.

"Which answer are you hoping for?"

She fixes me with a wicked grin. "Not sure. Still trying to decide how scandalous I'd like to be tonight."

"You look the perfect amount of scandalous."

"And you look like a sexy Steve Jobs," Darcy says, biting her lip and scrunching up her nose.

"Thanks," I deadpan, looking down at the black sleeveless turtle-neck dress I'm in. "That's exactly what I was going for."

Darcy laughs and gives me a playful shove as she sets her bass back down. I'm furious at myself that the press of her hand makes my heart leap, that such an innocuous, *friendly* gesture turns my insides out while she walks away unfazed, following the rest of the group out of the green room and toward the stage. With a deep breath and mental slap, I trail behind.

We stand in the wings as music bumps over the speakers, noises of the crowd pressing around me like a hand to the throat.

"This is it," Kevin says, turning to us. He drapes his arms over Harry and Kale to start some sort of huddle. Harry returns the gesture, looping Darcy in, but Kale stares at Kevin with a meaningful side-eye. Kevin clears his throat, removing his hand. "The big night, the start of everything."

I can see him digging deep within himself to make this as inspirational as possible. It's a sweet attempt to mark the moment, but I'm at risk of projectile vomiting on his shiny loafers.

"You all have worked so hard, not only these past few weeks, but for years. I know you haven't been together for long, but every step, every music lesson, every minute locked in your rooms playing something over and over has led to this. It's your time. You've got nothing to be afraid of. Take the moment and taste it."

There's a long pause.

"Kevin, did you just quote Taylor Swift to us?" Darcy asks.

Even in the dim backstage lights, Kevin's blush is obvious. "I . . . uh . . . It's . . ."

"That's one of my favorites by her," Skull says, soliciting a double take from Harry.

"Let's just go out there and play a good fucking show," Kale says with a roll of his eyes.

Harry nods appreciatively. "Not as poetic as Miss Swift, but gets the job done."

A stagehand gives us the signal that we'll be going on in one minute. *Sixty seconds.*

I want to melt into the floor. I can see a sliver of the crowd, the blue lights of their cell phone screens as they scroll and take pictures creating an eerie glow. My stomach twists into knots, wringing out spurts of adrenaline that burn up and down my body.

Thirty seconds.

I can already picture the comments. The tags and mentions telling me what a fake I am, how bad I am at singing, how I toy with precious boys, sucking the goodness out of them. I want to sprint far away from this murder of crows waiting to peck me to death.

Fifteen seconds.

I tremble, sound going fuzzy and distant as the world starts to spin in the wrong direction. I want . . . I need . . . I'm going to . . .

Suddenly, Darcy's there, her palm pressed between my shoulder blades. Something about feeling my breaths expanding and contracting against her stillness makes getting air down a bit easier, my head whirling at a slower speed, and it makes me want to cry in relief.

When I finally settle to a place where I don't feel like I'll suffocate in my own skin, she moves her hand, skimming across my shoulder to trace up and down my bare arm in a firm touch. Her fingers are callused, comforting and gentle in their roughness.

Time's up.

I'm swept onstage in the band's wave of energy, the rupture of cheers from the crowd building their excitement. Everyone makes a beeline for their position. I pick up my guitar in the center like it's a weapon, a shield, the only thing between me and my destruction. I stand at the frontlines, staring out at my opponent.

The noise of the crowd dips, and I know I'm supposed to say something, but I miss the natural beat, the silence stretching too long.

I'm losing them already.

The lights are blinding, making my eyes water and stomach pinch.

Say something. Anything. Don't fuck this up, don't fuck this up, don't—

"How're you all doing tonight?" Harry's words ripple through the mic, and the crowd erupts again. "We're Tea Time Tantrum, and if it's okay with you, we'd like to play you a little song." He smiles at the next surge of cheers.

Some people are natural performers, lit from within and radiating so brightly the entire room shines. That's Harry. Darcy. Dynamic people with an essence worth sharing, tugging you into their gravity. While I can't shake the feeling these people are here to watch me fail, I know without a doubt that they want to watch Harry win.

Whether I'm ready or not, the music comes in, Skull's drumming replacing my heartbeat, Harry on the keys adding something bright to Darcy's deep and consuming bass. My fingers automatically take their position along the neck and body of my guitar and I start to play. Kale's somber violin slides in, and my vocal cue is coming. Only a measure to go.

I clear my throat, then lean toward the mic. Nothing comes out.

The melody gets tangled in my throat, a rotten, wet mass of words I can't bring myself to say. The moment passes, my lips hanging open, a hollow wasteland on my tongue. The band recovers for me, circling the melody back to the start, giving me more time as I spiral deeper and deeper into the punishing bright lights. I feel my heartbeat pulse in my sweaty palms, fingers tripping over notes as the panic sets in, the weight of the crowds' stare swallowing me whole.

I slant an anxious glance to my right, hoping—needing—to see a reassuring face.

And Harry is there, closing the distance between us, keyboard abandoned, his pale blue eyes fixed on me. His hand slips along the curve of my spine as the intro comes back around, and he leans close to the mic, cheek brushing mine. He starts to sing.

> *I'm floating upside down,*
> *Can't seem to trace the sound.*

He takes a breath, pulling back for a fraction of a second and smiling at me before finishing the verse.

> *Of your whispers of forever*
> *And your footsteps to the door.*

His voice is rough, unrefined. Somehow perfect for its edges. His hand presses more firmly into my back, a grounding, warm weight as the next verse tumbles out of me.

> *Someone had to leave first,*
> *It's the ending of our story.*
> *I built a house on your lies,*
> *You built an empire off my worry.*

My hands return to my guitar, but his palm stays anchored on me, the other wrapped around the stand, holding us in a closed circuit. Our mouths are close, noses almost touching as we hover above the microphone. His crooked smile is charged, capturing all of my attention.

We trade a few more verses, the nerves leaving me with every strum of my guitar until something bright and golden sits in my chest. Harry's eyes stay locked on mine as we sing the chorus to each other.

> *Now you're back on my doorstep,*
> *My biggest regret.*
> *Sad smile and heart blue*
> *And I don't know how to tell you.*
> *I just don't give a damn,*
> *I'm gonna find myself a better man.*

I finally register the crowd again, their cheers echoing around us as the song continues to build through a few more verses. Harry's attention never falters from me as we give our everything to this moment.

The music swerves toward the end, Skull's drumbeat fading as Kale's violin haunts the stage, my fingers slipping up and down the strings as I continue to look at Harry.

We loop back to the end of the chorus, Harry winking at me at the change of lyrics.

> *And it's pretty easy to tell you*
> *I just don't give a damn,*
> *I'm gonna find myself a better man.*

There's one verse left, just vocals, but at the last moment, Harry steps back, my voice the only one echoing through the venue.

Just you watch, wait and see,
As I find myself the kind of man you'll never be.

The room swells with noise. I can't tell if they're cheers or boos or my heartbeat thumping in my ears, but it doesn't matter. We did it. Ripped that Band-Aid off. After a few gulping breaths, it becomes clear that the audience is clapping and yelling, and on a bubble of excitement, I float above the stage.

I turn to Harry, grinning at him. He drops his sweaty forehead to mine, and somehow, it feels more intimate than a kiss, sending a thunderbolt through my body. But he's got me, protecting me, shielding me from the world and its cruelty for a second.

The screaming grows even louder. Before I can overthink that, before I can dissect if that's the real reason, the only reason, these people are applauding, the band picks up the beat of the next song, Harry jogging over to his keyboard.

I know there will be pictures tomorrow; hell, there are probably pictures up right now—posts and stories and comments snatching that precious moment from Harry and me, warping it to fit whatever story they want to tell of us.

All the noise ricocheting through the space dissolves into my skin, and I let it wash away the sour pit in my stomach. Whatever this crowd's motivation for watching, it's the reason I'm up here, getting to play. I'm not going to let the shitty circumstances Connor built around the moment ruin this for me. Fingers strumming my guitar, I step up to the mic and I do what these people expect of me.

I put on a show.

Chapter 12

"Dream blunt rotation, go," Deja says a few hours later as we lounge in our nautical suite, the decor of which has become exponentially more charming and sensical as we pass a joint around.

Despite the rocky start and a few hiccups in the middle, the show was ultimately a success, all of us pressing our sweaty bodies together backstage when we finished. We convinced Kevin to make a pit stop at a dispensary on our way back to the inn, and we've been basking in the afterglow since.

"Do they have to be alive?" Skull asks, taking a drag then leaning over to shotgun it into Deja's mouth, her head in his lap. I'm either very high or it's the most romantic thing I've ever seen.

"Dead or alive. Fictional or real. No rules, just immaculate vibes," she responds.

He presses his lips together, passing the joint to Kale, who eagerly takes a hit. "Hmm. I would say, Karl Marx, Aristotle, bell hooks, probably Nietzsche . . . and Deja, of course."

We blink at him.

"Christ, not sure I'm smart enough to be smoking with you," Harry says, accepting the joint from Kale. Darcy laughs so hard she wheezes, resting her head on my shoulder, her giddy sigh tickling my neck. A thread of warmth traces down my throat, weaving around my heart then expanding with a delicate tickle to my fingertips and toes. I rest my cheek against her hair.

Deja claps with delight. "I love it. I think mine would be Pedro Pascal, Barrack Obama—Michelle too, crucial they come as a package deal—and Jennifer Coolidge, the centerpiece of the kief. Queen of the green. Oh! And Moo Deng. But in like, a totally ethical way, obviously."

Skull beams at her, placing a soft kiss to her lips.

"Who's Moo Deng?" Harry asks, voice slow and soft, eyes only half open.

Deja's jaw crashes open. "Wait, are you telling me you don't know the joy that is Moo Deng the hippo?"

"Are they a rapper?"

"She's only the greatest source of serotonin on the internet." Deja pulls out her phone and types wildly, giggling the entire time. She turns it to us, proffering a series of photos of an exceptionally chunky and adorable baby hippo.

"Wait, Moo Deng is an . . . actual hippo?" I ask, squinting at the screen as she taps on a video and I watch the hippo try to bite a stream of water, her rolls majestically jiggling.

"Well, duh," Deja says.

I stare at her for a moment, eyes traveling like treacle from her face to the screen and back, then laugh so hard Darcy's head bounces off my shoulder. Everyone else joins in until we're snorting and coughing.

Darcy resettles herself, head in my lap now, eyes closed and smile soft as she continues to giggle. My hands wind through her hair out of habit, feeling the slip of the silky strands against the sensitive skin between each finger.

This position—this closeness—is as familiar to me as breathing, and with my defenses down and brain fuzzy, it hits me like a blow to the chest how sharply I've missed it. How I'd do anything to preserve it—take back every moment that pushed her away so I can always keep her this close.

"How about yours, Harry?" Deja asks, choking on the words as she continues to laugh.

"You all aren't proving to be too bad, yeah?" he says, his smile broad and lazy as he looks around the circle. We boo his easy answer. "Jaysus, tough crowd." He tilts his head to the ceiling, smile only growing. "Let's see . . . Freddie Mercury—"

"Good one," Kale and I say in unison. If I were sober I'd be disturbed at our shared thought.

"David Bowie. Wanda Sykes."

"Also good ones," Deja says.

"Megan Thee Stallion. And . . . me mam."

"Your *mom*?" Kale says.

"Yes, my mammy," Harry says emphatically, head rolling forward to fix a look at Kale. "She's the funniest person I know. And Lord knows she deserves to kick back with a joint and Freddie Mercury after raising me and my sisters alone."

Kale holds up his hands, a serene tilt to his smile. "I respect it."

"Who's on yours, then?" Harry asks, nodding at Kale.

He ticks them off on his fingers. "Bowen Yang, Oscar Wilde, Jonathan Bailey, Frank Ocean . . . and Ina Garten. If the rotation devolves into an orgy, so be it."

"The Barefoot Contessa?" Deja shrieks, bolting up from Skull's lap. "From the Food Network? You want to be in an orgy with the Barefoot Contessa?"

"Well . . . no," Kale says slowly. I admire the fact that he genuinely seems to be considering the question. "I want to be in an orgy with the hot men I named. But I have no doubt that woman can rip cigs like no other and would provide the best snacks to replenish us after."

"That's rather brilliant," I say. "Didn't know you had it in you."

Kale tries to roll his eyes, but ends up laughing too hard, his face screwing up into a smile as we join in.

"How about you, Cub?" Harry asks, slipping the blunt to me. I take a hit, the smoke fuzzing my head further as I try to think.

"Elton John," I say, coughing on my exhale. "Fleabag. Diana Ross. Andrew Garfield because I feel like he'd get all giggly and make out with everyone—"

"So true," Deja says.

"And Mary, Queen of Scots."

"Bloody Mary?" Harry says with a guffaw. "Why the feck would you want Bloody Mary lurking around? That's the start of a horror movie."

"That's Mary Tudor, you knob."

Harry waves me away. "There's no keeping the lot of them straight."

"There absolutely is; this has been pounded into our heads since primary school. It's not like mixing up the random-ass Edwards."

"Ooh, add Edward Cullen to my rotation!" Deja squeals.

"What about you, Darce?" Harry asks.

I trace the pads of my fingers across her forehead, down the bridge of her nose to the cupid's bow of her mouth, and her lips curl up at the edges. Her eyelids slowly lift, and my breath catches in my throat as her gaze locks with mine, her entire body lazy like a cat in sunshine as she lounges on my lap.

She nods toward the blunt, and I hold it toward her. Instead of grabbing it, she lifts her head a few inches, taking the end in her mouth, her plush lips pressing against my fingers as she inhales, the tip of the joint glowing red, the heat traveling up my arm, circling my chest, flooding my cheeks, dripping low in my belly. She holds her breath for a moment, and it feels like she's stolen the air from my lungs. Without taking her eyes from mine, she tilts her head to the side, blowing out a stream of smoke. Like it takes some effort to do so, she finally pulls her gaze from me, head dropping back to my lap and neck turning as she looks at Harry.

"Mine is Cubby," she says, and I feel the stretch of her smile against my thigh.

There's a beat of silence. "Cubby, and . . . ?"

Darcy shakes her head, the movement rippling through me, a delicate swirl of pleasure that settles between my hip bones. She looks up at me again; my eyes haven't left her face. She lifts her hand, toying with the strands of my hair that fall around my shoulders as I lean toward her. "Just Cubby."

Something shifts in my chest, a vital piece notching into place, as everything around me evaporates in a pink cloud, Darcy's smile and big blue eyes the new axis my world revolves around. I let myself forget we're stoned and none of this is real. I let myself believe, only for a moment, that she means what she's saying. That she's choosing me, out loud and full-throated.

It's too grand to hold on to for long. It stings like a sunburn as the lightness of the idea drains out of me, dissolving into some alternate, beautiful universe that momentarily butted up against ours.

Despite the pain, I sit there, Darcy's head in my lap, my attention fixed on her.

At some point we all shift. I'm too lost in those eyes of hers to register it—everyone else retreating to their rooms, Darcy and I curled up like two halves of a heart on the destroyed big bed.

I watch her sleep, the way her eyelids twitch and flutter as she dreams, the rise and fall of her chest and soft flare of her nostrils as she breathes. I see the toothy seven-year-old I held hands with on the playground and the crying seventeen-year-old I held after her parents kicked her out—that time for dyeing the ends of her hair blue, the time after when they discovered she was on birth control. I see Darcy, my Darcy, and she's so beautiful, it hurts. An ache in my jaw. A crack in my chest. An itch in my hands to touch her.

It hurts so much, I have to look away, turn my back to her as broken tears slip down my cheeks. The afterimage of her glows behind my closed lids like I was staring at the sun, and a small burst of panic flares through me.

How do you ever unsee someone when they're as bright as Darcy is?

Chapter 13

After two chart-topping singles, Connor McCabe's much-anticipated debut solo album finally has a release set for the end of the month, with tour dates expected to drop soon after. There's no doubt that McCabe's unique sound and impeccable lyrics will be the soundtrack to the summer—

"Care to join us, Cubby?" Sigrún scolds via Zoom, making me jump.

"Sorry," I mumble, closing out of yet another article about how great Connor is doing.

"Streams are up," Sigrún carries on, voice fracturing from the crappy connection. "We're seeing a few local Boston news outlets pick up some media coverage of your shows too."

"And . . . ?" Every muscle in my body locks up. I now associate any form of media coverage as bad news.

"Reviews are *glowing*."

Kevin whoops, clapping his hands together before reaching over and patting Skull and Darcy, on the backs. Harry wraps an arm around my shoulders and squeezes, then does the same to Kale.

"Other tour stop venues are grabbing endorsements and ramping up excitement for your shows. You've sold out Kung Fu Necktie in Philadelphia, which is wonderful. And we've arranged some interviews for you along the way."

"What do the reviews say?" I ask, leaning toward the screen like a shark catching the scent of blood. I need to know more. Every positive detail. It's pathetic, but I'm made of crumbly clay, requiring someone to constantly pat me into place, build me up, before my legs give out. I can't stand on my own without the approval of others.

"I'll email a roundup later," she says, and I have to bite back a howl of anguish. "How's the tour bus? Everyone comfortable?"

My eyes flick across the interior of our home on wheels before landing on Darcy's similarly skeptical appraisal. *Comfortable* is not what I would call this. *Tour bus* is also an exceptionally generous term.

"Bit tight, but we'll manage," Kevin, the eternal optimist, says with a smile, grabbing the laptop from the unfinished wood table and swinging it around the converted school bus in a blurry tour for Sigrún.

Tight is putting on a pair of jeans a size too small; this is more like the seven of us living in a clown car as we zigzag across half this giant country. The kitchenette sits in a corner with some cupboards and drawers, but the area is so cramped, you can't fully open any of them. Built-in bunk beds line opposite walls of the bus, the mattresses so thin they may very well be repurposed seat cushions from the bus's school days. Compartments at the bottom of each bunk pull out for a third bed on either side. The problem is, bringing out both like we need to for all six of us to sleep (not even including Tiny Deja who is electing to spend her summer snuggled up with Skull in horrifyingly tight quarters) eliminates any floor space and creates the equivalent of one slightly-wider-than-a-twin bed for the two on the bottom to share. Darcy and I are notorious for excessively getting up to pee at night, and were graciously assigned to the ground.

And I'm not at all freaking out about having to pseudo-share a bed with Darcy for the next eight weeks. Not freaking out at all.

It's not like anything changed after last night. She woke up, red-eyed and rumpled, not mentioning a thing about her answer to Deja's silly question. Because . . . why would she? She was high and essentially said she likes smoking weed with me. I already knew that. It's not like she confessed she, I don't know, *wanted* me or anything. My tangled brain needs to stop creating something from absolutely nothing before I once again find myself looking like a vulnerable fucking idiot.

"Not to rush off the call," Kevin says, placing the laptop back on the table, which is so tiny the keyboard juts out over all sides, "but we better get going. We need to hit the road for Burlington."

"Where's that again?" Harry whispers.

"Vermont," Kale mumbles back.

"Yes, yes! Be on your way," Sigrún says, waving at the screen. "Keep up the great work. Oh, and Harry, your posts these past few days have been *wonderful*. Lots of engagement."

Harry slaps a hand to his chest, smile cheesy. "My mammy will be so proud."

"Cubby?"

I pop back into the frame.

"Try to bring more energy to yours, yeah? They're falling a little flat."

I want to *flatten* my head under one of the wheels of this ridiculous bus. "I'll work on it," I say through a tight smile.

"I'm sure," she says back, smile similarly strained. "Tonight will be a good opportunity to change things around."

"Tonight?" Our show isn't until tomorrow, and all I want to do tonight is indulge in some sensory deprivation and sleep.

"Burlington is one of those picturesque New England towns," Sigrún explains. "We thought it would be cute to get some candid photos of you and Harry exploring. There's a retro arcade in the downtown area that will be a great backdrop. You two playing pinball or something like that."

"I'm sorry, who's *we*?" I ask, indignation flaring. Am I ridiculous for thinking that I should be included in decisions that take up my time?

Sigrún gestures around vaguely. "All of us."

"I actually mentioned the arcade," Kevin pipes up, grinning. "I went once a few years ago and it was awesome."

"And who exactly will be taking these 'candid' photos?"

Sigrún sighs like I'm being exceptionally difficult. "I don't know. Skull?"

"I will be taking Deja to dinner," Skull says, leaving zero room for argument. "We have a real date planned. No time for fake."

"Kevin? Kale?"

"Absolutely not," Kale and I say at the same time at the latter suggestion.

"I have a conference call with a team on the West Coast . . ." Kevin hedges.

Sigrún looks skeptical, but she doesn't push. "Darcy? How about you? You've spent enough time with these two, I'm sure you know their best angles."

Darcy blinks, lips falling open and brow furrowing, something dark shuttering across her expression. But it's gone in a flash. "Of course I'll do it," she says, her brilliant smile fixed firmly in place. "Anything to prevent Kale and Cubby from killing each other before the show."

"Nothing guarantees that," I mumble. Harry elbows me.

"Thank you, Darcy. We all appreciate you stepping up for the team," Sigrún says, then signs off.

Kevin closes the laptop. "All right, gang, let's get this show on the road." He slides his palms together in excitement.

"Are we still waiting on the driver?" Kale asks, ducking to peer out one of the windows.

"Nope. You're looking at him."

We all slowly turn to stare at Kevin with varying degrees of horror.

"Kevin . . ."

"You're taking the piss."

"I'm not looking to die on this bus."

Kevin's face falls. "Not the reaction I was hoping for."

"Have you ever driven something like this?" Darcy asks, throwing her arms out to the sides. Her wrists slap against the bunk beds and she curses violently.

"How hard can it be?" Kevin responds, moving to the front of the bus and getting behind the enormous wheel. He cranks the engine and, with very little ceremony or warning, throws it into drive and hits the gas. And a curb.

The monstrosity is at risk of capsizing as he makes a sharp right onto the road, our bodies thrown to the side, Darcy crushing me against the partition that separates the beds from our comically small toilet. Kevin overcorrects, and we shoot to the other side, my ass colliding so hard with Darcy's solar plexus she wheezes and crumples, her chin banging on my butt cheek as she goes.

Lovely.

"Easy, Ms. Frizzle," Kale yells, clawing his way toward the driver seat. "This isn't F1."

"Bit touchier than I expected," Kevin calls back, doing what feels like a massive swerve and sending us all careening across the bus. "But never fear! I'll get the hang of it."

Kevin did not, in fact, get the hang of it. We spent close to four hours being tossed about like sailors on the choppy sea, and we're all green as we pull into Burlington, Vermont.

"Get me out of here," Kale garbles, pushing his way out the door and proceeding to puke on the closest patch of grass. The rest of us file out of the bus, Skull and Tiny Deja walking off hand in hand, completely unfazed by Kale's physical crisis, for their date. Harry takes a few laps, hands on his hips and chin tipped to the sky, his sheen of queasy sweat reflected by the sun.

Darcy and I plunk down on a wheelstop. I drop my forehead to my lap, waiting for the wooziness to pass.

"Traveling in the lap of luxury, we are," Darcy says after a few minutes.

I turn, my cheek resting on my knee. "We'll have to start calling it the vomit van if this keeps up."

"Retch ride."

"Barf bus."

"Upchuck—"

Harry walks up, clearing his throat and cutting Darcy off as he stops in front of us. "Sorry to interrupt . . . whatever nonsense this is—"

"Artists are never appreciated in their time," Darcy whispers with a solemn shake of her head.

"—but happy fake date night, fake girlfriend." He pulls his hands from behind his back, proffering a fistful of flowers at me. My lips part, eyes dancing between the blooms and Harry's bashful smile.

"W-where did you get these?" I ask, jumping up, hands flitting around the buds like a bumblebee too indecisive to land.

"Christ, Cub, don't look so impressed," he says with a rough laugh as I stare at him in wonder. "I picked them from what

I'm pretty sure was private property. Some of them are weeds, I think."

I continue to gape at him, taking the bundle of mismatched flowers. Sure enough, some dandelions are thrown in. "This is . . . so sweet of you."

"Have your standards always been this low?"

"I mean, I am reportedly dating you, so that should speak for itself."

Harry laughs at my jab, giving me a one-armed hug as he smiles down at me. There's measured vulnerability in his expression, a cautious tenderness, like he's cracking open a door to a secret room and inviting me to peek around the corner.

I can almost see what's on the other side, the comfortable closeness we've been building for years, this varnish of something new making it shine.

My stomach lurches, and I step away, turning to look at Darcy. She's scrolling on her phone, dull apathy on her features, and something about the disconnect twists with the unease in my chest, making me want to yell at her.

"I didn't forget about you, Darce," Harry says, pulling an orange lily from his back pocket.

She finally glances up, offering a brief smile as she takes the flower. "Right. Thanks. Gotta compensate the photographer accordingly."

A chilly distance wedges between all of us, my skin crawling at how wrong everything feels. They must feel it too, right? This awful tension that's so different from our norm?

"Well, come on, give me something to work with," Darcy says, popping up to standing, the sudden chipperness in her voice giving me whiplash. Her grin is broad and genuine as she pulls out her phone, rapidly taking pictures, getting super close to Harry's face with the camera and making him laugh. Harry's at ease like always, gently pushing her away and fixing his face up in a goofy look that makes Darcy giggle back.

. . . Well, maybe it *is* just me who feels the distance.

"Come along, lovebirds," Darcy says, pocketing her phone and heading down the block. "We have a date to fake."

Chapter 14

Synthy whirs and neon signs greet us we walk into the arcade, nostalgia heavy in the air. Brick lines the walls of the large space, a well-stocked bar and overstuffed couches and chairs in a corner for board games, everywhere else a maze of pinging machines surrounded by people. Harry buys us wristbands at the counter, chatting up the woman as she runs his card.

"I know we're technically here for work," he says, sidling up behind us and slinging an arm around our shoulders. "But what if, and hear me out, we take a well-deserved break and hang out for a bit."

Darcy and I share a quick glance then look up at Harry, saying in unison, "Drinks on you," before beelining for an open booth.

Darcy slides in on one side. I move to sit next to her, then hesitate, noticing she hasn't left the space for me she normally does, her palm flattened on the seat like a blockade. I stare at her hand, unease pulsing from the knot in my stomach.

Then I blink, and her hand is on the table, hips shifted over slightly, enough that there's technically room for me and I'm making up problems in my head. I glance at Darcy's face, but her expression is flat and unreadable. In a jerky movement, I sit across from her, back ramrod straight, feeling awkward and clumsy and invasive for instinctively trying to glue myself to her side.

"This is weird," Harry says, dropping the drinks on the table and sitting next to me, shoulder to shoulder.

"What is?"

He flicks a finger between me and Darcy. "You two sitting opposite. You always sit next to each other."

"We don't *always* sit next to each other," I argue, panic cresting in me like Harry's uncovered some great secret.

"Didn't know we had seating assignments," Darcy replies.

Harry rolls his eyes at our combative tones, taking a swig of his beer. "Christ, forget I said anything."

We sip our drinks in silence for a few minutes, Harry completely at ease, arm slung over the back of the booth and fingers toying absentmindedly with some of my flyaway hairs. His eyes make a lazy circuit of the arcade, a smile here and there when someone at a machine wins.

Darcy's inscrutable—bored being the closest thing I can decipher. Which is so not her. She's never bored, always filled with something to say, some joke to tell, an endless well of excitement for life. I don't recognize the apathetic person across from me, peeling the label of her beer bottle off fiber by fiber.

"What'll you do?" Harry asks, interrupting our quiet. "When we make it big, I mean. What'll be the first huge thing you do?"

Darcy perks up. "Like what would we spend money on?"

Harry shrugs. "Sure, if that's what you fancy. Whatever big, outrageous thing that we can't do now that maybe we'll be able to if we make it."

Darcy chews on her lip, eyes bouncing to me then back down to her beer bottle. "I gotta think. What's yours, Harry?"

Harry's grin is wide, color flagging his cheeks. He drags a hand through his hair, gaze turning inward like he can already picture the moment. "I'd pay off me mam's house for her first chance I get."

"The one she's currently in?" I ask.

He nods. "It's tiny, I know, and could be in a much better part of town, but she loves it. Loves her flowers in the windows and her bright yellow door and all her paintings she's hung on the walls." He's quiet for a moment, like he's taking a tour of the house he spent his adolescence in, smile soft and proud. "It was the first place I think she felt fully safe when she finally left me dad. I'd want her to know it's hers forever."

Emotion scratches at my throat and behind my eyes, and a quick look at Darcy lets me know she feels similarly overwhelmed with affection for Harry.

"Then I'd get myself an absolutely deadly flat of my own," he continues, face lighting up and voice rising. "Tons of bedrooms, incredible views, a balcony, probably a hot tub? Something real class that'll get me a ride regularly."

Darcy and I share a lasting glance this time, both of us rolling our eyes then laughing. "Going from your mum's flower boxes to you shagging your way through a giant flat was not how I expected that lovely speech to end."

"Found you sweet for a half a minute there," Darcy says.

Harry pouts. "You can't blame a fella for dreaming big." We boo him. "Fine. Let's hear your grand ideas. What'll you do, Darce?"

She takes a deep breath, letting it out slowly through her nose. "God, I don't know . . . I suppose I'd go on a trip."

"Where?" I lean toward her.

She shrugs, eyes back on the table. "The first flight to somewhere new. And another after that. A completely fresh start as often as I want for as long as I want."

I'm embarrassed that I immediately feel left behind.

"What about you, Cub?" Harry asks, curling his arm around my shoulders and giving me a playful jostle. I force a smile for him, but panic trips down my spine.

I don't know. I have no fucking clue. And that terrifies me.

How can I not know what I'd want to do if I could do anything? How do I not have a pie-in-the-sky fantasy to blurt out? The only thing I can think of is that I'd keep making music. And, given the chance, I'd follow Darcy on that trip.

Fuck, I'm pathetic.

"I'd pay Oliver to write a book," I come up with. My brother has one of the most wonderful minds ever made, filled with an under-standing of color that's nearly sacred, his explanations on its theory spiritual in intensity. "And any publishing costs or whatever to ac-tually get it made. Share his genius with the world, let everyone else catch a glimpse of the beauty he sees in everything."

"Hell, I'd chip in on a project like that," Harry says.

"Me too," Darcy adds.

I nod and smile, but I feel hollow, buried and separate from my friends who know themselves in a way I'm jealous of.

We finish our drinks in quiet contemplation, then Harry drums his hands on the table, pulling me out of my daze. "Break time's tragically over, I think."

He slides out of the booth and marches straight for *Street Fighter II*. I watch him go, wanting to curl up in the booth and never leave so I don't have to go back to pretending.

"No rest for the wicked," Darcy says sarcastically as she watches Harry melt into the game. "Poor fella must be knackered from all that hard work." I snort, picking at the calluses on my hands as I try to scrounge up the energy to follow him. "Come on," she says after a moment, standing from the booth, smile perfectly in place. It feels like a gut punch. "Go at least pretend to have fun so I can take a picture and then kick your ass at table tennis."

I search for a clever response, but only manage a nod, trailing after Harry, wanting so badly to be as fine as she is about everything.

I'm robotic at first, questioning every move I make, looking down at the scene from above my body, dissecting myself like I know I will be in the comments. I feel my brain wasting away, dissolving into this gooey obsessive blob that's leeched onto social media like a parasite.

I shake myself, trying to claw out of the pit. It would be foolish to waste this precious time I've been handed with my friends. I loosen up even more when Harry buys us another round of drinks after I demolish him at *Frogger*.

"Bet you a fiver I'll beat you at air hockey," I say to Darcy, nodding my chin toward the table in the back. Harry lets out a dramatic gasp.

"*Pft*." Darcy shoots me a challenging look, the vicious curl of her mouth into a smile making my heart beat double time. "You're on."

I lose, of course, but none of it matters, the three of us yelling and cheering over the synthetic noises, the flashing lights making us glow. Skee-Ball, *Galaga*, *Pac-Man*—we work our way through all of them, laughing and trash-talking.

Every so often, I catch Darcy taking photos, and I remember that's why we're actually here. But I'm taking photos of her too. And Harry. All of us having a good time like we used to before things got messy and so brutally public.

We eventually make it to the pinball machines, and I lose all sense of time, place, and self as competitiveness boils through me. I haven't blinked in god knows how long, my eyes wild and vision fogged with focus. I claw into the sides of the pinball machine, my middle fingers tapping the buttons like mad to keep the silver ball in place. I'm vaguely aware of Darcy breathlessly cheering me on from somewhere over my shoulder, Harry pacing behind as he watches my rise to victory.

I'm so close to beating his score. One hundred points away. If I can just keep the ball in play—

A cool stream of air shoots directly into my ear, and I jump, screaming in the process and slamming against the top of the pinball machine. I watch in horror, nose pressed to the greasy plexiglass, as my little silver ball of victory zips right between the flippers.

I blink, trying to recalibrate, every light suddenly so bright my eyes water. My gaze lands on Harry, his body curved toward me, smile villainous, mouth about ear level.

"You rat!" I scramble to my full height, then lunge toward him. "You dirty cheater!"

Harry laughs, sidestepping my attack. I spin on my heel and jump on his back, arms slung around his neck, wanting to wring it.

"All's fair in love and pinball, Cub," he wheezes, more from how hard he's laughing and less from any actual strength I'm bringing to this fight. He squirms from my grip, spinning me in front of him and grinning down at me.

"You're evil." I try to fix my indulgent smile into a scowl.

"Maybe so," Harry says with a laugh, hands cupping my cheeks as he drops his forehead to mine. "But I'm also a *winner*."

I let out an indignant growl, making him laugh even harder. "Can you believe this shit, Darcy?" I say, still mock-frowning at Harry, hoping to loop her into the swell of playfulness that feels like old times.

She's silent for a beat too long, and I slide from Harry's grip to look at her. Her eyes are fixed on the ground, mouth a thin line, something almost crestfallen scoring her features. A sudden knot of guilt lodges itself in my throat, and I don't understand why it's there.

"Darce?" I prod. She blinks, giving herself a quick shake, then looks at me, smile luminous as always. But it doesn't quite meet her eyes or crease the dimples in her cheeks.

"I think I got the shot," she says, passing her phone to me and Harry. Our bodies are still close, and her gaze bounces from our faces to Harry's arm lazily wrapped around me. I take the phone, but find it hard to look away from her face, hoping to unearth something there.

But her expression is smooth and serene. It's only my own fucked-up feelings that has me seeing anything different.

"That's a great one," Harry says, resting his chin on my shoulder as he looks at the screen. I drag my eyes from Darcy to the picture glowing at us, Harry's forehead and nose brushing mine as we both laugh. The knot in my throat tightens, and I swipe to the next.

Darcy took a bunch—in the heat of competition I forgot we actually had a purpose besides having fun—and they all capture Harry and I giggling or smiling in some capacity.

We look . . . well, we look like a couple. A happy couple. The kind you'd find on some aesthetic Pinterest board or in a rapid-fire reel that makes your teeth ache with how much you want that kind of happiness in your other half.

"These are so fucking cute," Harry says with a laugh, one large hand giving my arm a gentle squeeze. "Probably doesn't speak well of my romantic history, but fake dating you is easier than any real dating I've done."

I'm not sure why my stomach bottoms out like it does, the rest of my body clenching up like a fist.

But he's *right*. Harry is nothing but easiness. He's funny and charming and so kind it makes my head spin. Everything would be so much less painful if these romantic feelings weren't fake, if I wasn't so . . . so . . . *stuck* on some huge giant mistake made in the desperation of my loneliness.

Harry is the type of person I want to want. Why can't that be all it takes?

"Ah. That's class," Harry says, brushing my finger away and sliding back to the previous image. He zooms and my breath catches. The picture shows me on his back, wrapped around him in a blur of limbs, my grin the only part of me in focus. Harry's smile could melt even the coldest heart, so genuine and earnest as he turns to beam at me over his shoulder.

My pulse picks up as I look at the picture, the happy, carefree us.

The version of me that untied the protective mask of numbness for the evening. I wish I could be her all the time.

"If the bass doesn't work out, photography might be your calling, Darce," Harry says.

I pull my eyes from the photo and catch her look. Her smile is tight again, arms wrapped around her middle as tension radiates from her. I have the impulse to gather her to me and hold her until she relaxes. Awkwardness is so far removed from our dynamic that witnessing it feels like swallowing down the wrong pipe—sharp and unnatural and scary. She's not supposed to feel awkward around me.

I mean *us*. She's not supposed to feel awkward around *us*.

"I don't know about you two, but I'm beat," Harry says with a yawn. None of us have fully adjusted to the time zone yet. "Wanna head back to the bus?"

Darcy gives a half-hearted shrug, turning to follow Harry toward the door. After a few steps, realization hits her, and she pivots back to me, hand out for her phone.

Desperation tears through me, and I squeeze her phone tighter. I can't let it go. Can't let her go. If she walks out of here now like this, with this gloomy cloud eclipsing her usual sunshine, I worry I won't be able to fix whatever is wrong.

Darcy frowns, waving her hand and forcing a laugh. "May I?"

I start to shake my head, then realize how juvenile it is that I'm keeping her things from her. Slowly I extend it to her, ideas tripping over themselves on what I can do to salvage this night. I drop the phone in her palm and, without missing a beat, she turns toward the door.

Then it hits me. Her Achilles' heel.

I grab her wrist, spinning her back to me, her expression harried and confused. "I'm not ready to go back yet," I say, stepping toward her, into her space, our toes touching. "Let Harry go ahead."

She blinks a few times, eyes skimming down to our feet, then up the length of my body, a frown fixed on her mouth. "And we do what? Not getting the impression this town offers much in the way of nightlife."

I lean in even closer with a conspiratorial smile. Her lips part, color inking across her cheeks as one eyebrow flicks up in curiosity.

"It'll be our little secret," I whisper. Hand still on her wrist, I squeeze gently. "Let's get some ice cream."

Chapter 15

Darcy sits cross-legged on a bench under a streetlight, curled over a book in her lap. She sent me to get the ice cream while she secured our spot, and she's never without something to read.

I take a moment to look at her from a safe distance, the way her hair falls over her shoulder, thumbnail between her teeth as her eyes trail down the page.

"Whatcha reading?" I ask, pulling her out of her trance as I sit across from her on the bench.

She looks up at me with a cheeky smile, taking her ice cream cone. "Three guesses."

"More gargoyle erotica?"

Her lips quirk as she tries to keep a straight face. "No, I finished that one, but I did want to discuss incorporating a passage as a monologue between songs at our next show."

"Request approved. It will be a lovely surprise for Kale."

"Bold of you to assume he isn't the one that introduced me to the banging gargoyles."

"It wouldn't surprise me that he emotionally resonates with stone."

Darcy laughs, and the sound lights a candle in my chest. I try to cool it down with a bite of ice cream. "Next guess?"

I make a show of tapping my chin. "*Everyone Poops*?"

"Obviously. Have to stay in tune with the wonders of my ever-changing body." She waves a hand down her torso, and I have to keep my eyes glued to her forehead so they don't linger anywhere they definitely shouldn't. I grasp the wrist of her hand holding the book, turning it so I can see the cover. *Pride and Prejudice.*

I should've known.

I study Darcy's worn copy that she's had for years, its scars and cracks along the spine. Along with romance novels, she's one of those people who genuinely enjoys reading classic literature and somehow manages not to be pretentious about it, and *Pride and Prejudice* is her most read. It's how she got her name, after all.

Darcy's parents have told her from the time she was born how much they'd hoped she would be a boy. Mrs. Burton always finds a way to talk about how badly she wanted to raise a little boy to become a striking, romantic man like Fitzwilliam Darcy or some weird, emotionally incestuous shit like that. I can't think of anyone more opposite from cool, aloof book Darcy than my bubbly, insatiably charming real Darcy.

She's spent most of her life compensating for not being the perfect son her parents wanted by trying to be the perfect daughter they could tolerate. If a toddler could be classified as Type A, Darcy would have been the blueprint. When we were little she was rigid in her ways, playdates and tea parties held with a decorum fit for a queen. Schoolwork and grades came first, our music a guilty pleasure she hid from her parents as study sessions. It wasn't until year ten that she finally realized she could snap her spine in two for her parents' approval, and it still wouldn't be enough.

They've always quietly accused me of corrupting their daughter—her pink hair and septum piercing and love of music all my fault—and I secretly love the idea that maybe I did. Maybe I was lucky enough to play some small part in helping her unlock her cage.

"I haven't seen you read this in a while," I say, dragging the pad of my thumb over the worn edges of the pages. "Not since we tried to pierce our cartilages."

Darcy lets out a startled laugh, then sighs, taking a few licks from her ice cream cone. "God, that was a night, wasn't it?"

We'd just graduated from high school. Darcy had waited until the final hour to tell her parents she wasn't taking her spot at university and instead was going to try to make our music really work.

They'd kicked her out of the house on the spot, saying they didn't raise some useless lowlife. She'd shown up sobbing on my doorstep, makeup smeared down her cheeks, and I'd pulled her to me immediately, not needing to know any details, only that she was hurting.

That wasn't the first time they'd given her the boot for speaking up about what she actually wanted out of life. Every few months there was some issue or another that brought us back to this point—Darcy crying at their latest cut as I tried to stitch her back up.

After she'd filled me in, I'd swallowed down my rage at her parents and spent the rest of the night trying to make Darcy delusionally happy, which somehow resulted in us poking needles in our earlobes, neither one of us brave enough to get it all the way through, until we were both crying and laughing and holding each other with swollen, bloody ears. When we'd slipped into the quiet of our thoughts a little later, she'd pulled out her book, the sound of the turning pages like a lullaby as we both found a sense of peace—her in the book, me in her presence.

"I think about that night a lot," she says, voice rough and eyes fixed on her dessert.

"What about it?"

Darcy swallows, and I watch the movement of her throat, the flutter of her pulse at the hollow between her collarbones. I have the sharp urge to press my lips to the spot.

"I don't know . . ." She lets out a long stream of air between pursed lips. "Just how much it meant to me."

"Meant we had to get on antibiotics for our botched piercings," I joke, trying to escape the thick tension between us with a laugh. It's delicate and precious and my impulse is to break it before it breaks me, before I seek comfort in it only for it to be ripped away. She doesn't take the bait.

"I'm serious. It meant so much to me. *Means* so much to me," she whispers in a way that has me leaning toward her, hanging on every word. "I was choking on this idea of my life, losing myself more and more every day to try to be what they wanted. Something about that night . . . How you let me be sad and angry and impulsive and *myself* . . . You pulled me out. You were always pulling me out."

I see the pain crawl across her beautiful features, sitting heavy and hurtful at the corners of her eyes. I grab her hand, not wanting her to sink too far into the bad memories.

She stares at our hands, breathing hard. Then she settles her features, fixing a smile on her face. Lifting her head, she steals a bite of my strawberry ice cream and I squawk in outrage, pushing her away with my palm against her chest. She laughs, smile turning more genuine. With a puppy-dog look, she tilts her cone of maple bacon toward me as a truce, but I wave her away. I'm a habitual strawberry girl, the perfect mix of sweet and tart. Darcy has never ordered the same flavor twice, always trying something new and adventurous, and she instructed me to get her whatever seemed the weirdest on the menu. She consumes ice cream in the same way she consumes life, like there are too many amazing things to try for her to linger on a safe choice.

I take another lick, then flinch at a shock of pain that zips along my jaw from the cold.

No. Not ice cream. I can accept a lot of betrayal, but not from ice cream. I make a mental note to floss more (and by more, I mean at all) and brush better. It's gross, but I haven't been doing that simple act of hygiene as often as I should. I wake up feeling so empty and depleted every morning that it would take a Herculean effort to lift the toothbrush to my mouth, and I'm so drained by the time night rolls around I collapse face-first on my shitty mattress because neglecting myself is easier than trying.

"How are you getting on with the new song?" Darcy asks, tucking her book in her bag.

"Which one?" We have a dozen half-baked at this point that loop around my brain at all hours of the night.

Darcy takes a savoring lick of her ice cream, and my stomach swoops, heat pooling low and fast as the image of her tongue ingrains itself in my mind—the smooth glide, the perfect pink of it, the quick flick of the tip across her full bottom lip as she licks up a creamy drop. I clear my throat, looking away and shifting on the bench.

She starts to hum, and I clock the beat.

> *Ignorance is bliss, I'd lose myself to forget your kiss.*
> *Cuz these memories, they haunt me,*
> *All the things we used to be.*
> *It all slipped like water through the cracks of my hands,*
> *Now I'm dying of thirst in our no-man's-land.*

I'd accidentally typed the rough lyrics in our shared note instead of my private lyric folder, and she'd jumped on them, wanting to work out a melody as soon as she read them. She thinks the song is about Connor. I will go to my grave lying to her that she's right.

"I've put it away for now," I say with a shrug.

"May she rest in peace," Darcy whispers, making a quick sign of the cross and dipping her chin to her chest. We've buried enough unfinished songs between us that this is nothing new. "But also . . . why? It was so good. I loved the direction it was heading."

I shrug again, looking off to the side. A curl of wind blows my hair across my face, and I hope it hides the emotions burning along my cheeks. "It . . . it hurts to work on."

Darcy makes a sound deep in the back of her throat, and her free hand lands on mine, squeezing tight.

"It all hurts to work on," I whisper. I find the backbone to look at her, and understanding is etched across her face.

"I know, Cubby love."

I let out a shaky breath, shoulders slouching in relief. Darcy always gets it. Harry brings out my light and playful side, the parts people on social media like to see, but Darcy brings out *me*.

She leans forward, wrapping her arms around me. We get ice cream on each other, but neither of us care. All that matters is this warm hug on this old bench in this tiny town.

"Creating something always feels like breaking a bone just to document its healing," she says as she pulls away. "And sometimes it's hard to pick which bone to break."

I nod, then shake my head. "Yeah, but I don't think that's my issue. I know what I want to talk about. What sore spots I want to poke at and write down the results."

"Then write them," she says, catching the stray lock of my hair blowing in the wind and tucking it behind my ear.

I shake my head again. "It won't be anything but sad."

"Then let it be sad."

"Sadness isn't interesting," I say quietly, blinking up at the darkening sky. "It's not bright or dynamic or productive."

"Productive?"

"Happiness, anger, hate, love . . . Those are all kinetic, they're states of action. Sadness is stagnant and bleak and a place no one wants to linger. People don't want to hear a song about a sad girl sitting around being sad."

"I'm sorry but Phoebe Bridgers's entire discography begs to differ."

I laugh. "She's the exception, not the rule. My sadness is boring and bleh."

"Write about it anyway."

I bite my lip, voice barely above a whisper. "I'm scared."

"Of what?"

"That if I put the words down on paper they'll belong to the world. They'll stop being ours."

Darcy's eyes widen a fraction, and I realize I've said something too real. Too honest. I wave my hand at her. "I mean *mine*. Or like . . . ours because we cowrite a lot and . . . stuff."

I brace myself for the brush aside, the emotional retreat that's become our new normal since that night we pushed forward too far. I look down the darkening street so I don't have to watch the blinds close over her eyes.

Darcy surprises me by grabbing my hand again. Holding tight. She tilts her head into my line of sight. "Those words, those feelings, they'll always belong to you, Cubby."

My lips part, a whimper sitting at the back of my mouth, but I swallow it down. She smiles at me, broad and soft and genuine, causing my heart to trip over itself.

And it feels so good to sit here with Darcy, that indescribable understanding knitting us together. The reminder that no matter how alone I feel, she's still there. For now, at least.

My phone rings, breaking up the moment and making us jump. Then it beeps again and doesn't stop, buzzing in my back pocket and making the whole bench shake. I retrieve it like a dog following its owner's command.

I posted pictures of Harry and me while I was waiting in line for the ice cream but I've had horrible reception here with my cheap-ass SIM card, and notifications flood in all at once, every good feeling in me turning sharp and serrated as my mind flips to high alert.

I click my way to Instagram, scrolling through the overload of new comments and likes. Most of them actually seem . . . nice. Well, not most. But at least enough that I don't contemplate shutting off my comments section and/or walking into the sea.

"Whoa . . . people are really liking my latest post," I say, the pleasure center in my brain lighting up as I continue to scroll. I have to consciously stop my thumb from liking a comment near the top that says *omg connor who? Get it girl!!* and another that went so far as to tag Connor giving condolences for losing this round.

Good.

Fucking *good.* I hope he checks every mention. I hope it makes him replay all our happy memories, searching for Harry's presence in the mix, reliving the moments until he's twisted himself sick with jealousy and doubt over nothing. I hope it eats him alive. It's petty and vile and feels so damn good to imagine him feeling even a tenth of the hurt he's caused me these past few months. Hell, these past five years.

"I bet this will get us more streams too," I say, scrolling further. "Looks like a lot of people are sharing the post and adding our latest song to it."

Darcy's silent, and I eventually tear my eyes away from the screen to grin at her, excited to celebrate this new triumph. I'm shocked to find the smile drained from her face, a blank stare blunting her features.

"Ready to go?" she says, already standing and walking to the waste bin near us to throw away the hefty remainder of her ice cream.

"Uh, I guess. You didn't want to finish that?"

Darcy huffs in response, turning on her heel and heading down the street. I almost fall off the bench in my rush to follow after her.

"You okay?" I ask, jogging to keep up.

"Fine." Her tone is as bland as the word.

I have the impulse to push the matter, but it's not nearly as strong as the compulsive pull to get back to my phone. The notifications have a barbed lasso around my brain, my neurons shriveling up like dehydrated fruit, howling in desperation for another dopamine hit. I need to know what people are saying like I need my next inhale.

I slip back into my notifications, falling out of step with her as I respond to some comments with as much charm as my bitter self can muster. In a blink, we're back at the van, Darcy swinging the door open and letting it slam in my face.

Lovely.

"Are you going to tell me what's bothering you or should I learn to communicate in passive-aggressive scowls and grunts from here on out?" I ask after I let myself in. Harry and Kale's attention falls on me from their bunks, but I ignore them.

"Right, because you're the only one allowed to have an off night and be an asshole about it, right, Cubby?" Darcy says, a surge of venom in her voice as she rounds on me, knocking me back a step.

"Wow. Tell me how you really feel about me, then." I cross my arms over my chest. "Come on. Let's have it. Clearly you have some thoughts on the matter."

"That's exactly my point!" she yells, throwing up her hands. They smack against the bunks, and she curses as she cradles them to her stomach. "Not everything is about *you*. Sometimes people are just in a bad mood and it has nothing to do with you or your hurt feelings or your perpetual melodrama."

"She's got a point," Kale unhelpfully adds.

"Shut up, Kale," Darcy and I say in unison. It would be a beautiful moment if we weren't staring daggers at each other.

But it's a stand-off. A stalemate.

I blink first.

"Darcy," I whine, pushing harder at the gaping wound. "What's *wrong*?"

She glares at me for a moment longer before shaking her head, blinking up to the ceiling. "*Nothing*," she grits out. "But for the love of God just leave me alone."

She turns on her heel, marching the few steps to the bathroom and slamming the flimsy door.

The bus is silent, anxiety and anger and hurt churning through every inch of me with a terrifying roar. Darcy's never done this before, never iced me out so succinctly. Even when we fight, it's big and dramatic, but it's all laid out on the table, addressed then and there until we're both usually crying and apologizing.

Whatever. Fuck her. If she wants our friendship this way, empty and sterile and existing on the surface, she can have it. I don't care about Darcy. I don't care about any of it. Caring only leads to hurt. Indifference is better than looking like a fool.

I wonder if I'm too comfortable lying to myself, a tiny voice whispers to me. I decide not to care about that either.

Harry catches my wrist from his spot on his bunk. "Give her some space, Cub," he whispers, baby-blue eyes meeting mine as his thumb traces a circle across the back of my hand.

I shoot another panicked look toward the closed door, then shake myself, nodding at him instead.

"We're all tired and tense and trying to figure out what the hell we're doing," he murmurs, reaching out with both hands and massaging mine between his. "Give her a breather. Trust her when she says it's nothing. I'm sure everything will be smoothed over in the morning."

His soft, kind voice takes a chisel to my wall of anger, all of the bricks crumbling to dust, my bones wanting to fall with it as all the fight rushes out of me. I don't want smoothed over. I want Darcy's rough edges and raised voice and her *talking* to me.

But I can't make her do that. If space is what she wants, it's what I'll give her.

Harry tugs on my wrist, and I move toward him. He scooches over, offering me a sliver of his tiny mattress.

With a sigh and one last glance at the door, I curl myself in next to him. He readjusts so his neck is propped against the few slats that constitute a headboard, tucking me against his chest, my head on his shoulder.

"Am I safe to assume tonight's dramatics are over or should I keep my guard up for act two?" Kale drawls from above. With a shared look, Harry and I kick at the bottom of his mattress, snickering at his squeal of surprise.

Harry rests his laptop on his stomach and hits play on some dumb show he was watching before Darcy and I exploded in. He laughs at a slapstick joke, and the soft rumble of it ripples from his chest to caress my cheek, soothing me, unlocking my tense shoulders. The sound is so nice and safe and warm, it makes me laugh too.

But part of me is still focused on Darcy, ears perked for the slightest sound. Any opening for me to get back to her, push her to talk to me.

The show plays on, and I become more focused on the thump of Harry's heart against my cheek, its sure and steady cadence. Its interrupted pattern when he laughs again. It becomes a lullaby.

And that's how I fall asleep, to Harry's laugh and his heartbeat and my own stupid organ being split in two.

Chapter 16

"When did you know you wanted to be a musician?" Terry, a journalist for a Cleveland-based online magazine, asks Darcy and me in a café across the street from the Rock & Roll Hall of Fame.

Darcy and I share a glance, then look away. We haven't spoken since our fight two nights ago, only finding out as we rolled into Ohio this morning that we were scheduled to do an interview together.

"Music is my one true love," Darcy answers, voice bubbly and body language at ease, the wall of ice between us only for me to see. "It was the first way I learned how to escape."

"Escape what?" Terry asks, adjusting his wire-rimmed glasses and looking bored. He barely stifles a yawn as he sips his coffee.

"The real world, I suppose," Darcy says with a smile. "I wasn't allowed to listen to rock 'n' roll or pop music or really any type of music growing up. So the first time I heard it—heard what was being said in the lyrics, of course, but also heard what wasn't articulated, the emotion in the music—I was obsessed. Addicted, really. I consumed every type I could get my hands on, devouring it."

I remember this moment. Think about it all the time. We were probably eight or nine, around the age Darcy learned it was better to ask for forgiveness than permission from her parents when it came to walking over to my house. It was right around the holidays, and my family was decorating, my mums sipping wine and tending a fire while Oliver, Darcy, and I trimmed the Christmas tree. Mum put her old Joni Mitchell vinyl on the record player, skipping to "River" and turning up the volume. Darcy froze as Joni started singing, eyes wide and dazed, lips parted. She clutched a bundle of tinsel in her hands, the thin strips of silver shaking along with her.

By the time the song ended, Darcy had tears streaming down her cheeks, and she turned slowly to my mum, softly begging her to play it again. And again. By the fourth time, Darcy's smile was huge and she was singing along.

Mum's record collection became Darcy's first stop in our house from that moment forward.

"What about you, Cubby?" Terry asks, unmoved by Darcy's answer.

I hesitate, sneaking a look at Darcy from the corner of my eye. She focuses on her cappuccino. "I can't think of one specific moment," I lie. "There was nothing else I ever could be."

The truth is, while I've loved music since I was a baby—my mum takes every opportunity to talk about how playing a Tracy Chapman album was the only way to get me to stop crying—it was watching Darcy discover music, watching her fall apart and rebuild into something even brighter than before over the course of a single song, that changed me as a person. I knew, then and there, I wanted to do something like that. I wanted to create something that resonated with people that profoundly.

"Right," Terry says, adjusting the recorder in the center of the table. "Where does your inspiration come from?"

"Cubby leads the charge on most of our writing, so I'll let her take this one," Darcy says.

My mind flashes to the song I've been secretly working on, the early, raw scraps of music that feel so naked and humiliating—sounds plucked straight from my brain without the shield of collaboration, the protection of someone else having a stake in nurturing and protecting them.

"Every song is different," I say, choosing my words carefully so the answer can't be whittled down to either *Connor* or *Harry* for clickbait. "Some flow out of me nearly full-formed, lyrics tracing a story. Others are phrases punching at bars and measures for a melody that suits them. Most often, they're roughened beats plucking different instruments in my head until they find a chord progression that lets them breathe. Expand."

Terry blinks at me, his mouth breathing audible. I prattle on to fill the silence.

"People like Darcy and Skull have a much better vision for the finished products of songs and compositions, spending hours perfecting a track's final production. But toying and tweaking is part of my process, especially when something is lodged in my brain and refuses to leave."

The song currently up there is an annoyance, like food stuck in my teeth, and I want it out of me so I can focus on something—anything—else. But the stupid words have embedded themselves and are demanding my attention.

> *And it's a burning blush,*
> *I always feel too much.*
> *You're the fire, you're the storm,*
> *But if you let me, I'll be the one to keep you warm.*

It's about Darcy, obviously. Everything I work on or think about nowadays is.

"It's a pretty open secret that you use past relationships for most song content," Terry comments.

But say the word, and I'll chain up my demons.
We'll dive into the deep end,
I don't think I wanna be just friends.

"I wouldn't say that's my main source of inspiration."

One of Terry's untrimmed eyebrows quirk up. "I see. And what about you, Darcy?"

"Me?"

"While we know quite a bit about Cubby's romantic history, what about yours? Anyone special you're writing songs about?"

"No," she answers quickly.

"No one at all?"

"I mean, if Mick Jagger ever wants to take another shot at love, I'll give him my number."

I snort.

Terry gives us a tight smile. "Okay, moving on, then . . . So none of the members of"—he skims a page of his Moleskine notebook and yawns again—"Tea Time Tantrum—cute name—have any formal or classical musical training?"

"I . . . uh . . . I mean we've all had *lessons* of some kind," I say, eyebrows furrowing. I'm glad that Darcy's perplexed look mirrors mine. "Darcy and I have been playing together for over ten years. Our violinist, Kale, started when he was three or something absurd like that."

"Harry's mum taught him the basics when he was little, but he's one of those that's always been able to play any song by ear," Darcy adds.

Terry gives us a slow, patronizing smile. "Sure. Of course. Do you feel like social media and the age of rapid content consumption allows musicians without more significant training backgrounds to get further than they would otherwise?"

"Uh . . . I . . ." Darcy gives me a bewildered look.

"I . . . I don't know how to answer that," I finally manage.

"No problem," Terry says, lifting up his palms and browsing his notes. "I knew that one would be a thinker. Let's see . . . Ah, here's one. Your sound has been characterized as Bob Dylan mixed with Lana Del Rey but with heavy emphasis on her feminine angst. Someone else said it's like going back and reading their high school diary. Do those descriptors bother you?"

"Why would it bother us?" Darcy asks slowly, like she's tiptoeing around a trap.

Terry shrugs. "I mean, no one wants to be described or associated with the melodrama of teenage girls, right?"

"What's wrong with teenage girls?" Terry stares at me like I have three heads. "No, seriously. Explain it to me."

"A notoriously capricious and emotional demographic with grand theatrics that puts everyone in their vicinity through the wringer? You don't see anything a little overwhelming about that?"

"No. I don't."

That patronizing smile is back. "Really? You don't? Listen, I don't mean any offense or anything personal by the question. I'm simply reiterating other reviews of your work. But I'm also a father to two teenage girls, so you've got to understand how a description like that could be off-putting to a lot of people."

"Fucking Christ, tell me you don't say shit like that to your daughters," I blurt out.

"Excuse me?"

"I think what Cubby's trying to say is—"

"That maybe you're too easily overwhelmed," I cut Darcy off, staring at Terry and his ratty ponytail. He stares back.

"*I'm* too easily overwhelmed? One of your lyrics is '*I'm twenty-three and my life feels over / I look in the mirror and I don't know her,*' but I'm the one here that seems too easily overwhelmed?"

I shrug. "I don't know you personally so I can't speak to it, but what I do know is I am personally very *underwhelmed* by the lack of substance in your questions."

Terry's laugh is cold, the perfect adornment to his eye roll. "Yeah? Should I turn that statement back around on you now? Demand you explain it to me? Is that the choreography here?"

"Sure, I'll explain it to you, you dense prig," I say, my voice rising. Darcy places a hand on my arm, but I shrug her off. "Do you actually think any of what you've asked us is original? Our dating history and inspiration? Do *you* have any formal training in your field? Because that's about as stale as it comes."

A thrill zips through me as he indignantly slaps his notebook shut, color rising on his cheeks. He opens his mouth, but I steamroll over him.

"People have no problem poking and prodding at girls, barking orders of what we can and can't be and then sit there and judge us when we break ourselves into jagged, brittle little pieces trying to do what we're told; be diluted enough for the world to stomach. But it never works. We'll always be too angsty. Too emotional. Too entitled. Too meek. Bossy. Controlling. Conniving. So yeah, I'm underwhelmed by your questions that do the same thing that's been done to death. Does that clear it up for you?"

"We're done here," Terry says, gathering up his recorder and messenger bag.

"No shit, Terry," I sneer, clapping at his astuteness. "Have a nice day."

He storms out of the café, and my hands shake as I try to hold on to my iced latte, taking a few sips. All the fire rushes out of me, and I want to curl into a ball under the table and sob.

Suddenly, Darcy's hand is on my back, and I realize that a few tears have slipped out. I avert my face, but she reaches out, turning me to look at her. Her big blue eyes search mine, and, after a moment, she smiles. "You're my fucking hero."

"You're only saying that because you look very, very likable compared to me."

"I've always been more likable compared to you," she says dryly. "I'm a people-pleaser before a person."

I give her a sad smile.

"I'm sorry we've been fighting," she says suddenly, grabbing my hand and squeezing tight. "I'm sorry for the . . . weirdness." Her voice cracks on the last word.

My heart stutters. Does she . . . is she talking about what I think she's talking about? Is this it? The moment that I want so badly that my teeth ache, the conversation I pretend I don't play out over and over again in my muddled head? Are we finally going to talk our way back to how we were before?

"I'm so sorry," she repeats, a few tears slipping down her cheeks. I check the urge to brush them away. We stare at each other, the weight of so many unsaid things pressing down on us.

A dangerous feeling of hope trickles through my veins. I lean forward a millimeter, my gaze accidently skimming to her mouth and lingering for a moment too long before bouncing back to her eyes. Darcy sucks in a tight inhale, biting on the lush pad of her lower lip. Then she pulls back, breaking the spell.

"Weirdness from Vermont," she says, clearing her throat. "I'm sorry I was kind of a bitch." She lets out a watery laugh, looking at me with the expectations I'll echo it.

My heart sinks like a stone in water. "That's okay." I twist my face into something I hope looks like a smile and not devastation. "I'm kind of a bitch all the time, so we're even, I suppose."

Darcy laughs again, slipping her fingers from mine and pressing the heels of her hands into her eyes. "That might be the most self-aware thing you've ever said."

I scrunch up my nose. "I promise not to make a habit of it."

"Are we good?" she asks, not meeting my eyes.

"We're good," I breathe, wanting to scream the opposite. I would do anything in the world for Darcy except tell her how torn up I am over her. Over something we both silently agreed is *nothing*.

Nothing. Nothing. Nothing.

Nothing worth destroying our already teetering friendship over by rehashing.

A notification pings through on my phone, and I jump on it like the little lab rat I am. Yes, I have a Google alert set up for my name. Yes, I am digging my own grave one shovelful at a time. But it's easier to focus on strangers' opinions than all the nonsense in my own head.

I snort as I read Terry's latest post, showing it to Darcy.

IT IS VERY OBVIOUS CUBBY CLARK ISN'T PR TRAINED

She reads it, then rolls her eyes. "And thank fuck for that," she says, exiting out of the screen. "We wouldn't have any fun at all if you were."

Chapter 17

"Cubbyyyyyyyyyy!"

A sonic boom of a voice calls my name the second I get out of our ride back to the tour bus, and my smile is automatic.

Tilly.

I scan across the parking lot and find Oliver being led (dragged) by his girlfriend, Tilly, as she charges toward me. I meet them halfway, wrapping her in a giant hug before doing the same to Ollie.

I met Tilly a few summers ago in Copenhagen. She and Oliver were interns for the same company, and our paths crossed when we were doing our small shoestring Scandinavian tour. They've been dating ever since, and I'm not sure I've ever rooted for two people so hard. Things must be going well for them, since Tilly brought Ollie home to Cleveland to meet her family this summer.

"We're whisking you away," Tilly says, acting like a herding dog and pushing me toward her dinged-up car.

"I have a show tonight," I say, looking over my shoulder at everyone huddled by the bus. Kale glares at me, and I cheerily raise my middle finger. Harry offers a tiny wave while Skull and Deja kiss behind him. Darcy must have gone inside, and my stomach twists.

"Yes, yes, we're well aware that you're a giant rock star and need to sing to your adoring fans tonight," Tilly prattles on, placing her palm on the top of my head while she oh-so-lovingly shoves me in the back seat. "But you can spare us lunch, right?"

"There's no use trying to fight her on anything," Oliver says with a radiant smile.

Tilly keeps up a rapid stream of conversation the entire drive to the restaurant, her perpetual excitement for life so contagious, it isn't long before I'm smiling and laughing with the windows down and wind in my hair. It's nice to feel something other than gloom. But I keep catching myself glancing at the empty seat next to me, wishing Darcy was here.

"So, Cubby," Tilly says, when we're settled in the corner of a deli with our food, propping her elbows on the table and resting her chin in the cradle of her fingers.

"Yes, Tilly." I mirror her pose and she smiles.

"You seem to be having an eventful summer in the love department. And I demand details. *All* the details."

"I demand to be spared the details," Ollie says, eyes flashing with horror.

"I ought to make you suffer for how I had to pull your head out of your ass in regards to our lovely Tilly here."

Tilly cackles, throwing her arms around Oliver and giving him a big kiss on the cheek, his face erupting in color. I love them both dearly, but they were some of the world's worst communicators with each other and their feelings, and I wouldn't be a (twenty-seven minutes) older sister if I hadn't set him straight.

Oliver lets out the world's most dramatic sigh, sinking in his seat and waving me on. "Right. Yeah. You were helpful that one time, so carry on, I guess."

"You've come such a long way on social niceties, Ollie," I tease, kicking him under the table.

"I'm sorry, but if you don't fill me in on exactly what is happening between you and Harry in the next ten seconds I will actually scream," Tilly says, subtly redirecting the conversation.

"It's . . . it's not a thing." I shrug, eyes fixed on my plate as I focus on putting a single pea on each tine of my fork.

"Your pictures certainly make it look like a thing," Oliver says.

"And all the headlines and social media speculation doesn't really convince me you're telling the truth," Tilly adds.

"Well, that's the thing, isn't it? None of that is real," I snap. "Social media, these stupid headlines, none of it's real life. It's made-up versions of ourselves that we polish to round out any sharp angles or harshness and post in the hopes that people perceive us that way. It's empty, it's—"

"You sound like Mum raging against kids these days," Oliver says.

"But it's true!" I throw my hands up, collapsing back in my seat. "Harry and I never meant for our love lives to become a public conversation topic, but now that it is, we have to feed into it or we lose relevance. Become just another D-list band fighting to get anyone to listen. We've stopped being people and have become this . . . *spectacle*."

Tilly and Oliver offer me sympathetic looks, but I can tell they don't get it. I don't blame them. It's the price of putting your art out there, when it's all said and done. You aren't a human; you're the product you make, being rabidly devoured. It's hard to convey how lonely it is to be so known by name and reputation but not actually known at all.

What I don't tell them is how addicted to it I've become. The way I refresh my phone constantly like a rat in a psychological experiment hoping for a reward of someone saying something nice about me. How reading something cruel has become its own sort of rancid drug. A morbid hit. The all-consuming burn of absorbing those things, harming myself over and over again by seeking them out, validating and feeding that cruel voice of insecurities always clawing through me. I feel my brain rotting from the obsession of it all.

"What does Darcy think of all this?" Tilly asks, straw between her teeth. She dips her head and takes a giant gulp of her milkshake so the drink gargles. I catch Oliver looking at her like she's the most precious piece of art he's ever been lucky enough to witness. I'd rather they just punch me in the face.

"Why would you bring up Darcy?" I ask, jumping to defensive because that's easier to hide behind than admitting I have no idea what she damn well thinks of any of this. We don't talk that deeply anymore.

"Because she's your best friend?" Tilly says, face twisting in confusion. "Because you two have been inseparable since I've met you and have a tendency to finish each other's sentences? I mean, honestly, I'm surprised we got you solo for lunch and she didn't tag along."

I bristle. "Sorry I'm not good enough company on my own."

Tilly and Ollie blink rapidly, expressions so startled it's like I yelled at Bambi.

"Do we make you feel that way, Cubby?" Oliver asks, tilting his head.

"No," I admit, my nose tingly and a pressure building behind my eyes. I stare down at my plate.

"Then why would you say that?" he asks. He isn't being a dick; he genuinely wants to know. Oliver so badly wants to understand other people; it's one of the things that make him so beautiful.

"The questions might be a little overwhelming," Tilly murmurs to him before rounding the table and sitting next to me. She takes one of my hands in hers, but when she feels me trembling, she throws both arms around me, holding me close. I start to cry against her shoulder, screwing my eyes up tight in the hopes I can stop the flow of tears.

"I'm sorry," Oliver says, voice cracking with panic. He's so good-natured, it's almost comical, and I let out a choked laugh, looking at him.

"You didn't do anything wrong," I tell him, pulling away from

Tilly to wipe my eyes with the backs of my hands. "I'm the one being an asshole. I'm . . . I'm a mess," I say, more tears leaking out.

"A mess how?" Tilly prods, rubbing my back.

I grab a napkin, blotting at my eyes, then my nose. "In the . . . I don't know, messy way? Fucked-beyond-repair kind of way? I don't know what to do."

"Talking to us might be a good place to start," Tilly offers, one hand still fixed on my back, warm energy radiating from her palm into me. "Oliver is an *excellent* listener. Admittedly, listening isn't my strong suit, but I'm focused in and ready to beat up whoever has hurt your feelings."

I look between them, their earnest expressions cracking through any defenses I've built up. With a shuddering breath, I start at the beginning. I talk about my breakup with Connor nearly a year ago, the way I felt relief more than hurt to finally put it to rest, the way he revived all our pain with the greatest cruelty he could muster these past few months. I tell them about the stolen music and the night at the bar and what Darcy and I did after (an abridged version for my brother's sake). I tell them about that crushing morning and how that stupid picture with Harry upended all our lives and how stunningly vile strangers can be behind a screen.

I talk about how Darcy and I don't talk like we used to. How badly I want her to talk to me. How she's the only person in the world I actually want to talk to. I chronicle every up and down until my head hangs low and my shoulders slump, spent from rehashing it all.

True to Tilly's word, they both listen, Tilly offering noises of outrage or devastation when appropriate, Ollie holding my hand across the table through it all.

"Go on, then," I say with a disenchanted laugh, nose running and eyes swollen. "Tell me what to do. Tell me how to fix it."

"Cubby," Oliver says, voice rough. He looks at me like his heart is breaking. "You need to put a stop to this social media stuff. This isn't healthy. This isn't fair to you."

"Oliver's right," Tilly says. "You shouldn't be forced to carry that much hate."

"It's for the band," I whisper. "It's gotten us on the map. Gotten us this tour. It's for the good of the group."

"I'd rather see you never write a song again than have to deal with this," Oliver says, his voice rising in earnest. "Please, Cubby. Talk to Harry. Talk to your team. They'll understand."

I hear what he's saying, but I don't listen. I can't. I'm so out of control of everything—where I go, where I sleep, what I wear, what people think about me—that choosing to spiral, to lose myself, is the only form of control I know.

It's like my life is carrying on without me, like I'm missing every moment. Time ticks on and I'm stuck in the past as the future leaves me behind, hollow-eyed and numb as I scroll on social media, digging my nails into the festering wound.

Searching out how deeply rotten and necrotic public opinion of me is makes the damage *mine* to inflict. If I choose to hurt myself, no one else can hurt me as badly. I'll destroy myself before I give someone else the power to do it first.

"What do I do about Darcy?" I ask, not wanting to waste their time on things I know I won't change. "I miss my best friend. I need her."

"Have you talked to her?" Oliver counters. "If memory serves, that was your big advice to me when I was mucking things up with Tilly."

"She doesn't want to talk about it. She's made that much clear."

"But does she know how much everything is bothering you? I think if she knew how badly you were hurting she'd talk to you."

I shake my head. Talking to her about everything would require me to be dangerously vulnerable with her. It would hurt too much to have her reject me like everyone else.

"Are you sure you want Darcy as your friend?" Tilly asks.

I frown at her. "Of course I do. She's amazing. She's my favorite person in the world." Ollie slants me a glance and I roll my eyes. "Present company excluded."

Tilly raises her hands in surrender. "I didn't mean it like she isn't a great person to be friends with. I mean can you handle her being *just* your friend when you want more?"

Tilly's question stuns me, every word rattling my bones as my stomach bottoms out. "Who said I want more?" I ask, mouth dry and pulse pounding.

She tilts her head, fixing me with a knowing look. "Cubby . . . come on."

"I thought you like guys," Oliver pipes up, as if his girlfriend hasn't sent me into an utter tailspin and has me asking myself that exact question at an alarmingly loud volume.

Tilly scowls at him. "Your compulsory heteronormativity is showing, Oliver."

He rolls his eyes. "That's not what I mean, and you know it. It wasn't until I was ten that I realized not everyone has two mums. But, Cubby, you've always dated guys. It's not like you've dated many . . . I mean, Connor's been it, yeah? But I feel like any time you've talked about someone you've liked, it's been a boy."

He pauses for a moment, looking at me. I can tell by his frown that my face must mirror the circus of panic tumbling through my gut.

"I guess you didn't talk much about liking anyone, now that I think about it," he continues. "Connor popped up in conversations awhile back, but before that it's always been . . . Darcy. Your friendship with Darcy."

I bite my lip, tearing my napkin to confetti with shaking hands, trying to get my breathing under control. Oliver has a point. My mums are queer, so it's not like it would ever be an issue if I were too, but I've always thought of myself as straight. Although, I can't say I ever really thought about it much at all. It's rare for me to like someone to begin with. Connor is the first person I remember admitting to myself—and subsequently, Darcy—that I might fancy, but even that took many years of getting comfortable around him for anything more to develop.

I never gave my sexuality much brain space because I just . . . didn't think it was different than what most people were experiencing? I had my best friend and my band and this bone-deep urge to make music, to pour every bit of myself into those things. I mean, I've found people attractive. There are a few fit guys from our hometown that I'd nod in agreement about when Darcy talked about her crushes, and I've always noticed girls as almost ethereal creatures. Soft skin, shiny hair, rounded curves, good smells . . . What isn't to like?

But everyone feels that way. Right? Everyone wants to, like, touch a girl's skin and run their hands over her hips and braid her hair just to feel it between their fingers and cuddle and hug and giggle and touch and . . .

Holy fuck.

Do I like girls?

Am I . . . *gay*? Have I just, like, never known this very pivotal-seeming potential fact about myself? A tiny, hysterical voice in the back of my head shrieks with glee that hooking up with a girl was probably a good indication of such, but I smother that voice immediately, nerves swirling into a fury as the entirety of who I've always thought I was rearranges itself. It dawns on me—suddenly and confusingly and excruciatingly obviously—that these feelings for Darcy are exactly like a primary school crush . . . Although it feels more like I'm *being* crushed.

"Cubby?" Oliver says, giving my hand a squeeze. "Are you—"

"I don't know what I am," I blurt out, gaze bouncing between him and Tilly. "Holy fuck, I don't know what I am."

"I was going to ask if you're okay, but the answer to that seems fairly obvious," Oliver says, eyes widening with worry to match mine.

My breathing becomes choppy and short, the world tipping as I try to understand what's happening, a flood of emotions and ideas and memories previously explained away ripping through me like the opening of Pandora's box.

Oh my god. I think I like girls.

I . . . I know I like guys. At least, I think I like guys? Do I like guys? Do I like anyone?

"Cubby." Tilly cups my cheeks, tilting my face to hold her gaze. I've never seen her so still and steady. "You don't know what you are," she says in an even tone. Something about her unwavering focus unlocks my tense muscles a few degrees.

"I don't know what I am," I echo, not daring to blink.

"You don't know what you are," she repeats. "And that's okay."

"A wreck is probably the best word for it," I say with a harsh, self-deprecating laugh, a few more tears rolling down my face. She doesn't indulge me, and I feel even more pathetic. Instead, she wipes away the wet streaks with her thumbs, then gives my head a tiny rattle.

"A wreck is an okay thing to be too," she says, finally releasing me. "You're allowed to find peace in the perplexity."

"What's it like, dating Brené Brown?" I ask, turning to Oliver, trying to joke my way out of these ginormous feelings.

He gives me a blank stare. "I have no clue who that is."

Tilly knocks my shoulder with hers. "You're ridiculous." There's a weighted silence, then she clears her throat. "Are you okay?"

I shake my head, then shrug, folding my panic into a box and locking it tight.

"I need to get back for sound check," I say, glancing at my phone. There's a string of social media notifications, and I have the sick compulsion to dive in, wade through them so maybe I can feel something sharp and staggering that jolts me out of this painful daze of confusion.

"Okay," Tilly says, voice quieter than I've ever heard her. I'm so pitiful I even dim sunshine incarnate.

She drives me back to the venue, attempting to cheer me up

with some small talk at first, then letting the quiet linger. Oliver sits in the back with me, staring at me with that knowing, twin look of his. I choose to ignore it, pinching his ear to get him to stop. He wraps me up in a hug in response.

"Talk to the band, Cubby," he says when we arrive. "Save yourself from this. You deserve so much better."

I nod, slipping on a flippant smile. "I'll be fine, Ollie." I reach around the driver's seat and give Tilly a hug goodbye, telling them both how much I love them, then I walk to the venue's entrance, Oliver's words echoing with every step.

You deserve so much better.

At the front lines for us
I was ready for battle
I was ready for war
Put my dreams in a bottle
You left it on the shore
I was fighting for our life
You were keeping score

Chapter 18

Cleveland proves to be an outrageously fun show. We're the second of three acts at the House of Blues, but the crowd responds to us like we're the biggest stars in the world.

We close out the set with our newest song, which we released online about a week ago, and it quickly started trending. We weren't expecting it; the sound is a bit harsher than the folksy vibe we usually put out, but it's become a personal favorite and I sing it like my life depends on it, the crowd screaming with me.

> *You know I know you know you're never going to change.*
> *I find it funny that you find it strange*
> *That I'm a mess, when I'm the mess that you made me.*
> *Waiting on your love to come save me.*

The energy is intoxicating, a pulsing reminder of why I do this. My brain isn't wrestling with questions I'm scared to even ask myself, my focus centered on the pull of my vocal cords and bang of the band and the echoed words from the audience. It's like we're sharing a soul as we scream out words that do a small part to soothe

the hurt. We're all humans thinking of someone different, connected by that evergreen ache.

Darcy is absolutely killing it, performing like the night's energy has sunk itself into her bones and is radiating through her. I watch her step forward as she rips through a chord progression. She's both delicate and raw when she plays, her fingers dancing across the neck of her bass as she translates the confusion of emotions into the precision of musical notes.

Harry's feeling it too, singing with me from behind his keyboard. The recording circulating the internet has both our vocals on there, and he's delivering tonight. At a break in the lyrics, he steps around his instrument and strides toward me, a grin on his face. He's magnetic, a performer through and through. When he gets to me, he steps close, feet between mine, our thighs brushing. We smirk at each other as we prepare for the final verse, leaning in so our noses touch.

You call me selfish,
But your kiss makes me reckless.
I'd risk it all to crash and burn at the edge of your lips.

The music plays out, and we repeat the lyrics a few times, letting our voices trail off as the song comes to a close, the crowd screaming. It's hard to drag my gaze from his face—skin flushed and hair tangled, smile creasing his eyes and the bridge of his nose. He drops his sweaty forehead to mine, and I reach up, cupping his cheek. The way he looks at me makes my heart squeeze, like I'm the most important person in his world.

Finally, he acknowledges the crowd, turning his head and waving, and I follow suit. We take a minute to soak it all in, the noise and the amazing set and the absurdity that our dysfunctional group has somehow gotten to a moment like this, everything so perfectly synchronized. The audience slowly calms down, and Harry fixes his grin back on me.

As I do most nights, I go to hug him. But Harry does something that shifts my world off its axis. He curves one hand around my waist, the other at my throat, thumb tilting my chin so I'm looking up at him. There's nothing but heat and mischief in those ridiculously blue eyes of his.

Then he kisses me.

Onstage.

For everyone to see.

Chapter 19

"What the actual fuck was that, Harry?"

Surprisingly, this isn't coming from me. Darcy is the one who seems to be leaning into rage now that we're back in the green room.

Harry's expression is indignant, and he hangs his hands on his hips as she gets in his face. "It was a kiss, Darcy. Do you really need me to explain the mechanics of it to you?"

"No, I need you to explain what the hell you were thinking," she shouts, shoving a hand against his chest.

Harry scoffs, stepping around her and heading to the food table where Kale is already munching, watching the scene with a bored expression. "I was thinking, huh, that was a really class set and my fake girlfriend did a great job and looks rather fit so I think I'm gonna go ahead and give her a quick kiss. A kiss that you weren't remotely involved in, I feel I should add, since you're having an extreme emotional reaction here."

"I think everyone should take a breather . . ." Kevin says, but his voice is drowned out by Darcy's next argument as she stalks toward Harry.

"You didn't ask Cubby or run it by her. That was so messed up."

"Have you been living in a cave, Darcy? We've literally all kissed each other. There's like, a complete lack of any boundaries when it comes to touching each other in this fecking group."

"I've never kissed any of you," Skull says from the corner, Deja perched on his lap.

"Looking to change that now, are ya, Skull?" Harry says back with a wink.

Skull looks him up and down. "I could do worse, but I'm set, thank you."

"Would you all shut up?" Darcy yells. "What you did out there is not the same as us hugging or kissing each other's cheeks or whatever. That was onstage. That was public. You were using Cubby."

"As if you aren't all fucking using me," I snap, my voice echoing across the room. Everyone goes silent, slowly turning to look at me.

Darcy's face shifts from outrage to devastation. "Cubby . . . *What?*"

She steps toward me, but I back away, shaking my head. "All of this—this tour, this album, the social media clout—it's all because you've used me. And Harry, for what it's worth."

"Exactly," Harry says with a smug smile.

"Don't you dare pretend we're on the same team here," I say, turning on him, fingers curled into fists at my sides. "I'm not happy with you either. Just because we're both pawns in this stupid game doesn't mean you can't be as guilty as they are. What you did out there was fucked up."

His face falls, lips parting as he stares at me. "Cubby . . . I-I'm sorry. I got caught up in the moment. I—"

"I'm not really interested in your excuses. We'll talk about this just the two of us later," I say through gritted teeth, a sharp throb traveling down my jaw.

"But why are you exploding on *me*?" Darcy says, blue eyes wide with hurt and confusion. "I mean . . . us," she corrects, gesturing at the rest of the group. Kale rolls his eyes.

"Jesus. It's like . . ." I throw my hands up, searching for the right words. "Get off your high horse, Darcy. Did Harry take things too far tonight? Yes. But it's not like I didn't see the writing on the wall. Honestly, I'm surprised Sigrún hasn't asked for something like this sooner."

"Well, part of the allure of this whole thing was that nothing was confirmed or denied," Kevin chimes in. "The mystique and element of the unknown really contributed to the frenzy."

"Thank you, Kevin. That was so incredibly helpful right now," Harry says.

"My point is, Darcy," I say, temper still rising as I glare at her. The anger feels good. Justified. Way easier than any other feelings I've had toward her lately. "You don't get to be angry at Harry on my behalf when you're also benefiting from this whole thing."

Darcy flinches like I slapped her. "And you don't get to tell me how to feel."

"I would really love it if we could move on from the hysterics," Kale says, stretching out on the couch. "I'm exhausted."

"Yes, please, everyone. Let's make sure we're prioritizing Kale's comfort."

"As if you don't center yourself in literally every fight," Kale shoots back. He keeps me humble, I'll give him that.

"I'm out of here," Darcy says, ducking her head and furiously brushing at her cheeks as she darts toward the door, slamming it behind her. I have the impulse to chase after her, but I lock it back, anger still pulsing hot and raw through me. I'm done chasing after her like a pathetic puppy. Harry grabs my wrist, and I jump.

"Sorry. Sorry," he says, letting me go and raising his hands in front of him. "I'm sorry. Touching you was probably not the right move at this point."

I frown at him. "Glad to know you have at least one brain cell left." My eyes dart back to the closed door. I hate that I wish she'd walk back through it.

"She'll be okay," Harry says. I give him a look, and he raises his hands again. "I have a feeling asking to talk this through right now might not be a winning idea either?"

I arch an eyebrow. "Depends on what talking it through means."

Harry's face softens in earnestness. "I want to apologize to you properly. Can we go somewhere? Just the two of us?"

I stare into Harry's pleading eyes, then glance at the door once more, feeling like I'm being split in two. "Yeah, fine. Let's go outside."

We exit out the back of the building, the Cleveland night dark and humid. A light is on in the bus, and I'm assuming that's where Darcy escaped to. Opting to give her space, I lean against the side of the bus, Harry doing the same.

"I'm sorry," he says, turning to look at me, sincerity etched across his face. "I should never have done that so publicly without talking to you. I just—" He sucks in a breath, staring at the concrete as he rakes his hands through his hair.

"What?" I nudge his shoulder with mine.

He looks at me. "I got caught up in the moment. I'm an idiot."

My lips purse as I resist the impulse to smile. "You *are* an idiot."

His face falls, and he tilts his head down and to the side. I stare at him for a moment, my eyes tracing his handsome features, the lines of worry bracketing his mouth that's usually tipped up in a smile. I reach out, wrapping him in a hug.

"But you're my idiot," I whisper into his shoulder, his arms circling my waist, holding me tight. "And I forgive you."

We stay like that for a few minutes, swaying slightly to the sounds of the city as we hold on to each other in the dark. I breathe him in, familiar and safe and warm. With Darcy and I fighting again, he feels like the only one I have left. My constant, steady anchor. There's something so bright and special about the way Harry moves through the world, and I have a gnawing impulse to cling to him like he's a shield.

"Love ya, Cub," he whispers against the crown of my head. We've said this before, many times over our years of friendship, but something about his voice sounds . . . different. An undercurrent of intimacy that didn't used to be there. My heart picks up speed, gentle heat blooming across my cheeks as I realize something about it sounds . . . *good*. Clearing my throat, I pull away, pushing the back of my spinning head to the side of the bus, blinking up at the stars.

"Have you checked on the outcome of the frenzy you created?" I ask, not looking at him. "Or is throwing gasoline on the fire and running more your style?"

He chuckles, his elbow brushing my upper arm as he fishes out his phone. I'm not sure why my skin tingles on the spot. "You know I prefer the latter, but I'll check it out for you."

"I'm sure I have a few death threats waiting in my inbox."

Harry's eyes shoot wide in horror. "*What?*"

I try to laugh past the tiny bubbles of anxiety popping in my gut. "Yeah, I get some real winners in my DMs. Telling me I should off myself or that they hope I get hit by a car."

"For what?" Harry says.

"I dunno. Breaking Connor's heart, apparently. Toying with yours. The block button is my new best friend."

"Cubby . . ." Harry's voice is low, filled with worry.

I wave my hands, wanting to swipe away the dark cloud I created. "It's fine. Seriously. Don't worry."

Harry gives me a bland look. "Ah, yes, just like that, all my worry is gone."

"It's only because you're so bloody handsome," I say, trying to steer things to playful. I tickle my fingers into the spot below his ribs and he squeals. "Everyone foaming at the mouth for ya."

Harry grabs my hand, caging it against his hip so I can't move it. "Right. Because you're so hard to look at."

I scrunch up my nose, sticking my tongue out at him. Harry's smile is wide, and his eyes flick to my mouth, pausing there before traveling back up. He lets go of my hand, and we press our backs flat against the bus again, a weird chord of tension buzzing between us. He clears his throat and scrolls through his phone.

"Well, my notifications are absolutely blowing up if that's any indication of the kiss's impact."

"From Kristen Stewart and Dylan Meyer on the red carpet to Britney and Madonna at the VMAs, where does our impact rank?"

"Rachel McAdams and Ryan Gosling re-creating *The Notebook* kiss at the MTV Movie Awards," he says, pocketing his phone again and grinning.

I let out a sigh. "We are too powerful. Guess I'll have to pretend kiss my pretend boyfriend at a few more shows moving forward if we want this career to last us the rest of the summer." I expect Harry to laugh, say something silly or teasing. But he goes silent. I can't read this silence, why it's so heavy and loaded. Unease skitters across the back of my neck.

"What if we didn't pretend?" he whispers.

I jump, pivoting my entire body to look at him like he screamed the words at me. "What do you mean? Call it off?"

He shakes his head, color creeping up his cheeks as one side of his mouth notches up in a bashful smile. "No. We keep doing what we're doing. But what if it isn't pretend?"

My mouth goes dry, every thought whooshing from my head as I process what he's saying. "How . . . how would that happen?"

Harry looks at me—stares—those glacier-blue eyes sharp and honest. "Maybe it's already happening for me."

I shake my head, tripping backward. My ankle twists in a hole in the pavement, and I start to go down. But Harry's there, he's always there, reaching out, arm snaking around my waist, catching me before I fall. Gathering me snugly against his chest.

"Have I upset you?" he whispers into my hair.

I shake my head against his sternum. Nod. Shake my head again. "I'm not sure I know what you're saying."

"I'm saying I feel things for you, Cubby. Real things that we've been calling fake."

"But . . . why?"

He laughs at that, pulling back to look at me. Not sure how anything could be funny right now when he's turning my world upside down. Both of his hands trace up my back and around my shoulders, landing to cup my face.

"Because I like you? Because you're brilliant? Because I want to be with you as more than a friend?" His face scrunches up in a forlorn smile. "But I need to know if any part of you feels the same."

In this moment, I can see it, alternate universe me looking up into those electric eyes that she knows better than her own, that face she adores, the guy she trusts. She'd slowly drag her hands from where they squeeze his forearms, up his biceps, across his chest. Loop them around his neck. She'd push up on her toes, their gazes still locked, the tip of her nose brushing his. She'd suck in a deep breath, the familiar, comforting smell of her friend whirling through her system, mixing with her blood in an alchemy that switches from friendship to lover. And alternate me would smile, then press her lips to Harry's.

But real me can't. My heart clangs in my chest in a way that doesn't feel exhilarating or right. A way that doesn't feel like it does with . . .

It doesn't feel right.

I wish it did. Everything would be so much easier if it did.

"I'm not sure I can stop pretending," I whisper.

Harry's smile wobbles then steadies, equal parts sad and self-deprecating. "What if I told you I'm willing to wait around for you to decide?"

My hands feel shaky, like they're trying to hold on at the edge of a cliff, the only thing saving me from a free fall. I make a conscious effort to release my grip on him and step away, pressing my palms to my burning cheeks.

But what if? What if I loved Harry like that? What if I said yes to someone who actually wanted me? Someone who would kiss me and make love to me and not pretend it didn't happen the next morning? Someone who adored me and wrote songs about it being amazing, not a disappointment? Because that person is right here, right now, making me that offer.

We could be good together, I know we could. We could make each other laugh. Make each other happy. That's all a relationship really needs . . . right?

I shove away the voice in my head that screams no.

"Okay," I whisper.

"Okay?" Harry's smile is so wide and eager, I almost giggle.

"I can't stop you from waiting," I say with a shrug, trying and failing to hide my own wobbly smile. I don't know why I feel like I'm about to cry. "This is a free country, so they tell me."

Harry laughs, bumping my shoulder with his. "Always so romantic. You sure it's still a no to that love song?"

I snort. "I'm sure. I'll never make the mistake of writing one of those again."

"Should we practice?" he asks suddenly.

"Practice what?"

"Well, uh, the kissing bit."

"Novice, are you?" I tease, stomach clenching at the idea. Do I want to kiss him again?

No.

Yes.

No.

. . . Kind of?

It's so hard to be unwanted by the person I desperately need. I'd do anything for Darcy to offer me what Harry just did. I want the attention, I want the validation that I'm here and worth chasing after.

"Okay," I whisper again. I hear Harry's intake of breath.

"Okay," he murmurs, leaning toward me. I mirror the movement. We stare at each other for a long time, his eyes still shockingly bright even in the midnight darkness.

With excruciating tenderness, he places a hand to my cheek, then drags it along the angle of my jaw, down until it curves around the nape of my neck. His thumb traces the spot of my thrumming pulse before he gently applies pressure, my lips parting on the barest hint of a gasp.

It's so strange, Harry touching me like this, like I'm something precious, like he's played this moment out a million times in his head and he's savoring reality. It's made all the stranger by how natural it feels, like his touch belongs on my skin, these threads of intimacy as simple as our friendship's history.

He jerks forward like he can't hold his muscles back a second longer, closing the distance between us, lips pressing against mine in a way that's both gentle and consuming. Harry kisses me like he needs me, and it makes my blood burn in my veins.

I kiss him back like if I kiss him hard enough, I can convince myself I need him too.

Something inside me slices in half from the pressure of it all—the desperate want to be wanted, to throw everything I have into this kiss, to surrender to the promise Harry's offering, the lashing jolt that none of this is right. I push the latter away, wrapping my arms around his neck, kissing Harry harder like that will force the protesting parts out of me.

Harry matches my passion with equivalent passion, a hungry sound coming from his throat, vibrating against my lips. A few tears slip down my cheeks as I register how deeply present he is in the moment, how with each passing second, each closer press of my body against his, I float further away.

The sound of the bus door opening cracks through our haze, and we jump apart, swaying in opposite directions as a sharp gasp echoes in the night.

I shoot a guilty look over my shoulder and instantly wish more than anything that I had kept my eyes fixed on the ground. Darcy stares back at me, lips parted, face crestfallen, as the light from inside illuminates her like a vision.

I step toward her, mouth opening and closing on air as I try to speak, to say something, any desperate explanation, a ridiculous cry that she's the one I want to be kissing. But she doesn't hang around long enough to hear it.

"Sorry," she rushes out, voice cracking a bit. "So sorry." She disappears back inside and slams the door closed.

My heart shatters with the noise.

$$Chapter\ 20$$

We're in New York, one of the most exciting cities on the planet, a place where history-altering music is created and performed every single day.

And I don't care about any of it because Darcy hasn't talked to me since Cleveland two weeks ago, and I'm apparently unable to have a thought that isn't about her.

We did shows in Ann Arbor and Chicago, then looped back around to Pittsburgh before finally getting to the city. Harry's been booked up on interviews, my dismal attempt in Ohio solidifying him as our spokesperson. One did fairly well, an appearance on an internet show where he ate hot dogs with an incredibly hot host, and it did a lot to build excitement for our shows in the city. We've played two gigs here already: a sold-out spot in Brooklyn and a more meager (but still respectable) turnout in Midtown.

Harry's kissed me at all of them.

And that's good.

It's right.

Suitable, at the very least.

Because that's what we agreed to: a fake, whirlwind romance

surrounding our music, infusing it with the lore of what people want us to be. Things have gotten a bit out of hand on social media, though. The winds have changed, people now making Harry the center point of their obsession, tolerating me well enough as a tag-along to his glimmer. One post in particular from a recent show has gained a tremendous amount of attention, a carousel of photos from an audience member getting reposted to stories, fan accounts, and some media outlets. Objectively, it's not hard to see why the pictures have people feeling some type of way.

Scrolling through the series is like watching a timeline of the show. All of us walking out onstage, my hand raised in a wave to the crowd—Harry's eyes fixed on me, lips turned up in a precious grin that has his dimple popping. Harry during a piano solo, head bowed and eyes closed, mouth pressed close to the mic—me in the corner, guitar slung in front of me with one hand gripping the neck, the other at my throat as I watch him play. Another of us pressed close, singing together, him giving me a cheeky smirk while I playfully narrow my eyes up at him. One from the end of the show, his forehead dropped to mine, sweat curling the hair at our temples, the corners of our eyes and bridges of our noses crinkled from our smiles.

And, finally, the kiss. His palm cradling the angle of my jaw like his hand was created to fit there, his thumb brushing my cheek, entire body centered and focused on mine like he's putting every ounce of himself into kissing me. It's a picture of a man kissing someone he's head over heels for.

It hurts to look at him.

Darcy is in the background of every photo, usually a blur on the periphery—a pinkish smudge doing her best to avoid being captured. Except for the picture of the kiss. Half of her face is in focus like she turned her gaze away the second our lips touched, eyes downcast and teeth digging into her lower lip. It's a picture of someone I used to be able to read every expression of. I have no idea what this one means.

It hurts to look at her even more.

Social media users seem to have no problem looking, though.

> no but fr the way he kisses her??? Like he can't not?? most
> romantic shit I've ever seen
> God I've seen what you've done for others . . .
> i stfg if she hurts precious angel harry she will never know
> peace
> Okay but the way he looks at her HELP

The pictures have upped the energy at our shows, but tonight's crowd at a decent-sized venue on the Lower East Side is a new level. The venue manager warned us that the vibe might be a little extra, most uni students having gotten out earlier that day for the summer, but nothing could have prepared us for this.

I can't tell if the screaming is for us as a band or more the by-product of cheap drinks and heavy pours, but either way it's absolutely feral. We're all feeling it, the energy lifting us on a different wavelength, the music running in us, through us. It's our best show yet and we know it.

I shoot a grin to Darcy, who is somehow the brightest thing in this place. Both of our hands work up and down the necks of our instruments in beautiful harmony. It's only when we're onstage that things feel somewhat normal between us, like we shed the baggage of our real selves when we make music. The second the curtains close, it's back to silence and averted gazes. She bites her lip, putting her entire body into the way she plays. With a deep breath, I step back up to the microphone, fingers still strumming as I let out the last lines of the verse.

> *No, it's not water under the bridge, it's a hurricane, it's a storm.*
> *Sure hope hell keeps you nice and warm,*
> *And I'll rebuild myself tomorrow.*
> *Tonight I'm giving in to all my sorrow,*

Counting up the hours,
Drowning in cold showers,
The water touches me better than you ever could.

People scream, many singing along, and it fills me with so much pride, I could burst. We play the last bars of the song, Darcy harmonizing with me on the outro. The noise of the audience crashing like a wave against the stage. I stare at the writhing crowd, taking in the indescribably special moment I've shared with all of these people. Each one is someone. Some are hurting and some caused the hurt. Some are happy and some are scared and some are all those things at once. But, for one night, a few minutes, we've shared something dazzling.

Motion to my right pulls my attention, and I expect it to be Harry moving toward me like he always does.

But it's Darcy, bass gripped in one hand, the other outstretched in her wild dash toward me. I turn my guitar out of the way at the last moment before she crashes into me, rocking us back and forth as the cheers continue around us. She holds me so tight, I can't breathe.

I don't mind.

She can have all the oxygen in my lungs if it means she'll stay close to me like this.

"That was brilliant," she yells near my ear so I can hear her over the crowd. "*You're* brilliant."

She presses a quick kiss to my cheek—one that couldn't be mistaken for anything but friendly—before pulling back, grin huge and eyes glinting as she holds my gaze for another second, hands still on me. Eventually she steps away and waves at the crowd. My fingers fly to my cheek, holding that kiss in place like I can brand it to my skin. I have to keep my hand there because otherwise it would jerk out, gripping Darcy's dress, bringing her back to me until her lips land straight on mine. Where they belong.

Where I wish they belonged.

An arm wraps around my shoulder, and I'm in such a daze it takes me a second to recognize the familiar touch of Harry. My stomach clenches, sinking like a stone at his handsome smile, the joy he turns from the crowd to me. How genuine it all is.

It kills me.

He follows the normal routine, the choreography, giving me a squeeze before ducking his head for a kiss. I watch the descent of his mouth in slow motion like it's the arc of the executioner's sword.

I turn at the last moment, and Harry's lips fall where Darcy's were a minute before. And it feels so wrong, like he brushed away something beautiful, snatching its chance to grow into what it should be.

If Harry notices, he doesn't show it. "You're *amazing*," he says as he pulls back, tucking some of my hair behind my ear. Somehow, his kindness makes it all worse, nausea churning up my stomach, sweat prickling my skin. Harry reads something in my expression, tilting his head, reaching out for me again like he wants to fix whatever's broken in me. Instead of letting him, I turn, scampering off stage to outpace the slice of pain trying to take me out by the knees.

"Cubby!" Kevin booms the second I'm in the wings. "You all were unreal."

"Thanks, Kevin," I croak, gulping past the knot in my throat, the sharp tug of tears threatening to embarrass me.

Kevin's eyes are glinting, fixed over my shoulder as the rest of the band files off stage. He ushers us to the green room, making sure we're hydrated and fed as he gushes on and on about the show and the crowd. After a few minutes, Deja bursts through the door, jumping into Skull's arms and wrapping herself around him like an amorous koala, screaming the whole time.

"You're the next big thing. I can feel it," Kevin says.

I expect us all to scoff like we normally do when someone says that, almost as an exercise of luck. If you believe too truly you're the next big thing, the universe won't ever let it happen. But when I glance around, everyone looks like they agree with Kevin's statement.

There's a knock on the door, and a stagehand pokes his head in, gesturing for Kevin, who maneuvers through the tight space to him. They chat for a second, then Kevin grins, clapping the guy on the back before turning to us. "I'm sure you all are exhausted after that."

"'Bout to faint dead away if I don't get something besides this bird food in me," Harry says, chewing on a handful of mixed nuts. "Can we get burgers?"

"Oh god, a burger sounds amazing," Kale says, looking at Harry like he suggested a cure for the climate crisis. Harry winks at him, reaching out an arm and pulling Kale to his side so they lean on each other.

"I would love some chicken tenders, if you're taking an order, Kev," Darcy adds.

"Fries for me, please," Deja chimes in.

Kevin frantically waves his hands. "We can get all of that later—"

"Tiny Deja needs fries *now*," Skull says (speaking for the first time in a few days, I'm pretty sure). Deja giggles and reaches up on her tiptoes to kiss his cheek.

"Fine. Okay. I'll put in an order. But while we're waiting, what do you say to signing some autographs?"

We all look around, similar frowns on our faces.

"*Who* signs some autographs?" Darcy says, turning to Kevin. "Us?" She slaps her hand to her chest.

"No, the plumber from earlier. Yes, *you*," he says, waving at us.

"Does anybody, er, *want* that?" Harry asks, sharing a skeptical glance with Kale.

Kevin grins. "Apparently, a pretty good crowd at the back door does."

"What would we even sign?" I ask, nose scrunched up. "I don't know why my immediate thought was necks and tits."

"Oh my God, Cub, that was *my* initial thought," Darcy says with a giggle. "Could you imagine signing a neck?"

"Like feeling the pulse under the marker tip?" We both gag.

"I love you all dearly but as your manager I'm kindly asking you to stop talking and go sign anything and everything your fans out there want you to sign, including necks and tits. This will be great for publicity." Kevin whisks us out of the room and to the door that opens to the side alley where we parked the bus.

"Here we go," he says, pushing it open, a riptide of noise grabbing our ankles and tugging us out into the night.

The small crowd gathers around us in a semicircle, herding us against the brick wall of the venue. Rationally, I know it's not that many people—we aren't some massive celebrities like Harry Styles or the Rolling Stones—but it might as well be for how immediately overwhelming I find the moment.

So many hands and bodies and voices reach for us—well, Harry, mainly—yelling our names and snapping pictures on their phones. Markers are pressed into my hand, papers shoved under my nose. My wrists are grabbed, tugged, pulling me along in the chaotic energy.

The crush of it feels like sinking in quicksand, every nerve in my body pulled tight with fear as random cheeks press to my face for photos no one asked me if they could take.

I look around, and everyone seems to be handling it better than I am. Well, except for Skull, who is nowhere to be found so I'm assuming he's already miles away hunting down fries for Deja.

Kale has been corralled into his own little circle, signing in a methodical order (he's very lucky having a decent personality isn't a prerequisite for being a musician). Darcy has her arms around two women about our age, the three of them pressed tight as someone else takes a bunch of pictures. Harry is a natural, smiling and laughing and seeming to genuinely connect with the people swamping us. I can't stop staring.

How?

How is he so calm? How is he okay with being pulled in a thousand different directions, everyone wanting something different, something special from him? Doesn't he feel like he's about to break? Be pulled apart at the seams until there's no putting him back together again?

His head lifts from whatever he's signing, turning to me and catching my stare. Our gazes hold, and he smiles, flashing a wink. He must sense how much I'm drowning, because he maneuvers toward me, reaching out to give my hand a squeeze.

Someone notices. Of course they do.

"Oh my god, do that again," a person yells, their thumb moving in rapid fire as they snap photos of our parted hands.

"Any bad blood between you and Connor for you stealing his girl?" some douche with a grin asks, raising his eyebrows and giving me an appraising look that sours my stomach.

Harry frowns. "The only bad blood between us is for the shit way he's treated people I care about."

I glance up at him, my lips parting. He gives me a quick, sad smile before turning away, clapping his hands.

"Thank you all for coming," he says over the noise. "Tonight was amazing. You were amazing. Best crowd we've ever had. But we're all knackered and calling it a night."

Without further ceremony, he laces his fingers with Darcy's, places a hand on my back, and guides us inside, Kale on our heels, the door slamming shut behind us.

The noise is cut off, and the angry hornets of thoughts buzzing through my head start to calm. Kevin ushers us back to the green room to catch our breath, then makes good on his promises.

Half an hour later, we're scarfing down greasy fast food in a trance, sitting on the floor of the bus, lights dimmed and curtains drawn. The crash hits hard—an inevitable comedown from such a high. Despite the chaos of the signing, I can't shake the satisfied grin that etches across my mouth, eyes heavy as I sit on my mattress, back propped against the base of Kale's bunk, Darcy across from me.

Even when exhausted, Kale's fingers can't sit still, and he gently plucks his violin. Harry starts to sing along, an Irish folk song he's played countless times over the years. His voice is rough and flowing like water traveling over a bed of rocks. The combination of his singing and the strings is bright but haunting, the type of song that chases an optimistic ending to an otherwise sad film, never pushing out the melancholy, but coexisting with it. Deep comfort wraps around us, Skull and Tiny Deja already fast asleep on their bunk, cuddled close with an empty fry carton resting on the pillow between them. It makes my throat ache.

I grab my phone, trying to wake it, but the screen stays black. With a mild sigh, I reach along the floor for my charger and plug it in, tossing it to the side. Without the distraction of scrolling, my eyes fall to Darcy. I'm surprised to see her already looking at me.

Our gazes hold, my heartbeat keeping time with the music. Then, she smiles—slow and radiant—and something in me unlocks, a stream of languid joy tracing through my veins. Like we're tethered by a wire, we move at the same moment, pushing away from the base of the bunks to lay down on our sides facing each other. Kale's music turns slower, Harry's voice gravelly until he fades into a gentle hum.

In the darkness, Darcy reaches out, bridging the space between us and taking my hand in hers. Touching me so intentionally for the first time in a long time. Part of me wants to cry out at the relief of it, the instantaneous swell of safety. But the moment's too perfect, my eyes too heavy, to ruin it with such mortifying feelings, so I let myself drift to sleep instead, holding on to her hand as I slip away.

It's still dark when I wake up, everyone else fast asleep. Darcy's on her side curled into a tight ball facing away from me. For a second,

I think about scooting closer, letting my shoulder rest against the curve of her spine, letting her warmth and the rhythm of her breaths lull me back to sleep. But instead I grab my phone out of habit, squinting at the harsh brightness as I tap in my password and open Instagram.

The number of notifications is so absurdly large, I bolt upright, panic spiking. I bring my pillow to my chest, biting the edge and choking down a whimper as I scroll.

It's a video of Harry's response to the bad blood question, edited with a dramatic swell of music after he says it, a cut to us heading to the backstage door, a zoom in on his hand on my back. My stomach twists and head swims as I see it has almost a million views.

Not wasting any time, I turn to Google, typing in my name and Harry's. A slew of headlines pop up.

**Silence Broken: Harry O'Connell publicly confirms
relationship status with bandmate Cubby Clark after
weeks of PDA and speculation**

**What happened to bro code? Harry O'Connell
makes pointed jab at his new girlfriend's ex,
singing sensation Connor McCabe**

**Feud brought to the forefront: Cubby Clark
shamelessly flaunts relationship with bandmate,
and her ex's best friend**

How about this headline: Cubby Clark screams into the void so loud she rips open throat? Or maybe: Cubby Clark is sick of only being talked about in the context of men! Or, a true gem of a contender: Cubby Clark is hopelessly obsessed with her best friend who is not Harry but said best friend does not reciprocate romantic feelings! Oh and also Cubby is now completely questioning her sexuality and having a bit of an identity crisis to top it all off!

I skim one of the articles that looks slightly less sensationalized.

Members of Tea Time Tantrum find themselves in some hot water. The band first gained notoriety after front man Connor McCabe left for his soaring solo career. Becoming an overnight sensation, McCabe's hit song "grin and bear it" was rumored to be written about ex-bandmate/girlfriend Cubby Clark. Since then, Tea Time Tantrum has not missed an opportunity to capitalize on their unearned notoriety, hinting for weeks at a growing romance between its new leads, Clark and Harry O'Connell. While rumors seemed to be confirmed by the regular lip-locking of the pair at the end of their shows, O'Connell squashed any room for relationship deniers, speaking out against McCabe publicly and declaring his ex-friend mistreated Clark. The love triangle keeps getting messier, and it's hard to see if there's any end to this growing feud in sight. McCabe, for his part, has kept it classy, saving any animosity he has for his razor-sharp lyrics and brilliantly produced music videos.

Brilliantly produced? Razor-sharp? Do I live on the same planet as these people?

A whine rolls out of my throat, and I turn off the screen, hitting the corner of my phone against my forehead. I want to cry. I want to run. I want out of this ridiculous scheme and this endless cycle of relevance from what guy I'm supposedly snogging or torturing.

This can't be how life is supposed to be, how love is supposed to be. There's no way it's supposed to hurt this much, destroy me this profoundly. My phone vibrates as it makes contact with my skull, shaking my brain. Maybe it can scramble memories of the last few months out of my head.

With a sigh and no self-control, I check the notification.

Connor has started a live stream on Instagram.

Yes, I still follow him. Yes, I hate myself. But, in my weak defense, I was told it would look worse for me to unfollow him.

Because no one can dig their fingers into a wound quite like I can, I grab my earbuds, crawl to the bathroom, and click into the stream. Connor's sharp, handsome features fill my screen.

"Hello," he says quietly, Irish accent rolling the word to soften the edges. "Just giving everyone a minute to get on."

Several thousand people are already shooting up hearts from the corner. Dante has nothing on this circle of hell I'm living in.

"All right. Hey, guys," he starts. The man has never had an original thought, I swear. "So . . . there's no easy way to start this off, but obviously there's been a lot of talk about my personal life, particularly my dating life, recently."

He looks away, dramatically of course, like he's digging deep on what to say. He turns back to the camera, stunning jawline set in defiance, like he's busting through some invisible barrier he as a white, cis, het guy has been a victim of for a lifetime. "I've always tried to keep my personal life personal."

Liar.

"What comes out in my music—my *art*—is personal."

Then why is it out for public consumption, you prick?

"And whatever interpretations you have of that belong to you as a fan, but so much of it is being dumped on my doorstep in the form of rumors and feuds that, quite honestly, don't exist."

I will feud with you till the day I die, Connor McCabe, and that is a universal truth.

"All this to say: I'm taking a short break from social media. This isn't permanent, I promise, but I do need some time to focus on my mental health, especially with the world tour coming up."

Sublime humble brag there at the end, you rancid twat stain.

"You all have shown me so much support and love, and I pour it all back to you, our energy a beautiful, continuous cycle."

Great, now I'm dry heaving.

"And I appreciate the kindness and understanding I'm sure you'll extend to me for this too. I can't say I deserve your grace, but I cherish it."

With a gratuitous kiss blown to the camera that results in an eruption of hearts and comments, he signs off, and I swipe out of the app, tossing my phone on the cramped counter and biting down on my knuckles to hold back a scream.

I think it's interesting that Connor—someone who created this absolute shitshow by writing about me being a lousy lay and disappointing first love, someone who has never had a mean thing uttered about him on the internet—is the one given the grace and compassion for a social media break while I'm forced to pretend to be dating my friend while being ripped apart joint by joint online.

I bury my head in my hands and let out a muffled groan.

I. Hate. Everything.

My phone buzzes and I reluctantly drag it toward me, a delirious little rat in a fucked-up experiment. My stomach bottoms out, heart snapping like a rubber band up my throat as a name I never wanted to see again pops up on my phone with the text.

Connor.

With shaky fingers, I open the message, reading it over and over.

We need to talk

Chapter 21

I make terrible decisions.

In fact, I don't think I've ever made a decent decision in my life. And I'm fully aware of this. I'm so deeply self-aware that I drive myself absolutely mental with it, and I'm pretty sure everyone in my life, myself included, would be so much better off if I weren't so self-aware . . . and also didn't make such terrible decisions. Et cetera, et cetera.

But knowing I'm making a terrible decision doesn't seem to stop me from seeing it through.

I scream at myself to get away from the door I'm lurking in front of, sprint as fast as I can from this posh hotel and back to my dingy tour bus, do one single thing to protect my already battered self-worth.

But I'm a fool searching for some sort of humiliating closure. Which is why, with one more deep breath, I knock on Connor's door.

No answer.

Lazy fucker.

I knock (pound) on the door again, adding a rattle of the handle for good measure.

Still nothing.

I'm about to take this as a sign to leave well enough alone when the door cracks open, and Connor appears. He fixes me with a careless smile, eyes heavy-lidded and hair mussed like some girl has been running her hands through it for the better part of last night and most of this morning.

It's a look I'm all too familiar with on him. It's the same one he wore countless times on my doorstep after disappearing for a night or two when we were still a bunch of nobodies playing crap pubs. I'd glare at him, taking in his rumpled clothes, trying to push away the seared image of some random woman on his arm in his Instagram stories from just a few hours before. And he'd give me that half smile, both of us knowing I was too chicken to ask the questions I didn't want honest answers to.

Glad to know fame hasn't changed him.

"Hey, darling," he says, voice low and accent thick. I roll my eyes.

"You wanted to talk, yeah?" I say, hooking my hands on my hips. "Can we get on with it? I only have so many minutes on this planet and I'm sick of wasting them in your presence."

Connor lets out a laugh through his nose, smirking at me. He holds up his hands like he's calming an aggressive animal. "Down, girl. I'm not looking to fight."

"Keep talking to me like that and there won't be a fight, I'll simply push you out your posh window."

Connor's gaze flits over his shoulder to the floor-to-ceiling glass overlooking the city. "It is pretty posh though, innit?"

"The point, Connor?"

"Right, yeah. Come in, come in."

The suite is expansive and open, with white walls and gray art and red accents thrown in here and there. It's so cultivated. So perfectly sterile yet chic. A good fit for Connor.

There's an entire living room set up through an archway off the bedroom—couches, chairs, a desk in the corner—but Connor doesn't have the decency to lead us in there to talk. He plops on top of his messy bedsheets, legs crossed at the ankles in front of him and arms clasped behind his neck as he leans on the headboard. The only options he leaves me are to perch like an awkward, worried mum on the edge of his bed or sit on the floor and stare up at him. I opt for the nearest wall, leaning against it and crossing my arms over my chest. He scrolls on his phone as I stand there like the world's biggest dickhead.

"Something you wanted to talk to me about?" I eventually ask, hating myself for being the first to speak.

He glances up like he forgot I was here. "Oh. Right. Yeah. How's it going?"

"*How's it going?*" I gape at him. "Did you really drag me here to ask that? Fucking *stellar*, Connor. Time of my life."

He gives me that classic, pacifying smile of his. Like I'm predictable. Like I'm a capricious toddler lashing out. Like I'm too much. "I'm sure you can guess why I asked you to come by."

"You love taking the piss on your exes?"

He ignores me. "It goes without saying that you've got a bit of a celebrity presence growing, yeah?"

"Not for anything I'd like to be known for."

"Whatdya mean?"

I scowl at him. "People only mention my name if it's in the context of you or Harry. I'd much rather be known for my music."

Connor clicks his tongue against his teeth, waving me away. "Any press is good press, Cub. Which is actually what I wanted to talk to you about. Or, more so, my label wanted me to talk to you about."

"Your label?" My hackles rise, legs tensing. I'm a moment away from bolting.

"Right, yeah, here's the thing. You've caught the attention of some of the producers at my record company. Publicists too. They like your whole mopey-yet-bitchy vibe or whatever. It's stirred up some really good buzz for me."

I generally consider myself a pacifist, but everything about Connor makes homicide seem appealing. He's special like that.

"And when they first presented this idea, I told them to fuck off, but they're persistent and have made some really good points," he continues, looking at me like I should be fully aware of whatever points those were.

My brain recoils in my skull as a truly awful conclusion jumps to the front. "I am begging you to grant me peace just this once and not suggest what I think you're about to."

He smirks. "Come on, Cub. It makes sense. I created a stir, opened that door for you to stick your foot in, and you've created a stir right back. The next step is obvious."

"I'm sorry, you opened a door for me now, did you?" I feel my pulse pounding at my temples and wrists, face heating as I push away from the wall, storming the few steps between us and looming over him.

He's unfazed, yawning as he glances at his vibrating phone. "We collaborate. Lay down some tracks. Spend a bit of time in public together, give them something new to talk about."

I stare slack-jawed at him for a good ten seconds before letting out a laugh so shrill and loud, it's a miracle all of the shiny glass in this tacky room doesn't crack. "Why would I *ever* do that? Even knowing your name is an insult to my intelligence, let alone willingly spending time with you."

Connor, for once, has the decency to react beyond his usual apathy, his lips twisting and eyes darkening. "Why would you do it? Oh, I don't know, Cubby, maybe because I made you famous? No one would know your name if it weren't for me. And this is a way to grow that."

Rage streaks through my body so succinctly, it embeds itself in my bones, my cells, my DNA. I want to scream at him, claw off that hideous smile creeping back up his pompous face, tell him to rot in hell. But instead, the emotions swell into this grotesque blob, squeezing my throat closed, pushing pinpricks of tears at my eyes. I will die if Connor sees my cry.

He stares at me for a long moment, running his hands through his hair and letting out a deep breath. "I'm not trying to upset you, Cubby," he says, continuing to upset me. "Despite whatever lies you've convinced yourself of, I did love you. I still care about you. And this would help you as much as it would help me. Take both our careers to the next level."

"Is this supposed to be your apology? Because it's pretty shit."

"Apology for what?"

My mouth drops open. "You must be joking."

His face scrunches up like he's genuinely confused. "You aren't still on about the breakup, are you? That was ages ago, Cub."

"I'm not upset about the breakup, you walking trash can. I'm upset about you stealing my song. My music."

He has the gall to look affronted, and he gets up from the bed, taking a step toward me. "We wrote that together."

"I wrote it with you sitting next to me, that hardly takes effort on your part," I yell. "Those lyrics were *mine*, Connor. My art. My ideas. *Mine*."

He fixes me with a patronizing glare, letting out a scoff of disgust. "Jesus, Cub, it's just a song. It's words and notes. You're acting like I shat on your mattress and robbed your house. It's not that deep."

"Easy for you to say, you have the emotional depth of a puddle."

He lets out another humorless laugh, shaking his head. "You really love to pick on the past, you know that? I was there, wasn't I? I sang those words. Told you when something wasn't working."

I stare at him, anger churning in my gut. "You truly believe that, don't you?"

"Well . . . yeah."

Jesus fucking Christ. How do you reason with a brick wall? Apparently, I'm a glutton for punishment, so I push on. "If I went into your fancy studio and stole the song you were supposed to record tomorrow and played it for millions and claimed it was mine, would you not be a little pissed off?"

"I'm not recording tomorrow."

"What is it like to be utterly unencumbered by the thought process?"

"Cubby, like I said, I didn't invite you over here to fight." He reaches out, palm wrapping around my shoulder.

Red bleeds across my vision, his touch shooting hot rage through my body. "Well, tough. Because a fight is what you're going to get." I smack his hand away. "I've bit my tongue so many times with you, it's a miracle I can even speak, so you're going to hear what I have to say whether you want to or not."

"I don't."

"I don't care!" My voice is high and piercing, hands fisted in my hair. "I don't care about your opinion or your reasoning or how you talk yourself out of being the bad guy. I don't care what lies you tell yourself to fall asleep at night. Because you don't matter to me. You don't."

"Kind of ya, thanks."

"I care about my *music*," I say, gesturing in the space between us like the music is a physical being. "I care about this awful, wonderful, maddening thing I rip myself to pieces for over and over again to try and create something beautiful. Something real. And you taking that from me is the cruelest thing you could have ever done. You knew that. You knew that and you did it anyway. You wanted my words but never the person that came with them."

My throat is tight, face hot as emotions twist like a knife in my gut. He's snatched something from me—he and everyone else that plays his betrayal on loop—stole something precious that I'll never get back. He's led the charge in ripping any softness I had to shreds, any naivety that the world could be nice to a girl like me. This may be my only chance to exorcize the demons he seeded in me.

"I'm a real person, Connor," I say, voice fracturing. "I'm not the subject of your next pop song or some muse you can reference in interviews about your oh-so-profound lyrics. I'm flesh and blood and I have feelings and what you did to me hurt and it matters and you need to be told that so maybe you can stop treating people like disposable playthings. I know you don't care about my feelings, and hopefully one day I'll stop expecting you to, but you have to stop destroying people as you search for yourself."

He looks at me for a moment, stare hard and unreadable. He lets out a deep breath through his nose, tilting his face to the ceiling. It looks like real emotion is playing out across his face.

"You've always been so dramatic, Cubby," he says with a resigned sigh, gaze dropping back to me, boredom dulling his features.

If Americans weren't such huge fans of the death penalty, I'd strangle him right now, I really would. "You're a prick," I say, laughing in spite of myself. Connor smiles, and that smile exterminates any dark humor I could find in this moment. He'll never fucking get it. "I didn't deserve the way you treated me," I say, voice steady, chin lifting.

Saying it unlocks something in me, a cage door opening. The rush of it carves through my empty chest, scraping the bone, but the hurt feels good. It feels more real than anything I could ever hope for with this man. We stare at each other. I wish I could say unspoken things pass between us in the silence, something meaningful, something that could blunt the edges of this hard-to-swallow pill. But there's nothing but mutual disdain.

"Let me walk you down," he says at last, waving toward the door in dismissal.

"You don't have to, I'm fine," I say and, maybe, this time I actually mean it.

"It's the least I can do."

Well, that much is true.

The ride in the elevator is quiet, and I look at Connor in the shiny silver reflection of the doors as he thumbs through his phone, my eyes tracing the distance between our bodies. It's baffling that I ever felt close to him.

It hits me that, if things go my way, this will be the last time I'm with him, having to share air. And part of me, the sticky, clingy, spineless blob of me that relied on this guy for all my worth for all those scary teenage years, cries out, trying to latch on to him out of sick habit.

But the real me—brittle and coarse and bruised—straightens her shoulders. Takes another step away. Sucks in a full breath. I can breathe so much clearer without the weight of him pulling me down.

"What do you think went wrong between us?" I hate that I give voice to the thought, but I want to know. Were we broken from the start? Two drastically different people never meant to mix? Or did we really try? Was he unable to let me love him? Let himself love me?

Connor shrugs, then looks at me, searching my face like he's trying desperately to find something he lost. He sighs. "You're just so damn sad all the time."

The weight of the statement wraps around my throat, squeezing tight. "It must have been hard to love me."

"It certainly wasn't easy." His smile is pitying. I want to claw it off his face.

We both face straight ahead. Resentment pulses in my stomach, shame twisting through my chest, both battling for which can hurt me more. I want to cry, but not for Connor—not for the bullshit he's put me through—but for the fact that he's right. I'm not easy.

I never will be.

I'll always carry around gloom like a low-grade fever, it growing larger and heavier, dripping like tar from my joints and clogging my thoughts.

It's too much to ask for anyone to take that on.

The elevator doors slide open, and we walk down the glossy hall into the lobby. Eyes fixed on the exit, I plow ahead, but Connor catches me off guard, grabbing my shoulders at the last moment, spinning me around and pulling me into him. All the air shoots from my lungs.

He holds me flush against his body, arms cinched around my biceps so I can't worm away no matter how much I try. I'm so tired from our conversation, I can't say I try all that hard. After too many seconds, he pulls back, dragging his hands up my arms, one cupping my neck, the other cradling my jaw, leaning until his forehead touches mine. I flinch but he has me locked in place.

"Goodbye, Cubby," he whispers, thumb tracing across my cheek. "For now."

"Forever," I say back, managing to pull out of his grip.

His chuckle is dark and void of humor. "Something tells me this isn't over between us." He swoops in once and kisses my cheek. I jerk back so hard my teeth slam together and my vision spins, an electric burst of pain traveling along my jaw.

With one last flash of that lazy smile, he turns on his heel and slopes back to the elevator banks. I dash out the door, gulping down the stale city air as I try to soothe the anger flaring through me. I hate him so much it almost seems miraculous. With a shake of my shoulders, I take off toward the tour bus, scrubbing my face to erase the slimy feel of his kiss.

I'm halfway down the block when I register the number of paparazzi that were in the lobby.

she ate through the hole
like all good girls do
and under the wait
she finally did break
waiting on you
The dream that never comes true

Chapter 22

Philadelphia is a bizarre place.

Our tour bus barely made the trip from New York, and Kale—the only one of us with a US license—drove Kevin's dinged-up car behind us in case we broke down along the way. In perhaps the only stroke of luck we've had this tour, the bus sputtered to a halt as we pulled into an auto shop parking lot. Kevin turned it over to a mechanic who did not say a single word to us, just stared, a chunky gold cross hanging between the open flaps of his shirt to land on his exceptionally hairy chest.

Kevin had us cram into his shitty hatchback as he drove to a highly questionable motel near tonight's venue, the only affordable lodgings we could find on such short notice. But the "good news," as Kevin phrases it (he could find something lovely to say about a turd), is that the motel rate is so cheap we can afford for everyone to get their own room. I don't want to touch anything for fear of catching pinworms but hey, at least I'll have the opportunity to be murdered in my own personal space!

We're in a pocket of the city called Fishtown and the residents flaunt the name with pride, fish paraphernalia decorating wrought-iron fences, trash cans, and murals. The shops are equally as odd; countless storefronts with bizarre offerings and antique goods lining the streets. At one point, we even pass a bakery with an attention-grabbing window display of cakes shaped like boobs.

Tonight's show is at a wonderfully grimy bar called Kung Fu Necktie, every centimeter of the walls covered to its fullest potential with graffiti, stickers, and a stray neon monkey. I've been on edge since leaving the hotel yesterday, refreshing my phone over and over as I wait to see if Connor is really so evil as to plant a story, but a new problem has taken priority in my anxious brain: Something is horribly wrong with my mouth.

Staring in the mirror like some Sad Girl™ in an indie film, I poke at the angle of my swollen jaw, hissing out a breath. The pain is a sharp, throbbing ache that travels all the way down to my toes. Angry blotches of red slash across my cheeks, the rest of my face gray and sweaty.

Lovely.

I've been noticing a growing but sporadic ache along my face for a few weeks now, but I chalked it up to grinding my teeth to dust from stress. I'm starting to think it might be slightly more serious than that.

With a sigh, I lean closer to the mirror and open my mouth as much as I can, which isn't very much at all, and gingerly pull my cheek back. It's dark and hard to see in there, but the back right looks swollen and angry, a large bump forming where my lower jaw meets my upper. I try to touch the spot, but it's so tender I almost bite my own finger off as I jerk back.

Bracing my hands on the sink, I gulp down a few deep breaths.

Okay. This is okay. I splash some cold water on my cheeks. *Totally okay. This is tomorrow Cubby's problem. Not yours. So mind your own business.* With a final shaky breath, I straighten and head out of the bathroom to the small backstage area.

Only to discover there is something horribly wrong with my band.

"It's absolute bullshit," Kale yells into Kevin's face. "Wake up, man."

"You have to calm down, mate," Harry says, stepping between them. "Come off him, he didn't cause this."

"Don't tell him to calm down, he's rightfully upset," Skull says. I do a double take at the sheer passion in his voice.

"We're all fucking upset. Him screaming his head off won't do any good, though, will it?" Darcy snaps back. All four of them erupt into more yelling.

"If we could all take a breath . . ." Kevin says, his voice lost in the noise.

My attention flits from person to person, their red faces, phones clutched in their hands. I grab my electric guitar sitting in the corner, plugging it into a stray amp and spinning the knob all the way up. I play a shrill note, holding it close to the amp so feedback pierces through the room. The yelling stops, everyone clamping their hands to their ears and swiveling their angry faces to land on me.

"What the hell is going on?" I say, sweat pricking along my hairline as the pain in my mouth builds.

Kale, *shockingly*, is the first to respond, marching toward me. "You tell us, traitor."

"Excuse me?" I square up to him.

With a curled lip and a scoff, he throws his phone on the worn couch next to me, pointing at it like it's a smoking gun. Refusing to take my eyes off him, I reach out, picking it up and bringing it toward my chest. When I have no choice, I look away from the rage in Kale's face to the screen.

My heart sinks.

My own face looks back at me, a series of pictures of me in a posh hotel lobby . . . *embracing* Connor. A surge of pain zaps between my temples as I scroll to look at the headline.

Cubby Clark Crawling Back

The first few sentences have bile burning up my throat.

Cubby Clark, the notorious girlfriend of Tea Time Tantrum's leading man Harry O'Connell, can't seem to help herself as she's seen begging her heartthrob ex, Connor McCabe, to take her back, not only in the bedroom but onstage. Insiders report Clark orchestrated a surprise visit to McCabe's NYC hotel in an attempt to lure him back into a relationship, and to take her on as a supporting act as his stardom intensifies.

"It's just sad to see such a good guy toyed with," a friend close to the star tells us. "Cubby is so desperate to use these guys in her life to further her career. She doesn't even think about the emotional damage she's doing to them."

Desperate indeed . . .

"I get the picture," I say, tossing Kale's phone back on the couch.

"Yeah, we do too," he spits.

"I'm sorry, but why are you mad at me?"

He splutters for a moment, shooting a bewildered look around the room. I've actually rendered Kale speechless. It's a miracle.

"You're joking, right?" he finally manages. "You seriously aren't going to own it?"

"Own what?" I clap my hands after each syllable for emphasis.

"That you're two-timing us. That you're using us as a stepping stone to your next big conquest. You're in cahoots with Connor and waiting for the right moment to tell us you're leaving the band to go work with him."

It's my turn to splutter. "Are you cracked? You think I'd ever do something so degrading as go back to that asshole?"

"Up until I saw pictures of you doing just that, no, I didn't think you would. But the proof is right there. We all see it."

"There's nothing to see!"

Kale picks up his phone, flashing the article at me. "Really? Because, from where I'm standing, we can clearly see Connor, a fancy hotel paid for by his execs, and you having some sort of secret meeting with him. What else would you be doing there?"

"Obviously it wasn't so secret if all the paps got pictures, you prat. But that's not at all what it was. Connor texted me, he arranged the whole thing. And, yes, he asked me to collab with him—spewed some crap about his label wanting it for publicity—but I told him to fuck off."

"Why didn't you tell me about the meeting?"

It takes me a moment to remember there are other people in this room besides me and Kale, and I turn.

Darcy. Eyes wide, brow pinched, lip caught between her teeth. She clears her throat. "Why didn't you tell *us* about the meeting?" Her voice has a ragged edge, almost imperceptible unless you knew her normal voice well. As well as I do.

I push past Kale, to get to her. I reach out and grab her hands, trying to hold them to me, but she slips away, wrapping her arms around her middle.

"Darce," I whisper. "Come on. Not you too."

"Why?" she repeats.

I let out a humorless laugh, a few angry tears slipping out the corners of my eyes. Does she really need any more evidence of how fucking pathetic I am? Do I need to spell out how I was desperate for closure in at least one failed relationship? "Because it didn't matter," I say through gritted teeth.

"A major pop star asking you to join his band matters a bit, Cub," Harry says. "That's stuff you share with your band. Unless you're trying to hide something."

I drag my gaze from Darcy's hurt face to land on Harry's frown.

I shake my head slowly. "You of all people, Harry? Are you kidding me right now? Have you been awake for any of the events the past six weeks? The absolute circus we've been thrown in the center of? The media twists everything! How could you think that's real after everything we've endured?"

"That's the thing, though, innit? It *is* real. He really asked you that. You really took the meeting." There's a pleading note in his voice like he's begging me to say it's all photoshopped.

"It seems pretty convenient that the media has it out for you so specifically, Cubby." This time, it's Skull digging the tip of the knife into the wound.

"Yeah, interesting that you're always the victim," Kale says, coming to Harry's side and clapping a hand on his shoulder.

I go to open my throbbing mouth, but any arguments turn to ash in my throat. I stand there, gaping at the people I thought I could trust. What's the point in trying to make them see the truth? They were so ready to believe this, so ready to think the worst of me. Why would I bother defending myself when I have no one left to give me the benefit of the doubt?

A knock sounds at the door, drawing our attention.

"Five minutes till show," a runner says, popping her head in and ducking back out in a blink.

"I'm not going onstage with this lying snake," Kale says, turning to Kevin, who's hiding in the corner and, if I'm being honest, doing a horrible job of managing things.

"I think we all need to take a second," he says, face bright red and sweat ringing the collar and pits of his shirt.

"No," Kale says, crossing his arms. "I'm not going to do it."

The pulsating in my jaw intensifies, making my eyes water and vision blur, anger pumping through my blood and clawing at my muscles.

I glance around the room, desperate to find anyone to back me up. Skull sits on the couch, eyes fixed on the wall across from him.

After a heavy moment, he stands, setting down his drumsticks, and shoving his hands in his pockets. "Tonight isn't the night to play."

Harry's head is hung low, hands fisted in his hair.

"Harry."

He doesn't look at me.

"Harry."

Nothing.

Darcy at least has the decency to meet my gaze, but there's a mix of hurt and confusion on her face. How does she not get it? The one person that knows me the best. How can she not see how utterly humiliating it is that I even showed up at Connor's stupid room, desperately searching for pathetic closure? Why would I give any of them one more example of how pitiful I am?

Another shock of pain shoots down my jaw and up to my brain like barbed wire is cinching them together. I grab my cheeks, squeezing my eyes shut as I try to breathe through it.

This can't be happening. This can't be happening.

My world has been slowly crumbling for months, and this was the final blow. There's no coming back from this. Not when I don't have anyone listening to the truth. I dredge up my last bit of strength to collect myself, gaze sweeping to every single person in the room.

"Fuck this," I say simply. "Fuck you. All of you. Fuck this band and our stupid songs. I don't need any of you."

"Cubby." Darcy's voice is soft, but the warning echoes like a shot through my head. I don't care. I'm done holding myself together if everyone is so dead set on ripping me to pieces.

I stare straight at her, letting all the hurt, all the excruciating pain of the past few months play across my face. "I'm serious," I say, not blinking. "I'm done."

Chapter 23

After a huge, dramatic exit, I do the only thing a mature, independent twenty-three-year-old would do: I lock myself in my disgusting motel bathroom, curl up in the grimy tub as I blubber like a baby, and call my mums.

"Cubby? Are you all right?" Mum asks, picking up on the second ring. Her voice is thick from sleep, and I feel a curl of guilt at having woken her. She probably thinks it's an emergency. But, if my cheeks keep ballooning up at this rate, it might be.

"I . . . I'm safe," I press out, voice cracking. "But I'm not sure I'm all right, no."

"Oh, sweetheart . . . Hold on, Mãe is here too. I'm going to put you on speakerphone."

I hear rustling on the other end, Mum saying something along the lines of *Cubby is crying* before Mãe's warm, familiar voice fills the line.

"Talk to us, my love. What's wrong?"

I cry even harder. Where do I begin? "I got in a fight with the band."

"What about, darling?"

I grit my aching teeth as I play it back in my head, then get to the long and short of it. "Connor. He's an asshole. He set me up." I give them a brief overview of meeting up with him and the trap he set with the paps. "I hate him," I force out through choked sobs. "I hate him so much. And I hate all of them for believing him. I hate everyone for believing him."

My mums make a few comforting sounds, allowing me the time to cry. When my breathing starts to settle, Mãe speaks. "I am so sorry he has hurt you, Cubby. I would do anything—*anything*—to take your pain away."

"I know," I whisper, scrubbing my nose.

"But you cannot hang on to all this hate, my girl. Your heart is too beautiful to let the anger and hatred fester."

"He's not worth your pain or your heartbreak," Mum adds.

"What if you're wrong?" I sit up in the tub, more tears falling.

"Wrong about what?"

"My heart. You called it beautiful. What if you're wrong? What if it's not?"

There's a pause. "I don't understand, Cubby. How could it not be?"

My breathing turns jagged again. "My heart isn't beautiful. No part of me is. All I have in me is this massive, aching sadness. It's bleak and sticky and leaves me too numb to do *anything* beautiful with my stupid heart."

The silence stretches, and I close my eyes, rocking myself back and forth.

"Cubby, we had no idea you felt this low. How long has this been going on?"

I shrug, even though I know they can't see it. I don't have an answer. Even as a little kid, I've grappled with a heavy sort of . . . *bleakness*. Something in me that has the power to drain the vividness from life if I give it too much space in my brain. But I've always been good at tucking it away, plastering on a smile so other people wouldn't see that I'm a hollowed-out shell.

"I've been having a really hard time since Connor broke up with me last year," I admit, voice small. "And before that too, I guess. When we were still dating. It always felt so . . . hard. So draining." My mums are quiet again, but now that I've eased the cork off the powder keg, I can't keep words back. "And I feel selfish for feeling so sad. So numb. I don't have a right to it."

"What do you mean?" Mum asks.

"Look at my life. It's not perfect but it's objectively good. You two have always given me so much. I've never once questioned if you love me. I've never had to worry about not having enough to get by. How can I claim this sadness when I've never earned it?"

Mum lets out a deep breath. "Everyone has a right to feel sad even if they haven't experienced some big traumatic hardship, darling. You aren't put on Earth to overcome very natural human conditions, you're here to experience them. Sadness, numbness, bleakness, they're all a part of life. But it sounds like you're existing in those feelings for longer stretches than is healthy."

"When did you realize you liked girls?" I blurt out. My heart stops. Oh *fuck*. I did not mean to ask that.

"W-what?" Mum asks, wrestling with the whiplash.

"Cubby, are you . . ." Mãe clears her throat. "Are you exploring your sexuality? Is that contributing to these feelings?"

I groan, smacking a hand over my eyes. It jostles my swollen cheeks, and I groan again. "Please forget I said anything. My question was awkward enough without that follow-up." There's a beat of silence, then I hear my mums suck in a series of breaths. They're *giggling*. "It's not funny!" I say, my own voice cracking on an indignant laugh. They giggle even harder.

"I'm sorry, I'm sorry," Mãe says, pulling herself together. "I wish you could have seen the look your mum gave me when I asked that. You'd think I'd told the Pope to go to hell she looked so horrified."

"You can't dive in headfirst with your emotionally distraught child like that! Have some finesse, woman," Mum argues, still laughing.

"I imagine Mum's expression was pretty similar to mine." I trace the shower tiles with my nails, silently praying they'll answer my question.

"I've known for as long as I can remember noticing other people," Mãe says. "Even as a child, those innocent little crushes were always girls. It actually was very shocking to me to find out that some women are attracted to men. Your mum's experience was quite different, though."

Mum hums in agreement. "I realized a lot later. It wasn't until I was probably twenty-seven, twenty-eight . . . right before I met Mãe, actually. I only dated men as a teenager and in my early twenties. That was the status quo and I never thought to question it. I didn't have queer friends, no one was openly out in my school . . . It's hard to put a label on a feeling when you aren't given the words to describe it."

I gulp down the emotions starting to spill out of me, but Mum clocks the sound. "Why are you crying, love?"

"I thought this would be easier," I choke out.

"That what would be easier?" Mãe gently probes.

"My . . . my sexuality. I grew up with two mums, how do I not know what I am?"

"Oh my darling, why are you beating yourself up for having questions? For poking around your own brain to understand the wiring?"

All I manage is a frustrated hiccup.

"Growing up with two mums, in theory, and probably in practice, certainly makes you more aware of LGBTQ identities," Mãe says, slowly, like she's weighing each word before she gives it to me. "But that doesn't mean it makes figuring out *your* identity any easier. Your mum and I are in a happy, joyful, queer marriage, but that doesn't mean that everything else you're exposed to doesn't portray heterosexual relationships as the default."

Mum makes a noise of agreement. "TV, movies, books, music videos . . . most of those show a man and a woman. Of course that becomes ingrained as the default. You can't beat yourself up for not rising above society's setup while your brain is still developing."

"I want to have things figured out," I cry. "I'm so sick of being confused about everything. Who I am. What I like. Who I like. It's exhausting."

Mum and Mãe both let out small, kind laughs. "Cubby, my love, I am so sorry to be the one to tell you this, but life is nothing but confusion. Learning to embrace the joy in the awful mess of it all is what makes it worth living."

While that's a beautiful sentiment, it's a bit too sugary and optimistic for me to absorb right now. I want to believe them. I want to trust that all of this is as simple as asking myself a few questions. And, maybe, on a night when I'm not in a fight with the people I care most about (plus Kale) and being ripped apart on social media and sitting in a moldy bathroom crying, it can be that easy. But tonight is not that night.

"I have another problem," I say, needing to change the subject. I'm wrung out, too many feelings and teardrops filling this bathtub I'm curled in.

"What's that, love?"

"I think there's something wrong with my mouth. My jaw hurts so badly."

A confused silence follows, and I snap a quick picture of my puffy, red cheeks and another of the inside of my mouth, which is too dark to really make anything out, but text it to them anyway. They both suck in a breath.

"You need to go to the doctor, Cubby. Something's wrong with you," Mum says in horror.

I snort. "Title of my memoir."

"Cubby, I'm serious."

"I'll handle it," I say, before her panic escalates further. "I've got it under control. I better go."

"Don't ignore this, Cubby."

"I won't," I say as the pain intensifies.

"Thank you for talking to us about this," Mãe says gently. "We love you so much."

And I feel it. Through miles and wires and time zones, I feel their love. I swallow it whole, let it fill me and hold me and carry my voice as I whisper, "I love you too."

Chapter 24

I'm not sure anything is quite as mortifying as making a dramatic *fuck you* exit, then showing up on that person's doorstep a few hours later, but here I am, banging on Kevin's door. I must have left my last shred of dignity somewhere in Ohio.

"Cubby?" Kevin rubs his eyes, voice froggy with sleep. "What's wrong?"

"I'm not quite sure," I garble. "But my cheeks are a bit swollen."

Kevin blinks a few times, then his eyes shoot wide. "Oh shit."

"Oh shit?" I repeat, hands fluttering in front of me. "Don't say *oh shit*. *Oh shit* makes it sound really bad."

"Cubby, it *looks* really bad. Your cheeks aren't *a bit* swollen, they're alarmingly, massively blown up."

"Kevin, that is not at all helpful," I cry, panic mounting.

"I don't know how to be helpful, you look like a bullfrog!"

"You're supposed to be my manager! Managers don't panic and compare their clients to farm animals!"

"They do when said client looks like they took a hook to both sides . . . Also, what kind of farm has frogs as livestock?"

I let out a sharp whine, hot tears rolling down my inflamed cheeks. "What do we do? It feels like someone is twisting a knife into my jaw."

Kevin looks to be on the verge of tears himself, shifting from foot to foot as he bites his nails. "Is it a tooth thing? Should we take you to a dentist? Could it be your wisdom teeth?"

"A dentist? Kevin, I can feel my heartbeat in my jawbone, this is far beyond a dentist."

"They're never helpful, anyway," he mumbles, pulling out his phone. "Charge you for breathing. I got stuck with a five-hundred-dollar bill for my last cleaning. Can you believe that?"

"Can we talk about the inadequacies of American dental insurance later? It feels like my face is about to pop."

"Sorry," Kevin says, looking sheepish. "Give me a sec." He ducks back into the room, closing the door behind him, and I'm left blinking in the hall.

"I'll wait here, then," I mumble, my anxious fingers clawing at the base of my throat like they're desperate to rip out whatever is hurting me.

Kevin appears a minute later, pajama bottoms replaced with jeans, keys in hand. "Come on."

I follow him down the hall, the pain growing sharper, even the feel of air across my cheeks is enough to rip at the nerve endings. I follow him to his car and collapse into the passenger seat. "Where are you taking me?"

"To the emergency room." He revs up the car and pulls out of the extremely tight space. "There's a university nearby, Callowhill, and they have a really good med school or whatever. They should be able to help."

I nod, the pain turning to an echoing throb that travels down my neck and up to my temples. The drive isn't long, but every second is agony. Kevin is frantic, shooting me panicked glances and placing his cold hand on my forehead every few seconds. My mouth hurts so badly I can't even verbalize how annoyed I am. A true medical emergency.

We wait for an hour in the dingy lobby, my head cradled in my hands as I beg any deity listening to make the pain stop. Finally, a nurse calls me back and I'm so delirious I consider worshiping at his feet for a moment.

He takes me to a small room, introducing himself as Dev while taking my blood pressure and temperature.

"One-oh-two," he says, reading the thermometer, then touching around my jaw and neck. I hiss at a tender spot. "Running a bit of a fever. Your lymph nodes are swollen too."

"Am I dying?" I ask hopefully as a fresh new throb shoots through me.

"Open, please," Dev answers, flashing a light in my mouth as I do as he asks. He makes a humming sound. "Do you still have your wisdom teeth?"

I want to make a deprecating joke about not having an ounce of wisdom in my body, but the pain is so intense I give him a pitiful shrug instead. "I guess? I've never had them removed or whatever. Aren't I kind of old for that to be an issue?"

Dev glances at my chart, then shakes his head. "Nah, plenty of twenty-three-years-olds deal with complications. You'd be surprised by how many people in their thirties and forties end up having some sort of problem pop up because they never got them out."

"How comforting. I was worried I was somehow special or unique."

"Nope. Nothing to worry about there. I'm gonna grab an X-ray, then see if the oral surgeon on call can take a look. I think that might be what's causing this."

Dev takes me to a tall X-ray machine at the end of the hall, then sends me back to the room to count each pulsating second as I wait for the doctor.

"He didn't confirm you're dying, so you probably aren't dying," Kevin says, pacing the tiny space in three strides. "I'm fairly sure you aren't dying."

"If you keep stomping like that, you might be the one to kill me. I feel the sound of your footsteps in my cheeks."

He screeches to a halt, plopping down in the nearest chair. A firm rap on the door draws our attention as a woman in a white coat walks in.

"Hi," she says in a calm, soothing voice. "I'm Dr. Harper Horowitz, one of the oral surgeons on staff here. I'll be taking care of you today."

Despite her petite stature and looking rather young, the doctor exudes a commanding presence like she'd love for someone to make her day by questioning her authority. But there's also something inherently kind and warm about her, deep compassion in her alert eyes.

I decide I like her.

"Tell me a bit about what's going on," she says, rolling up her chair to where I'm perched on the table and giving me her full attention.

I launch into an abbreviated account of being in so much pain for the past few hours I simultaneously want to puke and die. For some reason, I find myself crying at the end. It's not a dignified, quiet type of crying either. It's a sobbing, wracking type of crying that has snot pouring from my nose and tears trailing down my swollen cheeks to my neck.

Dr. Horowitz takes my hand in both of hers, holding tightly and drawing soothing circles on the back with her thumb. I'm so mortified, I use my free hand to cover my face, unable to stop blubbering. It isn't just from the pain. The pain pushed me over the edge, beat me up on my way to rock bottom, but it's everything.

It's the stupid tabloids and the stupid band and stupid Harry and stupid Darcy and my stupid, confusing love for her. It's my hate for

Connor and my anger at the world and my silly, pathetic feelings being crushed over and over again.

It's life hurting so badly I've forgotten what it's like to feel good.

"I'm so sorry you're in pain," Dr. Horowitz says quietly. I know she means my teeth, but it soothes me like she means my everything.

"Thank you," I mumble, wiping roughly at my eyes.

"Do you mind if I take a look? Try to figure out what's going on?"

I nod, and she gets to work, repeating a lot of the same touches Dev did. She rolls over to her laptop on the counter, pulling up an X-ray of my mouth stretched like the grin of a scary clown.

"Pretty classic presentation of abscessed wisdom teeth," she says, tilting the screen so Kevin and I can both see. "Your lower third molars are partially impacted, and the overgrowth of gum tissue around them has led to a pretty bad infection on both sides of your mouth, hence the fever and swelling."

"Can I take antibiotics?" I ask, pressing the backs of my hands to my hot cheeks.

"Definitely. But that isn't a great long-term solution. You need these out. And soon."

"How soon?" Kevin asks, biting his nails.

Dr. Horowitz glances at her watch. "As soon as you're able. I wouldn't want to be walking around with an infection this bad in my mouth." I let out a little whimper of terror, and she has the decency to pretend she didn't hear me. She's literally an angel. "Let me go check with the triage nurses to see if we have an emergency spot open." She walks out of the room, clicking her pen as she goes.

It isn't until Kevin is in front of me, shifting his weight from side to side as he looks at me with a panic-stricken expression that I realize I'm crying again. This overt display of emotion is more traumatizing than the literal trauma in my mouth.

"It'll be okay, Cubby," Kevin finally says, surprising us both and giving me a hug. It's a bit awkward and stiff at first, but slowly, I soften into it, hugging him back.

I realize it's the first meaningful touch I've had in quite some time, and I forgot how much I needed it. Harry's kissed me and touched me onstage the past couple of weeks, but that's more confusion than comfort, both of us actors in some awful play trying to decipher reality from fiction.

This hug from Kevin isn't a Darcy hug—it isn't like plugging my drained battery into a charging port, sighing in relief at the contact— but it at least reminds me I'm not alone.

"I have some good news," Dr. Horowitz says, coming back into the room. Kevin pats my back, then steps away. "It's been a pretty calm night, and we can do it in an hour if you're okay with that."

My heart races, and I blink at her. "An hour? Like . . . in the sixty minutes type of the word?"

Dr. Horowitz nods, pressing her lips together and schooling her features when I can tell she wants to laugh.

"Would you . . . What happens during the, um, procedure?" I ask, digging my nails into the skin at my collarbones like I can hold on for dear life.

Dr. Horowitz turns serious again, fixing me with a steady gaze. "We'd put you under—you can be awake if you'd prefer, but I don't recommend it—and we'll extract the impacted wisdom teeth. I personally think if we're going in for these bottom two, we might as well extract the uppers as well before they cause problems."

Okay, so I thought I liked this woman, but now she's talking about ripping out four of my teeth and I'm far less comfortable in her presence.

"And . . . and . . . I feel like I should have questions. I feel like I should ask you a million questions if you are about to literally harvest my mouth bones from my body, but I can't think of any." I shoot a desperate glance at Kevin.

"She's a singer in a band," he says, slipping into his role as manager. "Will she be able to sing after the surgery?"

Dr. Horowitz purses her lips. "Technically speaking, the procedure doesn't impact your vocal folds at all, so she could sing right after. But there will likely be some discomfort and swelling, so I'd give it at least a week before really pushing it. Resting goes a long way when it comes to healing."

My face twists in panic. We're supposed to play four shows over the next week. I open my mouth to protest, but Kevin places his hand on my shoulder.

"Don't worry about it, I'll handle rescheduling," he murmurs. "Let's get you well."

I think about arguing, but then I remember the fight with everyone earlier, and realize Kevin might not even have a band to manage at his point.

"Are you okay to move forward with the surgery?" Dr. Horowitz asks.

I glance at Kevin and he shrugs helplessly. With a sigh, I nod.

Things move quickly after that, filling out paperwork and signing consents. I text my family group chat with a very brief synopsis, and both my mums proceed to call me and, when I don't pick up, send about five hundred worried texts. The one from Oliver really makes me laugh.

I'm sorry about your teeth and good luck with the surgery but please remove me from this group text because the excessive amount of notifications woke me up.

Love you too, Ol, I type back. He sends me a rainbow of hearts.

I think about messaging Darcy. Part of me desperately wants her here. I stare at her name on my screen until my eyes go fuzzy, but I can't allow myself to be vulnerable. I can't risk the embarrassment, no matter how much I need her.

Too soon, I'm escorted to a surgical room. Kevin is supposed to wait in the check-in area, but I refuse to let go of his hand, and the exhausted nurses don't put up much of a fight. The rapid beep of my heart rate on the monitor does nothing to settle my nerves, and my eyes flick around the busy room, the nurses and Dr. Horowitz laying out terrifying forceps and medieval-looking metal tools. My head starts spinning when they bring out the needle for my IV, hovering it over the crook of my elbow like a bee ready to sting. I bite into my lip in anticipation, but commotion in the hall draws our attention.

Through the tiny window in the door, I see a messy bun of blond and pink hair, hear a voice I'd recognize anywhere traveling through the wood. "I need to be in there with her."

"Ma'am, we've already told you, they're about to start, and it's family only to be in the actual room."

"Bullshit. I'm more her family than Kevin in there."

"Can someone get that handled?" the nurse holding the IV needle yells, then sticks me. I'm too confused to really register the bite of pain. I turn my wide-eyed gaze to Kevin.

"I texted her," he says, placing his hand on my shoulder. "I figured you'd want her here. That she'd want to be here."

Christ, I'm going to cry again, aren't I?

"Here we go, dear," Dr. Horowitz says, plugging a plastic tube holding a milky liquid into the open end of my IV. "Take a few deep breaths and count back from ten."

She might as well ask me to recite the *Iliad* in ancient Greek for how jumbled my head is.

The door squeaks open. "Sir, we're going to need you to exit the room and get this young woman under control. She claims she knows you."

Kevin steps toward the exit, and I want to reach out to him, grab his hand and make him stay. Make him explain the confusion that's filling my head like a swarm of hornets.

But my limbs are droopy and my eyelids heavy, vision swimming. I force my lids open, trying to see through the haze. I make out the pink hair again. Fighting against the drugs, her features fit into place like fuzzy puzzle pieces. The last one to slot into focus is her mouth, those full lips dropping open. My name rolling off her tongue.

My body doesn't belong to me anymore, but I feel myself smile all the same. I'll always smile at Darcy.

Then everything goes black.

Chapter 25

My forehead bouncing against cool glass tugs me out of the ether. A string of curse words muttered by someone next to me punctuates every hit, and I slit my eyes open, fuzzy light squeezing in.

Huh . . . I didn't expect to wake up in a spaceship. I don't remember being abducted by aliens, but, for some reason, it feels rather fitting.

"Take me to your leader," I mumble, voice rough as gravel as I continue to squint through the glass, my head spinning.

A tiny laugh echoes back to me. I didn't know aliens laughed. That's so cute.

"What are you on about now?"

Funny, that alien sounds a lot like my best friend.

With a deep breath, I open my eyes further, halfway at least (I'm so brave). Refocusing them from their bleary state, I stare first at my bandaged-up reflection, then out a moving spaceship window. How strange . . . Outer space looks a lot like a four-lane road, trees and the occasional wooden stand blurring past.

"All right?" the alien says in that far-too-familiar voice.

"D-Darcy?" I garble out, blinking at a series of signs that appear to be advertising pyrotechnics.

"Yes, Cubby love?"

I swallow through my dry throat, tongue and cheeks feeling thick and puffy. "Where are we?"

"About an hour into a state called New Jersey."

New Jersey . . . My head is still fogged, and my cheeks feel swollen like overripe plums, but that doesn't seem quite right. Outer space shouldn't have a place called New Jersey.

"Darcy?" I whisper again, closing my eyes as a dizzy spell curls my senses.

"Cubby?"

"Are you an alien kidnapping me?"

I know Darcy well enough that I can sense her every smile, and this one is wide. "Obviously."

A few minutes pass, the fuzzy streak of green out my window slowly shimmering into focus, sunshine poking through the foliage.

"Darcy?" I say once more, slanting a glance at her next to me, her jaw tense and hands gripping the steering wheel with white knuckles. An overwhelming sense of urgency floods through me. "Do you think other planets have trees? Do you think those trees tell secrets?"

"Cubby, as much as I *love* chatting with you—especially when you're high as a kite—I am fighting for my life to drive on the correct side of the road in this backward country."

"Whose car is this?" I ask, still loopy but more grounded in reality. I scan the interior. It's not luxury by any means, but has a decent stereo and leather seats. Practical with a touch of comfort. I highly doubt any car rental would hand it out to a twenty-two-year-old who struggles to meet even her homeland's traffic laws.

"Kevin got it sorted for us. Same with your hospital bill."

The surgery, and the pain leading up to it, comes back to me in a jolt, and I groan, gingerly poking my cheeks and the bandage wrapped from the crown of my head to under my chin. "God, what a nightmare."

"Yeah, I'll say. You scared the shit out of me. Are you okay?"

She risks a look at me when I don't immediately answer, our gazes locking for the first time since I went under. Her hands tighten on the steering wheel, and my heart speeds up.

I could look at her forever, that face more familiar than my own—the tiny scar on her forehead from an accident when she was a toddler, the dusting of freckles across her nose—but I instinctively glance at the road when it seems she won't be the one to do it.

"I'm okay," I say at last. It's the truth and a lie. But in this moment, alone with Darcy with my raw cheeks and misty senses, I really am okay. "Feels weird to have my mouth organs harvested."

"I don't think teeth are considered organs."

"Of course they are, they have nerves and a blood supply."

"That isn't what makes an organ an organ."

"Then what *does* make an organ an organ?"

Darcy throws up one hand. "I don't know. A bodily function? A purpose?"

"I'm sorry, do you not chew? That seems like a pretty important bodily function. If they aren't an organ, they should be."

She lets out a tiny laugh. "Why do I feel like Skull would have a lot to add to this conversation?"

"You just *know* he has some outlandish special interests." A smile tugs at the corner of my lips.

"Oh, for sure. We'd know all about them at this point if he didn't refrain from speaking for five to seven business days at a time . . . I love that weirdo."

"I do too," I say, meaning it. We sit in silence for a few moments, and dread weaves through me as I remember our fight. I clear my throat. "Where's everyone else?"

"Remember Harry's cousin, Joe?" Darcy's mouth kicks up in a

cheeky smile. "The really fit fella that used to visit him in the summer?"

"The one with the hot—"

"Half sleeve? It's a full now."

I groan.

"Anyway, he's in grad school at some uni outside of Philadelphia. Harry popped over for a visit."

"What's he studying?"

"Fine art, I think Harry said."

"That man is the embodiment of fine art. Does he just study himself?"

"I would, if I looked like that. I'd never leave the mirror."

I snort. "As if you aren't every bit as stunning." There's a long beat of silence, tension pulling my skin tight like a rubber band as I regret ever learning to speak.

"Kale went to see his folks in Ohio," Darcy says, taking mercy on me. "Skull is . . . Well, to be honest, I'm not sure where that enigma slinked off to, but I'm sure he's having a grand old time with Tiny Deja, wherever they might be."

My stomach pinches. "Are we . . . are we broken up?"

Darcy does a double take. It takes me a moment to piece together that she couldn't tell if I was talking about the band or . . .

She lets out a long sigh. "I think we all need a bit of breathing room from each other."

"They hate me." I turn back to the window, cursing the lovely blue skies and brilliant sunshine. It's a barbed pill to be so miserable on a beautiful day.

"Don't be dramatic. No one hates you."

"The entire internet hates me." A lump knots in my throat. It must be the drugs that have me so touchy.

Darcy purses her lips, tapping the turn signal before merging. "You don't fare well in the court of public opinion, I'll give you that much."

"Not sure I fare very well in our band either."

Darcy's sigh is empty of patience, and I'm surprised to see the anger flash in the look she shoots at me. "That right there. That's your problem."

Defensiveness is my default. "My *problem*?"

"You act like we're out to get you like the rest of the world."

"I'm sorry, but after our fight yesterday it kind of feels like you all might be."

Darcy looks at me again, this time her face falling in a pained expression so genuine, my chest aches. "Yesterday was . . . not good," she concedes, glancing back to the road. "We were all caught off guard and exhausted and moody and didn't handle it well. But you should have told us. It wasn't fair we found out how we did. We all love you. We wouldn't follow you around this bloody country if we didn't."

"Follow me around? How are you following me around? We're all equal members of this group."

"In theory, yes, but have you noticed we tend to crumble to pieces the same moments you do? You're our *leader*, Cub. Whether you like it or not. Whether you believe you're worthy of it or not." I go to argue but she cuts me off. "Music doesn't get made without your spark, your light. But your defenses are up so damn high all the time, you keep us in the dark instead."

I shake my head, emotions pulling me deep under. Her compliments bruise more than criticism. If I stop to listen to them, I may actually start to believe what she's saying, and that would make life hurt all the more. If I hate myself the most, it doesn't matter how much anyone else does.

"I'm nothing without you. There wouldn't be any music without *you*. I'm nothing more than a buzzkill," I mumble.

Darcy's cheeks flush a deep crimson with frustration, and I'm worried she's about to curse it all to hell and swerve us into a tree to get me to stop my incessant self-loathing. "Do we each have our strengths?

Of course. Harry regularly makes me cry with even a basic melody. Kale could be in a professional orchestra if he wanted. Skull has one of the keenest senses of musicality I've ever witnessed. But together? That's when it shines. That's when it's the brightest. And we all want that so desperately. And we want that *with you*. So stop getting in the way of it with your chronic pity parties."

"What about you?"

Darcy flinches. "What about me?"

"You mentioned the strengths of everyone else. What about *you*?"

She shrugs. "I don't know. I'm not bad on the bass. I keep you in line . . . sometimes. Not bad traits to bring to the table."

I scoff.

"What?" she says, voice icy. "Do you have something to say to me?" She keeps her glare fixed on me for so long, I have to reach over and turn her face back to the road.

"It's interesting you can say nice things about everyone else, but not yourself when you're the one that deserves the most praise. You're the best person I've ever met."

She's quiet for so long, I start to wonder if she'll ever talk to me again. At the GPS's sudden urging, she gets off the freeway and we pass an old wooden sign welcoming us to Cape May.

We navigate for a few more minutes down quiet side streets, eventually turning into the drive of a small, Victorian-style home. It's painted various shades of pink like a Valentine's heart. We face forward, staring at the house, the engine's hum the only noise.

"Rented this for a bit," Darcy says, not looking at me. She lets out a sad laugh. "I mean, *I* didn't rent it, Kevin convinced Sigrún to put it on the company's tab for you to recuperate. But it's ours for now."

I nod, swallowing past a dry throat, nausea brutally churning my stomach. I don't want to go in there. I'm so sick of sharing spaces with Darcy when we aren't ourselves. It creates a caustic ache in my bones, permeating out until my skin itches with it.

"Very nice," I murmur.

"I don't think I'm a good person at all," Darcy says suddenly, jaw set, hands still clenched around the steering wheel as her eyes bore a hole into the happy-looking house. I blink at her, tracing back the conversation. She's so tight, so uncomfortably wound, it makes my own muscles clench. I reach across the center console, turning the keys and cutting the engine, dropping us into pure silence.

After a moment's hesitation, I place my hand on hers, coaxing her grip to loosen.

"You are a good person," I whisper. It's one of the only truths I know. The moon orbits the earth, the earth orbits the sun, Darcy is a good person. They're all fundamental truths. "Why do you think you aren't?"

After a moment, her neck releases like it weighs a ton, head bowing forward as a small tremble ripples through her. I'm surprised to see tears tracing down her cheeks, landing in dark stains on her lap.

"Because . . ." A whimper breaks from her throat. I drag my hand up her arm to rub circles along the center of her back. She sucks in a shaky breath, then looks at me, mascara smeared, face red. She's so lovely it's staggering.

"Because why?" I lean toward her. She's poised there, on the edge of vulnerability. I'm right there too, gripping on to her, following whatever direction this goes—the safety of solid ground or the tumble off the cliff.

She licks her lips then bites the lower, the weight of the words dangling at the tip of her tongue bearing down on both of us. My hand traces up her neck until I cup her cheek. She nuzzles into my touch, eyes closing.

Somewhere close by, a car door slams, starting a frenzy of barking from the neighborhood dogs. Darcy jumps, wrenching away from me. Like the extinguishing of a candle, the intensity in her expression snuffs out, all the raw honesty disappearing like smoke.

"Sorry," she says, eyes back on the house. "I didn't mean to get all weird out of nowhere. Let's get inside; check the place out."

Before I can say anything—any desperate attempt to tug her back into our golden bubble where we say the things we think and mean them fully—she gets out of the car and unloads our bags, trudging up the walkway and into the silly pink house, leaving me with my blue heart in my hand and a lump in my throat, wondering if I'll ever get my Darcy back.

Chapter 26

"I'm going to tell you something you don't want to hear," Darcy says by way of good morning the next day, banging open the door to my room and standing disheveled like a banshee in the frame. It's absolutely mortifying how much my heart lurches at the sight of her.

I let out a long sigh. "Oh good. I was just thinking, 'You know what? I haven't received enough bad news lately.'"

Darcy rolls her eyes. "You don't have to be reserved all the time, you know. It must be exhausting to be *so* understated and undramatic in your approach to life."

She pads across the room to my bed, nudging me over before sliding in next to me and wriggling close. My pulse picks up like the wagging tail of an overeager puppy greeting its owner. Feelings are so embarrassing.

"What awful thing are you here to tell me?" I ask, resting my head on her shoulder despite knowing better. Her gravity is too strong for me to resist.

"We need to work on the love song for the festival. It's ten days away and we don't have anything usable."

"Kindly go fuck yourself," I say in the sweetest voice I can muster.

Her laugh bounces my swollen cheek against her arm and I wince, rolling away.

"Oh Cubby love, I'm so sorry," she says, turning on her side toward me. Her eyes are filled with worry, hands fluttering close to my skin but not touching.

"S'fine," I mumble, squeezing my eyes shut. Not from the pain in my mouth, but from the way she's looking at me. So soft and caring and like my hurt hurts her too. I need to stop seeing things in her face that aren't there.

"Will waffles make it better?" Darcy asks in a low whisper.

My eyes flash open. "I let you get away with a lot of crap, Darcy Burton, but don't you dare toy with me about the possibility of waffles."

She laughs again, nose scrunching up and dimple peeking out. "I wouldn't dream of it. I saw a mix in the pantry and there's a Belgian waffle maker on the counter. Place is pretty well stocked with food."

A needy noise escapes from my throat right as my stomach growls.

"I'll take that as a yes." She gets out of bed, taking a moment to stretch next to the mattress, and I instinctively scoot toward her, chasing the warmth she left on the sheets. "I'll go get started."

"Meet you down there."

"One condition." She plants her hands on either side of my shoulders, leaning close as she traps me with her gaze. Her breath travels over my lips, and my tongue traces the sensation, my pulse pounding and every nerve ending standing at attention at her proximity. I lift an eyebrow, trying to be cool. "After I pump you full of sugar, we have to work on the song for the festival."

"You're evil," I whine, half-heartedly trying to roll away. She keeps me caged, grinning as she tickles the tip of her nose against mine.

"The absolute worst," she says in delightful agreement, then turns and skips out of the room.

Despite waffles being god-tier-level food, they apparently don't help much with inspiration. We've been at it for hours, strumming our instruments and groaning in frustration as nothing sticks.

"*This is ass,*" I sing, playing a C chord from where I'm sprawled on the oversized chair in the living room.

"*You're just being difficult,*" Darcy sings back, plucking her bass.

"*No, love songs are stupid and everything is pointless and life is meaningless,*" I garble, my face still swollen from the surgery.

"*What rhymes with meaningless?*" Darcy trills.

"*Penis puss,*" I respond with bravado. We both giggle.

"*Now you're being difficult as well as disgusting,*" she croons.

For once, I'm not being obstinate on purpose. I know what this song should be, what people want it to be—some deep, meaningful confessional, about Harry and how he's fulfilled me in ways Connor never could. It's supposed to be about a sweeping romance and pale blue eyes and a guy I'd risk it all for.

It makes me itch, trying to attach that to Harry, when who I really want is here with me, lying on the floor, legs propped on the couch, bass almost bigger than her body as her fingers move along the slender neck of the instrument.

No matter what I do—however much I try to tune Darcy out, pluck her from my mind—she reappears with a lightning strike every time I try to tap into the lyrical part of my brain.

I sigh, setting my guitar to the side and then sliding to the carpet. "I'm calling it for the day. Muses aren't musing." More like I can't keep thinking about my muse or I'll get sad(der) and horny(er) and probably start to cry.

"I know what will inspire us," Darcy says, setting aside her bass and crawling across the carpet to rest her head next to mine, feet pointed in the opposite direction. I swivel to look at her, and she's already staring at me, a devious smile on her lips. She drops her forehead to mine and whispers, "Wanna watch *Bridgerton*?"

"I'm ready for Anthony Bridgerton to stop being a gentleman," Darcy says as the character cites for the thousandth time that that's the reason he has decided to create seven episodes of sexual tension instead of just kissing Kate Sharma.

"I'm ready for him to take his pants off," I add through a mouthful of pizza. Darcy cut it up into tiny bites for me so I wouldn't hurt my extraction sites.

"That too," she agrees. "Kate as well. Honestly, the entire cast, crew, and ensemble while we're at it."

"God bless the female gaze." We high-five, then giggle, our bodies vibrating together from our snuggled spot on the couch. The sofa is huge, more nest than normal seating arrangement, but we've sequestered ourselves to a corner of it, tucked up tight with blankets and pillows. It all feels so normal, so wonderful—this irresistible closeness like muscle memory, even after months of trying to break it. I'm terrified of this charge of happiness looping through my body after going so long without it.

Touch used to be second nature for us. A hug. Holding hands while we ran down the hallways at school. Legs tangled in front of us as we played music back and forth. Cuddled close as we ate junk food and watched movies on so many nights like this. I wish I could pinpoint the moment when touching her became so . . . *raw*. So brutally vivid. Like I'm plugging myself into a circuit board, something warm and terrifying running through me.

If I knew the moment, maybe I could go back to it, disarm the memory like a bomb, rework the wires of it so all of these touches didn't turn me inside out with nostalgia for a life I'll never have.

As if this isn't our fifth rewatch, we both shriek in horror at the dramatic ending to episode seven, rabidly hitting buttons on the remote to start the season finale. It takes about ninety seconds for us both to start crying at the drama on the screen.

"I needed this," Darcy says softly, snuggling closer. Her arms are wrapped around my middle, cheek pressed above my heart, while I toy with the ends of her hair. "No one else I'd rather binge-watch with."

"Me too," I say, so many unspoken words chafing my throat.

God, I want to tell her. Want to turn her face to look up at me and pour out every overwhelming feeling I have for her, exorcise all these soft, scary thoughts. Make her hear the awful, remarkable truth of it so I don't have to be the only one to carry it. I want to tell her that I can't stop thinking about her and that night and the stupid things we did and that stupid kiss from years before. I want to ask her if she ever thinks about it too. If she thinks about me in the almost painful way I think about her. And, if she doesn't, I want to ask how I can stop turning back to these thoughts as often as I do.

She picks up my hand, absentmindedly turning the rings around my fingers as she watches the TV, my eyes fixed on only her. I love the little divot at her wrist, the way her veins and tendons track the music living in her hands down to the callouses on her fingertips. I love the way they feel against me. I hate how I can never tell her this.

I love my best friend so much, I worry who I'd be without her, without this love that eats me whole, tethers me to Earth. I'd rather be on the sidelines of her life, growing numb around this aching heart of mine, than risk losing her entirely over a silly, devastating crush.

"I'm sorry I didn't stick up for you in Philadelphia," she says softly, eyes still fixed on the screen.

She doesn't look at me, her jaw clenched and eyes creased. I see the hurt there, the way it pulls her muscles taut with regret. I shrug, clearing my throat.

"It's okay," I whisper back. "You already apologized yesterday."

She surprises me by sitting up, grabbing the remote, and turning off the TV.

"No I didn't." She stares at me, brow furrowed and lips pinched like it's the first time she's seen me in months. "And it's not okay." The crack in her voice is as sharp as a knife. "It's all right for you to admit I hurt you. That I messed up. That doesn't make you weak."

"It makes the hurt worse," I admit, barely above a whisper.

"How?"

I swallow a few times, words getting tangled in my throat. "If I admit I'm hurt to someone else, I have to admit it to myself— acknowledge the pain—then it will fester and grow and stink. Why would I do that?"

"Did you ever think that admitting someone hurt you would let the wound heal?"

I shake my head, not because the thought never occurred to me, but because I know it won't work. I don't want it to. I *want* to hang on to these wounds from Darcy. They're horrible reminders of how deeply I feel for her. If I let them go, let them scab and scar over, numb to any sensation, I'll lose this last bit I have of her, poignantly sharp and damning. It's sick, but I refuse to give that up.

"I'm sorry," she says again, one hand gingerly reaching out to cup my cheek. Every nerve ending reroutes to where she touches me, the brush of her fingers cool against the heat of my skin. "I don't want you to forgive me easily. I want you to acknowledge I hurt you . . . keep hurting you." She goes quiet for a long time, her thumb brushing away the tears streaming down my face. "But I also want you to know I'm going to work to make things right."

I bite my lip, trying to look away, but she doesn't let me, giving my earlobe a gentle tug until my eyes are back on her, until she can see every cracked-open, raw emotion playing across my face.

"I'm not going to hurt you anymore, Cubby love," she says, a few tears of her own rolling down her cheeks. "I promise."

Chapter 27

My phone has gone missing.

Or, more accurately, it's been—

"I didn't steal your stupid phone," Darcy grits out for the third time this morning, hovering over me as I look under her mattress. Nothing but dust bunnies. "Can we please get to work?"

"Not until I find it," I say, sliding on my belly to look under her nightstand.

"If you find it, you'll just sit there scrolling on it being distracted and miserable. We might as well use this time to get some actual work done."

"Joke's on you, I'll be distracted and miserable regardless."

"I'm serious, Cubby. Leave it. We have to get working. We need to have something to send everyone in a few days so they can start getting their parts together."

The only thing I want to do less than work on this love song is have any sort of conversation or confrontation with the band after how we left things.

"Let me check the couch again." I scramble to my feet, hightailing it out of Darcy's room and into the den.

I'm about to lift the cushions for the umpteenth time when my toe catches on the leg of the coffee table, a sharp and bright burst of pain shooting up my leg. I cry out, crumpling to my knees, scraping my shin along the pointed corner of the table as I go. Every curse word in the books shoots out of my mouth as I bury my head against the edge of the love seat.

A stubbed toe shouldn't break me like this but goddammit why is everything such an ordeal? Why can't *one thing* go smoothly? I'm so frustrated, so tired of having to work so hard every single moment, and I want to scream at how utterly pathetic I am.

I bite into a pillow instead, the sharp, horrible feelings only growing.

I'm overwhelmed and tired and my mouth aches and my head is filled with bees and I'm sick of traveling and I'm stir-crazy after only being here two nights and I'm wrung out from tiptoeing back into closeness with Darcy when I know it's going to leave me broken again. I'm homesick for Iceland and homesick for my home home. I miss being a little kid and having someone else take care of everything, every decision, every meal, every step. I'm desperate to be left the hell alone and make my own way and be my own person without the scrutiny of the world and I'm so sick of feeling like I'm missing my life. I never know what I'm waiting for, *wanting for*, but the hunger of it carves away at me.

"Cubby," Darcy says, her footsteps quickening. She gently pulls me to her, and I go without a fight. "It's okay. Everything will be okay."

I don't say anything. I don't nod or agree or tell her I'm fine or that I'm being ridiculous. She knows it. I know it. I cry anyway.

Eventually, I lift my head from the base of her throat, scrubbing my cheeks with the back of my hands.

"I'm worried about you," Darcy whispers.

"I'm kind of worried about me too," I admit with a wet, humorless laugh. My throat tries to lock around my next words, keep them in, but I speak up. "I think I might be a little depressed."

This isn't exactly news, but I've always been afraid of admitting to the label out loud. It felt dark and ugly. A secret word to keep buried deep. *Sadness* is easier to say, with its sibilant softness, the universality of the experience. It doesn't make people flinch if you mention it. Depression is a diagnosis, one I'm scared to commit to, holding on to some fruitless hope that I can white-knuckle my way out of the numbness that often outweighs my simple sadness.

Saying it out loud, handing it over to another person to carry or recoil at, is terrifying.

Darcy's hands ease my rough ones away, and her thumbs brush my continued stream of tears. I blink a few times, then, with a deep breath, look at her.

She smiles at me, soft and simple. "No shit, love."

Silence stretches for the span of a heartbeat, then we start laughing. We're quiet at first, our shoulders shaking. Then our entire bodies. Next thing I know, we're tipping over on the floor, laughing so hard we're gasping for breath, our temples pressed together and hands locked in a hold.

When our giggles die down, Darcy turns her head to look at me. She reaches out, brushing a fallen strand of hair off my forehead and tucking it behind my ear.

"I have an idea," she whispers, a secret smile, all for me, curling her lips. "Will you go somewhere with me for a surprise?"

"It's rather demented you would use this to blindfold me," I say, dragging my finger across the gauzy fabric wrapped around my eyes, the same one the oral surgeon sent me home with to keep ice packs tied to my cheeks.

Darcy huffs. "Reducing, reusing, and recycling is actually very hot girl of me."

"I don't think that applies to medical materials."

"God, Cubby, are you *trying* to get canceled?"

I reach out, trying to shove her shoulder, but I make full contact with her boob. I jerk my hand back so fast I end up smacking myself in the still-tender cheek. I am ready for a black hole to swallow me up, thanks.

"I'm done with this," I mumble, ripping the bandage/blindfold off.

Darcy lets out a shrill whine. "Cubby, no! Put that back on. This is supposed to be a surprise."

"This entire town is four square kilometers, how big of a surprise can it be? I'm not really expecting the Empire State Building here."

"You might recognize a street from when we drove in."

"I was high as a kite!"

"Fine," Darcy says, nicking a curb as she makes a sharp turn into a parking lot and slamming on the brakes as she pulls into a spot. "Ruin the fun. See if I care."

I blink at her. "You are being so dramatic."

"And you're contrary for the hell of it," she says back, crossing her arms over her chest and fixing me with a glare.

"Something you've agreed to accept after over two decades of friendship."

We continue to frown at each other, but colorful movement out the windshield snags my attention. I tilt my head for a better look at the red building we're parked in front of.

"*Ice cream*? You made this big of a deal out of an *ice cream* run?"

"A *surprise* ice cream run," she says indignantly, her dirty look turning into an adorable pout. "And the surprise also includes eating it on the beach, so . . . there."

Our gazes hook, and we break into smiles.

"You're absurd." I lean across the center console to give her a hug. She smells like summertime and sunshine. She laughs, giving me a squeeze before letting go. It feels like my heart stays stuck next to hers as she gets out of the car and walks to the door.

I secure us a bench around back, facing out onto the rocky shore of Higbee Beach. The waves curl up the shore in a steady rhythm, the sound lulling me into momentary peace. I always wonder what waves are reaching for—their relentless charge at the sand, their inevitable retreat. It seems sad that a wave's purpose is only to crash.

"Here ya go." Darcy hands me a strawberry scoop as she plops next to me.

"What'd you get this time?" I ask, mid-lick, nodding at her similarly pale pink swirl.

"Strawberry shortcake," she says before dragging her tongue around the ice cream.

I balk at her. "That totally goes against our pattern!"

"What's our pattern?"

"I get strawberry and you get some wild, outlandish flavor, and we steal bites."

"I'll still be stealing bites from you."

"Why? We got the same thing."

"No, no. Strawberry shortcake is *loads* different than plain strawberry." She reaches over, licking the top of my scoop, then gives me a look as though she somehow proved her point.

"Still too close." I steal a bite of hers. They're identical. "You say you like variety."

"Maybe I wanted to follow your lead today," she murmurs, eyes still fixed on me. They slip to my lips then back up, and I catch a glimmer in the midnight blue that makes my stomach flip, heart beating up into my throat.

But I'm imagining it. Imagining some hidden meaning that's absolutely not there.

"So, was this a good idea or was this a good idea?" she asks after a few minutes of silence, gesturing broadly at the shore.

"Don't give yourself too much credit. We long ago agreed ice cream is always a good idea."

"Would you say ice cream is a better idea than pizza?"

I take another bite as I weigh this incredibly important question. "Well, it largely depends on the emotional state of the person coming up with the idea."

"Interesting. Let's say the person is anxious."

"Pizza."

"Experiencing an existential crisis?"

"Ice cream."

"Stressed?"

"Pizza."

"Angry at the world?"

"Both."

"I guess that takes care of our dinner plans for tonight."

Darcy scooches closer to me on the bench as we giggle, our hips and shoulders pressed together. She closes her eyes and tilts her face to the sky, the sun caressing the barely there freckles across her nose.

"This feels just about perfect," she says with a happy sigh, opening her eyes to look at me.

"Too bad I can't take a picture of us," I say after a few moments, slanting her a glance.

"Yes, too bad you're the only person in the region with access to a mobile device with a camera," she replies with a cheeky grin, pulling out her phone. She presses her cheek to mine as she lifts her arm, our squinting faces filled with sunshine and happiness.

Darcy lowers her arm, head bowed as she looks at the picture. She zooms in. "That's a keeper," she says quietly, placing her phone back in her bag.

We finish up our ice cream in contented silence, breaking it every few minutes to point out a swooping bird or a particularly big wave beyond the break.

"Wanna walk?" Darcy asks, taking my napkin and crushing it into a ball with hers, then chucking it in a bin.

I nod, and we pick our way along the boulders until we reach a long stretch of sand at the water's edge. Most of the coastline is rocky, so the beach isn't particularly crowded, only a few groups of people here and there that we're able to get a decent distance from.

A wave rushes the shore, wrapping around our calves, and we both shriek at the bolt of cold, running hand in hand toward safety. Breaths quick and bright, we glance at each other, and, in a moment of understanding, we race back toward the ocean, chasing the wave as it melts away, screaming and giggling as we go.

When our toes touch the retreating tide, another wave heading toward us, Darcy wraps her arms around my middle, and I hug her back, both of us tripping our way through the shallow water. The froth clears after another break, and something in the water catches my eye.

I untangle from Darcy and lunge as it starts to tumble out toward the sea, dropping to my knees and catching it just in time.

"What is it?" she asks, raising her voice over the wind.

Clutching it close to my chest, I push to standing. Rolling the smooth piece of sea glass between my thumb and forefinger, I hold it up in front of Darcy, her identically colored eyes shining behind it. She smiles as she looks at it.

"The ocean made a little piece of you I can keep with me," I say. Something in her gaze shifts, smile fading, lips parting as she looks at me.

I'm not sure I like that look, whatever emotion is behind it. I shift my gaze away before I actually have to read it, continuing our walk down the shore.

"Not to be a broken record," I say, after a few minutes of silence, "but if you really didn't take my phone, that means I've lost it. I either need to find it or get a replacement soon."

I expect Darcy to say something about helping me look at home or letting me use hers to contact my mums and let them know I won't be easily reachable for a bit. Usually, she's quick with a solution, like she can read my thoughts and already knows how to solve my problems. But her silence hooks my attention, and I look at her.

Her eyes are fixed on the sand.

"Darcy," I say quietly. "Are you sure you don't know where my phone is?"

She lets out a shaky breath. "Don't be mad at me," she says, face still turned away and features creased with guilt. "But I did sort of . . . hide it."

The annoyance is sharp and swift and tinged with mortification. I stop in my tracks, and she does too. "Why would you do that?"

She finally looks at me, eyes pleading. "Because you've been so stressed, and you had surgery and I wanted you to have a few days of the outside world not bothering you."

"You had no right to do that," I snap. "It's stressing me out more not knowing what's going on. What's being said."

"And I think that's pretty damn unhealthy," Darcy says with a raised voice.

"Well, I didn't ask your opinion, did I?"

"You're getting it anyway."

"All I want from you is my phone."

"*Why?*"

"Because it's mine and I want it. End of story."

Darcy scoffs. "What good will it do you?"

Heat flares across my cheeks. "None. But that stupid fucking phone is all I have."

"That's bullshit and you know it."

I glare at her. "It's *not*, actually. I wouldn't expect you to understand."

"Understand what? How much you like torturing yourself? It's sick, Cubby."

I fist my hands in my hair. "No. You know what's sick? How I've lost any control over my life. I have no say in what stories are told about me, what people think, who I'm supposed to be dating, in love with, toying with. What I wear. How it looks. How none of it is good enough. The only thing I have is staying on top of the judgment, knowing where I stand from one second to the next by scrolling those stupid apps. Otherwise, they'll eat me alive. They will tear me apart to the point I cannot recover. If I don't know what's being said, how am I supposed to live my life?"

"A life isn't meant to be lived for the approval of others," she yells, color flooding up her neck and across her chest.

"Lovely sentiment, Plato, but this is the real world, one that raised us on filters and social media and constant validation from strangers on the internet. I find it funny that you're suddenly so far above that when you encouraged me to play into this shit to begin with."

"Because I see it killing you," she says, getting in my face. "Believe it or not, it's pretty easy to parse out the danger of something when the person you care about most in the world is falling victim to it."

"You're so full of shit. Give me my phone."

She shakes her head slowly, face twisting in disgust. "Fine." She fishes through her bag, then shoves it against my chest, walking away.

I fumble it for a second, then get a grip. A part of me wants to drop the damn thing, use my heel to dig it into the sand for good measure, chase after Darcy, and tell her, rationally, I know that she's right but emotionally, I can't figure out a way to stop this brutal spiral.

But I don't. Like the wasted-away husk that I am, I start to click, doing my obsessive rounds of checking apps. Googling my name as I trail after Darcy along the beach as she marches toward the car, my eyes glued to my screen, the blue light fueling my manic obsession to absorb everything I've missed the past few hours.

What shows up makes my stomach drop, mouth going dry and pulse pounding at my temples. The headline reads: D-list diva status: The cringey drama continues.

My vision fuzzes at the edges. I click through and start to read.

While Cubby Clark—lead singer of Tea Time Tantrum—primarily has any claim to fame due to the men she's dated, that hasn't stopped her from fully embracing diva status, walking out on a Philadelphia show one hour before the start time and canceling the next night's performance without even a performative Notes App Instagram apology. The band has further canceled their next four scheduled shows. Clark's team put out a blanket statement about one of the band members needing a break due to a health concern, but it isn't hard to read the signs that Clark is throwing a tantrum of her own . . .

A fist squeezes around each lung, my chest pulling sharp and tight as I try to breathe past the mounting anxiety.

"Fuck," I whisper, scrolling through my notifications. I'm tagged in countless reshares agreeing with the article. "Fuck, fuck, fuck." My throat closes up, stomach pinching.

"I can't watch this anymore."

I glance up, then flinch to find Darcy on me. She rips my phone from my hand.

"Hey!" I lunge forward, trying to get it back, but my legs are wobbly and head woozy.

"You're rotting away," she says, sidestepping me. "I refuse to watch you keep hurting your own feelings."

"Hurting my own feelings? What are you on about? It's the trolls on the internet hurting my feelings."

"You're the one looking." She runs down the slope of sand toward the ocean, and I chase after her. "You're the one seeking it out. Searching your own name. Looking at Connor's profile."

"I . . . I'm tagged in most of it."

"Then change your privacy settings!"

She stops suddenly, and I rip past her, tripping over my feet as I try to turn mid-run, the sand giving out beneath me.

Darcy's a woman possessed, blue eyes blazing in the sunlight. She cocks her arm back, and I gasp as I see—like a waking nightmare—what's going to happen next.

With more force than I thought her small frame capable of, she chucks my phone, the screen lighting up with a notification as it leaves her hand, creating a brilliant arc across the afternoon sky. Landing in the Atlantic Ocean with a *plop*.

I stare for a moment, mouth gaping, then I barrel into the surf. The water cuts me off at the stomach as I trip into a hidden deep spot. I whip around searching for my phone, ducking under the waves and opening my eyes in the murky water to try to find it.

It's no use.

"Are you *mad*?" I screech, resurfacing and turning to Darcy. I start marching—as much as one can march in waist-deep freezing water—toward her.

"You're the one that's sick," she yells back. "I'm not letting you torture yourself anymore."

"Do you have any idea what you just did?" I scramble onto the shore, hands clenched into fists at my sides as I stalk toward her. Darcy has the decency to look a bit scared. She moves backward, away from me.

"I did you a favor."

"A favor? A *favor*? That phone had all our draft lyrics on there!"

Darcy's eyes go absurdly wide, darting about as she continues to back away from me. My pace picks up. "I . . . er . . . Did you not save them to the cloud?"

"I'm going to wring your neck!" I lunge for her and she tries to maneuver away, but I clip her shoulder, knocking us both off balance.

We tumble together, falling to the sand and rolling down the slight incline back toward the water. Darcy ends up on top of me, and she presses my swinging arms to the ground, face centimeters from mine.

"Let me go so I can strangle you," I growl, squirming beneath her. I end up digging myself deeper into the sand.

"*No.*" She presses more of her weight into my wrists. "You know what? I don't even care about the lyrics. I *don't,*" she says over my gasp of outrage. "I would erase every song in the world if it meant bringing you back to me."

I pause my thrashing, heart hammering up to my throat. "W-what?"

Darcy is silent, gaze searching mine. She shakes her head, closing her eyes and letting out a soft breath that dances across my skin. Suddenly, she pushes away from me, rolling off my hips to sit on the sand. "I *miss* you, Cubby," she says, voice jagged.

"I'm right here," I whisper, dragging my eyes from the sky to cautiously look at her. She stares at the shoreline, face lined. "I've been right here."

She shakes her head again. "You know that's not true. You've gone somewhere. I feel like I can't reach you."

My gut twists like a wet dishrag, shame dripping through me. I sit up, facing her, features fixed in anger. Anger is easier than shame. "Well, sorry I've been such a fucking drag. Didn't mean for my feelings to be such a buzzkill."

Darcy's eyes flash to mine, and her face crumples. "Don't insult our friendship—don't insult *me*—by pretending that's what I mean. You know it isn't."

I set my jaw, stacking bricks between us so her words can't hurt me.

Darcy lets out a frustrated growl, shifting to her knees and grabbing my shoulders. "You can't play this game with me. Like it or not, I *know* you, Cubby. I know your quirks and your edges and your too-soft heart. I know how much you love the world, and I know how painful it is to you in return. I know your joy and I know your dark times. And I *care* about you. When you're happy and when you're depressed and any shade in between. But this isn't *you*. This hollowed-out person finding another inch of herself to carve off and hand to strangers on the internet. I'm not going to let any more pieces of you disappear. So fuck your phone and fuck our songs. I don't care about anything but you."

Her words slice me open until I'm bare-boned and shaking. It's too much. I disappear back into anger.

"You want to talk about playing games?" I say, leaning toward her, getting dangerously close to the truth. "Then tell me what's been happening between us for months. You want to talk about disappearing? Where the *fuck* have *you* been, huh? Where did my best friend go? Where has she been this entire summer? Because I sure as hell could have used her help and support."

Her breath trembles, but she doesn't look away. Doesn't let me look away. Her grip tightens on my shoulders, and it spurs me on like a whip.

"Why don't we talk about what happened that night?" My fractured voice echoes between us, crashing like an anvil.

Darcy's lips part, words dangling on their edge, but she shakes her head, eyes wide and glinting with horror.

I wilt, my chest collapsing in on itself. I shrug out of her grip, adjusting my soaked clothes. This is fine. To be expected. *I* am fine. Like she said, I've been hollow these last few months, and however gutted I feel now, I know I can live with it.

It's better to feel numb than alone.

"Do you know why I got so mad when Harry kissed you onstage in Cleveland? Why I avoided talking to you after?"

I glance at her as my brain recalibrates to this new topic. "Um . . . because I accused you of using me after you tried to stick up for me?"

She ducks her head, turning to press her mouth against her shoulder. I can see the deep breath she takes, the way it pushes at her ribs, fills her entirely.

"No," she says at last, eyes flicking back to mine. "I got mad—*furious*—at Harry because he got to do the thing I want more than anything. I was jealous, Cubby."

I blink at her, my heart leaping up to my throat and spinning around like a hopeful tornado.

"I got mad because I want to be the one kissing you," she says, slapping her palm to her chest, something wild in the tension lining her face. "Onstage. In pictures. In dingy dive-bar bathrooms. On our shitty excuse for a bed on that ridiculous tour bus. I was filled with so much jealousy I couldn't even see straight."

I open my mouth, but words fail me. It doesn't matter, she isn't done.

"Then you went ahead and pointed out the bloody truth of the matter, how much I've encouraged this whole ruse, and that made me even madder. At myself. At you. At Harry. And then the kisses kept happening, and watching it night after fucking night felt like having my heart torn out on that stage and ripped into a million pieces."

"Why didn't you say anything?" Emotions claw like feral animals through my chest.

Darcy's face is pure agony, and she laughs. "What was I going to say? 'Hey, Harry, stop snogging my historically platonic best friend because seeing you touch your lips to hers makes me want to rip your face off?"

"Why didn't you say anything to *me*?" I ask, voice rising. "Why haven't you said a word to me about *any* of this? Not that night after the pub or in Cleveland or . . . or . . . You've given me *nothing*, Darcy."

She stares at me, a pleading look in those midnight-blue eyes. A stray tear rolls down her cheek, and I turn away before she has a chance to see my own fall.

"Because I'm scared." Darcy whispers the words—so soft, I could do her the favor of pretending I didn't hear them. Let her go. Not make her confront the questions of a broken, lonely person sitting on a patch of sand next to the ocean that connects us to home.

"Of what?" I ask, never able to leave well enough alone.

"I'm scared of liking you, Cubby," she says with force, hands back on my shoulders, making me look at her and her steady stream of tears. "I'm scared of *how much* I like you. I'm terrified by this huge, indefinable *thing* I feel for you. Because it's so much more than friendship. It has been for years."

I stare at her, my vision blurry as I continue to cry. "*What?*" It's the only word I can manage.

She shakes her head, eyes tilting to the sky, like the correct answer is written up there.

"Why didn't you tell me?" I ask, my hands falling to the dip of her waist, holding on like I'll float away if I let go.

"Aren't you listening?" Darcy says with another sad little laugh. "I'm scared, Cubby. I always have been."

"But of *what?*" I'm desperate to understand, desperate to find a reason for all this time we've wasted not acknowledging the truth.

"You know how hard it's been with my parents." Her voice cracks, and my heart squeezes in response. "I . . . They're so small-minded. So closed off. Liking you—liking a *girl*—was so far removed from anything I thought could be my reality. They're so loud, so vocal with their hate it doesn't even seem possible I could be . . . could be . . . queer." She trips over the word. "How can I have parents with so much ugliness in them and try to claim that identity, let alone even think about it?" She's sobbing now. Every word choked and tight as her fingers dig into my arms like I'm the only thing holding her up.

"Everyone always says love is the strongest emotion, but that's bullshit," she continues, voice ripping at the seams. "Fear is stronger. So much stronger. No matter how at odds I've been with my parents, how much I've disagreed with the way they think and view the world, there's still this huge tangled mass of fear in me. Fear to even admit to myself what I was feeling. I mean, hell, I've been petrified to tell you, and you're the one I tell everything to."

I gape at her. "You don't have to be *scared* of me. You know I'd never care if you're queer. I mean, based on some rather important recent events and a fairly dramatic call to my mums, I'm in a similar sexual-identity-crisis boat."

Darcy laughs, but shakes her head. "I know you'd never care, but that's not what I mean. That's not the fear with you. I'm scared to like you—to tell you—because I don't want to risk ever losing you."

Her head falls forward, a small, wet whimper breaking from her throat.

But I'm there, and I catch her slumping shoulders, hold her hard and fast to me, both of us crying together, the noise left to the roll of the tide.

When she finally calms down enough to breathe steadily, I pull back, one palm cupping her cheek, the other at her neck, tilting her chin up so she looks at me. Sees me.

I'm unadorned, every defense stripped away as I finally let the truth of my feelings for her overwhelm me, play across every cell in my body. I go to speak, but she beats me to it.

"I love you, Cubby. More than a friend. More than anyone has a right to love another person." She braids her fingers through my wet hair, a shiver tracing through me. "I love you in a way that's terrifying and consuming and I don't even care, I can't hold it back any longer. I love you and I want you and I'm not sure who I am without you and I don't want to find out. I'm done lying to myself and to you. I love you and I need you to know."

Silence stretches for a beat, her words soaking into my skin like the sun's rays, burnishing me golden. I know that our timeline will be marked by this moment. There will be a before, and an after. This is it, that step off the tightrope wire where I let myself fall and hope she's the net that can catch me. I lean in, lips almost touching, and I feel the way she sucks in a breath, captures the air from my parted lips. "I love you too," I whisper.

Then press my mouth to hers.

Chapter 28

The drive home is no more than three kilometers, but we might as well be driving to Spain for how long it seems to take.

The anticipation between us is charged and heavy. Darcy's palm on my thigh. My fingers laced with hers. A kiss to my knuckles before she grabs the steering wheel with both hands for a sharp turn, veering out of habit into the left lane instead of the right. We're breathless and giggling at the angry car horn and the way our bodies sling against the opposite side as Darcy overcorrects. It's dangerous and intoxicating and matches everything storming inside me.

When we finally pull into the drive, Darcy doesn't even wait until we're inside, doesn't bother to turn the car off, throwing herself across the center console the second the car is in park, kissing me like her life depends on it. I laugh into the kiss, pushing against her until she's back in the driver's seat and I'm straddling her lap. My mouth is sore but I don't care. I've been pumping myself full of ibuprofen and, quite honestly, this painful degree of want beats out any other possible sensation.

With clumsy fingers and my lips still locked with hers, I fiddle behind me with the keys until the engine cuts, then I open the car door. We tumble out in a knot, crawling over each other and barely managing to shut the door as we race inside. In the hallway, we're a mess of lips and hands and limbs until we finally tip onto the couch, bodies flush and grinding together.

"I love you." Darcy kisses along my jaw. My collarbones. The center of my chest after she rips off my damp T-shirt.

"I love you," I moan, hands tangled in her hair, skimming down her neck, her back, gripping an appreciative handful of her hips.

"I need you so much I can barely stand it," she rasps into the shell of my ear, and my head tips back as I get dizzy from the pleasure, her teeth and lips trailing down the column of my throat.

"I'm all yours."

She cups my breasts; my hands are only a second behind in the same discovery, thumbs brushing over her hard nipples. We both groan, and I give her more pressure, the slightest pinch.

Her gasp sends such a bolt of pleasure through my center, my thighs instinctively try to squeeze together to alleviate the building, needy ache. But she's between me, her pelvis bearing down against mine, a jerky rhythm as she lightly writhes against me. My hands abandon her breasts to grip her hips, pulling her firmly where I need her the most.

"Cubby," she says between clenched teeth, face flushed and eyes hazed as she looks at me. "I need—"

"Me too," I pant out as she rolls her hips in a way that has stars blinking in my vision. "B-bed. We need a bed."

With absolutely no grace, we break apart and roll off the sofa, sprinting like wild things into the closest bedroom. My room.

It takes all of point-two seconds for us to tangle on top of the sheets, our remaining layers of clothing stripped in the process. We kiss and touch and devour each other until we're both a shaking, sweaty mess. When we did this before, we were outside of ourselves, the comforting wrap of darkness stunting the sensations, giving us a layer of protection. Now I'm a raw nerve, so fully in my body, the good feelings are barbed with pain, like there's so much joy—beauty—that it almost hurts for my frame to hold it all, muscles and joints stretching with its magnitude.

I know her lips better than my own, their every smile, every frown. I know the corner she bites when she's upset and the spot in the center when she's holding back a laugh. I know how she purses them when she's frustrated and how they get cracked in the winter.

And now I know how they feel against mine when we're both so lost in these feelings that kissing is the only anchor we have.

She holds me as she kisses me, touches me with so much reckless tenderness, that I know I'm forever ruined for others.

I've always belonged to Darcy in some gauzy, shadowy way, but this feels so solid, as inevitable as magnets colliding, as fundamental as the Earth spinning on its axis. Darcy is my sun and I'm lucky to be captive to her pull.

"Can I touch you?" she murmurs against my breasts before sucking my nipple into her mouth.

I arch into her, babbling something close to *yes, fucking hell, please and don't you dare stop.*

She snakes her hand down my body to where I'm aching, groaning out "Fuck" when she feels the wetness already soaking my thighs. I go to mirror her movements, desperate to feel her too, but she stops me with a shake of her head and a bite to my breast.

"Me first," she says, gently soothing the spot with a kiss. "I've wanted to do this for so long, I can't have you distracting me."

For once, I don't argue.

She explores with sure fingers, tracing up and down, swirling at my entrance, teasing my clit until I'm panting so hard I'm scared I'll pass out. Finally, she takes mercy on me, pressing two fingers deep inside me while the heel of her hand gives me the perfect amount of pressure.

My thighs clamp around her wrist, holding her there as she moves her fingers in a luscious, torturous rhythm that's so damn good it feels like my cells are rearranging from the sensation. I grind against her, and she laughs, a soft, awestruck sound.

"Can I give you more?" she says into a kiss as I loop a hand around her neck and hold her to me.

I pull back the barest bit, giving her a questioning glance.

Her smile is equal parts devious and bashful. "Can I taste you?"

I'm beyond speaking, nothing but nerves and feelings and inarticulate garbles, but I manage to nod, and her smile grows like I just gave her a winning lottery ticket.

In a flash, she removes her hand, sliding down the mattress until she's perched between my splayed legs. She tucks her hair behind her ears, color flagging her cheeks and expression almost sheepish as she scans my body. The enormity of the moment hits me, how special this is. Connor never did this for me; he never did much outside of getting himself off, and he always made it seem like an outlandish request if I ever brought up him going down on me, like I was being gross and greedy for even thinking about it.

But Darcy, the way she looks at me, lips parted and hunger in her eyes, sends a throb of sharp tenderness through me. She looks at me like nothing will bring her more satisfaction than tasting my desire for her.

"I've never done this," she says, voice thick, dragging her eyes up my body. I feel outrageously smug when she gets caught for a beat longer on my breasts. "With a girl, I mean."

I giggle, for no other reason than I feel punch-drunk and giddy and so fucking special that I get to be her first. "I haven't either." I grab her hand that's clutching my knee, needing to hold on to her.

"I've . . . I've thought about it, though. A lot," she says, glance earnest and tinged with desperation. "With you, I mean. Have you . . . have you thought about it too?"

Even through my needy haze, I see with stark clarity what this is. A lifeline, a humble beg to know that she isn't alone in how overwhelming all of this is.

Sex isn't something I think about all that often—I can go months without giving it a second thought, and, up until recently, most times it popped into my head, it was with a sort of academic reflection of how lackluster being with Connor always was. I've never understood what all the fuss is about.

But being with Darcy—the way she kissed me and touched me that night that feels like a different lifetime—that's a memory I could trace forever, memorize every corner and facet of. I don't think about sex all that much but—

"I think about you," I blurt out, voice rough. "I think about you all the time. It's always you."

With a raw look of relief, she cups my hips, tilting my pelvis slightly. My legs are already shaking, a deep pulse radiating from my center, an ache right above where her mouth hovers as she lowers herself closer to me. But she pauses, looking into my eyes over the planes of my body, waiting for permission.

I should say *yes* or *please* or *dear god get on with it before I fucking die, thanks* but instead what comes out is a hoarse, "I love you so much."

I say it like it isn't the most obvious thing in the world, like it isn't written in my eyes and inked across the flush of my skin and translated in the way my hands grip her wrists where she cradles my hips, holding on to her because I can't bear to let go.

I realize that it's not the subtlest or sexiest thing to say, and embarrassment starts to burn through me, but it's snuffed out at the slow, stunning curl of Darcy's smile.

"I love you too," she whispers, the words ghosting across my sensitive, wet flesh. Then she dips her head, and shows me how much she means it.

She's slow at first, an agonized groan tumbling from her with the first swipe of her tongue. The sound vibrates against me as she tastes my need, and my own cry echoes it. She kisses me, dirty and thorough, mouth open and tongue making luxurious drags across every inch of me as she explores with growing fervor. We're both loud and panting, my heels digging into the mattress as my body begs for more. I'm startled by the sudden suction as she closes her lips around my clit.

It's intense, almost sharp, and my stomach muscles clench, back bowing from the bed. She pulls back a few inches, eyes searching mine. "Was that bad?" she asks, her lips wet and red. Pleasure spears through me as she absentmindedly licks her lips.

"That was amazing," I choke out. I curl up, scrambling until my palms cup her cheeks, and I give her a sloppy, hungry kiss, our moans of need harmonizing in our throats. "And I want you to do that again. Like . . . many times again," I say against her lips as we kiss some more, nipping the lower as she gasps against my mouth. "Just . . . just give me a minute to get to that point. I need to ease in a bit more . . . God, you're fucking amazing."

I feel her smile against me, one hand snaking across my ribs, fingers brushing my sensitive nipple before she splays her palm across my chest and pushes me back to the bed.

With the most sinful look I've ever seen, she resituates herself between my thighs like she belongs there, shoulders nudging me wider until my legs drape down her back. She parts me with her thumbs, taking a moment to stare at me, study me, her eyes glazed with pleasure and smile growing. I squirm, my greedy hips seeking her mouth, and the little huff of a laugh she lets out against me can only be described as triumphant.

She puts her tongue to me again, tracing up and down my slit, her eyes fixed on my face. She catalogs my every moan and whimper until I'm clawing at the sheets and crying out her name.

She returns to my clit, slowly adding more pressure as she laps at it, first with the tip of her tongue, then alternating with the flat of it. It isn't long until I'm blinking away stars, my entire body a live wire, every cell humming like a plucked harp string.

"Faster," I beg. "Please," I add, not wanting to be rude to the woman with her head between my thighs. She does as I say, and I worry my muscles will snap with the tension stretching through them.

She works me harder, until I'm gasping and sweating. The pleasure coils tight, an agonizing, beautiful thing as I spiral *up, up, up* to an unimaginable peak. Darcy keeps me hovering there, no matter how much I cry and beg and pull on her hair, her lips backing away for a moment right before I topple over the edge. It's so good and I'm so close and she's so beautiful with her hair splayed across my thighs and her eyes closed as she savors me that a few tears slip down my cheeks, my breaths short and sharp.

"*Please*," I beg, pressing my hips against her mouth until it feels like I'll melt into her. Finally, finally, *finally*, she takes mercy, giving me pressure and attention until I'm shaking and pulsing beneath her, repeating her name over and over and over as I come.

When the sensation becomes too much to bear, I pull her up my body and tangle together as I thank her over and over with messy kisses. When the world finally stops spinning, I roll us so she's pinned beneath me.

"My turn," I whisper into her ear before biting the lobe, tracking the shiver that runs through her frame. I kiss my way down her body, in disbelief that I can touch her like this.

Between her thighs, I'm suddenly timid—wanting so badly to make it good for her, to show her with my mouth how much I want her, need her—scared I won't do this sacred moment justice. But her desperate little whimper spurs me to action, and I press my tongue to her delicious heat, reveling at the taste, the outrageous pleasure of getting to love her like this.

It takes a few minutes and plenty of enthusiastic encouragements and moans, but I find a rhythm and pressure that drives her as wild as I was, becoming instantly addicted to the taste of her, the feel of her writhing against my tongue. As she did with me, I drag it out, and it's only when she's pulling my hair and cursing at the ceiling that I take mercy and give her what she's begging for.

With a victorious laugh, I kiss back up her body until our mouths meet, tasting each other and ourselves in the tangle of our tongues. Some dam of emotion breaks—maybe for how long we hid ourselves, or how amazing this moment feels, or how overwhelming this love is—but we start crying. We hold each other tightly, sobbing and laughing in relief and mourning for how long we denied the truth. As I hold her to me, kissing her slowly and reverently until my heart beats itself into dizziness, I know as much as I'm hers, she's equally mine.

And, because I can, I repeat myself. "I love you so much."

Chapter 29

History has taught me to fear the morning after big feelings come to light.

The night I told Connor I loved him, he'd been drinking, but he'd kissed me deeply . . . then sagged in my arms, piss drunk and passed out. The next morning when I angrily brought up him not saying anything back, he'd laughed in my face and said he'd thought I'd been joking.

The morning after that first night with Darcy, while not quite so pathetic, wasn't much better on the emotional validation front.

Which is why I have no plans to leave my bed today, pretending to be fast asleep any time Darcy pokes her head in to check on me. She's even placed her fingers under my nose to confirm I'm breathing. I give a little snore for effect (not like a grandpa-asleep-in-front-of-the-telly, rumbles-the-whole-house type of snore, but more like a tiny-fairy-curled-up-in-a-flower-for-a-nap breathy sort of vibe).

If I stay wrapped up like a warm burrito with the sunshine pouring in through the white lace drapes, nothing can touch me. No feelings can be hurt when you're this cozy. Yesterday was too perfect to taint, and I, quite simply, refuse to face the day.

"I know you've been fake sleeping for an hour," Darcy says.

My eyes flash open and land on her hovering at the side of my bed.

I blink a few times, then remember to act drowsy and disoriented. "W-wha . . . Huh?" I mumble, pretending to yawn.

"You're a terrible actress."

"I think I'm actually a very good actress, thank you very much," I say, giving up the pretense. Darcy grins at me, then hands me a steaming mug of coffee.

I prop myself up against the headboard and grab at the cup like a needy toddler. "Did you add—"

"An ungodly amount of sugar to it? Yes, I did. No wonder your teeth are rotted," she finishes.

I let out an indignant huff. "They were *impacted*. It's very different."

"All I know is I only add one sugar packet to my coffee and I've never been hospitalized for my teeth . . ."

I ignore her, closing my eyes as I savor the first sip. The mattress dips as Darcy climbs into bed next to me.

"Is there a reason you're avoiding me after spending the night exploring each other's bodies?" she asks sweetly, making me choke. She grabs my coffee and sets it on the nightstand before giving my back a hearty thump.

"Mainly to avoid awkward conversation starters like that," I wheeze.

Darcy cackles. "So we're gonna keep up our very healthy cycle, then? Gals just being pals?"

"You started it," I shoot back, leaning across her to grab my mug. I meant it to be teasing, but sadness drapes across her features.

"Sorry," she mumbles, tilting her head to the side, her hair falling across her face.

"Hey, no, no. *I'm* sorry," I say, hands fluttering around her, too afraid to touch. And then I remember that I *can* touch her, and I waste no time drawing her to me, tucking her messy hair behind her ears. "I was trying to be funny."

"Never been your strong suit."

"That's sweet, thanks."

Darcy laughs again, head falling against my shoulder. Her laugh is my favorite sound in the world. It starts tinkly, then turns expansive and rough, reverberating straight through my chest. I want to make her laugh forever.

I keep one arm wrapped around her, her cheek nuzzled below my collarbone, and we take turns sipping my extra-sweet coffee.

"How are you feeling?" she asks after a few minutes, turning her head to look up at me. She uses the pad of one finger to stroke gently across my still slightly swollen cheek.

"Better." In pretty much every way. The pain in my mouth isn't anything ibuprofen can't fix, and the fist squeezing my chest the past few weeks has eased. Even my brain has calmed down a bit. Now that I truly have no phone to connect me to social media, I have startling, sudden peace, even if it's fleeting. I'm sure I'll dredge up some anxiety on the matter later, but, right now, all that really matters is that I'm cuddled up to my best friend, her lips close enough to kiss, and, by some miracle, I'm allowed to do that.

Darcy smiles as I press my mouth to hers, and she holds me against her for an extra beat until my smile matches.

"What do you want to do today?" I ask, breaking away to take another sip of coffee. I can't compromise my priorities.

"You aren't allowed to do anything but help me write this song," she says with a stern frown. "Everyone is coming down here in two days so we can get tracks laid and everything sorted. We have to have something ready."

"Couldn't we go swimming instead?" I ask, giving her my most pitiful look.

She boops me on the nose. "Absolutely not."

I groan, pulling a pillow over my face.

"Well, there is one thing I'll permit you to do outside of work on music," she says, voice smooth and dripping with promise. I perk up, whipping the pillow away. Kissing? This sounds like a perfect setup for kissing.

"What's that?" I bumble out with as much chill as I can muster, which is to say, none.

Color curls up her neck and across the bridge of her nose, eyes going heavy-lidded as she easily reads my thoughts. She leans in, eyes fixed on me, mouth a whisper away. "You could"—I feel the air ghost from her lips and trace over mine and I shiver, closing my eyes in anticipation—"talk to me about your feelings after last night."

I choke on air, eyes flying open.

Darcy looks tremendously pleased with herself as I splutter. "What's wrong, Cubby love? Did you have something else on your mind?"

I grab the pillow again, smacking her across the head with it. She squeals, wrestling it from me and getting up on her knees, weapon poised in the air as she prepares to strike back.

"Not my face! Not my face!" I throw my hands up in protection. She drops the pillow, squeezing a ticklish spot above my knee instead. I thrash like a fish on land. "Never mind! This is worse! Go for my face!"

Darcy laughs, stopping the torture and sliding her arms up to wrap around my middle, her cheek resting on the center of my chest as she lies on top of me. It feels so obscenely good to be with her like this, silly and wild and like everything else can wait.

I feel her swallow. "So? What are you thinking? What are you feeling?"

"*Good*," I say adamantly.

Her smile presses against my sternum. "Oh wow, pulling out the fanciful adjectives and everything."

"Need another big declaration, do ya?"

"Yes, I'm high maintenance like that," she says primly, moving so her chin rests on my chest, eyes on me.

I tuck my lips against my teeth but there's no hiding my smile. "Fine. I feel amazing and giddy and scared. I think last night was one of the best of my life and I stayed in bed all morning fake sleeping to avoid the possibility we were going to pretend it didn't happen."

"I don't want to pretend," Darcy rushes out, face serious. "Never again. It hurts too much to pretend to feel less for you than I do."

I nod, swallowing past the lump in my throat. "You're my best friend. So astonishingly special to me. I'd be lost without you."

"Me too," she says, placing a kiss right over my heart.

Our gazes lock for a long moment, and then I clear my throat. "I do have one question, though." I drop my hands to my sides so she won't feel them shake.

"Hmm?"

"Are you . . ." Heat rushes to my cheeks, and I squirm beneath her, body tensing. Darcy senses the change, and she sits up, tilting her head in question. I lift up on my elbows, staring at the end of the bed, a stinging pressure building in my eyes.

"Am I what, Cubby love?" She places her hand on top of mine, and I rotate my wrist, twining our fingers together.

I clear my throat again. "Are you, um, my girlfriend?" I squeak out, wanting to sink into a hole of embarrassment. Why are feelings so *mortifying*?

Darcy is silent for a moment then asks, "Do you want me to be your girlfriend?"

The absurdity of the question snaps my gaze back to hers. "No. I only confessed my love for you in the most dramatic way possible then spent the night eating you out for us to stay platonic besties. Hope we're on the same page."

Darcy laughs, her nose crinkling, dimple creasing. "You were rather dramatic about it all, weren't you?"

With an indignant grunt, I try to roll away from her, but she pounces, caging me beneath her and holding tight despite my squirming.

"Of course I want to be your girlfriend, you silly thing," she says. "Do you want to be mine?"

"I've always been yours." The words pour out of me before I can bite them back. I'm worried they're too much. Too soon. Too true.

But instead of looking alarmed or horrified, Darcy smiles with her entire body, inhale expanding her rib cage below my palms, mouth wide and eyes sparkling.

"Well, now that that's settled," she says, dipping her head to kiss my shoulder, "I guess it's time to get to work."

If today had a flavor, it would be marshmallow fluff—deliriously sweet and delicious that had us in a euphoric sugar high. It makes writing a love song bearable when you can be honest about the inspiration.

"What about," I ramble, doing a silly twirl in the middle of the sitting room before resuming my pacing, "something about the quiet moments? Love in the soft pauses of life?"

Darcy is hanging upside down from the arm of the couch, tracing my path. "Say more."

"Sort of moody but bright . . . maybe even have Kale solo open with some pizzicato?" I balance on one leg, tipping forward as I stare at the paisley print of the carpeting, lost in the image being painted across my mind. "A sort of do-da-do-do-da-do-do like it's the sound version of sunshine streaming in through the white lace curtains of an open window on the first perfect spring day."

"With vocals next or are you imagining Harry comes in first?"

I switch legs, kicking the other out to the side. "I think vocals? A little bit reedy? Like you just woke up . . . Whispered love confessions are the first thing you're saying for the day."

"And the things said are . . . ?" Darcy says with emphasis. Ah, lyrics, the only minorly crucial foundation of the song we keep getting hung up on.

I drop to the floor, crossing my legs and throwing my head back, blowing a raspberry as I search for words. Darcy hums the beat I started, and I turn to look at her.

She's so damn cute it almost hurts.

"*I choose you when you're lying on my couch*," I quietly sing. A smile blooms across her mouth, and she sits up to look at me. "*Something-somethingsomethingsomething something*," I mumble to the beat, making her laugh. She props her chin in her hand, giving me an adoring look. "*I choose you because there's nothing else I could do*."

The blush across her cheeks gives me butterflies, and she starts curling her toes against the cushions, precious energy vibrating from her. I crawl across the carpet to sit in front of her.

I beam up at her as I sing, "*And when they ask me, I can say I'm doing just fine / Cuz my girl's kisses taste like strawberries straight from the vine*."

Darcy giggles like a punch-drunk fool. In a swift motion, she leans down to cup my cheeks, peppering kisses all over my face and hair. "I love this beautiful brain," she says, giving my head a little rattle. I grab her hand, kissing a trail from the tips of her fingers to the crook of her elbow simply because I can.

"Song's perfect, we can stop working now," I say, a hopeful lilt to my voice.

Darcy snorts. "Yeah, I really love the *somethingsomethingsomething* part."

"That's my favorite part too. Can't wait to show Kale."

"He texted me a little bit ago," she says, tapping her phone screen to life. "Said everyone should be here around noon tomorrow."

"Has anyone warned the good townspeople?"

Darcy laughs. "We have a lot of work ahead of us."

"Which is why we should quit now and enjoy our last few hours of peace."

"Twist my arm," she says, rolling her eyes and smiling at me. "What do you want for dinner?"

"Hmm." I tap my chin. "What food is a good idea when you're devastatingly happy?"

Darcy's smile puts the sun to shame. "Pizza and ice cream it is."

Fever flashes from the bat of your eyelashes
Every moment becomes a memory
Stains my cheeks
Makes me weak
Breathless just to hear you speak

Chapter 30

"I miss my mums," I admit quietly as we lie on blankets in the back-yard a few hours later, staring up at the vast expanse of stars. "Does that make me, like, a giant baby? Aren't twenty-something-year-olds supposed to enjoy independence?"

I hear the soft rustle of grass as Darcy turns to look at me. "I don't think so. I miss your mums too. Beatriz always made me the best pastel de nata."

I smile at the memories that flood me: Mãe in the kitchen rolling dough, the house filling with the decadent smell of pastries and sugar, Darcy and I hovering by the table like rabid animals waiting for her to tell us it was finally cool enough to eat.

I rub my aching chest. "I think I've been avoiding how homesick I've been. This has all happened so fast, and I wanted to be an adult and handle it all myself but I . . . I kind of miss them taking care of me. Are you homesick at all?"

Darcy lets out a laugh that's equal parts brittle and bitter. "More so for your home than mine, but no, not really. I . . . Never mind."

"What?" I nudge her with my shoulder.

She lets out a shaky breath, pursing her lips as she looks at the stars. "I never really miss my home. It was more a house than anything, you know? I never felt . . . wholly comfortable there. Like I couldn't ever let my guard down."

"What about at my house?" I ask, bones aching for how desperately I want Darcy to have the comfort she deserves.

I feel her shrug. "Yes and no. Your mums have always been so good to me, and obviously I love Oliver like he's my own brother, but I don't know if your house is exactly where I get the feeling of home either. I think home is more . . . I don't know. It's dumb."

"*What?*" I press, rolling on my side until I'm stretched against her.

"It's so *cringey*." She giggles, throwing her arm over her eyes. "You're going to laugh at me."

"Probably, yeah." I pull her arm away, making her look at me. Her smile is bright and vulnerable as she giggles again. I place a kiss to the center of her palm.

"I feel at home with *you*," she says, biting the corner of her mouth. "I feel . . . Christ, I don't know . . . free. Like I can actually breathe around you. Like something in me unlocks when it's just us, a realer version of me breaking through the surface after going so long without air. I've always felt that way, even when we were little. You've . . . you've always been my person."

She looks at me shyly, eyes downcast, mouth pressed into a precious pout like she's holding back saying more, like saying that took everything she had. I'm so full of love for her—it's so big, so unearthly—I don't know how to articulate it, where to put it, and words fail me.

So I kiss her instead, one hand in her hair, the other at her heart, both of hers gripping my shirt like if she lets go, we'll float away.

"And you've always been mine," I say against her lips.

She smiles into the kiss. "I know."

We pull apart eventually, letting the calm heaviness of night cradle us as we look back up at the stars. Darcy stirs next to me, hips shifting as she fishes something out of her back pocket.

"Come here," she whispers, gathering me to her. She tucks my head between her shoulder and jaw. I nuzzle closer, placing a kiss to the soft skin of her throat. I see a flash of light through my closed eyes.

"Needed to capture the moment," she murmurs when I turn my head to look at her phone hovering over us. I reach up, bringing the screen closer.

The picture is grainy and a little blurry and nothing close to flattering. The tip of Darcy's nose is the same color pink as her hair from the night's chill, her mouth stretched in an outrageous smile that's almost clownish, the red-eye adding an extra jolt of energy to the scene. I, on the other hand, have my face smooshed against her neck, hair wild and ratty, somehow looking both serene and absolutely feral for her.

"We look delirious," I say with a laugh, zooming in on her grin. "I love it."

"How's the forced social media detox going?" Darcy asks as she clicks her phone off, dropping it on the grass between us.

I let out a deep breath through my nose. "Good? I think? I mean, it's only been like thirty-six hours since you sent my phone to its watery demise so it hasn't been that long."

"That's longer than I've seen you go without checking in months."

"Fair. Pathetic, but fair." I watch the dark outline of a cloud pass across the sky, blinking out some stars. "I'm surprised I don't feel the urge to check more. Maybe it's because I physically can't? The silence is the weirdest part, though."

"What do you mean?"

I pick at my nails, trying to form the right words. "There's this constant snag on my attention, part of my brain always facing the screen and the endless stimulus of it. Not being able to check makes me feel off-kilter, a nagging sensation that I'm forgetting something important . . . It's almost like an itch? One deep in my chest I can't scratch. It's not comfortable."

Darcy turns her head to look at me, but I keep my eyes fixed on the stars as I continue. "At any given moment, I'm in the middle of fifty conversations in DMs and text messages and emails and Snapchats and it's all so much and yet nothing at all and I don't understand how I can talk to so many people all the time and still feel so . . . alone." Darcy reaches out, grabbing my hand.

"It's become this huge, uncontrollable thing," I whisper. "I don't know how it got so out of hand but it's this vicious cycle of refreshing app after app over and over and most of the time, there won't even be something new to see, but I can't stop. It's this fear of being out of the loop, of missing something. Of being alone with my thoughts for a minute. I can't even go to the bathroom without checking something."

"I'm sorry it's become this bad, Cubby."

I swipe at my watery eyes. "S'not your fault."

"That doesn't mean I'm not sorry for your hurt. I can't imagine how hard it's been."

"Why do you think it's not like this for you?" I ask, feeling embarrassed, like something is wrong with my wiring for needing validation so badly. She's quiet for a moment, and I find the courage to look at her.

Darcy licks her lips, staring up at the sky as she thinks. "Maybe it's because I wasn't drowned in it like you were? I use social media, obviously, but I never had a big presence. I like seeing what other people post but I've never felt the need to share much about myself, mainly because it never felt real or authentic. More like I was . . . I don't know, perpetuating some version of myself I was already burnt out from upholding with my parents and stuff. But not posting much means I don't get as much engagement, and I don't get the extreme high of the serotonin hit you do with how massive your reach has become. It's easier to avoid becoming addicted to something if it doesn't create much of a high for you in the first place."

"I never wanted to be like this," I whisper.

Darcy makes a cooing noise. "I know, love. And I don't blame you for it becoming the trap it has. Anyone under the scrutiny you suddenly were would have a fucked-up relationship with the internet. The entire foundation of social media is designed around hooking a claw into the psyche. It's human nature to want to be known . . . I just don't think we were meant to be known in such a curated, digital way."

I nod. "It's kind of sick. We aren't allowed to be vulnerable and flawed. Everyone talks about being 'real' on social media and all that shit but at the end of the day, we show moments of softness in the most artificial ways possible."

"Have you thought about giving it up altogether?" she asks.

I nod, letting out another heavy breath. "I have, yeah. Part of me really wants to, maybe just to see if I even can. But the other part of me is terrified of . . . I don't know, irrelevance? Like if I stop posting, people will forget about me. Us, as a band. Like any footprints I've made will be washed away in an instant. That sounds really conceited but . . . yeah."

"It's not conceited. A lot of pressure has been put on you to carry our digital weight. This whole thing has programmed you to feel that way. But you could think of it in the opposite."

"Whatdya mean?"

"Think of it from the mysterious angle. People love a mystery, especially from someone they had so much access to. If you suddenly *stop*, people will be rabid for whatever pieces they can get."

I blink, envisioning this version of my life where I shrug off this boulder of obligation on my back, watch it roll down the hill, people chasing after it. A version of life where I don't have the compulsion to curate moments to gain the most clout and chase likability. Give myself the freedom to simply be.

"Could you imagine?" I say, propping up on my elbows to look at Darcy. "Just . . . not posting? Even deleting the account?"

"You could do it," she says, shrugging.

"Oh, you know what would really be the ultimate way to go out?" I say, a delicious thrill shooting through me.

"A blaze of glory posting screenshots of Connor's most horrible texts?"

I laugh, rolling my eyes. "That would be good, but no. I post that horribly lovely photo you took of us. No caption. No tags. Just us unhinged in love and I log out forever. My final footprint on the internet. Me, truly happy, hard-launching our relationship then digitally disappearing forever."

Darcy jolts up to sitting, and I grin at her excitement. I only need a hint of encouragement from her and I'll do it.

"Cubby, *no*," she says instead, voice harsh and loud. Even in the moonlight, I can see the color drain from her face, the panic splash across her features. "You absolutely can't post that."

I flinch from the force in her voice. "W-why? The tour's almost over, I'm sure Sigrún wouldn't care that much."

"*No*," Darcy repeats, saying the word through clenched teeth.

"What's wrong?"

"You can't post about us," she says, voice cracking.

"I can't?"

"Of course not!"

"But . . . why?" I repeat.

"People can't know about us."

The silence is piercing, an atomic bomb of quiet as we both freeze. "Excuse me?" I whisper, a serrated edge to my voice.

"We . . . I . . . You weren't planning on going public about all of this, were you?" she stammers out.

"What else would I expect to happen? This is going to get out at some point." Even in the dark, I can make out her face, and she looks so vulnerable, so sick with fear, it rips my chest open.

"I'm not sure . . . I haven't thought about it that much. I don't think we should share this yet. At all. Even especially in public."

"I don't understand," I say, strain in my voice as I try to discern her words. I hear them, understand each one individually, but together they aren't making sense. "What . . . what does this mean for us? How does that work?"

"I don't know," she says, voice rising an octave as it wavers. "I don't . . . I don't want anything to change."

My heart sinks like a brick in a pool. "Darcy, I think everything has to change."

"No," she repeats like if she says it hard enough, vehemently enough, it'll be a universal truth.

Panic mounts, pulling me under like a riptide. I turn away from her, nausea throbbing through me as I try to parse this out. A secret? Is that what she's asking? Another lie I have to uphold?

"I need more time," she says, grabbing my arms.

"More time?"

"More time of this being just ours. No one else's. No social media, no statements, no touching in public. Just ours."

My face twists, world starting to spin. I slide out of her grip, scooting away and crossing my arms over my chest. "I'm not interested in being your secret, Darcy."

"I'm not asking that of you," she says, crawling to me. There's been so much distance between us for months, I shouldn't want any more of it, but I shrink away.

"Aren't you?" I ask, voice cracking. "You're telling me you don't want anyone to know about us. That's the definition of a secret."

"Cubby, please. Please try to understand where I'm coming from. It's taken me twenty-two years to even admit to myself that I'm . . . queer. I can't just . . . *tell* people about it."

I recoil at her words. "Don't you dare talk like what we have is something shameful. That our love is something to hide."

"I'm *not*, Cubby. I swear I'm not. I just . . ."

"You what?"

"I'm *scared*. My own parents won't even acknowledge me when they find out."

"You don't know that," I argue. But the horrible, repugnant truth hits me that she's probably right. Her agonized expression makes me regret trying to lie to her.

"I tried to tell my mum once," Darcy says, barely above a whisper. "It was awful, Cubby."

"Why didn't you tell me?"

"Because it went so badly telling her I wasn't about to have a second go at it," she says with a hysterical bubble of laughter. "I . . . I asked her how she knew she loved my father. She told me she *always just knew*. Said it with such firmness. So I asked her if she *always just knew* she only liked men, hinted that maybe I might . . ." Darcy shakes her head, swallowing and gasping as she presses the story out. "I couldn't get the words out but I *know* she knew what I was saying."

"What did she do?" I'm not sure I actually want the answer.

She shakes her head again. "Somehow, that's the worst part. She did *nothing*. She was silent. Completely silent. Blinked twice, turned away from me, clicked on the telly, and got back to folding the laundry. Not a flinch of acknowledgment that I'd even spoken. No pursed lips or raised eyebrows or anger or worry or gladness I was trying to talk to her about something so personal. Just two careful, controlled blinks. A complete dismissal.

"And I know it's fucked up, but God, I wish she had yelled at me. Sometimes I think that might have been easier to deal with— her being an obvious monster, giving me some sort of tangible proof that she's horrible. But that silence was so much louder than anything she could have yelled at me. It told me that if what I was hinting at was true, acknowledged, I would no longer exist to her. I would be as invisible as the words I'd said, lost as sound waves dissolving in the atmosphere. I'd have no existence if I told that truth again."

I sit there, helpless and insignificant as pain bears down on the woman I love. Darcy cries, that deep wound ripped open.

"What am I supposed to expect from the rest of the world when the people that are meant to love me unconditionally won't even look at me?" Rough sobs rip from her throat, her shoulders hunching as she looks at me. "Cubby. Please. I— Please don't leave me. I need more time. Give me more time."

I reach for her, gripping her tight against me, holding her as gasps rack her small frame. Darcy, my indomitable Darcy, feels so fragile in my arms, and my heart is shredded to ribbons at the idea of the world hurting her.

I see it all as she cries against me. The scrutiny and the outrage. The accusations and name-calling. The internet—the world—is cruel to girls. Cruel to queer people. The combination would have them tearing us at the seams when we're barely stitched together.

"I'm not going anywhere," I whisper into her hair. "This is new for both of us. We can take it at your pace. I'm sorry. I'm so sorry I upset you."

"It's not you," she says, pulling back and scrubbing her knuckles across her cheeks. "I wish I was braver. I wish—"

"I wouldn't change a thing about you," I say, tilting her face to look at me. "I mean it."

After a moment, she meets my gaze, wrung out and weary.

"I'm not asking this to add more pressure," I say, brushing away more tears from her cheeks. "But are we telling anyone in the band about this?" Harry's warm, kind smile pops into my head. Darcy flinches, and I make a soothing sound.

"I don't think we should," she whispers.

I nod, a wave of guilt swamping me. "Harry confessed he might have feelings for me."

"He told me too," she says. "Back in Cleveland."

"I can't string him along. I need out of this. Out of the lies. Out of faking something so integral to who I am. What am I supposed to do?"

"I don't know," she says, hanging her head, voice broken and weak as she clutches my shirt. "Please, give me some time to figure things out."

"Okay," I whisper, trying not to sink too deeply into the quicksand of emotions we've stepped into. "We'll figure it out. Together."

"Don't . . . don't leave me," she begs again. "I don't want to disappear."

My heart lurches, and before I can even think, I'm kissing her, one hand twisted in her hair, the other at her back, molding her to me. She returns the kiss like she's been starving and I'm the sweetest thing she's ever tasted.

Carefully, I lower her to the blanket, stretching over her. She shifts beneath me, and one of my hands hooks beneath her knee, lifting her leg to wrap around my hip. She does the same with the other, locking me to her, never close enough. I'm still not used to the overwhelming pleasure of getting to touch her like this, and with shaky hands I move under her sweatshirt, feeling her warmth against my palms. My fingers play along the divots of her ribs, the swells of her breasts. Breaking us apart for only as long as necessary, Darcy pulls her sweatshirt off, tugging mine away too. We both sigh when our bodies make contact.

With aching slowness, I kiss up and down her body. I kiss every inch of her as if the press of my lips to her skin—her wonderful, perfect skin—will solidify her existence.

You're here, says the kiss to her temple. *You're real*, says the one right above her navel. *You're wonderful*, the crease of her hip. *I don't want a world that doesn't have you in it*, says the press at her shoulder.

I see you, the inside of her knee.

I love you, a kiss to the center of her chest.

She touches me back, pleasure weaving us together until we're moving as one, shaking and whimpering and feeling each other like any single brush of skin against skin could ever be enough. We know better. A lifetime of moments like this still wouldn't be enough to sate this need, but we'll gladly waste all our hours trying.

Chapter 31

Seeing our dilapidated tour bus turn down the tree-lined street of the rental house—hitting some low-hanging branches along the way—makes me both queasy and excited. While our time apart has been much needed, it hits me how greatly I've missed these assholes.

Harry's the first one off, and he bounds over to me and Darcy, scooping us up in a group hug that has us giggling like little kids.

"I've missed you two," he says, squeezing us tighter. "You better not have had too much fun without me."

"I take it you aren't still mad at me?" I ask him, poking him in the ribs.

He pulls back, features fixed in a serious expression. "I was never mad at you, Cub."

"You thought I was fraternizing with the enemy."

He blows out a deep breath, blinking up to the sky for a beat. "I was overwhelmed by everything I was hearing, yeah. I didn't understand why you wouldn't talk to us about Connor contacting you, and I got caught up in the rumors and didn't know what to believe."

An indignant huff squeaks out of me.

"And, obviously, I should have believed you," he says, grabbing the point of my chin between his index finger and thumb, making me soak in his frank expression. "I know that. I'm sorry."

"I'd never fake cheat on you," I say with a half smile. "And I certainly would never abandon you lot to join forces with Connor," I add as the others join us. "I'd rather eat my own hand before stooping that low."

"Good to see you, Cubby," Kevin says, giving me a pat on the back. "And glad to see your cheeks back to an almost normal size. Think you'll look, er, better in time for the show?"

"Great to see you too, Kev. I've missed your gentle way with words."

"How are you feeling?" Deja asks as she sneaks in for a hug. Skull waves at me over her shoulder.

"Much better. Everything seems to be healing up well."

"She's a tough one," Darcy says, giving my cheek a soft pat. Every cell in my body lights up.

"Can we go inside or would you rather we sweat to death in the appalling humidity?" Kale drones, looking—what a shocker—put-out.

It takes everything in me to not roll my eyes. "Missed you too, you cruciferous veggie." With a tortured sigh, he takes the lead into the house.

"It's amazing none of us have strangled him yet," Darcy mumbles to me and Harry.

I laugh, but Harry clicks his tongue against his teeth in a sound that's almost . . . chiding?

"He's not all that bad," Harry says, eyes fixed ahead on Kale. "We actually met up over our break."

Darcy and I stop in our tracks.

"You willingly spent time with him outside of band stuff?" she asks, face scrunched. "Are you all right?"

Harry's chuckle is rough. "Believe it or not, we had a really good time hanging out. We . . . got close."

Darcy and I stare at him, red crawling up his neck and cheeks.

"Close?" Darcy repeats. The color deepens. "How close?"

Harry pulls a face. "Oh my God, come off it. Can we get inside? I have to piss."

"There's something he's not telling us," Darcy hisses into my ear. "I need to know."

"Let it go," I warn. "There are things we're not telling him." Her smile falls and my heart sinks with it.

"Right. Yeah. 'Course." She moves swiftly into the house, and I follow behind.

"Can we talk privately?" Kale asks the second I step through the door.

"I'd prefer to have witnesses."

He grimaces. "Well, I'm planning on being semi-nice to you, so I'd rather avoid anyone observing."

I can't help the shock on my face. "Uh . . . Well . . . We can talk in here." I lead us into the kitchen, and we take spots on opposite sides of the island, sizing each other up.

"Your cheeks are still a little swollen, huh?" he starts.

"I didn't have very high expectations for semi-nice you, but you still slid right under them, didn't you?"

Kale laughs, hanging his head. "I'm sorry."

And something about the sad, frustrated breath he lets out has me believing he might actually mean it.

"I don't think I've ever had a conversation go well," he continues, eyes still fixed on the floor. "All my life I've managed to say the wrong thing. I meant that in a concerned way, like I hope you're doing okay."

"I'm doing okay," I whisper. "Are you, uh . . . doing okay?"

Kale lifts his gaze to me. "Yeah. I'm doing okay."

We're quiet for a long time, the chatter and laughter of the others drifting in from the living room.

"I, um . . ." He drags his hand over the back of his neck. "I'm sorry. I've been kind of a dick to you all summer."

"You have," I agree. "But I haven't been much of a delight myself."

Kale smiles at that. "Not always, no."

Something unwinds between us, cords of animosity finding some give.

He clears his throat. "It's . . . Well, it's not an excuse, but I care about music. So much. It's the only thing I've ever found where I sort of . . . fit. I'm sure you won't be surprised to hear I don't have many friends, and my breakup with my ex was anything but amicable, and I've already told you how much I suck at communication and . . . yeah. Music is my way of being part of something. Connecting with others. So I'm defensive and protective of it. And then I sort of started to care about all of you and I . . . I panicked that it was going to get taken away. And I overreacted." He says all of this in a blur, color rising on his cheeks as he talks, not fully meeting my eyes like he's mortified to be confiding in me.

"I understand," I say when he takes a breath. "My brother is actually a lot like that. He wants so badly to connect with the world, but spoken words aren't his way. I'm sorry it felt like I was threatening something so important to you."

Kale swallows, blinking back to me. I reach across the island, leaving my palm up. He stares at my outstretched hand for a moment before taking it. We do an awkward little squeeze thing back and forth that makes us both laugh.

"Can we call a truce?" I ask.

Kale nods. "Yes. As long as I can still bring you back to reality when you're being dramatic."

"And as long as I can point out when you're being a prig, you've got yourself a deal."

Kale smiles, and we shake on it.

"We better get working on the final song," I say, letting him go. "You, uh, probably won't be very impressed with the virtual nothing Darcy and I have."

"Wow. You? Under-delivering on a deadline? Shocker." His smile is good-natured, and I laugh.

"I want semi-nice Kale back because regular Kale is about to get a swift kick to the bollocks."

"Did I say that out loud? I meant, I'm sure whatever progress you two made on this very important piece of music that could have lasting implications on the trajectory of our careers is perfect and way ahead of the curve and will only need some light, collaborative tweaking."

I give him a sugary smile before flipping him off. I turn to leave, but with my hand on the kitchen door, he says my name. Quietly. Frantically. Something like a plea in the way his voice lilts. I look at him over my shoulder.

"Is . . . is any of it real between you and Harry?" he asks, tone low and words rushed. His eyes flick to the door, then back to me.

My heart twists. How do I answer that?

"I love Harry very much," I say slowly. "He's one of the best people I know, and, maybe in some other life, he's somebody I'd end up with."

Kale's face is pale, a muscle twitching in his jaw. "But in this life?"

I take a deep breath, smile honest but wobbly as I meet Kale's eyes. "In this life, I'm lucky he's one of my best friends."

Chapter 32

A miracle has happened.

We finished the damn love song.

Darcy and I put the finishing touches on it a few days ago, spending the rest of the week laying down music and cutting a demo with the rest of the group at a recording studio in Asbury Park.

It's a beautiful song, but it has teeth, something about it digging into my skin when I think on it for too long. It holds a piece of me and Darcy, a crucial piece, and I have a pit in my stomach that everyone will associate it with a narrative that isn't true. But I guess that's kind of the thing about art—it's created as a reflection of the artist but exists as the interpretation of everyone else. I know what that song means and so does Darcy. That will have to be good enough.

But today isn't for moping over the bittersweet.

Today is all about Pride.

The Jersey Shore Pride Festival kicks off with a parade weaving through Asbury Park, and we're sweating in the heat as we walk. All the musical acts at the festival were invited to join, and this might be the most fun we've had all summer, decked out in rainbow gear and waving flags high in the air.

The sun is a physical presence, pressing on our shoulders, smudging its thumbs along our cheeks as we scream and cheer with the crowds lining the route. Having two queer mums, this is hardly my first Pride parade, but I'm experiencing it with a new vibrancy, feeling more alive than I have in months. The joy is palpable, a sense of radical dignity in every queer person protesting and dancing in the streets.

Darcy and I link arms through it all.

When we first started walking, I felt like an impostor, shame curling my shoulders, whispering that I didn't deserve to be here if I wasn't loudly and proudly owning a label. But as we marched on, surrounded by people so happy, so unabashedly themselves I realized that it's okay that I haven't found my voice yet. One day I will.

We were told ahead of time that the parade route ended near the beach, and our group shares a look when we reach it. A second later, we're sprinting across the hot sand, shucking off our clothes and down to our suits as we go. As my feet hit the water, Darcy is there, arm wrapped around my waist, mine at her hip, plunging into the cold waves with a shared gasp.

Deja and Skull retreat immediately to the shore, Kevin already there being the responsible one and setting up towels and an umbrella. Kale and Harry don't last much longer, cursing as the freezing water slaps their chests, and they scamper back to land after only a few minutes.

Not me and Darcy.

Heat radiates through me from her proximity, and we swim out to where only the tips of our toes can skim the sand, the murky green-blue of the Atlantic our shield as we hold each other under the water, touching like we can make up for all the moments we can't on land.

"I miss you," Darcy whispers to me right before a wave crashes over our heads.

I grab for her as we resurface. "Love you," I say back.

We stare at each other for a moment, her lashes clumped in spikes around those big blue eyes, the sun illuminating the freckles along the bridge of her nose. We bob with the tide, and she drops her forehead to mine, wrapping her legs around my waist. I love the way it feels to be surrounded by her smooth, warm skin, how she makes my cheeks burn even when my teeth chatter from the freezing water. It would be so easy to steal a kiss right now.

But Harry and Kale ruin the moment, finding the courage to swim out and pop up a foot away, splashing our faces.

Kevin, Deja, and Skull are still lounging on the sand, but the four of us laugh like little kids as we play in the water. Someone suggests a game of chicken and I'm ridiculously overjoyed (read: pathetically horny) to wrap Darcy's thighs over my shoulders and hoist her up as she takes down Kale.

"You good?" Harry asks in a moment that's just us, Darcy and Kale diving for a sand dollar they feel on the ocean floor.

"Fine," I say—it's a bit of a lie and a bit of the truth. "Are *you*?"

His lips press into a tight line, and he tilts his head at me in confusion. I can't shake the feeling that there's something he's not telling me. I keep catching him looking at me. Or, if he isn't looking at me, he's watching Darcy, a frown almost constantly on his face like he's trying to solve a calculus equation.

"'Course I'm okay," Harry says. "I'm about to wrap up an amazing tour at an awesome music festival in front of a huge crowd. What's there not to be okay about?"

I flick my eyes to the sky. "Carbon emissions, increasing puritanical values becoming mainstream, conservative politics . . ."

"On par with that, I feel like I have a bit of a pimple coming in. Just here," he says, waving at his forehead.

I poke him between his eyebrows, making him laugh as he catches my hand.

"I'm fine, Cub. Don't worry about me. You ready for the final show?"

"I think so . . . Kinda weird, though, isn't it? This whole thing coming to an end?"

"I blinked"—Harry snaps his fingers—"and the tour is done. Feels . . . I don't know."

"What?" I splash him a bit. He returns the favor, but his smile falters.

"I'll miss this," he says. "The tour. The new places. The chase of creation . . . I'll miss my fake girlfriend." He whispers the last words, and guilt slices through me.

"Harry," I start, wanting to tell him the truth. Tell him everything. But he shakes his head.

"We'll talk after the show tomorrow," he says, smile back in place as he gives me another splash. I'm sick with anticipation of it, but I nod, Darcy and Kale swimming back over to us. Harry's smile seems to widen as Kale swims next to him, knocking their shoulders together.

As the sun slowly sets behind the town, we reluctantly wade our way back to the shore with frozen limbs.

"Fireworks start in thirty minutes," Kevin says in breathless wonder when we get to the towels. There is no joy quite like that of a grown man witnessing pyrotechnics.

We settle ourselves in for the show as nighttime falls, Darcy and I close together, staring up at the sky. With the sound of a whistle through teeth, a tiny spark erupts over the shoreline, snaking through the sky. The world goes quiet for a moment, holding its breath. With brilliant color, the firecracker blooms in a shower of pink and purple, the heavy *BOOM* reverberating through my chest.

The show takes off, the sky a shimmering rainbow of color.

As the fireworks explode, Darcy traces her fingertips down my back, a shiver chasing her touch. Her hands stop at my hips, resting there. After a moment, she grips them, tugging me back so I'm planted between her legs. I turn, fixing her with a questioning look.

Was that an accident? Are we allowed to touch like this in public? Someone might see . . . Is it bad that I pray they do? Should I move?

Darcy's look—soft and open and illuminated by the flash of lights—is a question of its own.

How could you belong anywhere else?

Emotions brighter and louder than the fireworks erupt in my chest, and, with a small smile, I slowly turn back toward the water, nestling closer between her thighs, my head falling to rest at the base of her throat, her chin perched against my crown. I match her every inhale until our breathing becomes the same, until we're pressed so close we're a tangle of sun-burned skin and frizzy hair. She reaches her arms around me, her hands landing right above my heartbeat.

I hope she knows its rhythm is all for her.

Chapter 33

Today is the day. The biggest performance of our lives.

I'm fairly certain I am going to puke my brains out with nerves.

I pace the back room alone, trying to calm myself as every worst-case scenario plays through my head: I forget the lyrics. I trip onstage and bust my nose. Worse, I trip onstage and flash my ass to the crowd at an unflattering angle.

This show is different, bigger than anything we've done, and I feel that fact echo through my bones as I pray we don't screw it up.

A realization hits me as I begin another lap of the room, and I stop in my tracks, heartbeat picking up for a different reason. In the mix of all these nerves is . . . *excitement*. For the first time in a long time, I recognize that anticipation to perform, that rush of wonder at what could happen when we step on the stage. Sure, maybe people are still coming to see a spectacle and not a performance, but maybe I don't care about their reasons for being here. I know my own.

I feel *ready*.

A small knock on the door pulls me from my thoughts, and I turn as Darcy pokes her head in.

"All right, Cubby love?" she says, smile slowly growing as she looks at me.

"Yeah," I answer honestly. "I am."

Her grin solidifies, and my belly swoops at the intimate curl of it, all for me. She slides into the room, shutting the door behind her. She crosses to me, and I reach for her in my new automatic response when we're alone, one hand to her waist, the other to her cheek, lips sealing against hers in a kiss, a cascade of happiness shimmering through me.

"Can I talk to you for a second?" she asks, breaking away.

My heart drops at the serious edge to her tone. "'Course."

With a deep breath, she squares her shoulders, grabbing my hand and leading us to the small couch in the corner of the room. "I know you still haven't got your phone sorted so you aren't on social media or whatever, but I have something I want to show you." She takes out her phone, tapping it against my knee.

"Is this going to be bad for my detox?" I ask, aiming for sarcasm as dread trickles down my throat.

Darcy rolls her eyes. "Trust me, no one wants you to relapse less than me. I'll have to drop your phone out of an airplane next time."

"I'm sure that's covered by Apple Care."

"Will you shut up and look at what I'm trying to show you?"

I take the phone, touching the screen before it falls asleep. It's open to Darcy's Instagram, a preview of a drafted post. Darcy clicks on the picture, increasing its size, and I recognize it immediately.

It's from the parade yesterday. She's wearing a magenta crop top with a high-waisted yellow skirt, her left foot cutely popped behind her to show off her light blue sneakers. Overhead, she holds a flag with matching colors that billows in the wind. The colors are bright but nothing compared to the dazzle of Darcy's smile. It's broad and open, a laugh perched on the edge of those full lips, her eyes crinkled at the corners, and I can see the emotions held there—joy, fear, longing, love—as she looked at the camera. Looked at *me* when I snapped the photo.

I tear my eyes from the screen, giving Darcy a questioning look.

A few tears roll down her cheeks as she smiles. "Read the caption," she whispers, tapping her phone again. "I want to post this."

I scroll, so many questions building in my head it takes me a second to focus.

Happy Pride!

I've always considered myself an ally. Prided (pun intended) myself on it. I thought: of course I love and respect the rights of people to love who they want to love, to live their fullest lives identifying however feels most true.

While I knew as an unshakable fact that I love others who are gay, bisexual, pan, trans, and everything in between, I couldn't face the idea of loving myself for belonging to the LGBTQ+ community as more than an ally. You see, not all families are safe. Not all people are accepting. And the fear of facing that has kept me from admitting the truth to myself. My fear was so great and huge and awful, I used to think it was stronger than love.

But yesterday, surrounded by people who stared that fear down, and claimed their identity with full-throated delight, made me realize the truth. Pride is, and always has been, a protest, a commitment to being your truest self regardless of the bigotry, the risk of hate and violence, from others. I'm ready to make that commitment.

I'm pansexual.

I've been attracted to men.

I've been attracted to gender-fluid folks.

I'm madly in love with a woman.

I'm done hiding in the shadows and dimming all this love I have to give. So, hi! Happy Pride! Thanks for waiting as I found my self.

I read it over and over, tears streaming down my cheeks and plunking on the screen and my lap. Darcy clears her throat, and I turn to her. Her cheeks are flushed, and she bites her lip as she reaches for her phone.

"A bit cheesy, I know, but—"

I cut her off, throwing my arms around her like I can envelop her completely, fuse her into my chest right next to my heart. Frantically, wildly, I search for her mouth, hands cradling her jaw as I kiss her with everything I have.

With a sigh of relief that dances across my lips, courses through my nervous system, Darcy kisses me back, her fingers threading into my hair.

"Does this mean . . ." I mumble against her lips, nipping at the spot.

"I'm done hiding," Darcy says. She pulls back, meeting my eyes, color high on her cheeks. "I'm done living in fear and shame. I'm done wasting another second pretending I don't feel everything for you."

"What changed?" My voice cracks, and she brushes my tears away with the tips of her fingers.

"Being here, seeing these people so happy, so deeply content being themselves . . . I *want* that." There's a palpable force in her voice despite its wobble. "I want that with *you*. I want it more than I feel fear about my parents or hurt at already knowing how they'll react. Lying about who I am is a slow, torturous death. I'm ready to *live*."

"Are you sure?" I ask, gripping her wrists, searching her face. "Are you ready to tell your parents?"

"No turning back now," she says with a nervous laugh. "I'm ready to tell them if they want to know. But I also realize it's not really any of their business. I'm happy, and that's all that matters. I'm not living my life by some litmus test of their approval anymore."

"Darcy," I say, pulling her to me again. We kiss, her pulse quick and furious as a hummingbird's wings under my palm where it rests at her throat. We kiss like they're apologies for lost times and being stupid. We kiss like they're welcome homes, finally arriving where we belong. We kiss like two fools in love.

As lost as I am to Darcy's touch, a sound cuts through our golden haze. A knock precedes the door swinging open by half a second. A sharp intake of breath sounds like a record scratch in the heated silence.

We bounce apart, the back of my head hitting the wall. I blink, trying to focus my swimming vision, finally registering the source of the sound right as Darcy whispers, "*Harry*."

He's there, in the doorway, mouth open, hand poised on the handle.

"Sorry," he blurts out, blinking rapidly, color rising on his cheeks. "Sorry. I . . . I . . . I came to get you for sound check. I—"

I stand, hands shaking as I raise them in front of me like I'm trying to soothe a spooked horse.

"Harry," I say, my voice a cracked plea. For what, I don't know. For him not to hate me, probably. I slowly lower my arm, heart lurching at the confusion etched on his face as he looks at me. "I think we need to talk."

Chapter 34

We stare at each other for a minute, Harry's face blank, Darcy's flaming-red, tears streaming down mine as so many emotions I've kept locked up tight claw out of me, demanding to be felt.

"Harry," I repeat.

He shakes his head, dragging a hand roughly through his hair. "You . . . you don't have to explain."

"Yes, I do," I say, finding my footing. I walk to him. He traces my movement, then comes back to himself, meeting me halfway with jerky steps. We both hesitate for a beat, then he opens his arms, and I crash into him with a hug. The tears come even harder.

"Hey, now, what's this for?" he asks. He pulls back, tilting my face up until I'm forced to look at him.

"I'm sorry," I whisper, my chin wobbling. "This wasn't . . . this wasn't how we wanted you to find out."

Harry's jaw tics, and he looks from me to Darcy, then back again, lines etched along his forehead. "Don't say sorry, Cub. Honestly, I should have guessed as much."

I blink at him in suprise, and he lets out a long sigh, smile sad but reaching his eyes. "Let's talk, love."

I scrub my tear-streaked face as we all sit down, trying to pull myself together. I feel raw and exposed. Happy and brokenhearted. I've gone so long trying to feel nothing at all that it's like my body is forcing me to feel the gamut of human emotions all at once.

Harry clears his throat. "So, this—"

"We're in love," Darcy blurts out, hand reaching out for mine.

Harry's sigh is deep and wistful, and he looks off to the side for a long moment. I study his profile. That sharp nose. The long sweep of eyelashes across his cheek. The stray hairs that fall over his creased forehead. He turns back to us.

"I've had my suspicions of as much," he says slowly. That sad smile is back, and a tiny whimper tumbles from my throat, hating myself for putting that pain there. Harry shakes his head, making a *tsk* sound. "No more of the tears, Cub. I mean it. Everything is okay. You don't need to feel sad."

"Yes I do," I cry, my hand clutching Darcy's, my other reaching for him. "I've made a lot of mistakes this summer, and hurting you is one of my worst."

"I'll recover," he says, those devastatingly blue eyes filled with tenderness.

"You should be mad at me."

He tilts his head, a playful smile tugging at his lips. "Do you want me to be mad at you? At my two favorite people?"

"It would probably make this conversation hurt less," Darcy says.

Harry laughs. "I could never make it easy on ya now, could I? Where's the fun in that?"

I stare at him, my eyes watery.

"What's wrong?" he murmurs, wiping another stray tear from my cheek.

"I feel terrible for hurting you. For not . . . not feeling the same way and you finding out like this. You deserve better than that."

"Cubby, I love you. You know that."

I bite my lip, looking down. With the softest pressure, he uses his fingers to tilt my chin up. "I love you as more than a friend, but it's nothing close to the way you love Darcy. Or the way Darcy loves you."

I open my mouth, but Darcy beats me to it. "How did you . . . ?"

"Like it or not, I see you two," Harry says with another rough laugh. "I notice things. Small things. But you two also make it so painfully obvious. The forlorn glances, the sighs, the theatrics of it all . . . I'm not as dense as you might think. Like I said, I've suspected something for a while."

We stare at him as he chooses his next words with great care. "I was always kind of expecting you two to get together during school. Or you'd see what was right in front of you while Connor was jerking you about, Cub."

He takes a moment to frown at the memories, and I do too.

"There's something uniquely special in the bond you two have," he continues. "The closeness. It's been a long time coming, in my opinion. I was just foolish enough to see if the spark I feel for you could compare."

I watch him swallow, jaw tense as he continues, "My love for you both—the love you have for each other—far outweighs any skin I had in the game. I'd be lying if I said there wasn't some afterburn in this moment—it's never easy to love someone who doesn't love you the same—but any aches I feel are minimal compared to how fecking happy I am for you."

Darcy is properly crying along with me now, a sniveling mess, the pair of us.

"What about you?" I ask.

"I'll recover," he repeats, squeezing my hand, then letting it go.

"I want you to be happy. I want you to be loved as much as you deserve."

He tuts, giving me a chiding smile. "I'm twenty-three, Cubby, not one hundred and three. I'll find someone."

"Aren't you . . ." I swallow, shaking my head. "Never mind."

"Aren't I what, babe?"

"Aren't you scared of being alone?" I whisper. I feel Darcy at my side. She knows the darkness of loneliness as harshly as I do.

He laughs through his nose, tilting his head back and blinking up at the ceiling. "'Course I am . . . Isn't everybody? But just because I'm alone doesn't mean I'm lonely."

Darcy scrunches up her nose. "Christ, you're emotionally evolved. It's a bit disturbing. Cubby would've destroyed you with her cold, bitter heart."

I let out a gasp, a disgusting bubble of snot popping out of my nose, making my best friends recoil, then howl with laughter as I frantically cover up my mess.

"You certainly know how to stroke a fella's ego," Harry says, passing me a napkin from the nearby coffee table with a horrified look. "But if anyone's up for the challenge of this one"—he cocks his thumb at me—"it's you, Darce."

"I know," she whispers, giving my hand a squeeze.

"None of this changes us, I want you to know that," Harry says, turning serious. "You are my best friends. I don't want life without ya."

"I don't want that either."

"Not up for negotiation," Darcy adds.

We share a smile, sitting in comfortable silence for a moment. "What comes next?" I ask eventually.

Harry shrugs, glancing at the door. "Well, I reckon we go do this show, then start planning out our *Cubby Clark Is Madly in Love* album."

Chapter 35

"Five minutes," the stage manager calls, making us all jump.

"Christ, I'm nervous," Harry says, pulling on his collar. "This feels a bit bigger than usual, no?"

"I feel it too," Skull grumbles from the corner, tapping his sticks against his thighs.

"The crowd looks massive," Kale adds, craning his neck to see around the sound equipment and up the stairs we're sequestered behind.

Deja beams at us. "Y'all are gonna kill it."

"Unless the panic kills me first," Darcy mumbles, cracking her fingers with her thumb as she paces.

"I'm really proud of us," I blurt out. Everyone turns to look at me, and I cringe. I'm not one for motivational speeches, but I feel like I need to say this. "Like, really proud. We've done something pretty incredible with the hand we were dealt."

I look around at the band, my friends, and slowly they each nod in agreement. I want to say more, I could write an entire book on how lucky I feel to know them, but the stage manager is back, his hurried tone interrupting my thoughts.

"Two minutes," he says. "Please come with me."

We file up the steps and hover behind the giant curtain, the humid, sunny day beating on our shoulders. We're a late-afternoon show, the bigger bands closing out the night. The crowd is loud all the same, and we hear their cheers and chatter from our spot at the base of the stage.

"Maybe you know their folky sound from the backdrop of your moody social media posts . . . or maybe you know them from a certain juicy love triangle," the emcee says, the audience erupting in screams. "Regardless of how you found them, they are one of the hottest bands of the summer to follow. So give it up for Tea Time Tantrum!"

We run onstage to the booms of cheers, taking our spots and waving at the giant crowd. The sun digs into our skin, and I squint, taking in the enormity of what we're doing, the sheer number of people here to listen to us play. We pick up our instruments and the world pauses for half a second—everything going still and silent as our eyes meet from where we're spread across the stage. Each of our faces is etched with the same thought: *Holy shit, how did we get here?*

Then, with a deep, shared breath, reality rushes back in—the heat and the sun and the screams—and we do what we do best.

We start to play.

Because we aren't a headlining act, our set is shorter than usual, but I'm glad for that, as we've poured everything we have into each note. Harry and I share a mic as we sing the final verses on our second-to-last song. The energy is electric, and while our performance isn't perfect, it's one for the books.

The notes fade, and the audience cheers. Harry drops his forehead to mine, both of us breathing hard, as we take it all in. There's an eruption of screams.

He pulls away and his smile is knowing. He tucks his lips against his teeth like he can barely hold back the secret. Like he can't wait for the world to hear it. My heart twists up into my throat, and I have to check the impulse to hug him. I might not love Harry romantically, but I love him just as deeply, just as genuinely. And I know he loves me back in equal measure.

He retreats back to his keyboard, and I'm left alone at the front with the mic, bare-boned and raw, my guitar the only protection from the mass of eyes staring at me.

My pulse pounds in every joint, blood rushing in my ears as I look at the sea of people, all of them waiting for me to fulfill the role they cast me in. I clear my throat and lean in.

"You all were promised a new love song tonight," I say, and the screams are so loud, it's like I'm blasted out of my body.

A small quiver runs through my frame as I try to find steady ground. I turn to my left, gaze locking with those midnight-blue eyes. In an ocean of a million people, Darcy will always be the one I land on.

"I've been thinking about love a lot lately," I say into the mic, eyes still fixed on my best friend. The audience whoops, and my stomach dips in response. I start strumming my guitar, giving my nervous fingers something to do.

"Been thinking about it more than I'd like, if I'm being honest." I glance at the crowd, hoping, at least for a moment, they really listen to what I have to say. "See, I was forced to suffer the aftermath of a breakup very publicly. Very embarrassingly."

No whoops this time, and I physically feel the energy dim. I don't care. It's everyone else's turn to be uncomfortable. I keep plucking some basic chords.

"Love, I'm learning, is never what you expect it to be." I turn back to Darcy, and she's beaming at me, heart on her sleeve. I give her a quick wink.

"You search for it in the places you think you're supposed to find it, twisting until you break your back to fit what you think it's supposed to look like."

The sun and the spotlights are heavy. I close my eyes for a moment, Darcy's face burned into my retinas. "But that's not real love," I say into the mic. "Love doesn't hurt you. It doesn't break you down into pieces with sharp edges that are impossible to carry. Real love, true love, strips you bare and holds you close, never asking you to be more than the person you already are."

I play the first few notes to our new song, preparing my fingers.

"You all were promised a love song," I repeat, my voice rough as I turn back to the audience. "You were given hints that it was about a certain Irish fella with blue eyes that would tempt Jesus to sin."

The crowd cheers, hooking back on to my words, safe ground to fulfill their fantasy of what my relationships should look like. A small echo of Harry's name rolls through the venue.

"Well, this is a love song," I say, a laugh in my voice. "It's probably my favorite song I've ever written."

I clear my throat, trying to calm my racing heart as I give words to the important part.

"But it's not about a boy." A small murmur rumbles through the crowd, and I let their questions build. "It's about the person I love the most. The person I don't want to spend a day without. In fact, that person helped me write it, helped me pluck every word from my scribbly brain and create something beautiful." I strum another few chords. "That person is Darcy Burton. She's my muse and my torment and my best friend and the love of my life. And this song is for her."

With one more deep breath, the noise of the crowd sinking away, I step up to the mic and start to sing.

Heartbeat flicker of the twin flame,
So lost in you, can't remember my own name,
But that's okay. I don't need it anyway.
I'll wear yours no matter what they say.

My eyes are fixed on her, only her. It will always be for her.

> *You're my anchor, my heart, my crush.*
> *Quick rush, slow burn, each twist, each turn*
> *Led me to your door . . .*
> *You're the only home I need anymore.*

My fingers dance along the neck of my guitar. The band waits another verse, then joins in. Skull first. Then Kale. Harry's keyboard rounding off the sound as I continue through the song.

> *You are the storm, you are the fire,*
> *Breathe me in, fuel my desires.*

Darcy stares at me as I continue to sing, her lips parted and tears in her eyes, hands limp at her sides as her bass section comes and goes. I grin at her.

> *You dance us across the tightrope,*
> *I beg, don't drop my heart of hope.*

The verses loop twice, then we flow into the bridge, and I take a shaky breath as I open up the vein. *I love you*, I mouth before I lay it all out there.

> *And you know I slice through life like a knife.*
> *My pain is impatient and I get complacent.*
> *Pacing my room all too consumed*
> *Of how I'll mess up and lose you.*

> *But you hold me close, you fight off my ghosts,*
> *And tell me, baby, it'll be okay.*

And this time I don't overthink it,
I chain up my demons, we dive in the deep end.

The music slows and quiets, my voice coming from some part deep inside of me.

Because, for once, my happiness isn't pretend.

I strum the chord progression again, singing the chorus one last time, playing the final notes. The music fades, tears rolling down my cheeks. Even from here, I can tell Darcy is crying too.

It takes me a moment to process the sound that breaks around us like a wave crashing on the shore, loud and forceful.

It's applause.

I flinch as I reenter the world, eyes scanning the crowd of intruders, their unexpected cheers at me handing my heart over to the girl I love. My gaze flashes back to Darcy's spot, needing to see her, needing to be anchored back in our connection. But she's already at my side, lips wobbling as she stares at me with those big blue eyes.

Then she smiles, the moment splitting open, my heart erupting into a thousand butterflies.

I take the two steps separating us, one hand snaking to her lower back, the other dragging through her hair, cradling the back of her head.

Our eyes lock, happy tears streaming down our cheeks.

"I love you," she whispers, voice shaky.

"I love you." I say each word with conviction, using my thumb to tilt her chin up.

Then I kiss her. For all the world to see.

Epilogue

One year later

EXCERPT FROM *ROLLING STONE*'S MAY COVER STORY

It would be easy to mistake the five members of global music sensation Tea Time Tantrum for a ragtag group of early twenty-year-old burnouts arguing in the corner of the deserted London pub they asked to meet in.

"Best chips in the city," lead bassist Darcy Burton explains through a mouthful.

"She would know, she's tried them all," Harry O'Connell, the band's keyboardist, adds with a playful wink.

The group erupts into teasing banter, sans moody drummer Skull Helguson, who watches with a bored expression, the only indication he's even listening a subtle twitch of a smile when lead singer Cubby Clark refers to violinist Harry Kale as bitter roughage.

"Is it always like this?" I manage to ask the band when they pause long enough to take a breath.

"Like what?" Cubby asks, those sharp slashes of eyebrows

furrowing with a frown as if the group hasn't spent the last quarter of an hour bickering.

"This . . . much . . ." I say at last, waving at them. They share a look; a heavy pause.

Then erupt into laughter.

"Pretty much, yeah," Cubby says. "We're like a family."

"A dysfunctional one, but one nonetheless," Kale adds. No one argues the point.

The young band is rather notorious for their convoluted interpersonal dynamics, landing on the map after musician Connor McCabe blasted Cubby in a song that was just last year lauded as a masterpiece, but has since been dissected on the internet for its undertones of misogyny, toxic masculinity, and inappropriate references to his past sexual relationship with Cubby.

"It bothers me that it's taken people this long to realize it," Cubby states when I broach the subject of the Cancellation of Connor McCabe. "I was ripped apart on the internet, forced to face constant reminders of this really toxic relationship, and now that I've finally moved on, everyone is realizing the truth of the situation and expecting me to be some spokesperson for how cruel the world can be to women. I've made my peace with that chapter of my life; I'm not looking to open up old wounds."

Cubby, and the rest of the band, would be best described as a closed book. After teasing a relationship between Harry and Cubby last summer, the group shocked the world by Cubby and Darcy announcing their relationship at the Jersey Shore's Pride Festival with a now record-breaking love ballad and a passionate kiss, then going radio silent for the better part of a year. This interview with *Rolling Stone* is the first they've agreed to sit down for since the infamous performance.

"We don't do it to be some sort of clickbait for trolls," Darcy says, when I ask why they've all taken a vow of social media silence and if the mystique of being offline is a ploy to generate interest. "The world is a painful enough place as it is. Making music forces us to confront a lot of that pain in a deeply personal way, and then people you've never met convince themselves they know you because of a silly photo you post on an app, then proceed to judge you for it. We put enough of ourselves into our music; we don't need to share every facet of our lives for mindless likes too."

"What was the experience last summer like for you?" I ask Harry. "There was a lot of speculation that Cubby broke your heart."

Harry rolls his eyes, giving me his trademark smile that could win over even the most jaded of people.

"Heartbreak is such an interesting concept," he says, leaning toward me. He has a way of making you feel like the only person in the world when he talks to you. "*Love* is an interesting concept, innit? It's both common and the most spectacular miracle on earth. Do I love Cubby? 'Course I do! But my love for Cubby became this public spectacle, and grew into something not ours. Somewhere during that summer, our story was being told *to* us. While the love I have for Cubby will always be real, it isn't the love rumored or expected of us by the public. Cubby is my best friend, the love of my platonic life. That is no less special than the romantic love that was rumored between us."

"Kissing Cubby onstage would classify it as something a bit more than a rumor, no?" I ask Harry.

He gives me that smile again, this time a little sheepish. Darcy shoots him a pointed look.

"Just some fun between friends," he says innocently, smile growing. "Kale gives me the shift all the time!" (Note for our non-Irish readers: *The shift* is apparently a slang term for open-mouthed kissing, and had I known this at the time of the interview, there would have been quite a few follow-up questions).

"So this is a band of friends? Is that all?"

Cubby and Darcy share a knowing look. "Gals just being pals," they say in unison, erupting into giggles.

"We're all extremely close friends," Cubby confirms, eyes scanning the group. "Darcy and I just happen to also have romantic love on top of that, and that's all we plan on saying about the matter."

"It's ours to know and understand," Darcy adds. "No one else's."

"What comes next for the group? Any new music on the horizon?"

They all turn giddy at the question, bursting with easily-guessed-at news. This is the most energy I've seen from Skull all afternoon.

"Not much," Kale deadpans.

"Just a new album release," Harry adds.

"And a world tour, no big deal," Darcy says, her smile infectious.

Cubby loops her arm around Darcy's waist, nuzzling her nose against Darcy's cheek as she says, "With a set list full of love songs."

Author's Note

Cubby's was one of the most drastically stubborn stories I have ever worked on. In true Cubby Clark form, her journey to the book you now hold took many shapes and forms and iterations, none feeling quite right. This book has been written and rewritten extensively for more than three years. The original idea for the book was a light, carefree young adult/new adult follow-up to my YA novel *Tilly in Technicolor* about a band touring around Iceland and having road trip mishaps that was supposed to come out in the fall of 2024. It was fun and silly and a story that, in theory, felt like it would be easy to write. But Cubby—my complex, complicated Cubby—there's nothing easy about her. She pushed and chafed at the saccharine circumstances I tried to place her in.

And it pissed me off. I so badly wanted to skim the surface with her, create something fluffy and escapist, and she absolutely wouldn't let me. None of what I was writing for her was genuine, and she refused to be forced into anything inauthentic. The problem, I realized, was how deeply scared I was to explore the intersection of depression and creative burnout, because that would require me to admit I was at my own personal crossroads with these beasts. Art is one of the most radical endeavors we can pursue—it's creation for the sake of creating, it's the holding up of a mirror to the world or, even scarier, to your own soul, it's the manifestation of things you need to say or the path to discovering what you think. But when depression knocks on your door, it can feel impossible to say anything through the fog, let alone create art. Cubby never let me go, and even when it felt impossible, I knew her story was one I had to tell, if for no other reason than the young, lost, and sad me of seasons past needed a story that shows that light exists with the darkness, and something beautiful can always be born from the stubborn determination to push on another day.

Acknowledgments

After seven books under my belt, you'd think I'd have the process down pat, something streamlined and hiccup-free that took some pushing but didn't feel like brain-birthing an entire family of characters. You'd be wrong. I have no grace or poise during the publishing process, and I'm so thankful to everyone who tolerates me through it.

To my editor, Eileen Rothschild, thank you for your patience on this book. I honestly don't feel like I was exaggerating when I sent you the email "Cubby attempt 501," but we got our girl over the finish line eventually, and I'm so grateful for your steady belief that we could do it through my kicking and screaming.

To my amazing agents, Claire Friedman and Jessica Mileo, thank you for putting up with me even when I send unhinged emails about torching a book a few hours before it's due (and the similarly unhinged ones on any other given day or time).

Thank you to my fabulous team at St. Martin's Griffin: Kejana Ayala, Char Dreyer, Alyssa Gammello, and Brant Janeway. Thank you for all that you do, especially all the thankless things behind the scenes that make publishing a book possible.

Amber D'Ambrosio, I have no idea what I would do without you, but I imagine it would involve a straitjacket and a lot of tears. I owe more to you than I could ever put into words, and I appreciate you endlessly.

Korina Bachman, my biggest supporter. Thank you for beta reading and convincing me that Cubby's story was one that needed to be shared. I am so thankful for your endless encouragement. To Jessica Joyce and Ava Wilder, I'm not sure I can ever have a Google doc without it being shared with you two. You are two of my favorite writers of all time, and I'm inspired by your art in ways I could never fully explain, and I always try to write something that would make you proud (is that codependent? That's probably codependent . . . sorry!). To the readers, booksellers, and librarians who support my books, give me countless opportunities, and keep showing up for me in ways I can never properly thank you for. This career of mine would be nothing without you.

To my best friends, Serena Kaylor and Megan Stillwell, who are so funny and so hot and get me through it all.

Mom! My mom! You are on my dream blunt rotation, for what it's worth. Thank you for always having the VH1 Top 20 Video Countdown on and not whupping my ass when you heard me swear for the first time singing along to P!nk. Your look of horror is cemented in my brain and one of my earliest memories. You are my favorite person in the world. Dad, I can trace my love for music back to the sound of you singing *Born to Run* to me since I was a baby. From dancing with you in the kitchen to Elvis to you handing me the Killers' *Hot Fuss* album and saying you had no idea who the band was but I wore you down with my begging for the CD.

And to Ben. You've seen Cubby in almost all her forms, and you were invaluable in helping me get her to where she is. Driving in the car, windows down, music blasting, and us singing along is my happy place. I love you so much.

HEADLINE ETERNAL

FIND YOUR HEART'S DESIRE...

VISIT OUR WEBSITE: www.headlineeternal.com

FIND US ON FACEBOOK: facebook.com/eternalromance

CONNECT WITH US ON X: @eternal_books

FOLLOW US ON INSTAGRAM: @headlineeternal

EMAIL US: eternalromance@headline.co.uk

RAISING READERS
Books Build Bright Futures

Dear Reader,

We'd love your attention for one more page to tell you about the crisis in children's reading, and what we can all do.

Studies have shown that reading for fun is the **single biggest predictor of a child's future life chances** – more than family circumstance, parents' educational background or income. It improves academic results, mental health, wealth, communication skills, ambition and happiness.[1]

The number of children reading for fun is in rapid decline. Young people have a lot of competition for their time. In 2024, 1 in 10 children and young people in the UK aged 5 to 18 did not own a single book at home.[2]

Hachette works extensively with schools, libraries and literacy charities, but here are some ways we can all raise more readers:

- Reading to children for just 10 minutes a day makes a difference
- Don't give up if children aren't regular readers – there will be books for them!
- Visit bookshops and libraries to get recommendations
- Encourage them to listen to audiobooks
- Support school libraries
- Give books as gifts

There's a lot more information about how to encourage children to read on our website: **www.RaisingReaders.co.uk**

Thank you for reading.

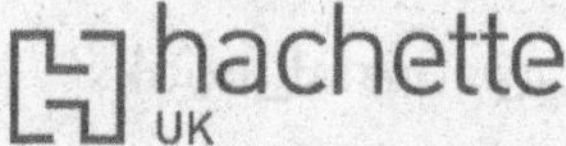

[1] OECD, '21st-Century Readers: Developing Literacy Skills in a Digital World', 2021, https://www.oecd.org/en/publications/21st-century-readers_a83d84cb-en.html

[2] National Literacy Trust, 'Book Ownership in 2024', November 2024, https://literacytrust.org.uk/research-services/research-reports/book-ownership-in-2024